Paul D. Escudero

Arizona
Alien
Adventure

WHEN THE ZHRAKZHONGS ARRIVED

WORKBOOK PRESS LLC
187 E Warm Springs Rd,
Suite B285, Las Vegas, NV 89119, USA

Website:https://workbookpress.com/
Hotline:1-888-818-4856
Email:admin@workbookpress.com

Ordering Information:
Quantity sales. Special discounts are available on quantity purchases by corporations, associations, and others.
For details, contact the publisher at the address above.

Library of Congress Control Number:
ISBN-13:   978-1-957618-88-3 (Paperback Version)
             978-1-957618-89-0 (Digital Version)

REV. DATE: 02/03/2022

Arizona Alien Adventure
When the Zhrakzhongs Arrived
Novel
By Paul D. Escudero

Chapter One

When the Comet Arrived

With the world focused on North Korea, Russia, the American President that was relentlessly under attack by his political enemies, the greatest and saddest moment in Human History quickly unfolded in the most unpredictable manner.

NASA, ESA, and other international space agencies picked up the large comet that was no threat to Earth, and it didn't seem all that bright. At least it wasn't nearly as bright as Haley's comet. Right at what was perceived as the closest point of approach, the comet's tail suddenly started shrinking. To NORAD's consternation, the velocity of the comet changed. It was slowing. The relative motion quickly caught the attention of the entire scientific community. One thing all the astrophysicists knew, comets didn't slow down!

The comets tail virtually a million miles long slowly dissipated as one would think the contrails of an airliner passing overhead.

Dr. Brandenhagen who had been laughed at because of his Mars reports, was suddenly sought after for comment. In just the prior few days, he was considered the laughingstock of the scientific community, even though he was a former nuclear weapon developer at the Livermore Labs. His comments were not too pleasing to those pesky reporters who lambasted him often in the past. Now suddenly there was a new electricity in the air as the comet continued to slow and the tail shrank proportional to the decrease in velocity. Within 48 hours it was only 500,000 miles long, cut nearly in half.

The rugged surface of what they could see on the comet looked as what would be expected. But comets do not slow down. They do not have brakes! Excitement grew and grew, and before you knew it Dr. Brandenhagen was speaking on the various news channels.

"Doctor, do you think this could be an alien ship?"

"I would have no way of knowing what it is, but I will offer you this: The comet's tail has shrunk in half and all the rumors coming out of NORAD, ESA, NASA, and a few other places are that the comet's velocity has already slowed in half. That I think is quite spectacular and we should be prepared for the inevitable."

"And what is the inevitable."

"I would say visitors or a revelation like a lot of governments are not going to like."

"You took a lot of criticism from the scientific community concerning your comments on Mars being wiped out by nuclear explosions. Are you ready to receive similar treatment over your comments about the comet?"

"Let me answer you this with a question which will answer what you are seeking in your question to me. NASA has given the size of the comet in their reports and its very large. If it were to strike earth, the amount of energy given off would cause 2000-foot-tall tidal waves and release energy equivalent to one million atomic bombs. So based on what NASA has stated concerning the comet's size, you agree its huge right?"

"Yes Doctor, we all understand the comet is huge."

"Now then, let me ask you, us just assume based on the size of the comet, if it were solid rock, it would weigh somewhere in the neighborhood of 500 trillion Pounds. How much energy would it take to slow something down that weigh 500 trillion Pounds, from a reported 250,000 miles per hour already down to 125,000 miles per hour in the span of 48 hours?"

"I would have no way of knowing how to calculate that Doctor."

"Well let me give you some guestimates, Okay?"

"Sure."

"It would take all the energy of every single nuclear power plant operating on this planet combined, and you still would not have enough energy to slow it down as much as that so-called comet has slowed down."

"What do you think that suggests, Doctor?"

"It suggests intelligent life is controlling that thing that NASA has classified as a comet."

"You mean alien life forms?"

"Let me say this, if you look at the current trajectory, it almost looks like it is approaching an orbit to our planet. It will become a small moon soon enough, then we get to find out what is in it."

"Doctor don't you think that if it contained intelligent beings, it would have attempted contacting us?"

"Yes and no. It depends on how they travel."

"Explain."

"Our airliners fly to their destination in auto-pilot. The pilot doesn't have to touch the controls at all. The computers on the airliners can take off the plane, land it, and if necessary, taxi all the way to the gate without the pilot ever touching the controls."

"So, what does that have to do with the comet?"

"If it's not a comet and a space craft of some sort, it could be flying in autopilot and the crew is in suspended animation, to be woken up upon arrival."

"Doctor, can we quote you?"

"I'm a public figure, I don't expect privacy, but if you do quote me, be sure and be accurate in how you do it."

"Doctor, you think it's an alien ship and not a comet?"

"Ms. Buchannan, I would have no way of knowing if the comet is an alien ship. But to observe this thing slow in half in just 48 hours when comets never slow down, suggests it's not a comet."

Rebecca Buchannan, a smoking hot reporter for Consolidated News Network, wasn't really much after a story as she was simply working on her air time. Her ratings fluctuated by the length of the dresses she wore and quite often operated on the fringes of yellow journalism. Her news cast later in the day would not show Dr. Brandenhagen in the best of light, as society was nowhere near ready to what just about was ready to occur.

The Zhrakzhongs were far more advanced than Earth people could imagine. Advanced beings figured out the best way to travel long distance was to put propulsion systems on a large asteroid. If the asteroid was large enough, they could carry substantial amounts of food and water to cover long distance travel. Their purpose for approaching Earth was not conquest, they merely shared the planets they found suitable for their own needs. Their goal was to spread their civilization through 1000 or more solar systems to insure survival of the species.

Zhrakzhongs were not morally or ethically better than humans, though they did feel superior in many ways. Earth people had never left their planet, thus were categorically estimated as extremely backwards compared to most of the rest of the galaxy. Earth had been living on borrowed time. Their first major mistake was not embracing the United States Space Force concept quick enough to mitigate the disaster that now unfolded.

The tail of the comet blocked out much of what would soon alarm Earth societies. The rear of the comet didn't need protection like the front area. A Trillion pounds of material that acted like a battering ram protected the intricate maze of passengers currently all snug in their transportation capsules, kept in suspended animation until arrival. This form of travel protected their psychology and prevented excessive utilization of the resources on board. When they arrive at a planet's destination, they can live off what they carried for nearly a generation, so finding a food and water supply wasn't critical. Though they purposely chose planets that appeared to have a hospitable atmosphere which their drones had successfully surveyed including electronic surveillance on the civilization that existed there.

The Zhrakzhongs knew a lot about planet Earth. Not everyone was placed in suspended animation. A certain number of crew members deemed necessary for safety and surveillance for the ship and its contents were alive and coherent during the 10 years of travel to Earth. Part of their responsibilities included continual education on planet earth and learning as much as possible to help with planning and operations upon arrival. They would also be responsible to prepare the passengers to descend to the planet. Their reward for staying awake and helping the others gave them priority on transport to the planet's surface, though many of them elected to stay aboard the comet until all the planetary issues were resolved.

On the rear of the comet, which Earth would not see until it was too late was a huge sprawling surface providing transportation access to dozens of space ports and some very strange objects were propulsion nodules capable of accelerating this massive object at incredible speeds. The comet tail resulted from debris burning off of the comet surface as it approached planet Earth, when solar winds struck the surface. As the Zhrakzhong planetary transport slowed using gravity waves in breaking, in due time the far side of the comet would be observable if America had not foolishly delayed the space force out of political partisan bickering. Unfortunately, the moment of vulnerability had manifested because nobody on Earth knew those space ports on the comet would be disgorging numerous craft that would soon descend upon the Southwest American desert areas of Arizona and New Mexico where the first Zhrakzhong settlement was planned.

In due time, Communists, Muslims, Christians, Jews, Atheists, Hindu's, and Buddhists would come to realize the Zhrakzhong arrival as their worst nightmare. The Zhrakzhongs had their own views on intelligent design and the Pagan Earth religions as they were viewed would not be tolerated in their zones of occupation. And since no Earth Space Force existed, there would be no means of preventing the Zhrakzhongs from deciding exactly what conditions they would impose on the inhabitants of planet Earth.

That evening as Rebecca Buchannan televised the Dr. Brandenhagen interview on TV, she did her usual defamatory methodology and as everyone went to bed that night, most of her audience surmised that the scientist was a goofball putting out ridiculous information.

Dr. Brandenhagen was all smiles watching the presentation because just before the Consolidated News Network televised the interview, his friend working over at the NRO had called to inform him the comet had now slowed to a little over 25,000 miles per hour and people were scrambling because the current trajectory would place it in an Earth orbit of approximately 50,000 miles, nearly one half the distance to the moon. Dr. Brandenhagen knew by tomorrow morning, his phone would be ringing off the hook by other news organizations wanting an interview, asking what he now thought.

The Zhrakzhongs would be awakened in segments. Military forces would be the first to exit suspended animation because as soon as the first planetary lander departed their transport, it was assumed planetary response would come and they had to be prepared to repel any attacks.

Earth had really no ability to attack the comet and the genius design was all that huge mass protected the Zhrakzhongs as any weapon would simply detonate harmlessly blowing away a small amount of rock and debris on the surface of the huge rock.

But long before and type of Earth weapon would get near the Zhrakzhong transport, it would be destroyed by advanced technology such as plasma debilitater weaponry. Earth people had never seen any such weapons nor observe the destructive power.

In space battles, usually the first ship to successfully target the other wins. Space weaponry like the plasma debilitater had such destructive forces, there was no protection against it. Thus, it was a quick draw, the first to shoot wins.

A million times hotter than a laser, the plasma debilitater melted through the skin of a ship, melting anything it touched. If combustionable material existed near the strike zone such as liquid hydrogen fuel or chemical rocket fuel, a horrific explosion occurred as the plasma superheated the material into explosive temperatures.

In the morning as reality struck home and Rebecca Buchannan was begging Dr. Brandenhagen for another interview, he even declined sexual offers for one. One could easily tell there was fear in a lot of people. In recent years, Christians were stating it appeared conditions set forth in Revelations in the Bible seemed to indicate "end times" was nearing us. The comet slowing down and entering an orbit around Earth fit into their narrative quite well.

Churches had been emptied in recent years. Suddenly thrust out of this new narrative, there were no empty seats and people stood against the walls in the isles as priests and preachers gave their sermons.

Out of nowhere came a phone call to Dr. Brandenhagen. It was a Chad Wentworth from Department of Homeland Security.

"Dr. Brandenhagen?"

"Yes that's me."

"Hello, I'm Chad Wentworth, I work for the Department of Homeland Security."

"What can I do for you Chad?"

"Dr. Brandenhagen, there will be a couple of our agents visiting you in a short while, just so you know this is all legitimate, they will be reiterating what I'm going to now tell you over the phone."

"And that is?"

"Doctor Brandenhagen, we know about your buddy over at the NRO and he told you a few things he shouldn't have. So, you already know the comet has slowed down considerably, and the administration as well as other world governments are getting concerned about all this comet business and what it might mean. We are asking you to not make any further comment on it to the press. The agents that will be arriving soon, are to provide you security as well as prevent anyone having access to you without our permission."

"This is totally unacceptable; I'll never agree to any of this horseshit. I have first amendment rights."

"Doctor Brandenhagen you of all people should know what the implication of such a huge body slowing down and entering Earth's orbit might mean. We have enough problems as it is and we can't afford to have the public in mass panic."

"So that's what this is all about."

"You should know how Doctor Brandenhagen your one little interview with Ms. Buchannan has already caused the administration a lot of grief."

"I thought Ms. Buchannan made me out to look like some kind of nut."

"Well Doctor, unfortunately for Ms. Buchannan, there are a number of journalists worldwide who have taken your comments to heart and we now have foreign governments demanding the President's attention. You rattled a few nerves and with what has happened to the comet since the interview, we are already close to a panic, and that's why we will be keeping you away from the media and will have to relocate you for your own good."

"You are going to arrest me?"

"No, take you into protective custody. Our agents will be ringing your doorbell in about 5 minutes. Cooperate with them and we'll make your life a lot better than what it otherwise will be."

"Where are you taking me?"

"The agents will explain all that. Goodbye Dr. Brandenhagen and please cooperate with our agents. You will first go to a Federal Building so you will know this is all legitimate and you will receive a briefing there and you might be asked to help in some way."

"I will always do whatever I can to assist the government on matters such as this."

"We appreciate that. Our agents are arriving. Thank you for your time."

Suddenly there was a dial tone and a moment later the doorbell rang.

This is not going to be a good day, Roger Brandenhagen thought.

Having been around high security settings in the

past such as area 15 (nuclear test zone that surrounds area 51 and Livermore Labs), Roger knew it would be futile to resist the goons that were ringing his doorbell. He was dressed casual and only had to put on a jacket and a ball cap since he knew he would be leaving with them.

Roger looked through the spyhole at his front door and observed four men wearing suits. No doubt they were Cash in Advance boys coming to get him to silence him. *Would they kill me or just keep me under wraps?*

Roger put on his favorite alien ball cap, and jacket then opened the front door.

"Mr. Brandenhagen?"

"Yes, that's me."

"My name is McClusky. Someone from the office just called you and said we would be taking you for a little ride."

"I figured as much."

"Would you please come with us?"

"Show me the way."

Roger Brandenhagen calmly followed McClusky and two of the Cash in Advance guys fell in behind Roger which made him surrounded and least likely to attempt escaping. They led him over to a couple black Chevy Suburban's with tinted glass windows.

Roger thought, these Cash in Advance guys are not very clever. They drive cars that easily identify them as who they are to our enemies.

A door was opened for him in the trailing SUV which he instinctively knew to *get in.*

In a brief while they were traveling through city streets then merged onto route 66 which was very familiar to Roger. It didn't take long before the took the Dulles airport exit and were heading near the airport, but when they approached a series of new office buildings, they turned into a parking garage.

When the Cash in Advance boys got out of the SUV, agent McClusky said, "We are getting out here."

Roger exited the SUV and followed the men out of the parking garage into the nearby building. Like many buildings in this vicinity, it had corporate signs on it, which in no way conveyed its purpose for existence. That was more evident in the lobby of the building that had ample security and a security screener metals detector machine just like at the airport that could detect firearms.

McClusky and his associates pulled out badges but Roger was asked to walk through the metal detector and place all his personal items in a small plastic tub that had a conveyor belt and took his billfold and car keys through the X-Ray machine.

After the security screening McClusky took Roger up to the 14th floor and into an unmarked office that had just a room number on it.

Inside the spacious office where it appeared 20 or more people worked, they walked into a room with a glass wall people could see in from the outside that had a long table and a television set and several flat screen monitors showing video piped in from the internet.

"Have a seat," McClusky said then gestured towards the long conference table where Roger sat down in the middle.

A moment later several individuals entered the room, carrying legal notepads and sat down across from Roger who was sitting with the video equipment and television to his right. The television was showing network TV but the audio was turned down. Roger could see the newscaster was talking about the Comet that was approaching Earth and getting a lot of public interest.

One of the individuals who entered the room, a female very well dressed grabbed the controller sitting on the table and turned on the video monitors that were showing live satellite feed from a KH-14 satellite Roger had no idea existed.

Roger knew from some experiences he had going out to area 51 while working on technology put in the Champ missile, this woman might be dressed up looking pretty, but she was no doubt one tough bitch a biker dude would not want to meet in an alley.

The woman seemed to be in charge. The men who followed her in had nothing to say at first until the woman introduced herself.

"Mr. Brandenhagen, I'm Sally Fairbanks. We brought you in here today for several reasons. First of all, we want to discuss the comet that has arrived and some of your comments you made with the news reporter Rebecca Buchannan."

"Okay." Roger didn't quite yet know what this was really about but his curiosity was nevertheless elevated by his welcoming committee.

"And the second thing we wanted to inform you of is that even though you currently are not employed by the government, you retain your Q clearance which you required while doing your work at Lawrence Livermore labs and Area 15. As such you know you are bound by security requirements."

"Yes, I'm well aware."

"First question I have for you Dr. Brandenhagen, just exactly why do you think that comet is ferrying aliens here?"

"The most obvious reason is comets do not slow down. This thing was doing 250,000 miles per hour two days ago and appeared to be on a trajectory where it would barely miss Earth. By the time Rebecca Buchannan interviewed me on TV, it had slowed down to approximately 125,000 miles per hour which for such a huge object would require lots of energy to do so, but yet there are no conventional rocket exhausts one would have to conclude more advanced propulsion such as the use of gravity waves or some other means."

"So, you think this is some kind of transporter for Aliens?" Sally Fairbanks asked in a very serious manner.

"It's the only thing obvious to me right now and if it goes into an Earth orbit, we will soon discover their intentions."

On one of the flat screen monitors, Roger could see it was a classified NASA channel which was showing the track of the object in relation to a graphic of the Moon and the Earth. It was now evident to Roger this thing had slowed even more as NASA was posting 25,000 miles per hour and it was now between the Moon and the Earth.

Sally Fairbanks had a lot of concern on her face as now reality was sitting in. The Majestic 12 group had already given her team the word to put a clamp down on information no matter what happened. However, Sally being a very bright Harvard graduate knew that in a few more hours when Earth Suddenly had a second moon traveling in the opposite direction, the public would be clamoring for information and it would be unlikely they could then silence Dr. Brandenhagen.

The video capability of the KH-14 satellite put up in space specifically for the detection of Aliens was rather astounding. The detail of the Comet was quite impressive, but it had no indications it was anything more than just a comet other than it slowed down and was not approaching Earth in what seemed to be like a controlled navigation system.

"Is that the comet?" Roger asked.

"Yes, it is."

"NASA indicates it's now only traveling at the velocity of 25,000 miles per hour. That's quite extraordinary don't you think."

"Yes, and that's precisely why we brought you in here."

"If I were a betting man, I would say looking at that graphic that by this evening the world will know it went into orbit around our planet."

"Even so there is no indication of any sort of life on it as it appears totally baren by the video."

"We've never encountered anything like this before, and we have no idea what is ostensibly inside that comet."

"What do you mean by that?"

"The comet could be hollow and as large as it is carrying a very large population."

"How could a mass of people survive inside that comet for a lengthy period. It seems there would be food, water, and sanitation issues."

"Hollywood has already figured it out."

"How so?"

"Suspended animation. Most of the beings are probably sleeping until they awaken by their caretakers."

"Hollywood fiction has no basis for reality of what is occurring with this object."

"If my guess is correct, they are waking up those multitudes right now and within a few more days, you will discover how many are coming when they show up on our planet."

"There is nothing to say we will allow them to come down on this planet."

"You have no idea what kind of technology and weaponry they have, I would suggest you operate with great restraint because they may have more firepower than you have ability to deal with it."

Roger looking up at the NASA display made the intuitive comment, "Looking at that display, I would suspect NORAD will be advising the joint chiefs within an hour or so the calculated orbit around the planet."

"They do have some extraordinary tracking ability as they now track 25,000 objects."

Roger thought now would be the golden opportunity to get to the essence of his visit and came right out and asked, "What is it exactly you want from me?"

Sally Fairbanks must have anticipated Roger's question and had an immediate answer:

"Mr. Brandenhagen, we are going to stipulate you stay away from the News Media indefinitely. We know how your Mars report has caused a lot of hysteria, and even if you are correct in your assessments, the administration needs time to cope with this event and determine its best course of action."

"You can silence me for a while, but when those beings start descending down on the planet, the public will be clamoring for information. I'll be happy to tell all the news media who comes up to my face with camera's that you have silenced me and they need to turn to you for comment."

"You may not be given that option."

"What do you mean by that?"

"You can do it our way, or you can do it the hard way." Sally Fairbanks stated finally showing her fangs.

"I assumed you would bring me here to threaten me."

"Dr. Brandenhagen, your public comments with Rebecca Buchannan have already stirred up the public."

"And you think the new Moon showing up isn't going to have more impact than my comments?"

"Like I said, the administration needs time to cope with this ordeal and your public comments will only cause mass hysteria."

"Okay, I get it. You silenced me. But one thing I will predict, withing 24 to 48 hours you will have a very bad day when these beings descend upon the planet."

"What's that supposed to mean?"

"I'm not saying this will be like the movie Independence Day where the aliens came to wipe us out. But then again you never know what their intentions are. And another thing I will caution you on. To move such a huge mass like that for such a far distance means they have incredible technology which we are not prepared to deal with. If you do something dumb like attack them, they you will set up a scenario you will wish to hell you never did when they defend themselves. Just to get that object here alone requires technology that will make our nuclear weapons seem like cave man arms in a very short period of time."

"What do you recommend we do then?"

"I would try to communicate with them, ask them what their intentions are and weigh all your risks before you make any dumb moves."

"What makes you think we can communicate with them?"

"Earth has been sending out radio waves for 120 years thanks to Mr. Marconi. They have had plenty time to study us. For the first 60 years it was probably rough to figure out what we were saying, but when they started receiving our Television signals with visual images, they quickly grasped the essence of who we are and what our recent history is."

"Why would they pick our planet?"

"I know the government likes to cover up all these UFO (UAP) sightings, didn't it occur to you that some of them could have been probes sent here long ago to study this planet and determine its suitability to support their type of life forms?"

"That's all speculation on your part and has no bearing on this case."

"Typical bureaucratic bullshit. You guys are terrified you have painted yourselves in the corner with Majestic-12 policies and now these aliens which I'm sure they are, will force you to deal with the public who will no longer tolerate all your coverup and harsh treatment of individuals who came forth and told the truth."

"Do you feel like we did that to you on your Mars reports?"

"I've first hand witnessed your disinformation campaign. You are very slick at the way you work it. But I wonder how you can sleep at night knowing the people you destroyed in doing so."

"All we are asking you to do is to not make public comment."

"That's easy to do, you know why?"

"Why?"

"I no longer need to make any public comment, the Aliens shuttling their people down to the planet will create a spectacle like you never dreamed of. And all those people that have put the clamp on are going to have a very bad day."

"We have no indications there are any living entities on that comet and all you think is just wild speculation."

"Think about this: those beings have been traveling for quite some time. We have no idea how long it took them to get here. Obviously if they are in suspended animation, they are being woke up now and like you say, it doesn't have the ability to sustain life for a lot of beings for long, hence their next actions are quite logical, they will shuttle people down to the planet in areas they have already selected and in a few more days, the public will have a full grasp on it. The "cat" will be out of the bag then and the administration will have some explanation as to what actions they took."

"We have no idea where they intend on landing."

"That's absolutely right, and if they land in China

or Russia, what do you think we can do about it? Those are sovereign nations with powerful militaries who would not appreciate us trespassing."

"Mr. Brandenhagen, we are going to take you home now. For your own well-being stay away from the press and all will be well for you."

"Yea, you can silence me. But you are in for a rude awakening. One thing I will advise you on since you know I've studied the nuclear annihilation of Mars, if you do not want to see Earth turn into another Mars with the atmosphere stripped away and a dead planet, I highly recommend you tell the administration to keep their powder dry and view these aliens as a severe threat and if you attack them, it will be worse than a nuclear war."

"We'll take you home now, Mr. Brandenhagen."

Chapter Two
Arizona Sunset

The evening seemed cooler as the heat wave appeared to lesson up a bit. This was the first night in a long time the medicine man *Binii 'ligaii* (Screeching Owl) could be outside his dwelling around sunset to view the beautiful Azure Sky as the night unfolds.

The *Béésh Łigaii Atsu* (Silver Eagle) Native American Tribe that lived in a rugged area with only one dirt road in that washed out every few years during monsoon cloud bursts, was made up with half breeds from Navajo's and Hualapai. Many Navajo's and Hualapai considered them outlaws kicked out of the tribes as troublemakers and undesirables. The truth of the matter is, they only had one sin. They married a person from the other Tribe.

But they were a proud people and good people. They lived off the grid and figured out how to survive without government assistance or interference from outside.

There were no alcohol abusers and the families respected each other and cared for one another. Every time Navajo's or Hualapai ejected their trouble makers, they ended up with the *Béésh Łigaii Atsu,* many times for a period of time before they disappeared making their way to Phoenix or elsewhere to learn to live in the industrial society. If there was any type of substance abuse it was a form of peyote *Naakai Binát'oh* smoked with a peace pipe for ceremonial affairs. The medicine man grew the special plants that produced the *Naakai Binát'oh* in a garden where he also grew his medical herbs.

As the sun set that special night when the medicine man *Binii'łigaii* (Screeching Owl) enjoyed the sun dip below the horizon and the nice gentle cool breeze, he saw the image of a second moon appear. It appeared half the size of the moon which was also now visible to the East.

Binii'łigaii knew this was some sort of omen. Even though they lived off the grid, they had windmill generators and electricity as long as there was wind or a breeze which powered lights or one of the few radios, they possessed obtained by trading relics to tourists 15 miles down the dirt road where a two-lane paved hiway existed and orientated in a North and South direction. They had some awareness of the world and all their children learned English and their native language. In the simple central Arizona news broadcasts, nothing appeared out of the ordinary other than some kind of a buzz about the comet losing its tail and where did it go?

Binii'łigaii reached into his small pouch around his waist and pulled out a bag that contained probably two or three ounces of *Naakai Binát'oh* and grabbed a good size pinch and stuffed it into his pipe and lit it with one of those stick matches he obtained in trade at the hiway entrance. But he knew if he had to, he could get one of his bows, a stick and his fire starter stone and start a small camp fire to light up his pipe.

The breeze carried his smoke to his cabin and his wife *Nizhóní Ch'ilátah Hózhóón* (Beautiful Flower) knew he was smoking the *Naakai Binát'oh* again which she wasn't thrilled about since he might want wild sex afterwards and she wasn't in the mood.

Binii'tigaii didn't like using his wife's full name, so he just called her *Nizhóní* (Beautiful), which she kind of enjoyed.

But tonight, to *Nizhóní Ch'ilátah Hózhóón* surprise, *Binii'tigaii* did not come back into their well-kept home for quite a while as he sat on one of his favorite rocks looking up to the sky and the stars trying to decipher the message the gods sent by bringing in a second moon. He would be even more perplexed the following evening as the gods then showed their true intent.

Nizhóní Ch'ilátah Hózhóón walked outside and knew where to find her husband. It was around midnight. She walked up to him slowly and quietly to not disturb his serenity as she could see this proud warrior looking out to space.

When she stepped next to him, he didn't notice her even though she was bathed in moonlight and his eyes were fully night adjusted.

She observed him for a while and he appeared like he was in a trance fully engrossed at what he was looking at. At this point she looked to the heavens to see what he was looking at. To say seeing the second moon didn't somehow elevate *Nizhóní Ch'ilátah Hózhóón's* emotions was an understatement. She herself suddenly wanted answers, and here she was standing by the wise man of the tribe, the medicine man who knew more than anyone in total silence. But she needed answers and had to ask the question.

"Why are there two moons?"

Binii'łigaii, didn't answer for a while, but he heard the question and was searching his own mind for answers. At the present time he had no answers. In fact, this was probably the first time in his life that he had no answers. All he could mumble is, "I think the whole world is searching for answers."

And searching they were.

As CIA Agent McClusky pulled up in front of Dr. Roger Brandenhagen's home, there were a couple news media trucks already parked on the street. This is what they hoped to avoid, but now all he could hope for was to get Dr. Brandenhagen inside his home with a couple security guards posted outside the home to prevent "visitors."

The news media people might be assholes but they are smart assholes. When they see these black SUV's, the idiots drive around in blowing their cover, they obviously are someone connected to someone with some authority. Pulling up in those black SUVs especially in front of Dr. Brandenhagen's home after that news cast was a really dumb thing to do. But Robots take orders and never think outside the box if they want to make sure they keep their good paying jobs.

The two SUVs stopped on the street, and just like a carefully planned choreography, the suits got out and with two in the front and two in back of Dr. Roger Brandenhagen, they made their way to his front door even though they had to shove a couple camera's out of their faces.

There were numerous questions the reporters were throwing at Dr. Roger Brandenhagen.

"Doctor Brandenhagen, are there aliens inside that comet?"

"Doctor Brandenhagen, will the comet strike Earth?"

"Doctor Brandenhagen, who are these men escorting you? Are you in some kind of trouble?"

As soon as they got Brandenhagen inside his home, they all left except the two men left at the front entrance there to tell anyone who wanted to ring his doorbell, he wished to not be disturbed.

The other Cash in Advance men quickly high tailed to those idling SUV's which pulled out immediately after the delivery.

Dr. Roger Brandenhagen was in his home no more than one minute when his phone rang. It didn't shock him that Chad Wentworth was calling.

"What now?" Roger asked as soon as he saw the caller I.D.

"Thank you for ignoring the reporters' questions on the way home. We just wanted you to know there are people in front of your home as well as in the alley behind you to protect you."

"That doesn't make me feel a lot more secure tonight knowing tomorrow will probably be the day they come down for a visit or an invasion."

"The administration is working on all that now."

"I suppose they will be just as successful as that goat fuck pulling out of Afghanistan?"

"There are reasons for everything we can't divulge because if the public knows it, then so does the enemy."

"Does that mean the enemy from within?"

"What are you making by that comment?"

"The perception is you're A-Team had too much trouble handling the former President's JV team he talked about. So, tell me Chad Wentworth what do you guys' plan on doing when you discover these Aliens are not the JV-team that beat you in Afghanistan and are the A-team you can't handle?"

"Dr. Brandenhagen, this is all speculation on you part. All we can see with our great optics capability is a comet. There are no signs of life or signals on that rock. We of course are curios as what caused it to slow down."

"Chad, the only thing that can slow down such a heavy object like that comet is brakes and propulsion. Since breaks don't work in space that only leaves one option: propulsion."

"Dr. Brandenhagen, we have not seen any signs

of propulsion or rocket exhaust to suggest any such nonsense occurred."

"Well Chad, thank you for calling me but before I hang up, I just want you to know that with probably 24 hours you will have all your answers then call me back so I can tell you, see I told you so."

"Dr. Brandenhagen this will all be over soon, so please continue to refrain from talking to those reporters outside your front door."

"I understand fully, I'm under house arrest and one day muzzling me will be something your agencies wish the hell they had not done because I might have some ideas on how to handle and mitigate the disaster, I think this administration will do, especially if those aliens chose to land somewhere in America."

"Dr. Brandenhagen, that is not going to happen."

"Well thank you for setting me straight Nostradamus."

"Good bye." Chad Wentworth then hung up knowing he wasn't getting anywhere with Dr. Brandenhagen but at the same time he didn't have a warm fuzzy this administration knew what the hell they were doing.

Roger then walked to his kitchen window and looked out towards the back yard and the alley way behind it. Sure, enough there were a couple goons out there in suits, fully locked and loaded just in case.

Roger walked into his front room and turned on the TV and selected Consolidated News Network which now had live reports over the growing public concern about the comet and the wishy-washy information coming out of the Administration. To say they lost a lot of public support over the Afghanistan debacle didn't help their case with the comet was an understatement.

Roger was smiling though, he knew in the morning when the administration had to start explaining the presence of a second Moon, how they would look so clumsy.

I wonder if we'll see a new white house spokesperson who's a better bullshitter tomorrow?

Chapter Three
Beltway Bastards

For some reason the following morning the TV coverage seemed to take on the appearance of the media gobbling up the administration like they did during Watergate. While Roger was making his morning coffee, he looked out his Kitchen window and there were two goons like yesterday, but it was obvious they had a shift change. Roger was so smug in his prediction he knew that probably by the evening the goons would be gone because by then the aliens would have landed and it would no longer be a secret, but more of another public relations disaster this administration could not afford.

Roger sat the coffee down on the light stand next to his recliner chair in front of the TV where he took a lot of naps, then walked over to the front door and looked through the security visor and saw two suits were at his front door and a couple news media vans were still parked on the street. *They are probably waiting for my appearance when this all blows up in the administration's faces.*

What Roger didn't know since he wasn't in the loop is it already started. During the night out in

Arizona as *Binii'łigaii* (screeching owl) and *Nizhóní Ch'ilátah Hózhóón* (beautiful flower) were watching the two moons, the smaller new moon played a magic spell. It started breathing fire. They were observing the Zhrakzhongs invasion team swing into action.

The Zhrakzongs needed to send down air defense squadrons and special assault troops to take care of any interference from Earth governments. The first phase of their operation would place a contingency not far from the *Béésh Łigaii Atsu* (Silver Eagle) Native American Tribe dwellings.

They were very mindful not to harm or disturb the locals, plus in this rugged area, even lizards and other desert creatures had a hard time existing. Water was precious. The *Béésh Łigaii Atsu* tribe had the only viable water well in 25 or more miles.

By sunrise to say *Binii'łigaii* wasn't a changed man was quite wrong. Not long after the 2nd moon spit out fire, there were objects that descended and came down probably a mile south of them. By morning the two moons were no longer visible and *Binii'łigaii* led *Nizhóní Ch'ilátah Hózhóón* to their home where it would not be as comfortable sleeping when the sun came up.

The three-foot-thick walls helped keep the home in a reasonable temperature with all the doors and windows shut. But the kids would be up soon making a lot of racket thus they knew they forfeited their nights sleep for this magical moment they experienced. About five seconds after *Binii'tigaii* laid down, he was in a comfortable sleep.

As soon as the kids started their morning routine which included a lot of noise, *Nizhóní Ch'ilátah Hózhóón* got up and directed them to stop making noise or go back to their beds because their father needed his sleep.

Her wonderful children complied and sat motionless waiting for the go signal where they could raise hell again. Nevertheless, the neighbors' kids were yelling, screaming, playing games and having fun. Then suddenly around 10:00 a.m. it was silent.

Silence is also a warning signal. It troubled *Nizhóní Ch'ilátah Hózhóón* who got up out of bed to check out the situation and make sure her kids were in the house and safe. They were looking out the window at the other kids who were looking at something almost appearing terrified.

Nizhóní Ch'ilátah Hózhóón opened the door and went outside and stood by the neighbors' children to gauge what drew their attention. In the matter of a few seconds, she was terrified. She now knew her wise husband was correct last night when the second moon started shooting fire that gods had spoken.

South of their settlement was a formation of Zhrakzhongs along with their exoskeletons and other apparatus that made them all look so terrifying.

This was not the Zhrakzhongs first time of landing on a planet evaluated as a pushover. The Zhrakzongs were establishing a perimeter defense and had extremely advanced weapon systems.

Norad not too far away up in Colorado Springs tracked the Zhrakzhongs to their landing sites in Arizona and down in a desert in Mexico. The Mexican landings would take some diplomacy because Mexico didn't want any American intrusions in their air space. But the Arizona site was in U.S. territory, so the beltway bastards could do whatever the hell they wanted.

The Zhrakzhongs took on much more powerful nations than the USA. They were not concerned. They knew we had nukes that could do a lot of damage, but none of them would ever get near the target. The air space around the Zhrakzhongs was sealed off. Airliners were escorted around it and made numerous reports to the FAA upset that belligerent Air Force Officers were diverting them with no justification. What the airline pilots didn't know those were not American officials talking to them.

To make matters worse, the Cowboys at the Pentagon flew two squadrons of F22's from their temporary base in Nevada to the landing sight to identify and take on the Aliens if necessary. None of the F22's that showed any signs of hostilities made it back to base. The Zhrakzhongs quickly discovered half the pilots were Cowboys and the other half Chickenshits who made it back to the base safely.

The Zhrakzhongs engaged the F22 squadrons long before they were in range of visual observation of the growing Alien settlement where the newcomers were now arriving.

One group of F22's came in low below what was assumed below radar. The Zhrakzhongs operating the air defense exoskeletons shot them all down like shooting ducks in a barrel using their Plasma Debilitater weaponry. No missiles, no anti-air artillery or any other conventional defense methods were used. The pilots had virtually no warning and only discovered bad things were happening to them when on board electronics started malfunctioning just before the craft blew up in the plasma field. In one case the pilot was ejected from the F22 but unfortunately the Plasma Debilitater weapon took his life moments before he was ejected only due to equipment malfunction and was not initiated by the pilot. His lifeless body floated to the ground in the Arizona desert where his remains were discovered days later by Native American Tribesmen long after the desert life obtained what they wanted from his remains.

Everything that Dr. Roger Brandenhagen unsuccessfully warned them about now manifested.

Suddenly the Aliens in Mexico no longer mattered for the time being. The Arizona situation was a glaring indictment to the administration. It's one thing to have a colossal screwup half around the world, it's another to have one in your own back yard.

When their husbands did not return home that day after "routine flights" the squadron commander was ordered to do something that disturbed him greatly. He was to round up every family member of pilots that did not return, seize their cell phones and put them into quarantine until further notice.

The pilots who returned were not going to put up with that bull crap. The base was placed into threatcon Delta and locked down, but that did not stop the pissed off pilots from leaking it to the press.

Nor could they do anything about the eye witnesses from the ground that saw how our F22 Raptors were no match for these highly sophisticated aliens.

Some discussions including dropping a hydrogen bomb on them. But suddenly clearer heads prevailed as one lone dissenter in the room, CIA analyst Sally Fairbanks raised her voice and said, "Dr. Brandenhagen warned you all something like this was going to happen."

"We dealt with Dr. Brandenhagen," one of the CIA analysts commented.

"All you did was silence him," Sally Fairbanks stated in the tersest manner.

"Yes, we did under orders from up above."

"He also gave you another warning that if you approached these aliens with hostile intentions, bad things could happen."

"And the Aliens apparently are very hostile considering what happened to the F22's we flew down from Nevada."

"Right now, the only damage you got is the F22 squadrons shot to pieces because some god damn Cowboy made his macho move."

"I like the idea of nuking them because it will send a message to them that we also have some powerful weapons."

"Even if you are successful at dropping a nuke down on them, we have no idea what the reprisal would be."

"They are currently centered in just two areas that we know of, in Arizona and down in Mexico. We need to hit them before they land more forces on the planet."

"Look to the skies, there is a second moon up there full of surprises we have no idea what is in it. Now is not the time to be cavalier and arrogant. We need to send diplomats in to talk with them to find out what their intentions are, because we sure as hell probably do not have the means to do anything about it otherwise."

"We do not have any diplomats that are prepared to deal with Aliens."

"Certainly, we do, Dr. Brandenhagen."

"He's currently not a government employee."

"He can be immediately contracted by one of your Beltway Bandits then he would be covered administratively, by the contract."

"Who would you suggest?"

"EG&G"

"They don't exist anymore. They were taken over in a Merger."

"That's not true. A part of them remains but doesn't have much visibility since they do not operate in the military support role."

"What exactly does this spinoff group do?"

"They were our interface to the Monroe Institute in developing Hemi-Sync for our agents that work behind enemy lines."

"How quickly could they be turned on?"

"You give me the authorization, I'll have them contracted within an hour, and they will have Dr. Brandenhagen hired within two hours."

"What makes you think Dr. Brandenhagen would be willing to take on such a task?"

"I think I got him figured out. He would do what is necessary to protect this planet and prevent an intergalactic war."

"How would we approach him?"

"As soon as EG&G is awarded the soul-source non-bid contract, I will personally pay him a visit."

"They will probably ask for a blank check."

"It would not be the first time Cash in Advance gave out blank checks."

"Yea, Obama was very cooperative with the CIA."

Chapter Four
Everyone Has a Price

The meeting quickly broke up so that all those involved in manning the crisis center could get back to Special Activities Command Center right away. This SCI cleared area had all the latest toys and display capability, partially augmented by artificial intelligence (AI). In essence it figured out the questions you need answers for usually before you formulate the question.

Because of the sophistication these aliens appeared to have, the Special Operations Group the SAC maintained was experienced in quickly setting up paramilitary operations in the briefest periods of time.

J. Grant Foster, the person from SOG who initiated the F22 flights down to Arizona was already packing his bags for China which is one of the two exclusive areas people were sent if it deemed, they screwed up.

Foster was an extreme innovator. The F22 Raptor squadrons had been sent out to Nellis Air Force Base where they could train using new ordinance developed for what was expected if things blew over in Taiwan and American Carriers were threatened in the South

China Sea. F22's flown from Okinawa could patrol over Taiwan where they had some safety margin, then if the big showdown happened these new weapons were a force multiplier. In essence one jet now had the fire power of ten. J. Foster Grant figured the same attributes would work dealing with the Aliens, and when the pilots took off that morning it wasn't for surveillance purposes since the KH-14 did all the surveillance the SOG needed.

Fighter pilots are usually type A personality with a great deal of determination, almost to the point they were sociopaths. To make matters worse, this hand-picked squadron from Virginia was rated as THE MOST AGGRESSIVE squadron in the entire United States Air Force. It was needless to say they would have more than their fair share of Cowboys.

The chickenshits who made it back to base alive in a short period of time wished they hadn't because some of the recorded voice channels fed via satellite clearly showed their cowardice including squadron commander condemning them as his own world was quickly disintegrating.

Sally Fairbanks knew much of the story as she was in the Special Activities Command Center CIC at the time of the incident and watched it all unfold via satellite feed and the various voice and video the modern air battlefield can provide, some of which was from space via the KH-14.

Sally Fairbanks knew her agency was going in the wrong direction and had been doing so since the early 1960's when Richard Bissell, Tracey Barnes, Allen Dulles, and Frank Wisner left the scene. The agency was now full of advocates instead of information seekers like they should be. It was Sally's firm belief the paramilitary operations should be left to the military and the Cash in Advance boys should just stick to providing INTEL. She believed that such a posture would not only improve what they do, but also, they would get more buy in from the military if they stopped all paramilitary operations and turned that over to the Pentagon where it should reside.

Nevertheless, Sally Fairbanks was a team player, never seeking notoriety, and always thinking in terms what is in their best interest not only short term but long-term consequences.

One of her biggest challenges of her life was now to go mend fences with a distinguished scientist, Dr. Brandenhagen who they humiliated and beat down with a heavy hand and convince him to be a negotiator in a sense with these aliens if it was even possible.

Sally wasn't dressed to badly that day and certainly wasn't a hag like some of the older cold warriors in the office. As an expert in social engineering, she felt if she worked at it hard enough, she would get Dr. Brandenhagen to go out to Arizona with her today and set the stage for discussions they should have attempted long before that dick head J. Grant Foster cowboyed up and sent those F22 pilots to their deaths. She could only imagine what was going on with the families. She knew first-hand the consequence of casualties as a few of her former coworkers got nailed shortly after getting out of a Sikorsky UH-60 Black Hawk helicopter in a paramilitary operation where the DEA was trying to take down one of the most dangerous drug cartels in Central America.

The families of the dead Americans thought their loved ones were white-color analysts on an assignment for a few days. They had no idea the kinds of treacherous work they often did and they were all close nit family people which makes the loss even harder to take.

Sally knew that particular case all too well. Another Cowboy with too much power and control executed a crappy mission that was half ass planned and conducted with arrogance until the bad guys gave them a taste of their own medicine. One day the agency will learn from the British: you can't Cowboy it and rush things. They are successful in many areas we fail at because long ago they learned to be subtle and patient, and to not to get into someone else's business aka military.

Sally walked into her office made a few phone calls and went down to the front entrance where a vehicle that didn't stand out waited for her.

Away they went and thank God it wasn't during Rush hour or it would take up to two hours to get there.

Driving through DC and the beltway is lovely if you hit it while everyone was at work and a few hours before they are scheduled to go home for the day.

DC is another one of those well-planned public transit disasters. People with good intentions spent a lot of money, but in reality, they didn't produce what the public needs since it was designed as if everyone lived near the tracks or the bus route. Something as simple as building more parking garages at public transportation hubs would have a remarkable improvement to utilization. It doesn't seem to get through the thick skulls of some of the designers, people are not going to walk 3 miles after they park their car to get on a train.

In due time the car pulled near the front of Dr. Brandenhagen's home. With a lot of rumors and leaks coming out of pissed off pilots in Nevada, there were now double the number of TV reporter trucks with antenna's double parked on the street waiting for Dr. Brandenhagen's appearance.

Sally instructed the driver, "I'm going to get out here and walk up to his home."

"What are you going to tell the reporters as you approach his door?"

"I'm his daughter coming over for a visit."

Sally got out about three houses away and walked up the crowded sidewalk. There were a few people crowding and shoving, but Sally's looks and charm easily gave her a free pass to get past the riffraff.

She walked up the stairs and the Cash in Advance boys there acting as sentries easily identified her by sight and simply moved aside to give her plenty of room to ring the doorbell and meet with Doctor Brandenhagen.

After about 3 rings, Doctor Brandenhagen yelled from his recliner, "Okay I'm coming, please stop ringing the doorbell."

Roger was surprised as he looked through the security lenses to see Sally Fairbanks at his front door. He opened the door and said, "Please come in."

Roger certainly didn't want the crowd to see him talking with Sally Fairbanks or hear what the two might have to say to each other.

"What's the special occasion that brings you here?"

"I assume you have already figured out by now a lot of things you warned us about has already manifested, and the agency now has a case of red ass."

"I assumed it would all come down to that. But I could read about that in the news, I can't believe you drove all the way over here just to tell me that."

"No, indeed not. You are a very perceptive person Dr. Brandenhagen.

"If I were a betting man, I'd say you came all this way to ask me a favor."

"I knew you would think that."

"Well then, what is it?"

"I might as well lay my cards out on the table now and see where it gets me."

"That's usually the best policy."

"Dr. Brandenhagen, I want you to accompany me out to Arizona and meet the Aliens."

"When do you plan such a trip?"

"Right now. Come as you are, we'll be going directly to Andrews Airforce Base where we have transportation waiting."

"What is it exactly you want me to do?"

"You have been promoted to diplomatic service."

"How could you do that; I no longer work for the government."

"That's true, however you have just been hired by a Beltway Bandit company, and they will take care of all he messy paperwork after we come back from the trip."

"I'm not looking for a full-time job."

"This will be a temporary assignment with a fat paycheck and you will not be compelled to work for more than 30 days I would suspect."

"How much money are we talking?"

"Probably four times as much as you made in the past, but I will sweeten the deal a bit."

"How so?"

"There are a lot of things you and the public do not know about Mars and what we have done there including bringing back a number of samples. I know that based on reading your work and observing your YouTube videos, you could advance all of your theories on the Martian nuclear disaster if you had soil and air samples. If you agree to take on this assignment, I will get you access to those soil and air samples as long as you are willing to sign a non-disclosure agreement for the diplomatic services and any information gleaned from the air and soil samples."

"It doesn't do me much good to have the air and

soil samples if you are not going to allow me to access it."

"Even if you can't disclose it, merely by discovering the truth and the details can bolster your Martian theories and then you will know how valid your prior comments happen to be. If you know the answer, then you will figure out how to get the data provided in a manner that would allow you to release it to the public. We just can't allow you to identify us as the source.

"That's fair, I suppose I could do it."

"Get your hat and your jacket and us go."

"That's a long way to Arizona, you sure I don't need to bring anything?"

"Everything you need will be provided. We have a lot of gophers to get what you need."

"What do you mean by gophers?"

"Go for this go for that."

"I see what you mean, ok let me turn out the lights. By the way I don't mind those guys out front keeping potential burglars out of my home while I'm gone."

"You will leave through the back entrance of your home. We can't allow the media out front to see you leave with me."

"Yea that would be scandalous."

"They think I'm your daughter."

"I can imagine."

"Keep an eye out your kitchen window. When you see the blue Toyota pull up, it will be us, come out right away, we need to get you in the car and out of here before the media guys figure out you are going somewhere."

"Alright."

Sally Fairbanks walked out the front entrance, then down 3 blocks where a policeman was having a little talk with the driver of the blue Toyota. Sally walked to the passenger side and got in the car, then she pulled out her FBI badge given her for the joint task force she supported part time, and told the police officer, "Thank you officer for protecting our car. We now must leave as we have urgent business to attend."

All along Officer Leroy Jackson thought the driver was bullshitting him and he was about to write him a ticket, but now he just grinned and shook his head. It's not the first or last time Leroy had to deal with spooks.

"It might be better if you back up and go down the side street to the alley where we will pick up Dr. Brandenhagen."

"We are lucky the police officer diverted all the traffic around this car, its currently open behind us."

The driver, a nice-looking man named Rodriguez, started backing up leaving the police officer Leroy Jackson in the middle of the road. After about 3 more houses, the side road existed they turned into and then smartly went to the alley way and up to the area where two Cash in Advance guys were standing."

Sally Fairbanks asked Rodriguez, "Could you please roll down your window I need to inform these guys."

After the window rolled down Rodriquez informed the man closer to them, "Sally wants to tell you something."

The man approached the car window. He knew who Sally Fairbanks was and she informed him, "We are taking Dr. Brandenhagen on a little trip. You guys are to remain here and act like he's still inside the house."

"All right."

About that time Roger Brandenhagen opened his

back door and proceeded to the gate that opened to the alley where his trash containers were sitting waiting for pickup. The Cash in advance man closest to the car, opened the rear door for Roger who immediately got in, then the car sped away. Turning away from his street and down a side road to get to the beltway where they would make their way out to McClain Virginia where a Sikorsky S-97 was waiting for them to transport them to the special hanger at Andrews that only saw Air Force One or CIA jets.

The S-97 traveling at 250 knots took a short time to get to Andrews where it landed right next to the hanger. Roger and Sally got out of the helicopter and were escorted through a side door into the hanger where a nice and pretty Gulfstream 650 with no markings was parked and the ladder extended down for passengers to get on. Next to the ladder was a female CIA officer Mable Potter who was in effect the executive officer for the Aircraft and controlled all its movements and cargo. Sally led Roger over to the jet and climbed up the stairs into the aircraft with Roger following her and also noticing she had a particularly well shaped posterior.

Mable Potter waiting by the GS650 ladder, followed the two passengers up inside and immediately retracted the ladder and closed and locked the door. She then walked forward and informed the pilots; the passengers were aboard and they were ready to leave.

She then looked back into the cabin and observed Roger and Sally sitting in isle chairs across from each other. She had flown with Sally before so she knew she didn't have to give the flight attendant speech because Sally would make sure the other passenger knew what to do in all instances.

As soon as the door to the aircraft shut, the ground crew knew it was time to open the hanger doors and the tug driver hitched to the GS-650 waited until the ground crew cleared him to tow the plane out of the hanger then made a 90 degree turn so the jet could start its engines without blowing the exhaust into the hanger.

The plane already had preflight checks completed on the assumption things out west would require transportation real time, and flight plan filed with the FAA the pilot and co-pilot restarted the engines even though 30 minutes prior had been checked out and shut down and secured, then went through an abbreviated check list and were soon moving on the ramp near the end of the runway 19L where they quickly lined up for takeoff.

With only 2 passengers on board the Air Force Officers, former jet-jockeys were happy the plane would be light with no cargo and take off with a full fuel tank with no stops on the way. They would be flying into Tucson Arizona, Davis-Monthan Air Force Base, where a reconditioned Sikorsky UH-60 Black Hawk fully recertified with crew ready to ferry them to nearby the aliens. It was sometimes rare they got to take off with such a light load where they could do a nice high-performance takeoff and get to altitude quickly and feel the G force all that nice thrust of the two Rolls-Royce BR725 engines, each producing a maximum thrust of 17,000 pounds-force.

Mable Potter sat in the seat facing Sally Fairbanks offset from Roger. The two-women chit chatted until the plane leveled off at cruising altitude then Mable got up and walked to the galley to prepare coffee for the pilots and the guest.

Roger had never been on a corporate jet like this before. Traveling at Mach 0.9 at 50,000 feet made it a comfortable flight with little or no turbulence. The pilots were briefed to get the passengers to Davis-Monthan Air Force Base safely and as fast as possible, because they wanted them to have time on the helicopter flying in daylight hours.

During the flight Mable Potter provided Sally Fairbanks a CIA notebook that automatically erased all new files when it was shut down for security reasons. The laptop was hooked up to the internet via satellite and she was getting all the mission planning information live including satellite imagery. The satellite provided the alien defense perimeter showing all the elaborate hardware set out to protect the site and the helicopter steered around them. Ultimately the only place they could find to land the helicopter was on that 10 mile dirt road that led to the *Béésh Łigaii Atsu* (Silver Eagle) Native American Tribe village.

After a few phone calls to Arizona and discussing the plan with retired Marine Corp Navajo's, they were asked to go out to the *Béésh Łigaii Atsu* village to inform them a helicopter would be sitting down on the dirt road a couple miles from their village and to please be kind to them when they arrived to talk with the Aliens.

Retired Sargent Hawthorne would no doubt think this was some kind of joke or a farce, had it not been for the fact a Marine Corp General called him and asked for his assistance in the matter. The General was introduced to him by another Marine he knew who was still on active duty. To say he wasn't the least bit astonished was an understatement.

Sargent Hawthorne had seen some hot fire fights in his days in the Marines and he felt it was expected of him to assist his country if he were in a position to do so.

The other purpose for sending Sargent Hawthorne in was to make sure there were no children or individuals on the dirt road that could get hurt by the helicopter or worse yet alien fire if it erupted.

From about 10:00 until the helicopter arrived the entire *Béésh Łigaii Atsu* tribe lined up by their settlement and surveyed the strange looking alien hardware south of them.

The Aliens knew they were simple indigenous people and not a threat, but they were professionals and didn't try to communicate or mingle with them because they were here for business and based on the threatening behavior and subsequent air combat this morning, they were not expecting a friendly welcome.

It took about an hour for Sargent Hawthorne to

drive his Jeep down the 2 lane Arizona State Hiway and turn down the dirt road to the village. He brought along some nice things for the villagers because he felt sorry for their poverty and thus brought along the most precious materials for them: bottled water cases.

The *Béésh Łigaii Atsu* would enjoy the clean drinking water plus some of the mothers would give their children some extra clean bird baths that day. They would be cleaner than they had been for weeks.

Binii 'łigaii wasn't expecting anyone and when the jeep pulled into the village, he turned to his wife *Nizhóní Ch'ilátah Hózhóón* because he recognized the Jeep and said, "That's Hawthorne, I wonder why he's here?"

In due course the Jeep stopped in front of *Binii 'łigaii* and Hawthorne got out and approached him.

Hawthorne had not been looking for aliens, he was more concerned about driving safely on the rugged dirt road and make sure he didn't run over children or animals. As soon as he got near *Binii 'łigaii,* the medicine man pointed to some of the Alien devices parked about a half a mile away. That's when reality hit Sargent Hawthorne like a ton of bricks.

Navajo and other Native Americans have ancient stories handed down concerning alien visitors in the past. One theory about the disappearance suddenly of Native Americans that disappeared from Mesa Verde in the four corners area, is they were abducted by aliens.

Sargent Hawthorne nevertheless assumed those stories were just folklore and preposterous. And now here he was facing the real thing knowing that in probably an hour or less, an Army helicopter with a couple civilians would be landing two miles up that dirt road to talk with these aliens.

Sargent Hawthorne knew this was a tumultuous time and these simple Native Tribesmen were not psychologically prepared for what was in store for them. So, he did the most humane thing possible to distract them from the events unfolding before their eyes and he said, "I thought you guys could use some bottled water. Could you help me carry this to your home?"

Sargent Hawthorne knew *Binii'ligaii* was a fair and decent man and as the Tribe's medicine man would dish it out equally among all the households, so it seemed the most logical thing to do was to first just get all those cases of water to his home.

The wife, kids and several other males jumped in and helped carry the cases of water bottles. As they got near *Binii'ligaii's* home, he directed those other males to take the water bottle cases they were carrying to their own homes. They all liked that idea. In five minutes or so the Jeep was unloaded and he aliens were observing with very powerful optics and watched all this unfold. They of course were curious as to what they were carrying until the tribe's people all took water bottles and enjoyed the moment drinking from them. The high-powered optics easily helped them figure out they were drinking the liquid, which was most likely water.

After the Jeep was unloaded, Sargent Hawthorne informed the villagers, "An Army helicopter is going to land up on the dirt road. I'm going to find a good flat spot up there for them to land on and park my Jeep there. Please keep all the children away from my Jeep because we do not want them to get injured when the helicopter lands."

"Allright," *Binii 'łigaii* said, then asked, "Would it be ok if I wait with you up there?"

"Actually, that's a good idea, if any of the villagers come up you can ask them to return to the village."

Binii 'łigaii gave instruction to the villagers directing them all to stay near their homes and to not go up the dirt road. He then hopped in the Jeep with Sargent Hawthorne who then found the best spot on the road about a mile up and parked his jeep next to it.

Flying at mach 0.9 (666.99 miles per hour) on a bee line course got the GS650 to Tucson Arizona took them about three and a half hours, with plenty of sunlight lit for the rest of their day. The GS650 landed and the air traffic controllers directed them over to the operating Sikorsky UH-60 Black Hawk ready for takeoff as soon as the passengers boarded.

There is a lot of beauty in Arizona, unfortunately you can't see it all from roads and hiways, but on a helicopter flying at a few thousand feet you can see it all. The serenity that hit Roger as he looked out of the open helicopter door gave him a feeling that would no doubt improve his disposition when he came in contact with the aliens.

"Are we going to have to go through some type of quarantine after we meet up with the aliens?" Roger asked Sally.

"Most likely."

"Can I do the quarantine in my home?"

"I'm sure we can work something out."

"I appreciate that."

The helicopter pilot flew on a course with coordinates fed to him he could dial into his GPS assisted navigation system. In effect he was flying auto pilot the entire distance. The Zhrakzhong aliens were carefully monitored the helicopter for the first sign of hostile intentions would shoot it down. The fact the helicopter never came within 10 miles of the aliens until it turned down the dirt road off the Hiway went far to ensure the safety of those onboard.

The Zhrakzhongs were of course curious why this single aircraft with no exposed weaponry was flying along their perimeter. The Earth people obviously knew the boundaries and were not attempting fate.

Sargent Hawthorne had called the General on his cell phone and informed him he was parked East of a nice flat area on the hilltop where it would be best to land the Helicopter. He also offered to drive the visitors to the Alien perimeter in his Jeep. The General relayed that to the crew on the helicopter so as it flew over that dirt road in a short period of time the pilot spotted the Jeep and an X marked on the dirt road by Sargent Hawthorne to signal a landing zone. The pilot was instructed to shut down his engines as to give a more accommodative appearance to the Aliens they knew would be watching every move they made.

Before the helicopter came down the dirt road,

the Jeep had been turned towards the village which would give them the best approach to the Aliens now hunkered down about a half mile south of the village in some flat and smooth pastureland that provided livestock food for about 3 months of the year. Oddly there was a dirt trail down that pasture the tribe's people had used from time to time to haul hay in to feed the livestock which could be sheep or cattle.

As soon as the helicopter shut down its engines, Sally Fairbanks who was in charge of the operation directed the crew, "Wait here until we come back."

The pilot asked, "What if they kill you and you don't come back?"

"If they were going to do something like that, they would have shot your helicopter down an hour ago."

To the Helicopter pilot this was a surreal event because up on the hilltop he could spot some of the alien hardware out there and when he looked through his binoculars at the aliens the first thing, he spotted was aliens looking at him!

It was as if the pilot was somehow imbedded in a science fiction movie. The battle-wears the aliens wore gave them a surreal appearance fitting for a movie.

The Alien devices looked nothing like a Jeep, Humvee, Tank, Bradley Fighting vehicle or Soviet Tanks. And at this distance it was slightly difficult to gauge the dimensions of the stuff he was looking at.

The group was lucky there was a cell phone tower just a few miles down the hiway, so they had cell phones and internet access. They all exchanged phone numbers just in case that form of communications was desired.

When they got out of the helicopter, they approached Sargent Hawthorne (retired). This was a proud Native American, and he exemplified the reality of the Marine Corp: Once a Marine Always a Marine. Some of his very best friends were guys he met in the Marine Corp and served with living in San Diego and Los Angeles. As a Marine, this was probably the most important mission he ever participated in. And he would do his very best. Since he was of Navajo blood, he had no fear of the Aliens. Because of Navajo Folklore it was more or less expected that one day the Tribe would encounter Aliens, but nothing like this was imaginable.

"I'm Sally Fairbanks and this is Dr. Roger Brandenhagen."

"Pleased to meet you, I'm Sargent Hawthorne, USMC retired."

"Thanks for assisting us, Sargent Hawthorne."

"My pleasure. I'm doing it for the Marine Corp."

"Yea I'm sorry we had to arrive in an Army Helicopter. I'm sure you would have preferred we arrived in a Marine Apache Helicopter."

"That's okay. I got a lot of rides on Army helicopters in my day."

"I bet you did."

"I assume I'll drive you down to the meeting."

"By now I'm sure they are figuring we are coming for a talk."

"I imagine so. Please hop in and us get going."

After they all got in the Jeep, Sargent Hawthorne headed down the dirt road into the village then turned south through the pasture and headed for the Aliens. Nobody knew what to expect, but Sargent Hawthorne figured he would wave at the aliens to convey there was no hostile intentions. His actions went a long way to save their lives as it gave a signal to the Aliens, they reported to their leaders now located about five miles south of this location.

The Jeep pulled up about 20 feet away from the nearest Alien device. It was unknown what it did nor did the appearance convey what its purpose was.

The three exited the Jeep and walked towards the Aliens and a moment later several Aliens exited one of the devices and walked towards the Earth people.

Now for the biggest surprise of all, the Aliens had translators.

"Hello and greetings. I'm Sally Fairbanks this is Doctor Brandenhagen and Sargent Hawthorne," which she gestured to at her side.

The Zhrakzhongs had mostly been in suspended animation for 10 years and not been with a woman in all that time. They are fond of female beauty and the Earth people had a remarkable resemblance to Zhrakzhongs which would make this migration a lot more desirable. One would say that Sally Fairbanks would be rated in the top 5 percent of beautiful Zhrakzhong females.

The fact the Earth people sent a beautiful woman to meet them helped to overcome the anxiety those F22 Cowboys created in the morning.

The senior officer for this sector stepped forward with another Zhrakzhong and said something to him in standard Zhrakzhong language. The person he communicated to then said, "Hello Sally Fairbanks, Doctor Brandenhagen, and Sargent Hawthorne."

"My government has asked me to come here to make introductions and have a few discussions." Sally stopped to give the translator time to repeat what she said in English to the Zhrakzhong language for the officer.

The officer then gave the translator a series of statements which he soon repeated in English:

"We came in peace but your welcoming committee this morning conveyed to us this might turn into a nasty struggle, but your appearance and demeaner here changes a lot."

"I'm surprised you can communicate to us so well. How long have you studied English?"

The translator repeated what Sally Fairbanks stated and then turned to her and responded, "I've studied English, Russian, Chinese, French, and German for 25 years."

About That Time Chills Went Up Sally Fairbanks spine as she now understood vividly *these Aliens had been studying them for a while and because Earth was such a pushover, it was time for them to move in.*

The officer then gave some statements to the translator who then repeated it in English, "Would you please follow us to the back of our Command Rover so that we can communicate with our superiors about your presence here."

They followed the two Aliens and noticed another thirty or so Aliens were watching them. Another visual Sally quickly discovered: even though the officer and translator were about their height and build around six feet, these other aliens were all about seven or eight feet tall! *Oh my god! They are Giants!*

Sally Fairbanks didn't know the average Zhrakzhong was built about the same size as most humans. These were shock troops from the Empire used for planetary invasion and plunder.

At the back of the Alien device a large door was open. The space inside would easily fit a couple large tanks. It was obviously some sort of command vehicle with no tires, wheels, or apparent means of travel. The officer walked up the ramp inside and directed the translator to tell them, "Come inside with me."

Very soon it became apparent why as the Alien spoke to a black box and suddenly a holograph popped up. This was another surreal moment as the holograph looked real as if the person was standing on the small black box.

There was a short discussion between the officer and the individual who appeared but was just a holograph of some sort.

The officer then asked the translator to provide

the Earth people the translations of what General Níngsī just said.

"General Níngsī would like us to take you to his headquarters so that you can ask him questions and he can explain why we are here."

"Thank you, that would be very helpful," Sally Fairbanks responded with a smile.

The translator then turned towards the holograph that would project his image to General Níngsī as he repeated what the Earth woman stated in standard Zhrakzhong.

The holograph suddenly disappeared and the officer said and the translator repeated in English: "Please have a seat." He then gestured towards several comfortable chairs which the three visitors sat down at.

Within a moment the rear ramp of the alien craft lifted up and a false wall came down covering it, no doubt to prevent dirt and debris from coming into the craft.

The three Earth people could not see what was happening but the *Béésh Łigaii Atsu* (Silver Eagle) Native American Tribe observing from their village observed this strange object lift off the ground and moved quickly south and was soon out of view. There were no wings or sound or any reason to suspect this thing could fly. It seemed like it was only a few minutes, and the device sat down and the false wall lifted up and the ramp lowered and the officer said to the translator which he repeated in English, "Please come with us."

Sally Fairbanks is a very intelligent woman.

She fully understood that if an Alien race showed up in a space craft a fraction of the size of the Moon, it would not be wise to tempt your fait with them. The technological differences between the Aliens and the Cosmic Cockroaches – Earth people took all recourses out of their hands. Now the question simply was, to what extent was this planetary invasion and what's the end game. Sally was feeling a little trepidation especially when she looked at the thing, they were walking towards that seemed a hell of a lot larger than a nuclear-powered Ford Class Aircraft Carrier.

It also had a large ramp and was no doubt one of the things that brought what she just traveled in to this planet.

The officer and translator led them up the ramp and through a doorway that was the access to an apparent elevator they rode up to near the top of this beast.

Inside they walked into what must have been an Alien Combat Information Center CIC. A quick assessment by Sally Fairbanks this large room was probably five basketball gyms wide. There must have been 1000 Aliens in here working all well dressed and professional acting. In the very center of this complex was a platform that had a circular staircase around it which the Zhrakzhong Officer led them up. In the middle of this platform was a wide chair and suspended from above appeared to be a number of sheets of glass. But as they walked into the center of this platform, they discovered those glass sheets were displays showing lots of videos, not only around this Alien landing zone, but a number of segments in outer space including images of the mother ship disgorging shuttle craft. In the span of 15 minutes over a million Zhrakzhongs left the mother ship, coming down to Earth and their new life.

Sally Fairbanks had no idea what Norad was observing, if she did, she would be a lot more depressed and not so perky acting. At this very moment she felt so blessed she arranged to have Doctor Brandenhagen with her to give her some psychological support because she was way in over her head and after looking at just this one Alien craft, she knew it was most unlikely Earth could do much or say much about the Alien invasion that caught them by surprise. The likelihood they could have mitigated the situation by any means was doubtful.

The General stood up and approached the Officer, translator, and the three Earth people. The Earth female was dressed very nicely, but the two others were plain clothed and certainly didn't appear to be diplomats like he expected.

The translator informed the General in Standard Zhrakzhong, this is a representative from Earth Governments Sally Fairbanks and her associates Doctor Brandenhagen and Sargent Hawthorne. General Níngsī then said in Standard Zhrakzhong, using English words his teleprompter was providing.

"I'm General Níngsī Zhrakzhong Supreme Commander."

Besides his teleprompter he also had an earbud inserted which coached him into saying words in English. Aboard this glorious Zhrakzhong Command

Ship there was more computational power than all the computers on Earth combined. Out on the perimeter by the *Béésh Łigaii Atsu* (Silver Eagle) Native American Tribe they needed an actual translator, but here on the Command Ship, he wasn't required, but General Níngsī knew it was wise to have the translator at hand to ensure there was no misunderstanding on either party.

Zhrakzhong Intelligence reported to General Níngsī in his earbud "We traced this woman back to Washington DC on replay and data reduction of surveillance video."

They also gave General Níngsī the precise time the Gulfstream 650 left Andrews Air Force Base.

"Tell me Sally Fairbanks, how was your trip from Washington DC?"

"Flying via helicopter from Tucson up here was a pleasant trip, from the air it had a very nice appearance of the wide-open country."

"That's precisely why we decided to land here and also a spot down in Mexico."

"Do you plan to land elsewhere on the planet?"

"No, this area and the Mexico site have all the land we need."

Sally Fairbanks could see on the video displays a large number of people walking off transport space craft. Her guess was perhaps a million or more.

"General Níngsī, how many Zhrakzhongs are coming down to the planet?"

"We brought a Billion Zhrakzhongs with us."

"And you can fit them in the limited space you have cordoned off in Arizona and down in Mexico?"

"Yes, we will build three dimensional. You Earth people are still in the two-dimensional building mindset."

"We have some tall buildings."

"Yes, I've seen images of many of them, but compared to my world those are extremely small and waste a lot of Air Space."

Sally asked the obvious question: "Will you build buildings a lot taller than what exists on this planet now?"

"In a way we will, but most of the construction will be underground."

"Why underground?"

"You primitive Earth people have not yet learned there are very bad creatures out there in the Galaxy and its best to show the smallest foot print possible. That's why after our construction you will not know we are here."

"That brings me to the question why did you come to Earth."

"You are only observing a small segment of our Empire. We have no desire to capture your planet and take over. What we are doing is simply scattering our civilization across the galaxy in case we lose the ongoing conflict with the Xīnguī in hopes that our civilization will not die out."

"How long do you think this conflict will last?"

"The Xīnguī struggle been ongoing for about 500 years, but the end is near one way or another."

"When will you know the results?"

"We expect about a year from now."

"You are going to build two large infrastructures and you may abandon them in a year or so?"

"We have to assume we could lose. If we do then we will not be leaving the planet."

"What plans do you have for this planet then?"

"We do not want to change it in any way except for these two small areas where our civilization will either park for a while, or if necessary, stay longer until we figure out our next move with the Xīnguī."

"Could you explain what that means?"

Even though we are scattering our people around 100 or more solar systems which makes it too difficult to wipe out the Zhrakzhong civilization, we could reconstitute the Empire in exile and in a few centuries go back and reclaim our worlds."

"Don't you think the Xīnguī will be waiting for you and put up a strong defense?"

"Since there will not be any fighting in a very long time, they will grow complacent and lazy. In two centuries, they will be pushovers."

"How do you know that plan will work?"

"We know it will because it happened to us."

General Níngsī then called his assistant up to the Commanders platform and in Zhrakzhong language said, "I'm going to my quarters for a while to entertain our guests and get something to eat, continue the landing operation and inform me if you run into any snags."

The assistant Zhrakzhong Supreme Commander was no doubt a seasoned warrior and did not need General Níngsī's presence as he knew his own talents were more than what was required for the job. One of the major developments which eased a lot of tension was the fact this pushover planet must have taken some smart pills and realized they could not in any way interfere with the immense power of the Zhrakzhongs.

General Níngsī then turned towards Sally Fairbanks and said to her, "I would like you and your two associates to come with me to my private quarters where we may further discuss this and have something to eat because I am a little hungry as I've been on watch now for 20 hours without a break."

"We would be delighted to go to your quarters General Níngsī."

"Please follow me."

He then informed the translator to come with him. But he said to the other officer who brought the guests here, "Go back to your unit. I will contact you when it's time to come back and get my guests and return them to their transportation device."

"The Officer bowed and said something in

Zhrakzhong language that appeared to show respect and acknowledge his orders, before he turned and walked off the platform down the circular stairway.

General Níngsī then stated, "Please follow me." He led them over to a large yellow circle on the platform. As soon as they were all standing on the yellow circle, a glass circular barrier rose from the floor about waste high. Then suddenly the yellow portion of the floor sank down below them to a lower floor and stopped and the glass panel then recessed into the floor. General Níngsī then walked through a hallway that was incredibly decorated. Sally Fairbanks thought the last time she saw such an amazing wall was at the Moscow subway where the artwork and decoration designed by the top architects of the world back in the 1930's created such an eye-opening imagery that created such resplendence. This further triggered more thoughts in Sally a history buff who read Stalin slept in the Moscow subways during the battle of Moscow back in 1941 while the Germans were shelling Moscow from the outskirts of the city.

Along the hallway every twenty meters, was security guards with strange looking weapons.

Sargent Hawthorne liked the way the weapons looked and asked, "Excuse me General Níngsī, I'm curious, how do those weapons work your soldiers are carrying?"

The three Americans were not aware, artificial intelligence on board his command ship was constantly down loading and analyzing all the information they could obtain from either satellite communications or nearby microwave towers and cell phone sites. As such they were building an impressive lexicon and performing analysis on every word spoken by the Earth people. They informed General Níngsī the question Sargent Hawthorne asked.

General Níngsī stopped in front of one of the security force personnel and in Zhrakzhong language directed the soldier, "Take Sargent Hawthorne off the ship and demonstrate your weapon."

He also directed the translator, "Go with them to explain everything in English language and after the demonstration bring Sargent Hawthorne back to my private quarters and to translate to him what I just said."

The translator responded in Zhrakzhong to General Níngsī, then he explained it to Sargent Hawthorne who shortly left with the two Zhrakzhongs to go out and demonstrate his weapon.

They made their way off the ship and the only target the security force person could spot was one of those large Saguaro Cactuses (Carnegiea Gigantea) that was out of the way with no people or craft behind it to avoid.

The security guard explained and the translator said in English after brief delays, "This is a dual mode weapon. It has a laser for general combat, but in the event, there is a breach in the front lines while fighting where a large number of Xīnggui attacking, we have the built in Plasma Debilitater."

He then demonstrated and it took several shots

to knock down one of the saguaro branches using the laser. He then demonstrated the Plasma Debilitater. He took one shot at the middle of the Saguaro Cactus which blew it in half leaving only the stump of the Saguaro Cactuses.

"Wow! Why not just use the Plasma Debilitater?"

"We get over 100 shots on one charge shooting with the laser only."

"For each Plasma Debilitater shot it eliminates almost 20 laser shots. Most of the time we can kill enough enemy with the lasers so we can save the power pack by not shooting the Plasma Debilitater."

The security guard then asked Sargent Hawthorne, "What type of weapons do you use?"

"I've been retired for a few years, but when I was part of the Marine Corp I qualified as a sniper. One of my weapons was a 1903 M4 Springfield Rifle that shot ballistic rounds."

The translator who was familiar with American weapons and ballistics was able to explain it to the Security Guard who was quite amused because he had only seen lasers or Plasma Debilitater weapons for surface warfare.

"Thank you very much for the demonstration. If I ever need protection, I will come get you!"

The translator explained those comments to the security guard who smiled and thought the comment was mildly flattering. The translator then suggested they all proceed to General Níngsī's private quarters.

In due time the group was all back together again and the security guard was back at this station looking professional, but was also hand-picked for his impressive skills he demonstrated in protecting the General.

General Níngsī was showing some artwork and some imagery of his city back on the planet Boku. The cities looked sparsely populated because everything was underground.

"On Boku you hide most of the civilization underground?" Sally Fairbanks asked.

"We attempt to, but just like on this planet we also have traitors who provide secrets to the Xīnggui."

"How large is the Zhrakzhong Empire?"

"I left the capital at Boku 10 years ago. A lot of time has passed. We are now too far away to receive deep space transmission. We really do not know what the current status of the Empire is. Nevertheless, when I left Boku, we had our civilization spread across 100 planets."

"How many other of these transfer operations to other planets did you do?"

"You being a representative of your government obviously knows there are state secrets that cannot be divulged for the sake of society. I can't give you any details but I commanded the very last mission to take Zhrakzhong civilians to far off star systems to spread them out for protection."

Sally Fairbanks had a frightening thought just

then which she pressed General Níngsī. "General Níngsī I realize your first encounter with us when some idiot sent two F22 squadrons at you is uncharacteristic of who we are. The person who ordered that attack has been demoted. What he did was clearly stupid since the Zhrakzhongs have shown no hostile intent, and I gauge you as peace loving people based on how you have conducted yourselves. All you did was defend yourself from a stupid plan that never should have happened."

"I appreciate your comments with regards to all that," General Níngsī replied.

Sally Fairbanks then pressed home the point she wanted to make. "You are obviously in conflict with the Xīngguī and it seems to me based on what you have said and all the precautions you are taking to hide your civilization across numerous star systems, the Xīngguī are most likely very dangerous and evil people."

"That they are."

"Okay General Níngsī, I must ask this question and please be as candid as possible because it's something I feel compelled to advise my government on."

"And what is your question Sally Fairbanks?"

"General Níngsī, is there any chance the Xīngguī followed you here putting Earth at risk?"

"Sally Fairbanks," General Níngsī delayed allowing him to gather his thoughts because it was a critical question and he suspected it might come up in their discussions.

"Please just call me Sally."

"Alright Sally."

General Níngsī looked directly into Sally's eyes because this was a come to Jesus' question.

"If I told you that I knew for a fact the Xīngguī did not follow us here with probes or a Fast Frigate, I would be lying. There are many ways your enemy can track you. In fact, because of Xīngguī spies, they may have arrived here before us to be in position to make their reports."

"General Níngsī, if the Xīngguī do arrive and attack Earth will you attempt to help protect us?" Sally Fairbanks asked know the complicated situation they were now in.

"Sally, by the end of the day we will have 500 million Zhrakzhongs in Mexico and 500 million Zhrakzhongs here at this site. We would have to attempt protecting you because you and Mexico have populations that exist not too far from where we landed."

Sally Fairbanks knew she had some very hot information she needed to get back to Washington but before she had a chance to request transport back to the Jeep, General Níngsī said, "I've ordered a Banquet for us. In a few minutes my staff will be setting up and you will have the opportunity to sample some of the best foods of the Galaxy."

Sally Fairbanks knew she was stuck there for a while and Doctor Brandenhagen had not had much to say, and he appeared to be ready to get verbose by his body language.

Within moments offset in this very spacious room, Zhrakzhongs arrived in mass carrying an assortment of devices. Within 5 minutes what used to be an open area suddenly had a large table probably 20 feet long. Then came the padded chairs and a third wave of workers arrived with place settings, decorations, flowers, and bottles containing liquids. Then suddenly more tables sprang up and soon silver containers were brough in and placed on all of them.

Almost as if on que, a person dressed in a very ornate uniform approached General Níngsī and said something in standard Zhrakzhong, then turned around and walked over at the end of the table.

General Níngsī stood and said, "Our meal is prepared, please come join me."

To everyone's surprise a small placard was placed at each setting on the table identifying where everyone was to sit. Sally Fairbanks and Doctor Brandenhagen were identified to sit next to General Níngsī. Sargent Hawthorne was to sit on the right side of Doctor Brandenhagen.

This might be interesting, Sally Fairbanks thought.

The waiters also wearing ear buds were used to getting foreign languages piped in to help them communicate. In anticipation of life on Earth and dinner parties, they also received English training, but did not have quite the expertise as the translator.

General Níngsī stated, "In our Empire, we have 54 religions and 109 dialects. When we begin a meal, we have a moment of silence so that we do not interfere with others religions, they can communicate to their gods in the manner they are accustomed."

General closed his eyes and bowed his head. All the servants copied his action. There was suddenly no noise in the room.

Sally Fairbanks had an uncanny ability to commence counting silently in moments like this to give details in her reports on such matters as how long the silence lasted and was there any indications of anything of importance exposed during the process?

General Níngsī nodded at the head waiter standing beside his chair who intern nodded at all the other helpers who immediately began serving. It was a small helping of something exotically green. First thoughts Sally had was, *"Am I going to die from Alien germs tonight?"*

The food tasted very delightful. There was a reason for the small serving, they had 24 more courses yet to enjoy.

By the time they were eating, the AI in the computer banks of the Alien Fleet had already gathered any available information on the three visitors. No computer security on the planet was safe from this alien force that had computer hacking skills that were really very far into the future for any domestic spies.

They had all of Sally's OPM files and her service record plus any electronic correspondence she ever made that had not been erased.

The Zhrakzhongs also did data mining of Doctor

Brandenhagen and had observed all his Youtube videos and read all his books. They knew he was interested in what happened to Mars 900,000 years ago.

The three guests had no way to know what to expect. Each serving of a new dish was typically two or three spoon full of substance. Everything served tasted very delightful. General Níngsī could have spent the entire evening discussing what they were eating, but he felt there were more important things to talk about so he didn't bother explain what they were eating, and in some cases, it was human flesh. They might all start puking if they knew about half of what they were eating, so there was no point to explain it.

General Níngsī an excelente bluffer played dumb but at his fingertips he had everyone of their life stories. However, he knew it would not benefit him by showing all his cards any time soon.

"Tell me Doctor Brandenhagen, what exactly do you do?"

"General Níngsī, I'm a nuclear physicist."

"What do Nuclear Physicists do?"

"We design power plants and other devices."

"Like weapons?"

"Unfortunately, yes."

Sally Fairbanks then chimed in: "Dr. Brandenhagen has been studying the planet Mars."

"Did you discover anything interesting about Mars?"

"Yes, I believe it was wiped out 900,000 years ago."

General Níngsī then said, I'll have my people check the records, but I think there was a planet around this area of space wiped out 900,000 years ago."

"Any idea who did it?"

"If this is the case I'm thinking of, it was the Jupitorians."

"Are they from the planet Jupiter?"

"No, they are in a solar system about 10 light years away from here."

General Níngsī would only divulge information he felt vital to his mission. Just 30 years ago he visited Proximas Dyafalious and the ruthless leader their Grand Constabulary. *Whatever became of him?*

Do you know how they wiped out Mars?

If this is indeed the correct planet, thy used nuclear devices with incredible yields.

"Do you know why they did it?"

"The Grand Constabulary was upset with Martian Forces who wiped out part of his fleet."

"It was an act of retaliation?"

"More or less, yes."

Dr. Brandenhagen's interest spiked as all this information was really a subject, he spent the last 15 years studying. And here he is with Aliens who know a lot about the history of Mars to fill in the blanks he hoped to one day reconcile.

General Níngsī, how long did it take the Jupitorians to do all the destruction?

"Doctor Brandenhagen, Mars was wiped out over the span of just two hours. The following day, Atlantis here on Earth was also wiped out."

"What is the connection between the two worlds and why did the Jupitorians wipe out Atlantis?"

"At the time, Atlantis was the only civilized area on the zoological reserve planet. All the beings that lived in Atlantis are descendants of Martians. There was also a settlement on Venus it too was wiped out."

Dr. Brandenhagen now understood the horrors associate with modern technology that brought about some of capabilities of destruction the world could not contemplate.

"General Níngsī do you have any knowledge of how the planets were destroyed?"

"Dr. Brandenhagen, you were correct on your analysis of huge hydrogen bombs used."

"You know about my works?"

"Dr. Brandenhagen, we are an advanced society compared to Earth. We have the ability to scan your internet and all your communications systems. As soon as we had our introductions, my artificial intelligence used internet resources and other means to fully vet you and discover exactly who you are and what you did at Lawrence Livermore Labs and elsewhere. We know your life story and more about you than Sally

Fairbanks knows."

Roger Brandenhagen realized the enormity of all this. The aliens knew everything about them but they didn't know much about the aliens. He hoped his worst nightmares did not materialize. And here he was with the leader of the Aliens that arrived and he knew more soon would unfold, especially after they unloaded a billion beings on this planet.

"General Níngsī, in the future do you think the Zhrakzhongs and the Humans on this planet will eventually co-mingle?"

"Doctor Brandenhagen, the billion people arriving know why they are coming here. The whole purpose is to hide them until the war with the Xīnggui is over, mainly so they don't perish as part of collateral damage.

"We can always rebuild our cities, but we could never replace the people if they were to get wiped out like what happened on Mars 900,000 years ago. If we prevail in this war and wipe out the Xīnggui who have not relocated their population, we will insure we'll have at least 50,000 years of peace. We'll move our populations back to our Empire so there is no need for Zhrakzhongs to socialize with Earth people since we anticipate in less than 100 years, we will all evacuate the planet and send everyone home."

"General Níngsī, 100 years is a long time. How can you stop curious Zhrakzhongs from comingling with Earth people?"

"Doctor Brandenhagen, there is too big a gap

between our cultures. Your religions are vastly different than our own. Our culture and our value systems are significantly different. The Zhrakzhongs would not be interested in Earth people and the minute they arrive on this planet, their only thoughts are how soon do they get to go home to their own planets, hopefully before they grow old."

"If you have to wait 100 years to go home, by the time they leave here most will already be dead or old people."

"We hope we do not have to wait 100 years, but we also have to plan for worst case and are willing to be patient and wait until the war is finished and we can return back to normal."

"General Níngsī, I hope your dreams come true soon."

The food was incredible, the tastes and effects were strange and it seemed the sequence of the courses was all designed to accentuate each different serving.

The carte du jour had been approved by General Níngsī. One of the 24 courses was a succulent meat specially prepared for General Níngsī came from the shank of a Xīnggūi General defeated in the Battle of Huátiělú.

Maybe one day I will inform Doctor Brandenhagen where that meat came from so that he understands a little of our traditions, General Níngsī thought.

By the time they finished the 24th course, General Níngsī knew some of them probably need to use the restroom, so he had the English-speaking waiters, mostly female take them to several restrooms that were available to the General and his guest and explain how the strange alien contractions operated. Roger and Sargent Hawthorne were quite amused when the females demonstrated how the machine held their body so they could feel comfortable in the process and how the machine cleaned them afterwards. The females suggested, "You will be more comfortable if you take off your clothes and do it like this. Part of their demonstrations they disrobed in the demonstration without the least bit of embarrassment as this apparently is something they had done repeatedly before for General Níngsī's guests not familiar with the devices. The Alien women had attributes that made them look very appealing and their sweetness was icing on the cake.

After the three amigos were freshened up and brought back into General Níngsī's private quarters, they discovered the table had been cleared and taken away and four comfortable reclining chairs were in the middle of the room facing a wall. They were in for a big surprise.

"Sally Fairbanks, since you are the spokesperson for your government and I know you are anxious to get back to your transportation and have important reports to make to your government, I thought it would be worthwhile to take another 30 minutes of your time to show you a video of who we are and where we came from."

"We can wait another 30 minutes, as this is probably important for us to see," Sally Fairbanks responded.

"Also, I want you to know, even though I know this is going to be an inconvenience to your government with us being here, you can be sure we have no intentions of staying forever. Our Empire is a long distance from here and we all want to go back. We have no desire to relocate here. We want to go home to our own worlds and our own culture. As soon as its possible, we will leave."

Sally's biggest fear was they were followed here and worse yet, just like in America they too have spies so even if they were not followed here, there was a possibility the Xīnguī might know their location which would be a terrible consequence for planet Earth.

"Please have a seat and recline for better viewing.

As soon as they were all in their reclining chairs, the light in the room slowly dimmed and a holograph appeared. The holograph was true three-dimensional video, better than any of them ever saw at a movie theater.

The holograph showed video taken from something probably a probe flying to their planet and to one of their cities.

Their worlds looked clean and prosperous. It was as if they were looking into the future thousands of years. The three Americans were moved by what they saw. After 15 minutes of viewing the culture and the planet the probe that took the video then flew to the heavens and out into space. The film was no doubt doctored for their consumption as the probe video then transited to a random place in space and slowly what came into focus was a great space armada.

These no doubt were Zhrakzhongs Space Warships as far as the eye could see. To strangers who know nothing about Zhrakzhongs or Xīnggui it would be hard to gauge size and scale. This was no doubt an actual war video recording showing the two fleets converging and then the violence started.

It wasn't clear exactly the point General Níngsī was making showing this video, but he obviously had a purpose in it. Most likely it was a warning to Earth governments the savage of space warfare and to send the message that to get involved might end up very costly and devastating. Hearing the exchange between Doctor Brandenhagen and General Níngsī was unsettling. Even though it went a long way to demonstrate Dr. Brandenhagen was right all along and his critics were way off base, knowing it was true did not do anything towards calming nerves and reducing the terrible thoughts of what happened.

And now as these two fleets clashed with huge laser weapons, Plasma Debilitater weapons and other devices created a spectacle they didn't bargain for. Observing 40 or 50 of these advanced space fleet assets disintegrate in sparkling debris created a visual effect and a surreal impact to their psyche. The psychoacoustics created by the probe recording added to the impact of the video that left no doubt in their minds the lethality of space warfare with advanced beings.

After a dozen minutes it was evident one side was winning the battle and the other group departed.

The lights slowly came back on and the holograph faded. The Earth people had just witnessed something that most Zhrakzhongs had never seen, the *Battle of Huátiĕlú.*

General Níngsī spoke first, "What you just witnessed was a defining battle in our war with the Xīnggui."

"It seemed something unlike anything we could imagine," Doctor Brandenhagen spoke.

"That video was taken about twelve years ago, just before we developed our plan to evacuate everyone out of the Empire so they might live. We understand we are trespassing on your planet. But it is out of necessity. We plan on not being a burden to you and we will isolate our people to make sure they have no impact on your society. We picked two wilderness areas where virtually nobody lives except for that small Native American Tribe where you came from."

"General Níngsī, we have a special place called Area 51 North of here 300 or more miles. It's closed off by the government so they can do research on advanced aircraft and they do not want our enemies knowing the capability of what we produce. A lot of Americans think there are Aliens up there and are constantly trying to break in to see it for themselves. As soon as it becomes known you are here, these crazy people will attempt to break in to your area as well to see your people."

"We have non-lethal devices that will convince them to turn around and not approach. By tomorrow evening there will be a 10-foot fence around the perimeter with lots of sensors. Nobody will get in."

Sally Fairchild looked at her wristwatch and knew it would be getting near sundown soon and had some anxiety about getting back on the road and General Níngsī understood she needed to leave right away.

"Let me escort you to your transportation," General Níngsī said and smiled.

General Níngsī led them off this huge craft and parked out in front of it was a strange looking thing. It didn't look like a space craft or military vehicle. As soon as they got near the device probably the size of a city bus, what appeared to be doors slid open sideways and a ramp deployed down onto the ground.

"I will take you to your transportation," General Níngsī stated. They followed him into the craft. There was plenty room inside and appeared to be set up to take at least 20 riders.

As soon as they were seated, they could feel movement. In less than five minutes they felt a slight movement as the craft sat down a few feet from Sargent Hawthorne's Jeep. The two doors slid open sideways and General Níngsī escorted them off the craft.

Just before they all piled into the Jeep, Sally Fairbanks said, "I'm not sure if I will ever be coming back to see you again General. When I get back, they will probably put me into quarantine because of my exposure to you and possible pathogens we Earth people can't handle."

"Not to worry. We know a lot about you earth people and we have no dangerous pathogens. It's us that have to worry about you."

"General, others may be coming soon wishing to talk to you. Our military leaders will most likely send an envoy."

"Sally, please pass on my comments to your leaders who wish to have discussions. If they want to have successful discussions, I advise them to send you and Doctor Brandenhagen back as their messengers because we get along very nicely."

"Thank you for your nice comments General, and I do appreciate your hospitality."

The three then got into the Jeep and retraced their path back to the *Béésh Łigaii Atsu* (Silver Eagle) Native American Tribe then up the dirt road to the waiting helicopter where two nervous pilots sat wondering if their passengers would come back alive and they would be allowed to fly out of there without being shot down.

As soon as the Jeep pulled up to the helicopter and the three got out, Sally Fairbanks said to Sargent Hawthorne, "Mr. Hawthorne you help is very appreciated. We are grateful for your service and we are also grateful that you were instrumental in assisting us today."

"It was all my pleasure Ms. Fairbanks."

"Just call me Sally."

"As you wish Sally."

Sally and Roger Brandenhagen climbed in the helicopter that immediately started up and in less than five minutes was airborne heading south.

As they were heading south, the Alien compound was now lit up and could easily be seen from a distance. No doubt travelers going down that two-lane country hiway would get curious as to what's over there and try to find a way in. The only way in was on that dirt road they were just on and by tomorrow morning there would be several Army guys with Humvee's blocking the road to anyone except tribal members.

After briefings from Sargent Hawthorne, the Army knew to take a lot of cases of bottled water when they came to relieve the watch.

That night Sargent Hawthorne drove his Jeep down to the village where the medicine man was observing from a distance the fence the Aliens were putting up that you could not see through. However, if you went up the hill where the Army guys were now guarding the road, you could see some of the compound, but since it stretched for miles, there was much of what you could not see.

"You met the Aliens?" *Binii'łigaii* (screeching owl) medicine man asked.

"Yes, they were very nice and courteous to us," Sargent Hawthorne responded.

"I bet your military training helped you deal with the Aliens?"

"It sure did. First thing they teach us is to respect others and that usually prevents a lot of issues."

Binii'łigaii pulled out his pipe and stuffed it with *Naakai Binát'oh*. He lit it with one of his stick matches.

Sargent Hawthorne made the mental note to bring a couple boxes of stick matches with him the next time he came this way.

After they each had a couple nice long puffs on the pipe and started feeling good, *Binii 'łigaii* asked, "What are those Aliens like?"

"They are very advanced and they are very nice. Their Military people appear to be seven to eight feet tall. They are giants."

"I knew one day this would happen."

"Why did you think that?"

"The elders talked about the people from the sky visiting. Everyone thought they were crazy and spouting nonsense, but now we know they were telling the truth."

"Did you think they were talking nonsense?"

"As a medicine man you learn a lot about what is in people's minds and their hearts. It all is used in their treatments for various diseases and to remove evil spirits from the body. By the time most of the elderly died off I got to know them very well and they never lied to me a single time. I believed everything they said. And now we see proof of what they were saying most likely happened."

"The aliens have put the fence across some of your land, there isn't much you can do about it."

"I understand that but I also know one other thing."

"What's that?"

"They being there makes us safer because I know they are watching over us."

And it was true. General Níngsī ordered his troops to keep an eye on these indigenous people and if there were ways to help them, do so.

As it turned out, Sargent Hawthorne delivering the bottled water helped out the *Béésh Łigaii Atsu* (Silver Eagle) Native American Tribe by a good margin. After the Zhrakzhongs watched them drinking the bottled water and the area was extremely dry, they most likely needed water.

The Zhrakzhongs themselves had water issues and applied their technology. Even though it doesn't rain much in this part of Arizona, on many days a lot of water vapor does pass overhead, but because of the high-pressure zones and other atmospheric conditions rain clouds cannot form. Hence it becomes a desert. The Zhrakzhongs knew how to create low pressure atmospheric zones which sucked in water vapor from the Sea of Cortez and the Pacific Ocean. They did this mainly at night so that Earth people would not accuse them of altering the climate even though that's exactly what they were doing.

Part of their scientific ability included vortex precipitators that created a vortex almost the size of a Tornado, but instead of lifting debris up in the air, it all came downwards along with condensation and compression of water vapor into a stream of water. One of their vortex precipitators could produce 8 million gallons of fresh potable water a day. To supply half a billion beings, they needed a dozen vortex precipitators spread around the compound which with its ragged edges measured approximately 200 square miles.

In the northern sector the vortex precipitator provided much more water than what was required so they had a surplus and a couple days later the Zhrakzhongs ran a four-inch pipe out to the tribe with a valve on the end of it providing the tribe pure water.

Binii 'ligaii (screeching owl) medicine man had a surreal experience the day the Aliens came forward with the pipe. Using specialized microphonic pickups, the Zhrakzhongs monitored the conversations in the *Béésh Ligaii Atsu* (Silver Eagle) Native American Tribe village. Artificial Intelligence in their vast computational domain quickly determined these *Béésh Ligaii Atsu* spoke a Navajo dialect. By taking the lexicon of the Navajo Language and tweaking it to the dialect, within a week, they had a fully functional translator which allowed them to effectively communicate with the *Béésh Ligaii Atsu*.

The *Béésh Ligaii Atsu* were proud people but they lived in poverty. They chose not to be victims of the welfare system and wanted to stand on their own two legs and take care of themselves. They would rather be poor than dependent upon someone else. Nevertheless, a number of the tribal mothers one day got together and cooked a number of servings of food for the Aliens to show their appreciation for the abundant fresh water. It seemed like they could use as much as they wanted. The dusty area slowly evolved into a much greener and cleaner area and when Sargent Hawthorne came for a visit and observed they had a water source suggested they plant some trees!

The medicine man believed he would only see cactus living near him. He never thought plush green trees would ever exist here. After a few trips to Home Depot, Sargent Hawthorne had at least a dozen trees including assiduous and fern trees and even a couple fruit trees planted and growing.

The following day, a group of Alien soldiers arrived on some sort of Hovercraft. There were several boxes with them which they carried to *Binii'ligaii* observing them, and with the use of the ear buds stated in perfect *Béésh Łigaii Atsu* dialect, "We really enjoyed the food you provided us. So we have brought you a sample of our food and hope you like it."

Binii'ligaii called out to his wife *Nizhóní Ch'ilátah Hózhóón*, "*Nizhóní* come here."

Nizhóní and her young tikes came out of the home and walked up to *Binii'ligaii* and was instantly frightened by the four giants standing by her husband but came nevertheless.

"These men brought us some food to thank all the women of the village who cooked them a meal yesterday. Take some to each of the villagers so they may enjoy it."

The Zhrakzhongs had taken a liking to *Binii'ligaii* (screeching owl) medicine man.

The medicine man was a lot wiser than people can understand because his tribe passes down through generations the magic that he performs to rid souls of evil intruders and diseases. He was so over joyous with the free water and now this wonderful gesture of Alien food, he proposed to the four Zhrakzhongs they would smoke his pipe in celebration of the friendship.

Like all security troops, these had body cameras and microphones. Artificial Intelligence monitored everything. By now Artificial Intelligence had done extensive research into the Navajo and surrounding Tribes and their customs. When *Binii'łigaii* pulled out his pouch of *Naakai Binát'oh* and started stuffing his pipe with it and lit it, the Zhrakzhong artificial intelligence quickly analyzed this was peyote. Because the Zhrakzhong were very sensitive to the impression they made upon the Earth people, they knew they could not turn down the offer of the smoke. However, their squad leader was directed as well as the others who also all had ear buds, the driver is not to smoke the pipe. You will be drugged when you smoke that pipe therefore as soon as you finish, report back to the compound right away.

Binii'łigaii inhaled a big gasp of the *Naakai Binát'oh* he then handed the pipe to the squad leader who followed his actions who intern passed it down the line to everyone except the driver.

The Aliens have their own elixirs which can be far more potent than *Naakai Binát'oh*. But there is a time and place for everything and taking mind altering substances while standing duty is normally not tolerated, however for the sake of diplomacy, this carefully orchestrated event allowed the activity to proceed.

After a couple tokes on the pipe the four men were ordered back to the compound. They excused themselves and shook *Binii 'łigaii's* hand as they left.

Because of the lack of water, the tribe could only graze cattle on their land three months of the year. It was too difficult for them to handle the cattle themselves, so they simply rented the grassland to other ranchers.

With this ample amount of water, which had a significant amount of water pressure, Sargent Hawthorne figured out they could put sprinklers out and irrigate their trees and the grassland. With the long hot Arizona summers, if you have plentiful water, grass can grow amazingly quick. Sargent Hawthorne knew if the tribe raised their own cattle, they could make far more profits and decrease the amount of poverty.

As such he personally bought a steer from a rancher and had it delivered and gave it to the tribe as a gift. In due time the Zhrakzhongs who knew all about cattle because they had by now an extensive database on anything Earth, understood the Tribe was raising the cattle possibly for their own consumption.

A few days after the cattle delivery, the Zhrakzhongs sent a representative to *Binii 'łigaii* to ask him what they planned to do with the cattle. After *Binii 'łigaii* explained he was raising it to sell it, they immediately offered to buy it. They asked him if he would take gold in payment.

Binii 'łigaii stated he wanted equivalent of $1000.00 which was the going market for a 750-pound steer. The Zhrakzhongs said they would be back shortly with the gold and take possession of the steer. Shortly *Binii 'łigaii* had five ounces of gold in his hand and watched the Zhrakzongs load the steer up in a type of

Hovercraft and went to their compound.

Later that day when Sargent Hawthorne arrived to see how the steer was working out, *Binii 'łigaii* explained he already sold the steer to the Aliens and showed the five ounces of pure gold received in payment.

Sargent Hawthorne asked *Binii 'łigaii*, *"Do you know how* much gold sells for these days?"

"No, how much?"

Sargent Hawthorne pulled out his cell phone and quickly got the figures and announced, "Gold spot market today is $1,750.00 per ounce."

"I wonder why the Aliens over paid for the steer?"

"I've learned a lot about the Zhrakzhongs in the short time they have been here. They know they are trespassing on your land. I think they over paid because they look at you as a special person and tribe. I feel that you mean something to them. Perhaps because they miss their home world so badly, they have an emotional connection with you. That's why you have the water and that's why they over paid for the steer."

Binii 'łigaii pulled out his pipe and filled it with *Naakai Binát'oh* and lit it and took a good gasp then handed the pipe to Sargent Hawthorne who took a toke.

Binii 'łigaii then handed the gold to Sargent Hawthorne and said, "Take out your cost in this transaction because I want to pay you back, and with what is left over, could you buy me another steer and have it delivered?"

"Not a problem."

The Aliens soon had a supply of beef for their northern sector which helped greatly with their food supply which reduced the need to consume stored foods.

The following day after the gold transaction, Sargent Hawthorne showed up with a rancher delivering five steers. When they were stopped at the checkpoint the Army guys at first didn't want to let them pass. They took their orders seriously!

Sargent Hawthorne introduced himself. "I'm Sargent Hawthorne USMC retired. In a minute I'll have someone on your chain of command to talk to you."

As soon as the General answered Hawthorne stated, "General, I'm at the road block on the dirt road leading down to the *Béésh Łigaii Atsu* village, could you please tell these soldiers to allow us to pass."

With the speaker phone on the Army guys were quickly surprised who was giving them orders.

"Sargent Hawthorne I will make sure their company commander knows to let you always pass as you are a special interface to the aliens and the *Béésh Łigaii Atsu* Village.

"Thank you General."

After offloading the five steers and the half dozen bales of hay, Sargent Hawthorne said to *Binii'łigaii,* "You probably need to put up a fence now on the dirt road to keep these steers in here."

When they came back the next day, the steers

were gone and *Binii 'łigaii* was all smiles. "Twenty-five ounces of gold."

The village was now the most watched location on the planet. The CIA's KH-14 satellite was watching it, the Aliens were watching it, the Chinese Yaogan (遥感卫星) satellite was watching it, Cosmos 2547 was watching it, the Native tribe had no idea, they were now the focus of GLOBAL ATTENTION.

The Aliens had camouflaged the 200 square miles extremely well, both electronically and optically. Nobody could see in. Drug Cartels were now being paid to surround the Mexican complex, not even coyotes could get in.

General Níngsī had a unique curiosity about the *Béésh Łigaii Atsu* (Silver Eagle) Native American Tribe and he was very positive about Sargent Hawthorne who he had his INTEL people fully research all his military records and every shred of information about him. The complete picture was therefore provided to General Níngsī.

Today as Níngsī observed the surveillance video of Sargent Hawthorne visiting the *Béésh Łigaii Atsu,* he decided it was time to bring Sargent Hawthorne back to his ship for lunch, but he also wanted *Binii 'łigaii* to come with him. Sentries were directed to go out in a Hovercraft and ask them to come visit General Níngsī.

As the two men were having a friendly discussion using their native toungues, off to the distance they heard a rumbling, a gate opened to the Alien compound and a Hovercraft came towards them.

"I wonder what that's about. They were just here an hour ago picking up the cattle."

The Hovercraft came to a halt a respectful distance from the village and the Zhrakzhong eight-foot-tall giants got out and walked towards Sargent Hawthorne and *Binii 'łigaii*.

With their ear buds they could communicate effectively now using the *Béésh Łigaii Atsu* dialect.

In the *Béésh Łigaii Atsu* dialect, the leader of the Zhrakzhong troops said, "General Níngsī requests Sargent Hawthorne and *Binii 'łigaii* come with us so we can take you to his command center for lunch."

Sargent Hawthorne looked at the medicine man and asked, "Would you like to go there with me?"

"Sure, maybe we can smoke my pipe with the General?"

Sargent Hawthorne said, "Yes we would like to go."

Binii 'łigaii asked, "Would it be alright if I brought my wife, *Nizhóní Ch'ilátah Hózhóón* with me?

In his earbud, the artificial intelligence quickly responded, "Inform *Binii 'łigaii* General Níngsī desires that *Binii 'łigaii* bring *Nizhóní Ch'ilátah Hózhóón* and also inform him that if he would like them to bring their children they are invited as well.

The quick decisions that followed produced the decision to leave the children with the Tribe as this was probably too much for them.

Sargent Hawthorne, *Binii'łigaii,* and *Nizhóní Ch'ílátah Hózhóón* stepped into the Hovercraft via a large open door and were immediately on their way to the Zhrakzhongs compound not knowing what to expect.

The Zhrakzhongs are expert builders. They had already built General Níngsī an underground command center.

The Hovercraft went inside the compound, the gate shut and it stopped, they all got out of the Hovercraft, and there was a transport waiting for them.

The Zhrakzhongs camouflage was ingenious, it was suspended several thousand feet in the air by great pillars allowing essentially an under-tent city with enough headroom to allow transports to fly within.

Sargent Hawthorne and the *Béésh Łigaii Atsu* couple were escorted inside the transport and it quickly departed for General Níngsī's command center. They could not see out nor have any idea where they were going. It was all fly by wire. Artificial Intelligence flew the craft, therefore there was no need for windows. It was more or less a horizontal elevator.

In about five minutes the transport stopped inside a building the Zhrakzhongs had built very rapidly. They were fantastic engineers and designers. They had built the galaxy's best in record time.

The group had an escort waiting for them who ushered them into the underground cavern where they went into General Níngsī's new command center. His former command center space craft was now hidden under camouflage on Mars with a crew aboard to respond to any exigencies.

Sargent Hawthorne and the *Béésh Łigaii Atsu* couple were soon led into an elaborate conference room where General Níngsī's was there to greet them. He was smiling and friendly.

Nizhóní Ch'ilátah Hózhóón was mildly shocked when she saw the eight-foot-tall giant. General Níngsī was an extremely intelligent man. This room just like on the ship had fantastic holographic technology.

General Níngsī said, "While we wait for them to set up our lunch, I would like to show *Nizhóní Ch'ilátah Hózhóón* and *Binii'łigaii* a little video of my home world and what our life is like there."

Just like on his command ship there were some nice soft reclining chairs pointing towards the holographic presenter and General Níngsī said, "Please have a seat here it reclines for the video so you get the best view and feel comfortable.

Nizhóní Ch'ilátah Hózhóón and *Binii'łigaii* followed Sargent Hawthorne's example and set back in the chair and watched how he simply attempted to move backwards and the chair automatically adjusted to the proper angles.

The lights slowly dimmed and to the side the staff were busy setting up the banquet with utter perfection using their special glasses that were designed for the ultraviolet light that used like a night light. The room appeared dark but to them it was bright as daylight with their special glasses.

Soon the video began showing the Zhrakzhongs civilization and many aspects to their worlds. To these impoverished tribal people who lived off the grid, this seemed more or less like heaven. They were quite animated by observing all this. The psychoacoustics of the holographic equipment and the visual effects created a memory they would never forget. It was a once in a lifetime event for them.

Binii'łigaii he was enamored by all this. In his tribal experiences and as medicine man, when you experience one of those once in a lifetime event that raises your consciousness and touches your soul, you give something back. The only thing he had to give was his wife and he would. If General Níngsī wanted to experience his wife he would direct her to please the General, but that wasn't going to happen. General Níngsī could have all the concubines he wanted. He even declined the green skin women from the Plastras Nostras worlds with purple eyes, red hair, and vagina's full of exotic chemicals and amino acids that create fantastic orgasms for men.

If the offer came, he would simply decline by saying, "Your presence is very precious, that is all I could ask of you."

And he would feel that way as he looked very affectionately at these Tribal people who were beyond any form of corruption. They were a breath of fresh air. Simple but real and genuine.

Binii'łigaii was happy he believed his grandfather who said one day something like this would happen.

He would put his faith in General Níngsī because

he would like to solve the mystery of what happened to the 55,000 people who lived in Mesa Verde who suddenly disappeared with the evening meals left on their plates. At the appropriate time he would ask the question. Nevertheless, he would quickly wish he had not asked the question.

The lovely three-dimensional documentary of life in the Zhrakzhongs worlds that left them all mesmerized ended and General Níngsī was informed via his ear bud, they still needed about 15 minutes to set up.

To give a slight delay he asked in perfect *Béésh Łigaii Atsu* dialect of the Navajo language, "Would you like to see some of our space battles?"

The answer was a unanimous yes, and so the next holograph video of spectacular Space Warfare video with psychoacoustics applications began.

Sargent Hawthorne had not seen this holograph. He was in for a big surprise.

General Níngsī was expecting Sally Fairbanks back any day. He had his holographic experts put together a dog and pony show for Sally because he assumed she would be bringing along other dignitaries for more formal and discrete discussions now that that shell shock of Aliens invading was over.

This would be a good experiment to see how this neutral group viewed the contents of this video which was not meant to be a threat, but just to articulate, what galactic warfare is about and why America and Mexico needed to just conduct themselves as if the Zhrakzhongs were not even here.

General Níngsī made it perfectly clear, *this was a stopover, not an invasion.* It might take them 100 years to leave, but they will eventually be gone.

Thank God this was the last planet to deposit Zhrakzhong. Some of the others did not turn out so well, so it became an invasion because the locals would not allow their trespassing under any conditions.

At the present time it appeared an invasion wasn't necessary, however if the Americans put up a fight, that would be a huge mistake for them. If they stopped to think for a moment shooting those F22's down like shooting ducks in a barrel was a big deal, they were in for a rude awakening if they tried something else.

The Zhrakzhongs had the ability to determine if a missile or bomb or projectile or anything else had fissionable material in it. As such it would be immediately destroyed, so the possibility of America nuking the Zhrakzhongs was slim. General Níngsī really didn't want to have to go heavy on America. He wanted no casualties, but if some stupid General pulled another F22 stunt like on day one, the base that launched them would be destroyed immediately.

Submarines, Aircraft Carriers, B21 bombers, TR-3B's were all sitting ducks with Zhrakzhong technology. Hopefully calmer heads would prevail and this short duration experience would soon be behind them.

The 15-minute video was quite impressive. In this particular video one could better understand the size and scale. Early in the video they compared one of the Zhrakzhong Assault ships five times longer than the U.S. Navy's Nimitz Class Aircraft Carrier. The firepower was immense.

A number of those Assault ships were hidden all over the solar system just in case they were followed here.

General Níngsī had met and commanded a lot of forces in his days. He was what would be referred to as a Gray Beard. He wasn't in charge of the Zhrakzhong Military. He was just the task force commander with the assignment to deliver another billion Zhrakzhongs to another planet far away from the space battlefield to ensure their civilization did not die out in the event they lost this war. But he was also augmented with a large attack force in the event the Xīngguī showed up which he intended to make sure it happened and end this war as soon as possible.

By spreading everyone out the hope was eventually they could reconstitute the Empire and comeback stronger and regain their once proud existence, especially if they lost an epic battle.

Chapter Five

What do we do now?

As the helicopter flew south to take Sally Fairchild and Doctor Brandenhagen back to Tucson to get back on the Gulf Stream 650 so they could make their reports back in Washington, it was nearing sundown. This was not a big problem for these combat helicopter pilots now flying at 15,000 feet who had plenty of battlefield experience.

Within 15 minutes after taking off, two UFOs flew very close to the Helicopter and immediately the pilots were informed via their radios, "We are here to escort you to Tucson to make sure you get there safely."

The pilot and co-pilot already knew they were in deep shit, but this was something else. Their religious beliefs were now being challenged like never before.

The pilot quickly discovered he had no control of the helicopter. The Aliens said, "We have control of your helicopter so we can fly you directly to Tucson so you don't have to waste your time flying an extra 100 miles.

As the sun set down on the Arizona Desert,

the pilots were now realizing they just experienced something in their lifetime few others would. It was an incredible moment flying in formation with two exotic UFO's. The co-pilot snapped a few pictures of the UFO on the Starboard side which was painted nicely with the sunset.

He would not share those pictures with anyone because they would not believe him. Plus, if the military knew he had those pictures they might confiscate his cell phone.

Eventually with Tucson lights up ahead the Aliens stated, "We are restoring control of the helicopter to you now. You are at your destination. We enjoyed flying with you today."

The UFOs then darted to the North. Everyone onboard knew exactly who they were. The KH-14 satellite was also tracking them and feeding live video to the NRO at that building in Dulles where Sally Fairbanks departed from.

As they were flying into Tucson Arizona, Davis-Monthan Air Force Base, the Gulfstream 650 was warming up its engines and going through its preflight check list. The pilots were updated and now told, "The inbound helicopter is 5 miles away, will be here momentarily."

Since there were no expect aircraft takeoff and landings in progress, Air Traffic controllers directed the helicopter directly over to the hanger where the Gulfstream 650 was waiting.

In due time the helicopter came down 50 feet

from the Gulfstream 650 that had engines running on idle and Mable Potter standing by the ladder to the aircraft.

Once the helicopter landed where it was informed it would be tied down for the night meaning the pilots could go home, they shut the helicopter engines down.

Mable Potter walked up into the GS650 aircraft as soon as soon as the two passengers were aboard and pulled the ladder up via electric control then shut and locked the door.

The pilot already had permission to proceed to the end of the runway and take off when he was ready.

Ten minutes later the GS650 was airborne and soon swung around on a course of 075 heading towards Andrews Airforce Base at 50,000 feet cruising along at Mach 0.9 fully fueled while it was at Davis-Monthan Air Force Base.

On the way back to Andrews there were a few phone calls and Mable got out a CIA laptop so Sally Fairbanks could do a couple conference videos. Her hopes of a nice naptime back to Andrews quickly evaporated. By the time they landed at Andrews it was almost 4:00 A.M.

Luckily there was a limo there to take them home. They first deposited Doctor Brandenhagen to his home, then they swung around and dropped Sally Fairbanks off at her residence.

Tomorrow came quicker than everyone thought. They received wakeup calls at 8:00 A.M. and notified a driver would be outside their homes in 15 minutes to pick them up to take them to Crystal City to a beltway bandit office for a conference.

This turned out to be an ultra-secure location, and after they got out of the Limo at a drop-off point in front of the main Crystal City Plaza, men in suits were there to escort them to the elevator and then up to the XYZ beltway bandit office spaces for the debrief and discussions.

The Generals and Admirals came in wearing civilian clothes. This location was picked because if they did it over at the Pentagon, they feared it would end up on Television news later that evening. The Joint Chiefs, CIA director, NSA director and a couple high ranking FBI persons were all present showing their badges once they got into the security area.

Most of the government offices had cleared out of Crystal City because the rents were too high, but this organization had long term lease on this portion of the office building so there was no point in leaving. Plus, most of the juicy stuff never happened over at the Pentagon because they could not keep secrets for some strange reason. Competing contractors knew not to take their business over there because their competitors were often given special briefings and exposure to all the goodies.

The Generals were in for a rude awakening.

"Are they here to stay?"

"No."

"How long will they stay?"

"They think upwards to 100 years."

There was a gasp and silence suddenly in the room

"Why did they come here?"

"To hide from their enemies."

"Is there a chance their enemies followed them here?"

"We do not know, but you have to assume the possibility exists that they did."

"What does that mean?"

"It means a galactic scale conflict will grip this planet."

It was no longer a political military. It was no longer Democrat verses Republican. It was a come to Jesus' moment. The joint chiefs almost felt paralyzed.

The briefer quicky surmised, "The earth is ill prepared, then you don't know the medical significance."

While the meeting continued Russia maneuvered the Cosmos-2542 currently following a KH-13 American Satellite registered as USA-245 to get a good look at the 2nd moon back side. Just like our moon that always has the same side facing the planet, the Alien mother ship rocky front side faced the planet.

It was a tricky maneuver and some Russian military chiefs bitterly opposed it because it would burn up so much fuel it would never be able to be put back in position trailing KH-13 to be in position to blast it out of operation in the event a war started.

A tactical force remained aboard the mother ship to operate the intricate defense systems in the event the Xīnggui showed up or Earth forces decided to take a shot at it.

CIA's SAC group sometimes referred to as SAD to mislead the public had been secretly tapping the telemetry from Cosmos-2542 and deep within the bowels of Fort Meade had engineered a decryption algorithm. Thus, these cryptologists were real time reading the imagery. The SRG group which reported to SOG performed this function and were watching the live streaming video thanks to the Russian providers. America was in the throes of sending up a TR-4C to look at the back side of the new moon, but policy makers were trying to come to grips with the possibility the Aliens would destroy the craft killing the 3-man crew. If the Russians were able to obtain a look at the Zhrakzhong mothership backside, there would be no need to risk a crew.

The SRG people were patiently watching the video and getting reports from NORAD who notified SAC that COSMOS-2542 was relocating. This maneuver helped the Space Force in another manner. By sending Cosmos-2542 the series of commands to relocate, SRG was able to catalog those commands which most likely were used in other satellites that would allow SRC personnel to maneuver them in the event of hostilities. That's the aspect of espionage that always worries planners. You never know what you lost most of the time and the enemy will probably capitalize on that discovery when it hurts you the most.

The SRC operation was ongoing while Salley

Fairchild was discussing her experiences with Zhrakzhong supreme commander General Níngsī. Her verbal report was fed into a voice to text translator allowing a printed report to be prepared for higher ups in a very short period of time. She was also video recorded and the video went into the secret archives that would no doubt be purged in a short period of time.

"All of the Alien craft appeared to be well camouflaged. The military members all seem to be within seven to eight feet tall. We don't know if that's the general make up of their civilization or just hand-picked for size since the Zhrakzhong is vast comprising over 100 inhabited planets."

"Did you get to see many of their spacecraft?"

"There were many and due to their size, it was hard to figure out exactly how many there were and how far away they were from each other."

"How big was the command ship do you think?"

"I've been flown off a Nimitz Class and the Gerald Ford a few times for missions, and I would estimate the command ship was taller and perhaps five times longer than those carriers."

There was a gasp in the room. As hard as they tried, nobody had obtained pictures of these military craft.

"What do you think the Command ship was like compared to our Navy Ships?"

"They seem to be like our Amphibious Assault

ships with a large cavity to carry the numerous attack craft that were stationed around the perimeter."

"Did you get a good look at the attack craft?"

"Yes, but all the weaponry was concealed. They appear to be flying boxes."

"You didn't get to see any of their weapons?"

"Sargent Hawthorne, the Navajo retired Marine who helped us got a demonstration of one of the soldier's weapons. I can ask his friend the General to contact him and do an interview to get the details of that weapon."

"Were there any significant revelations provided by the Zhrakzhongs?"

"I'll wait until Doctor Brandenhagen arrives to brief you on the discussion he and General Níngsī had, but I'll now describe a remarkable event we all experienced."

The room was now so quiet you could hear a pin drop. All eyes were focused on Sally Fairbanks, who looked professional yet attractive in her business attire. She was one of the types of women that didn't need makeup on to accentuate her natural beauty. She had to be careful to not over dress to give men around her the wrong idea.

"General Níngsī has some highly developed holographic technology. If you can imagine what a holograph might appear like when it's the size of a movie theater, that's what we experienced all this with. The video also had real sound recorded at the time to give an even greater impression and all that revealed to us in the 30-minute holograph in the three-dimensional viewing made you feel like you were in space personally viewing it all."

"What did you see?"

"What General Níngsī presented us was a 30-minute time slice of probably the greatest space battle they ever fought."

"Do you think you could work with Agency animators and help them create a video describing what you saw?" the SAC Director Mark Rebman asked.

"Sure, I can help them come up with a video because some of our movies in the past had a similar appearance to some of it."

"Go on and tell us what you saw?"

"Sure, there were spacecraft stretched as far as you could see. The Zhrakzhongs were the only visible ships in the beginning and I would estimate as many as 500 visible as far as one could see. The two opposing fleets approached each other at incredible speeds so there were no visual sightings before they started shooting their weapons, some being lasers and others beam weapons. I would say in the span of a minute I witnessed 10 or more enemy ships explode with spectacular sparkling debris, better than a 4th of July fireworks display."

SAC Director Mark Rebman asked, "How confident do you feel this was the real deal and not some fabricated video that you know Hollywood is quite capable of producing?"

"There is really no way we could vet the video without having someone there during the event. Assuming its actual Space War video and audio, it depicts with size and scale to which mankind has never experienced."

The room was eerie quiet, as at least six or seven people in the room who knew Sally Fairbanks quite well, knew her field reports were very accurate, she didn't embellish anything, and she never attempted to take credit for anything. She was the consummate team player. Therefore, if General Níngsī convinced her this was all legitimate and a recorded history account of their greatest space battle, then they would have to side with Sally's interpretation of the event.

Sally's next statement really hit most of the meeting attendee's hard in the gut, "God help us if the Xīngguī followed the Zhrakzhongs here."

SAC Director Mark Rebman picked up on that real fast and knew he had to ask Sally the next question, "Assuming the video is real, those types of space battles occurred, how long would it be before we discover the Xīngguī *did* follow the Zhrakzhongs here?"

"It took the Zhrakzhongs ten years to get here. Unless they were followed by a sizeable force ready to attack, a scout ship would have to transit to Xīngguī areas to make the report and the attack plan would then have to be formulated, so because of the long distances, I would think it would take quite a while unless they were chased here."

"I'm probably going to have to send you back out there to ask a few questions. One question I have you need to ask General Níngsī after you lay out this scenario to him, we need to know if they have sensors that would allow them to know if they were being followed by a large military force to confront them in the near future."

"He may or may not wish to divulge that to us."

"You still have to ask the question."

"What's your other question?"

"The second scenario you talked about, where a scout ship followed him here, knowing what their enemy is capable of doing, how long do we have before we need to be concerned about the Xīngguī showing up?"

"I think he would be more willing to answer the second question. But I could see where using strategy, the Xīngguī would most likely transit here at an angle or offset to make it hard for surveillance to detect them. They would be no different than our Navy in the past did not point the target and go on a straight line and give up the element of surprise."

"I have a third question to ask him. If eventually our worst fears are manifested and the Xīngguī do come, is there any kind of weaponry or techniques they would assist us with to make our own security and situation better under the circumstances?"

"Before I ask him that question, I want you to hear from Doctor Brandenhagen concerning his discussions with General Níngsī. What he's going to tell you might give you the notion there is nothing we can do to protect ourselves and we are strictly at the mercy of the

Zhrakzhongs, and if a space battle happens here and they lose, we will all be dead."

The meeting took place inside a vault that was inside a vault. The SAC Director Mark Rebman then said, "We will shift the discussions away from the information we just discussed and bring in Doctor Brandenhagen for his comments. He's not entitled to know anything about what we just discussed and he is not to be informed of any of what has been said prior in this room."

SAC Director Mark Rebman then nodded at his assistant that went over and keyed in a passcode and the electrical drive mechanism spun the worm gear that opened up the one-foot-thick steel door that appeared to be about six feet in diameter which some of the attendee's had to duck under to get into the room.

Doctor Brandenhagen was not dressed as casual as he was going out to Arizona. He knew he would be facing the crem da le crem in the INTEL world in this meeting, so he dressed accordingly with suit and tie. In the Beltway if you don't show up to meetings dressed appropriately, few people would take you seriously.

Doctor Brandenhagen was escorted over to a position on the conference table that had his name placard on it facing directly at the SAC Director Mark Rebman, who with his slightly shaded glasses appeared to be one of the evilest looking men Roger Brandenhagen ever faced. He also knew this man had ordered the deaths of people and under the rules did not require Presidential Authority, only Presidential Briefing after the fact. Many of the terrorists hunted down and killed after 9/11 were handled in this fashion. It had been reported in various media reports, George W. Bush set up this arrangement after 9/11 and some news analysts thought he did so to have perceived presidential deniability.

"Doctor Brandenhagen, thank you for your services and assistance in this matter. I have a few questions I would like to ask you."

"Of course, Director, I'm ready to answer your questions."

"Doctor Brandenhagen, when you had a discussion with General Níngsī you asked him some questions and he filled you in on various pieces of information you were interested in. Can you please tell us about that?"

"Certainly, Director. I'm well known by the UFOlogy community, and other organizations. concerning my reports on Mars being wiped out 900,000 years ago."

"Yes, I'm painfully aware of those reports."

"As you probably know I was called in by NASA to analyse air samples taken from Mars, and later soil samples we mysteriously figured out how to get off Mars. NASA was interested to figure out how the Xeon-129 got into the Martian Atmosphere. Later soil samples taken near the location on Mars identified as Cydonia, had an amount of Xeon-129 in the samples as well. Eventually with my assistance and their hard work we figured out the Martian atmosphere is saturated with Xeon-129 and there are two known hot spots on Mars where the soil samples show concentrations of Xeon-129."

"For those in the room who do not know anything about Xeon-129, it does not occur in nature and we have never found any traces of it except in the vicinity of where a Hydrogen Bomb test was made in locations at the Nevada test site, Pacific Islands, and in Australia where the British conducted their tests."

"After studying and confirming the hot spots on Mars I concluded the atmosphere was blown away from the planet leaving it a dead planet and the concentrations of Xeon-129 left behind as a way to discover what happened."

"Doctor Brandenhagen, you discussed this with General Níngsī?"

"Yes. I asked him if he knew anything about it. He confirmed that 900,000 years ago the Jupitorians wiped out Mars for reprisal after the Martians attacked their fleet and destroyed a number of their combat space craft."

"Are these Jupitorians from Jupiter?"

"No, they exist in a solar system far away from here."

"Any chances they will come back to our solar system."

"Probably not because aside from destroying Mars, they also wiped out the only highly advanced Civilization on Planet Earth at the time, Atlantis. They have no reason to come this way again."

"Atlantis is not fiction?"

"Atlantis existed and was more advanced than we are now."

The SAC Director Mark Rebman then chimed in and asked, "Doctor Brandenhagen, would we then expect the Xīnggui could wipe this planet out in a similar fashion as the Jupitorians did Mars?"

"Yes sir, I believe that to be the case."

"Doctor, Brandenhagen, I'm going to ask you to accompany Sally Fairbanks back out to Arizona to talk with General Níngsī again and determine if there was some way, we could prevent the Xīnggui from wiping us out like the way it ended for Mars."

Director, I will be happy to go, but my thoughts on this are: The Zhrakzhongs have skin in the game. They brought a billion people with them to hide them here until the current war is over. They have no reason to protect us because they owe us nothing in their mind, however they will do everything in their power to protect those Billion Zhrakzhongs transported to Mexico and Arizona.

"Is it possible the Zhrakzhongs could lose the war with the Xīnggui even without there being any combat in this area of the galaxy?"

"Then we would be stuck with them forever."

"At least for our lifetimes."

"We'll arrange transportation for you and Sally right away."

"Director, I didn't get much sleep since we arrived here about 4:00 A.M. Would it be possible to travel tomorrow?"

"One day will probably not make much of a difference, but we need to put together a briefing for the President as soon as possible. I will make the arrangements for you to leave here tomorrow morning to give you enough time for the helicopter ride and get back to Tucson before it gets dark."

"I'll be ready to go by then."

"Thank you Doctor Brandenhagen, you are excused and will be escorted to the entrance and given a ride back to your home."

"Thank you, Director, for your consideration."

"No problem."

After a few minutes, a man came into the vault and whispered something into the director's ear. SAC Director Mark Rebman then made the statement:

"Everybody without a Q and V clearance please leave the room."

Half the room stood up and left, and right afterwards the assistant closed the vault door. Sally Fairbanks was the only female left. The ones that just exited the room either had a Q clearance or a V clearance, but not both.

"Jim, go ahead and turn on the video monitors so we can watch this."

There it was, a space craft of sort the size of a

small moon. The Russians were steering Cosmos 2542 to the far side of the "Zhrakzhong Ark" as the Russian technicians called it.

Cosmos 2542 is a sphere-shaped satellite with two big ugly cameras on one side. As more and more of the backside of the Ark was observable, the Russians reorientated Cosmos 2542 putting the camera's directly on the Zhrakzhongs Ark.

"My god it looks like something right out of our recent Space War movies!"

The Ark was observable for probably a maximum time of one minute then all of a sudden there was a very bright flash and the video ended.

"What happened?"

"Russians are telling each other they lost telemetry."

"Maybe that bright light was the Zhrakzhong destroying Cosmos 2542?

"Contact Norad and see what they got on Cosmos 2542."

The assistant with a name tag: Jim, walked over and grabbed one of the red phones sitting on a phone shelf with a dozen phones that had labels as to where they connected. These were very expensive dedicated landlines that utilized single mode fiber to go long distances without too many repeaters.

When a person picks up the phone it automatically connects to NORAD and a red light is lit up at the other end with an alarm alerting the Air Force technician a high priority phone call was coming in usually during a crisis.

The obvious answer came back real fast: NORAD says Cosmos 2542 disappeared. They believe the Zhrakzhongs destroyed Cosmos 2542 with some type of energy beam weapon.

The reason why people in the room at to have a V clearance is the next piece of information that just came in on a purple phone. One of our spies inside The Russian Space Forces (Russian: Космические войска России, tr. Kosmicheskie Voyska Rossii, KV) reported the Aliens blew up Cosmos 2542!

"They were not quick enough; we got a peak at their backside for about a minute. I don't care how long they have to work tonight; I want our analysts do a careful look at everything they could see on the backside of the Zhrakzhongs Ark and if possible, identify what they think it is."

SAC Director Mark Rebman looked at Sally Fairbanks and knew tomorrow would probably be a rough day when she confronted General Níngsī about a lot of things. However, she would probably play dumb about Cosmos 2542. Unfortunately for the SAC, the Zhrakzhongs Artificial Intelligence knew the Americans were watching the Cosmos 2542 video and with all their break-ins into Pentagon and CIA networks were well aware America and Russia knew the Zhrakzhongs blew up Cosmos 2542.

Within days the Russian leader and the American President each wished the hell they had signed a Space Defense Agreement a long time ago. If nothing else the Zhrakzhongs arrival proved we need to share the responsibility of protecting this planet. One nation alone does not have the financial ability to build the infrastructure necessary to protect the planet from Alien invasion, just like the one that just happened.

Hours later it didn't take NORAD to figure what just happened when all of a sudden, our second Moon started moving away. Perhaps it was the Cosmos 2542 incident that forced General Níngsī's hand or it might simply be conincidental. One thing that was apparent with the SAC's analysts: the Zhrakzhongs had probably already offloaded all one billion people so there was no longer any reason to keep the second moon here attracting attention. So away it went.

It takes 248 years for Pluto to make one orbit around the sun. Currently Pluto is on the far side of the solar system away from the direction the Zhrakzhongs approached Earth. It would be another 120 years before Pluto would be on the side of the solar system closest to the approach to Earth from the Zhrakzhong Empire. General Níngsī believed the Xīnggui War would be over within 100 years so by the time Pluto got near the transit lane to Earth the outcome of the conflict will have been made. There was no hope for a diplomatic settlement. Too much blood had been spilt, thus a military victory was the only solution in the minds of the Xīnggui as well as the Zhrakzhongs.

Pluto was currently 39.5 astronomical units (AU) from the sun. Pluto's distance to the sun varies based on its orbit which can be from 49.5 AU down to 29 AU. One AU is the distance from Earth to the sun which requires 8 minutes for sun light leaving the sun to reach earth because the Earth is 92.96 million miles from the sun. Pluto was currently 3.16 billion miles from the Earth.

NASA tracked the Zhrakzhongs ARK as the Russians termed it. And before long the comet's tail reappeared as it gathered speed approaching 250,000 miles per hour. The ARK continued increasing speed to approximately 500,000 miles per hour.

In about 263 days the Zhrakzhongs ARK would become a Pluto moon, if it wasn't recalled before it got there.

General Níngsī hoped the final battle that would end the war between the Zhrakzhongs and the Xīnggui happened sooner than later. Even though it put him and the billion Zhrakzhongs on this planet at risk, the turmoil and stress worrying about their future had a significant drain on their personal psychology.

Thanks to General Níngsī's Artificial Intelligence in his computational networks, he knew he was going to get a surprise visit by Sally Fairbanks the following day. He was eager to see her, as he liked her. He wondered if he would be too large for her to have romantic intercourse. Maybe one day he would find out as she did seem a little perky.

The Army wanted to provide Sally Fairbanks and Dr. Brandenhagen a Humvee and a driver to go down to the Alien Gate. They were a little butt hurt when they discovered the Cash in Advance boys wanted Sargent Hawthorne and his Jeep.

"Those guys don't look too friendly today,"

Sargent Hawthorne said to Sally Fairbanks sitting in the front passenger seat of the Jeep.

"Their upset we prefer riding in your Jeep."

As they came down the hill towards the *Béésh Łigaii Atsu* (Silver Eagle) Native American Tribe village, Sally Fairbanks noticed the five steers delivered Earlier that morning. Then she got her next big surprise, the water pipe running from the Alien compound to the village. Sargent Hawthorne filled her in on the details of what transpired since he left.

The Artificial Intelligence knew the three were arriving via surveillance video and as they approached the gate thinking they would have to stop and get out, the gate opened and one of the security guards waved them in.

As the Jeep got inside the compound the impressive changes that occurred in the short time they were gone, underscored the expertise and efficiency these Aliens exhibited in almost a frightening manner.

Sally Fairbanks in the back of her mind, would not rule out there was more to the story and that planetary conquest and invasion was a component of what was really going on. As long as the Zhrakzhongs stayed inside their fenced in area covered up by extraordinary camouflage all would be well. But if they suddenly deployed millions of soldiers that spilled out of here and Mexico expanding their grip on the planet, then it was over for the humans who occupied the planet for now. They most likely had no means of defending themselves. After watching the holographic video of their space battle, it was a foregone conclusion that no

ICBM, cruise missile, or Jet Aircraft would get near this area with hostile intentions. The Zhrakzhongs would destroy any military hardware coming at them just as quickly as they did the Cowboys coming in with the F22 Raptors, our finest fighter bomber (the public was aware of).

There would never be a surprise attack. The Zhrakzhongs knew every move we made and knew what would be coming their way long before it got here.

To provide propulsion to a small moon that accelerated it to 500,000 miles per hour in a brief period of time further exposed the very advanced technology they had. The space battle holographs were a grim reminder to Sally, Earth cannot do anything about it and we are simply at the good graces of these Aliens and hoped General Níngsī stated his intentions exactly how he planned.

After they drove approximately 100 feet into the Alien compound, Zhrakzhong military personnel standing in front of their path indicated to halt. About that time the officer they previously met stepped forward and came to Sargent Hawthorne's side of the Jeep and said, "We'll take a shuttle to General Níngsī's compound."

The group exited the Jeep and followed the officer to the same device the traveled in the previous time.

Sally Fairbanks marveled at the intricate camouflage and how it rose so high up in the air. The *Béésh Łigaii Atsu* tribe loved their new view that appeared like a mountain range right next to their village.

Just like before they felt movement, but there were no windows to look out as Artificial Intelligence flew the flying box for about five minutes then sat it down. They had no idea how fast they were going and inside the flying box there was no cell phone service.

The false wall slid up like before and the ramp came down and they walked out of the flying box towards the entrance to General Níngsī's new command center. None of the multitude of ships they saw before was present. For their own security, General Níngsī would not inform them how all those space craft were now parked on planets throughout the solar system with good camouflage with crews in case a battle suddenly erupted by the Xīngguī entering the solar system. One axiom of war that General Níngsī knew: "You don't defend your planet on your planet, you defend it somewhere else so that your planet avoids getting hit. If a battle were to start here it would begin on places like Mars and Saturn and Jupiter. Decoys would be deployed there to be the magnets for the dangerous Xīngguī weapons to distract them and divide their efforts.

The group was escorted down to General Níngsī where he had made preparations to entertain them.

"Hello everyone, I'm glad to see all of you again."

"Thank you General Níngsī, we are glad to be back," Sally Fairbanks said with a slight amount of embellishment in her response.

"What would you like to discuss today?"

"General, we probably should have asked these

questions while we were here before, but sometimes you don't know what to ask until you think about it for a while."

"I understand that completely. I assumed you would be back seeking answers. Tell me, what is most on your mind?"

"General, I'm sure you realize all of this can be frightening to us backwards people. To say we were not ready for it, is the truth."

"You are lucky your solar system is a good distance away from the center of the galaxy where higher concentrations of stars exist along with numerous civilizations. Distance has been your friend up to now. However, that is all changing now as various civilizations are expanding their Empires and it's only a matter of time before they come this way."

"Well, you certainly came this way."

"I can tell by the look on your face you have a serious question to ask, so please do not hold it back, I'm ready for any question you might ask," General Níngsī stated knowing his Artificial Intelligence was at the ready to feed appropriate answers into his earbud to make sure he answered it in accordance with what they wanted him to state.

"General, we understand you are in a do or die conflict with your enemies. We feel for you actually and to me I feel sad that you had to go to such extremes to protect your people. When you came here, do you think there is any possibility your enemies followed you here which could create a war zone in this part of the galaxy?"

"Sally Fairbanks, I am currently reassessing all possibilities. We never know for sure because as you can imagine if we have an enemy who could chase us all the way here, they also use elaborate means to find us."

"This next question is from people I work for. I think it's a fair question. If the war zone was to come to this region and we suddenly were confronted with the possibility the Xīnggui would attack this planet, is it possible they can wipe us out like the Jupitorians did the Martians?"

"The Martians were no match for the Jupitorians who did that despicable act. However, the Martians were arrogant and never should have attacked their fleet. It's been broadly accepted by a number of Empires the Martians brought it on themselves by their own actions. You Earth people have never done anything towards the Xīnggui. They would not have the same motivations like the Jupitorians had."

"But you are on this planet and you are their enemy, does that then mean we can become collateral damage and wiped out as a result?"

"The Martians had no means to repel the Jupitorians or to stop the types of weapons deployed that destroyed the planet. It's different because we can repel the Xīnggui and we also have the means to neutralize the types of weapons they might use of the type that destroyed Mars.

"Are you sure about that?"

"Unless they come with everything they got, it would be stupid to attack us here. Furthermore, if we do see their approach, we will send out very fast ships that can outrun them to other outposts to bring in a reserve force to crush them with."

"Can your reserve force get here quick enough to make a difference?"

"Our moon size transport is a slow ship. It's not a warship. It was designed to ferry one billion Zhrakzhongs here. Our warships that came with it had to go slow to protect it along the entire route. Our warships are capable of speeds that are much faster. It would not take our warships ten years to get here like the transport.

"I know this question might sound ridiculous, but remember I'm just the messenger."

"I understand that Sally Fairbanks."

"In the event Earth is attacked, are you willing to give us some weapons we can help you fight with to help save ourselves."

"Sally Fairbanks that is very wonderful that you asked such a question and it has a lot of meaning. I understand why you asked that question and if I were an Earth person, I would feel the same way. But the reality is, most of our fighting is done with Artificial Intelligence. Our personnel are merely systems monitors to make sure the Artificial Intelligence is operating correctly and obtaining the results we want."

"That concept is very far in the future for us, but I understand how an advanced society like the

Zhrakzhongs would deploy weapon systems in those manners."

"If the Xīnggui come here to attack me, I would be quite happy to take along a few Earth observers to watch the Space Battle."

"I'm not sure who we could send to go on such a mission."

"It's clear to me, I'm looking at least 3 of them. I would insist you stand by me on the bridge of my command ship so you could see it all. I would also be honored to have Sargent Hawthorne standing beside me during such an event."

"Thank you General Níngsī, it would be an honor," Sargent Hawthorne said.

General Níngsī then turned towards Doctor Brandenhagen and said, "Doctor Brandenhagen, it's amazing that you figured out what happened to the Martians. You are a deep critical thinker. You also have a way of articulating your findings in the most honest and correct fashion. You are the type of man the Zhrakzhongs respect. In case you don't know, we have the means to read all your research and all your publications. My Artificial Intelligence has read and studied every document you ever produced and made public and some documents you didn't make public."

Roger Brandenhagen looked into General Níngsī's eyes and knew he was looking at someone that Napoleon, Caesar, Genghis Kahn, and others would not measure up to. This was an extraordinary leader. It was no doubt in Roger's mind of why General Níngsī is their leader.

"Doctor Brandenhagen, I can understand why your leaders may not believe the holographic video I showed you is a live recording of the event. Your Hollywood film makers could probably do a video of similar footage but not three dimensional holographic. The reason why I would want you with me also on the bridge should that unfortunate day occur, I want someone like you as an eye witness to watch it all unfold and to create the report in the way I know your capable of. You can thus report how this all manifests, if we prevail in the battle."

"What if you lose the battle?"

"If we were to lose which I don't believe is possible then there would be no purpose of a report."

General Níngsī only had Sargent Hawthorne's buy in on the offer to be a part of it and witness the results, but he suspected if he shanghaied the other two, they would be glad in the end they got to see it all from his command ship that has spectacular video capability.

"When you go back to your superiors and make your reports about our discussions, please convey to them to double up the number of soldiers they have at the roadblock, because if space combat happens, I will invite half of them to go with me."

"I would not be surprised if all of them volunteered to go with you," Sally Fairbanks responded.

We can't take them all, we need some of them to remain and protect the *Béésh Łigaii Atsu* Tribe.

In due time the three visiting Earth people were at a fabulous meal at the same time watching beautiful dancers and performers. It was apparent the dancers were not tall like the military which further expanded Sally's speculation the Zhrakzhongs selected the tall people for the military and most likely a lot of them were typical sizes found on Earth.

The entertainment ended as soon as the meal was complete. The General was pleased to see Sargent Hawthorne enjoyed eating the flanks of his enemies. *Perhaps one day I will tell him about the Admiral.*

Sally didn't want to ask the question, but General Níngsī knew it was coming thanks to the best espionage in the Galaxy.

"General, do your Space Warships have sensors on them that could inform you that the Xīngguī were following you here?

"Sally Fairbanks, just like you Americans have secrets like the KH-13 satellite the Cosmos 2542 was trailing, we can't divulge that to you because if some time in the future our enemies took Earth and placed it into their portfolio of Empire assets, then they would find out. I will tell you that we have excellent sensors, however there are many clever ways of trailing a task force without being detected."

Sally Fairbanks stared at General Níngsī and he was an expert at evaluating body language. He knew his next statement was not going to please her and she already was stressed.

"So even with the best eyes in the sky, it's still

possible our enemies could follow us here without our knowledge."

"But can they follow you close behind with a major tactical strike group without you knowing?"

"If it was a task force large enough to hurt us, we would know they were coming long before they got within reach to strike us."

"How comfortable are you with that statement?"

"Very."

"Alright General Níngsī, I think you answered all my questions."

"It was my pleasure."

General Níngsī then turned to Doctor Brandenhagen and said, "Doctor Brandenhagen, your analysis of the Mars tragedy is well advance of most of your Earth Scientists. I want to congratulate you on figuring it out by offering you a trip to Mars whenever you wish to go."

"I'll be busy for a couple weeks helping Sally put out a report on all of this, but once I'm finished, I will be certainly ready to go, but I do have one request."

"What is your request Doctor Brandenhagen?"

"I would feel a lot safer if you bring Sargent Hawthorne with me to provide me protection from possible Martians we may encounter."

"If Sargent Hawthorne wishes to go, there will be plenty of room."

General Níngsī had taken a liking to these three. A commander cannot fraternize with his subordinates or he could lose control. Hence a commander is a lonely person. That may also have played into his interest with the *Béésh Łigaii Atsu* (Silver Eagle) Native American Tribe.

It seemed like after General Níngsī escorted them to the entrance of his command center, they were back at the Jeep in five minutes. When they all got in the Jeep, Sargent Hawthorne made a comment: This Jeep has never been this clean before. Sally and Roger didn't pay attention to cleanliness coming to the Alien Compound, but since Sargent Hawthorne mentioned it, the paint looked newer and there was no dirt or debris anywhere. The Aliens had sparkled his Jeep for him.

Chapter Six

The Xīngguī

In the Xīngguī province of Màichōng desperation was sitting in. Bombing evacuated cities where no enemy ships or warriors existed wasn't going to win the war. It seemed like the Zhrakzhongs were always on step ahead of them evacuating their population and removing all military assets. The leadership of the Xīngguī hunkered down in this picturesque capital, had terrible memories of the Battle of Huátiělú.

Had the Zhrakzhongs just kept coming they could have ended it then, but thanks to lack of good intelligence and their overly cautious approach, they didn't press home the attack and departed the space with their fleet. But since then, Zhrakzhongs executed this strange new method of repositioning their population and slowly reducing their foot print they protected while repositioning their populations and preserving their forces for another battle. By not having such a vast territory to defend they could better concentrate their forces into a smaller area to create a much stronger defense.

There was a sizeable force defending the few

remaining planets that were not abandoned and the Xīngguī were reluctant to attack them for fear it was another elaborate trap that could be far more damaging than what happened during the Battle of Huátiělú. They needed to find out what happened to most of the population and where the rest of the Fleet went.

Precious information often derives a fat payday. Throughout the galaxy a number of free lancers existed who were in the business of data mining and espionage. They played both sides. Xīngguī and Zhrakzhongs had used their services many times. Sometimes the information changed hands three or four times before it made its way to the final destination.

The Zhrakzhongs Fleet vanishing for 10 years without any indication where they were, caused a lot of consternation with Admiral Aete. In the meantime, the Zhrakzhongs did a number of pinprick attacks to keep the Xīngguī off balance. It was now time for the big showdown, if the **Xīngguī** could just locate the marauding Zhrakzhongs Fleet, they could certainly wipe them out. Then they could scramble back to attack Zhrakzhong remaining populated Home Worlds and end this war once and for all, and take their fair share of the hegemony.

Tytrone Philosophers from an ancient sect had warned the Xīngguī they were on the wrong side of morality in this war. From the very beginning the Xīngguī who used to be the Zhrakzhong major trading partner were fighting recklessly for Hegemony. The Zhrakzhong who were fighting for survival and long ago ended any imperialistic tendency. Once they were the pariahs of that area of the galaxy. Just like the Ming Dynasty in China that ushered in the most advanced and moralistic civilization that ever existed on Earth until the Qing Dynasty in the 1600's, the Zhrakzhongs morphed into a similar mindset, where Culturalistic principals surpassed militarism and imperialism.

The Chinese Ming leaders had the largest Navy in the world with ships twice as large as any the Spanish built who were considered the Maritime champions in the west until that fateful day when the Spanish Armada was destroyed in England due to a combination of a wicket storm and English fire ships.

One could make the analogy the Xīnggui were copying the modus operendus of the Spanish Armada.

In the fog of war often critical factors are lost and never made public. Those engaged in the battle never learn of it.

The Xīnggui made a huge mistake of ignoring the Tytrone Philosophers. And they even went so far to attempt silencing them. Their brutal attacks that left most of them lifeless, did not kill the spirits of those who survived. And just like many examples we see on Earth, the Tytrone Philosophers merely went underground and as part of their survival and retaliation, they undermined the Xīnggui at every opportunity.

Tytrone Philosophers who could easily pass for a Zen Buddhist Monk, were always paying attention to information and in some cases had to be information peddlers themselves in a quid pro quo fashion for their own survival. The enemy of my enemy is my friend always applies.

In some cases, these free lancers get in trouble and are hunted down and killed in the most savage manner, especially if their activity hurt powerful forces, which happens in wars.

A number of the free lancers have an exit strategy or know where to go to hide out until the heat is gone. In some cases, it might be the Tytrone Philosophers who were mortal enemies with the Xīnggui ever since after the big purge that killed so many of them.

Many of the free lancers being espionage experts know those enemies are sources of huge payments. One particular freelancer on the run with some very hot information was desperate fearing arrest any moment and found his way to the Tytrone Philosophers but the only form of payment he had available was that juicy piece of information.

In order to survive, the freelancer was going to have to give up the payday and give the information to the Tytrone Philosophers or risk being captured any moment. There would be times in the future when he could data mine information for a fat paycheck, but for now he needed basic survival. The Tytrone Philosophers were very pragmatic. They knew taking in this free-lancer and hiding him created extreme risk. Unless he had some good information, they would turn him away.

In the heat of the battle, he disclosed the highly desired information.

"I know where the Zhrakzhongs have hid their fleet."

The free-lancer had mildly tainted information put out by Zhrakzhongs as disinformation ploy. Planet Earth was identified as the secret hiding place. General Níngsī did this on purpose to set up an elaborate trap. He felt bad that he was using planet Earth and making them a potential victim, but he had to win because he had skin in the game with the billion Zhrakzhongs who would also fall victim if he lost this battle.

The Tytrone Philosophers had a number of monks in the Xīngguī's Chǒulòu prison in Màichōng. They would now make the Xīngguī Emperor Shāyú pay for this transgression. Not only did they pass on this tainted information for the release of their Monks, they also altered it slightly which they didn't know helped General Níngsī's more than he could hope for as it further expanded the elaborate ruse to suck in Admiral Aete into a sophisticated kill zone.

What General Níngsī hoped to create was a set piece space battlefield with assets hidden until the trap was sprung allowing close range firing of their Plasma Debilitater weaponry.

The information had locations of Zhrakzhong Fleet assets spread out on 20-star systems and General **Níngsī** their arch enemy was on planet Earth with a small detachment and most of his generals. If they could capture General Níngsī with most of his Generals, they could end this war abruptly and force terms of the treaty to give them all the hegemony they ever wanted.

The planners went to work right away formulating their approach and methods to achieve a fast victory. If they had to, they would lay waste to planet Earth. Their concern for these primative people did not exist. They were simply on the battlefield that would soon erupt in fire as they destroyed General Níngsī and make him pay dearly for the humiliation at the Battle of Huátiělú.

Freelancers were soon selling information that Admiral Aete was at the same time concentrating his forces at Màichōng preparing to attack General Níngsī's Earth hideout.

That information soon found its way into General Níngsī hands as an ultra-fast Frigate made its way to the Jupiter detachment which immediately forwarded it to General Níngsī who now knew the Xīngguī are falling for the ruse. If he only knew how much help he was getting from the Tytrone Philosophers, he would be really smiling.

With the information presented, Artificial Intelligence was hard at work figuring it all out. In the Xīngguī province of Màichōng desperation over ruled common sense; when it's too good to be true it usually is.

Chapter Seven

The Red Barn

General Níngsī with his Artificial Intelligence was also preoccupied with another one of his pet projects, the *Béésh Łigaii Atsu* (Silver Eagle) Native American Tribe.

Artificial Intelligence was doing a vast study on American farming techniques on behalf of General Níngsī who wanted to improve the lives of the *Béésh Łigaii Atsu*. They were slowly figuring out what the *Béésh Łigaii Atsu* needed to help improve their situation.

One thing clearly evident was: they needed a barn.

Americans have no idea the extent a million bored Zhrakzhongs were willing to do. As soon as General Níngsī asked for a few craftsmen to help build the *Béésh Łigaii Atsu* a barn, he immediately had several thousand volunteers.

Using surveillance video with accurate ranging tools to pinpoint exact positions, the semi-flat rise just east of all the *Béésh Łigaii Atsu* homes appeared to be the best position to place the barn.

Because of security concerns they could not be out in the open all day building the barn. It was obvious they were going to have to build a prefabricated barn.

All day long the construction went on inside the compound. The Barn was fully assembled and then taken apart in sections to relocate after dark very quietly while the *Béésh Łigaii Atsu* tribe was sleeping.

With their security rover craft they could fly interlocking cement slabs out for the floor of the barn. These slabs also had bolting fixtures built into them to fasten the barn on. Around midnight, the work began with orders to be very quiet to not awaken the *Béésh Łigaii Atsu* tribe or alert the Army guys up at the road block.

With Alien precision and magnificent engineering expertise, a red barn was put together in an hour. The 50-foot-long cement slabs joined together had the weight and strength for a very good foundation and using alien technology they were quietly anchored. The rest of the pieces of the red painted barn were flown out with the security rovers acting as sky cranes. Finally, the roof that would not leak for 100 years or longer was lowered on the perfectly constructed barn and efficiently bolted together by some of the finest machinists in the galaxy.

With all that gold Sargent Hawthorne obtained that he had no use for, he decided he needed to buy some things to help the tribe and an I-phone was first on the list so that *Binii'łigaii* (screeching owl) the medicine man could reach him if he needed help.

In the morning, Sargent Hawthorne drove his Jeep to the *Béésh Łigaii Atsu* (Silver Eagle) Native American Tribe. As he was coming down the hill past the Army guys who seemed excited for some strange reason, he caught first glance of the new Red Barn. He was just here yesterday. To ask if he wasn't a little bit spooked, was a good question.

As he pulled into an area where he usually parked his Jeep, he saw most of the tribe walking through the barn which had a hay loft which would be nice and handy.

He walked up to *Binii 'tigaii* (screeching owl) medicine man who quickly said, "It looks like the Aliens built us a new house."

"That's not a house, it's a barn for your cattle and a place to store all your tools an equipment."

"It's far nicer than our homes, why don't we just move in here?"

"*Binii 'tigaii,* you are making a lot of money supplying beef to the Aliens. In a short period of time, you can afford to build new homes."

"Seems like a terrible waste to put cattle and tools in there."

"Do you see that door at the top in the front?"

"Yes."

"That is for a lift so that you can lift bales of hay up there. That's a hay loft to store your hay in the dry period or in the winter."

"Interesting."

"Oh, by the way, I bought you a cell phone so that you can contact me if you need help. Your phone number is taped to the back in case you want to give it to someone. Your passcode to protect it in case it gets stolen is your birthdate which I know but few others do, month, day, and year two digits each. You were born in January 15, 1990 therefore your pass code is 011590. I programmed my phone number in it so if you touch this little circle, then type in 011590, then the menu is available. If you want to call me press the telephone and then you will see my name. Just touch it and it will automatically call my cell phone."

"Can I try it now?"

"Sure."

The medicine man was very intelligent and a fast learner. He just jumped ahead a couple centuries in a few days.

General Níngsī's Artificial Intelligence reported, "Sargent Hawthorne just gave *Binii 'łigaii* a cell phone to allow him to contact him if he needed any help."

"That's good to know maybe I will call him on this new Cell Phone my INTEL guys gave me so that I can call Earth Officials."

"I'll program *Binii 'łigaii's* phone number into your cell phone so that you can call him when you want."

"Also, program Sargent Hawthorne, Sally Fairbanks, and Doctor Brandenhagen's numbers in it please."

Chapter Eight

They Meet Again

Just like before, Sally and Roger flew back to Tucson with an Alien Escort and the pilots were too scared to tell the passengers the helicopter was in autopilot because the Aliens were flying it!

The benefit of the Aliens flying his helicopter is they would take the most direct route to Davis-Monthan Air Force and he felt safe that no Alien would attempt to shoot them down.

They were going back earlier today so there was plenty of sunlight left to enjoy the majestic view of the Arizona mountains and hills. People who happened to be outside and photographing would find the two craft going with the Helicopter seemed kind of odd. The aircraft flying in formation with the Blackhawk didn't look like anything anyone had ever seen before.

In due time the pilots looking at their GPS supported electronic map and their familiarity with the local hills and mountains knew they were getting close to Tucson. It was about this time the Aliens stated, "We are returning control of your aircraft to you. We are leaving you now. Have a safe trip home."

The pilot would have to work now and the co-pilot with his goggles would be looking for air traffic ahead of them as a safety measure, because Air Traffic Control doesn't have complete control of the skies, especially weekend warriors lacking proficiency out on a joy ride.

Just like before, Air Traffic control vectored them directly over to the Air Force Hanger where a new jet, a Gulf Stream 700 waited for them. The pilot shut down and tied down the Blackhawk right where he landed because it just happened to be his destination.

Roger and Sally Fairbanks climbed out of the Blackhawk and walked a short distance to the GS700 pointing the service ramp with Mable Potter standing by the ladder waiting for them to return.

Sally climbed up the short ladder into the GS700 followed by Roger, then Mable who pulled up the ladder using electrical controls and shut and locked the door. She then proceeded to the cockpit to inform the pilots they were ready to leave.

As part of the preflight checks the pilot has an indication in the cockpit showing the door was shut and locked so they knew it was time to head out.

The GS650 is an excellent aircraft. The GS700 is

even better and had a dozen years of development since the GS650 first flew.

It seems like the CIA wastes a lot of money upgrading aircraft as often as they do. But there is a logical reason to do so. In some missions, the cost of failure of the mission could be more than the price of a new GS700. By incremental upgrades and giving the older Jets to the Navy and the Army and other government agencies, they still get many more good years of service so the taxpayer money isn't wasted. By putting forth the effort to fly the newer jets with a lot less hours on them, they are not prone to break down at a critical time when an agent's life or a foreign leader may be at risk.

Bean Counters working in the bowels of Federal Purchasing departments do not think tactical. They think how many beans are involved and all too often the tactical advantage is overlooked for the economy of scale.

In the case of SAC, who often rides on a razor edge of danger, they can't risk a mission because the purchasing officer can save a few more beans. Often it seems like it can't be justified. Unfortunately, the purchasing agents are not cleared to know the missions. Nor would they ever know the stress Sally Fairbanks experienced and her severe vulnerability meeting the Aliens after the Cowboy incident. That first meeting could have gone either way and cost her life.

Thanks to things working smoothly today, they were heading East at a decent hour and they would touch down at Andrews before midnight and get some sleep before the grilling started in the morning.

Sally Fairbanks truly hoped the Agency would leave her alone for a few hours so she could take a nap. Roger was least likely to be disturbed.

When they pulled up to the Hanger at Andrews, a limo was there to give them a ride home. They were lucky they lived relatively close so that neither party would be dropped off at a much later hour.

Even with the excellent transportation, morning came too early. And as expected they were summoned for meetings.

The seating arrangement laid out about the same as it was a couple days ago. Sally Fairbanks was facing the Director again. She expected more grilling and as she fell asleep on the plane, Mable did her a favor and turned off her cell phone for her. It appeared the director was slightly pissed because he had to wait until everyone else to hear the highlights. Theoretically it was after hours and she didn't have to have her cell phone turned on, but she knows how the game is played. There are some written and unwritten rules, and she just violated the hell out of one of the unwritten rules: Keep your cell phone turned on and nearby at all times.

The meeting began and the Director asked, "What was General **Níngsī's answers to your questions?"**

"He refused to divulge any technology that would detect a possible trailer."

"Did he elaborate?"

"He said the obvious which we too should have

figured out, there are means of finding other space craft and so it would be impossible to know for sure if they had been spotted transiting to Earth."

"Which means we are potentially set up for a huge disaster."

"It's apparent to me there isn't much we can do about it," Sally Fairbanks responded.

"Then what is he planning?"

"He made it perfectly clear they are only here on a temporary basis and as soon as this is all resolved, the Zhrakzhongs would all depart and its unlikely they would venture back this way anytime soon."

"Do you believe him and how do we know this isn't some kind of elaborate invasion?"

"We really do not know anything about the Zhrakzhongs other than the Holographic videos General Níngsī showed us and the exposure we get inside his compound that was developed rather remarkably."

"Any other events you remember you can inform us about?"

"One is they had dancers for us for entertainment while we were eating a 24-course meal, and a promise General Níngsī made to Doctor Brandenhagen."

"What was that promise?"

"Why don't you ask him that question when he comes in next."

Sally Fairbanks knew the director was pissed and being very pushy in his questions because he didn't get the information ahead of the crowd. She was starting to feel slightly resentful, because she really did need some sleep and there was nothing Earth Shattering for her to report.

The first briefing was over so they called Doctor Brandenhagen into the secure conference room and the Director jumped on him as well, he always turns off his cell phone.

"Doctor Brandenhagen, Sally Fairbanks informed us General Níngsī made a promise to you. What exactly was that?"

"Director, as you know I have published a number of articles and books about Mars being wiped out and these Aliens have confirmed time and date and have said who did it. General Níngsī was quite appreciative that I figured it out without outside help that he promised to take me to Mars on a trip whenever I'm ready."

"We can't let you go to Mars."

"Are you afraid I will claim to be the first human to land on Mars?"

"You are not, so you can't make that claim."

"Any reasons why I shouldn't go to Mars?"

"Many reasons which you are not cleared to know about."

"I've not given General Níngsī a date when I want to go, so its currently not planned."

"Keep it that way."

About that time the assistant came over and whispered something in the director's ear and immediately the director said, "Everyone not cleared Q, T, and Y, please exit the room now. Dr. Brandenhagen you will stay, we'll hand you a non-disclosure sheet to sign after the meeting."

After all the non-cleared people left the room and the foot thick steel door was shut and locked, the director grabbed the remote control and turned on all the Video display monitors.

"Did you guys see the Red Barn while you were out there?"

"No."

"It was built over night; we assume the aliens built it for the *Béésh Łigaii Atsu* (Silver Eagle) Native American Tribe."

"That's Amazing."

"Sure is, looks like the Aliens are turning the Tribal village into "Green Acres.""

"Over the next couple days, I would like you two generate a report for the record and try to get in it all you can remember of the visit."

The meeting was soon adjourned and Sally Fairbanks was sent home to telecommute, to prepare the report. Doctor Roger Brandenhagen now working as a consultant for a beltway bandit went home as well and prepared his comments which he would send to Sally Fairbanks to include as an addendum to her report.

There had been a news blackout about the Aliens

because there was no opportunity for the media to get near the Aliens who picked an excellent location for their compound since there were no good roads near it and the only dirt road one could take had the Army roadblock not allowing anyone except Tribal members or approved visitors in.

Nevertheless, the News Vans were parked on Dr. Brandenhagen's street attempting to get access during daylight hours had to contend with the four security men guarding the house 7/24. The news crews were never able to get to Dr. Brandenhagen because the CIA always brought him home through the alley way and opened the back gate designed to allow an RV access to park in the back. As soon as the vehicles were in the yard the gate was shut and the car could reach within 15 feet of the back door making it impossible for the news media to get to Dr. Brandenhagen who felt he was under house arrest. It didn't bother him because he was paid well by the Beltway Bandit, and he had a lot to work on as well.

Because of the hassle to go shopping Roger Brandenhagen simply had everything delivered, sometimes including hot meals from restaurants who delivered. His experience with Uber Eats was also positive.

After arriving home after the latest meeting which gave Roger Brandenhagen the impression the SAC Director was extremely agitated about the notion of him traveling to Mars. The Director was clearly under pressure and he wasn't handling it too well.

But what is the real reason? What are they hiding on

Mars?

The next couple of days, Roger Brandenhagen and Sally Fairbanks worked getting all their recollections into a word file Sally would soon be emailing to the Director and she realized he would be mad as hell because they omitted some information at the meetings. Unfortunately, a person who went through and experienced all they did with sleep deprivation may not remember it all at once.

The Director's time line and agenda was too aggressive. Sally had heard rumors before the Director was always paranoid about the NSA trying to embarrass him. He almost seemed like he was in a panic to get a report to the President before the NSA slipped one in on him.

The problem was the Director wanted a finalized vetted and proofed report. If he had more common sense, he would have allowed the "quick look" report like they did with the previous director who was much easier to work with. Unfortunately, when the White House changes so do all the political appointees such as the DCI and people who worked directly for him.

The director who was a former FBI manager and an SES over at the DOD, wanted a shot at a cabinet position and he was kissing any ass or sucking any you know what to get there.

Three days after the last meeting Roger did the final edit and changes Sally requested, he make for his narration of his roles in the Alien visits. He was finally done and Sally said it was *good enough*. Roger was also thinking timing was perfect because he had the weekend coming up and nothing scheduled to do, so he would try to figure how to escape his house and go out and have some fun.

He hadn't been over to Eads Street in Crystal City for a while where a few friends and he met up at the sports bar there on 23rd Street and played pool while drinking copious amounts of fantastic craft beers. Perhaps he would give Jack and Ben a call and see if they were busy.

Just as he grabbed his I-phone to call his buddies, it rang. The caller was unknown, but it had an Arizona area code. Normally Roger didn't answer phone calls from unknown people, but since it was from Arizona, he thought it might be Sargent Hawthorne or someone like that.

"Hello." Roger answered.

"How have you been Doctor Brandenhagen?" The voice was unmistakable. General Níngsī had a very distinctive voice, probably caused by Alien vocal cords not exactly like Earth People, plus he was eight feet tall.

"Is this General Níngsī?" Roger asked even though he already knew the answer.

"Yes, it is Doctor Brandenhagen."

"I'm surprised to be receiving a call from you General."

"Yea, I know these backwards gadgets you Earth people use is not as convenient as one of our holograph communicators, but that's all you have in your home."

"General Níngsī, I'm actually quite surprised to

hear from you and a busy man like you would not be calling someone like me if it wasn't important."

"Yes, it is important."

As Roger was trying to think how General Níngsī acquired an I-phone and was using it, he asked, "What can I do for you General?"

"Doctor Brandenhagen, when you were visiting me, I asked you if you wanted to go to Mars, and you indicated in the future you would like to."

"Yes, I did."

"Doctor, right now the street in front of your home is fairly empty, there is no traffic to speak of, so in about 10 minutes, walk out your front door and your ride will be there to pick you up."

"What about those news vans?"

"They are all gone, they went home for the night. They are obviously bored looking at your two security sentries out in front of your home."

"What if the security men stop me from leaving my home?"

"Doctor Brandenhagen, we have advanced technology, and we have neural interference devices. They will have a lost time event and not know you left. You will be long gone before they realize you are not at home."

"Alright General I will be ready and walk out of my home exactly in 10 minutes."

"We'll pick you up then."

In five minutes, two pedestrians walked down the sidewalk not far from Doctor Brandenhagen's home. They looked innocuous with nice business suits and brief cases. This was not uncommon for Washington DC, especially in this upscaled neighborhood for this time a day as many professionals were coming home about this time after a good happy hour at nearby bars. At one minute before Dr. Brandenhagen was expected to escape his home and get some temporary freedom from the goons guarding his front door, the men with the brief cases stopped directly in front of Doctor Brandenhagen's home and just stood there. Artificial Intelligence in the transport just set off Whitehouse alarms that occur when an aircraft violates the no-fly zone also controlled the brief cases that were now beaming the neurological disrupters on the two security men. In essence it was like what hypnotists do when they neutralize the left side of the brain. It's also key to hemi-sync which Monroe Institute developed for the CIA. The security men's body functions and motor functions continue working and they stood in a docile position without any knowledge of the world around them.

A minute later as Doctor Brandenhagen opened up his front door, the men were standing there staring forward as if they had no cognitive function. As Doctor Brandenhagen approached the city sidewalk, one of the two men in business suits said, "Doctor Brandenhagen, your ride has arrived."

At that moment the transport stopped out on the street in front of his home, eerily silent with no noise. The propulsion mechanisms were extraordinary to not give off a sound but yet have the ability to travel very efficiently. Doctor Brandenhagen thought he would one day ask General Níngsī for the physics that allowed this gadget to work.

The door to the transport opened and the two men in business suits escorted Roger Brandenhagen into it, then it immediately went vertical.

The KH-14 and the Cosmos 2549 stationed in synchronous orbit over Washington DC to support clandestine activity recorded this event.

One of the artificial intelligences projects the CIA did was to link up KH-14 records with anything to do with any threat to the White House including violating the no-fly zone. Any private pilot who made such a blunder would quickly be visited by the FEDS. Any terrorist who entered the zone unlawfully would have a very bad day.

Like all good Artificial Intelligence, there are automatic reports sent to appropriate parties including the CIA watch officer 7/24 staffed by some of the most professional people in government service. All of them would take a bullet for the President.

The watch officer then is required to notify specific department heads that the event may fall under their jurisdiction. In this case this particular artificial intelligence program registered two CIA men were stationed directly in front of where this possible UFO (UAP) parked for a moment with 3 people getting on board. Artificial Intelligence then performed data reduction tracking the 3 men where they came from. One of those persons exited Dr. Brandenhagen's residence between the two CIA men standing there appearing to be staring off into space.

This operation concerning Doctor Brandenhagen and the two CIA security men was clearly under SAC Director's purview so he immediately got a text message to immediately call the watch officer. If he did not respond to that text message within five minutes, they would call his phone and if he didn't answer send a car over in case, he was sleeping to wake him up. God help him if he was in a bar drinking with a couple cuties and didn't pick up on the phone.

SAC Director Mark Rebman being so paranoid and full of agenda, jumped at the text message and called the Watch Officer who then notified him, he had to come into headquarters to a SKIF where the level of classification required where he would be informed of what it was about. Until he got the report, he had no clue or any idea what he had to do.

SAC Director Mark Rebman was pissed off, he was going to miss his favorite TV shows and not get a chance to polish off a couple craft beers before he went to bed.

Because of the Alien situation he also knew this could be something very bad, like the enemy just entered the solar system and a space war would happen right here and very soon. It was all very unsettling.

SAC Director Mark Rebman arrived at headquarters, taken into the SKIF and shown all the video provided by the KH-14.

Meanwhile since it was daylight in Moscow in

the morning, at Lubyanka Square in the Meshchansky District of Moscow several high-level FSB (KGB) managers were getting reports and watching Cosmos 2549 video and thanks to google maps already knew the residence where the man left. This same residence was the location of the news media vans and the circus outside Doctor Brandenhagen's home. It didn't take a rocket scientist to figure out the man leaving with the two men in business suits was probably Doctor Brandenhagen.

The Russians and the Chinese are excellent data miners. Most Americans fail to grasp some of the best computer scientists in the world are in Moscow.

China has so many brilliant people it's actually scary. In 10 years, China will be the world's leader in Robotics, Artificial Intelligence, and Signal Processing. Whether or not China has a Yaogan 31 series satellite in synchronous orbit above Washington DC is probably a good guess. So, they also would know what just happened.

The CIA's artificial intelligence was working on video splicing with other sensors in an attempt to discover where the thing that landed on the city street and went straight up into the air went.

It took about an hour and the best analysts could figure out; is it went into space.

The SAC Director Mark Rebman is a smart guy. He would never have been put in that position if he didn't have above average intellect and social engineering skills. He also had to have a lot of determination and quick wit to handle the complexities of the day-to-day routines that would freak out America if they only knew the half of it.

Since Doctor Brandenhagen was involved and the thoughts of what transpired the past few days, he suddenly realized where these Aliens were going, in spite of his orders to Doctor Brandenhagen not to do so.

The group that was called into support were in for a big surprise.

"Everyone not Q and Y cleared, please leave the room. Half of the six people who worked the evening shift stood up and walked out and shut the cipher locked door behind them.

To the other three who remained he said, "The Aliens are taking Doctor Brandenhagen to Mars. Get Sally Fairbanks in here right away. I want to know if she had any previous knowledge of this little joy ride before this happened."

Sally too was perturbed she was summoned back to work, and at this time of day if they think she's going to put on makeup and a dress, they are in for a big surprise!

Thirty minutes later, there they were, for the big showdown.

"Did you know about Doctor Brandenhagen going to Mars?"

"I put it in the report and I'm on record for informing you General Níngsī offered him a trip to Mars. Since I was with Doctor Brandenhagen the entire time except once when he used the bathroom and so did

I, that we were not together where I could hear what he said. There was never any discussion of time and date as to when such a visit would be scheduled."

"Would you like to take a polygraph so we can help your memory?"

"Are you threatening me?"

"Its within my responsibility to vet all our spies including you anytime I think it's necessary."

"Sure, go ahead and hook me up to a polygraph, I have nothing to hide, but I will tell you this. I will immediately start looking for another job because I do not like to be treated unfair. You are relatively new here. You don't know how many times I put my ass on the line for this agency. What you are doing is alienating the people you need the most, and I do not need this job. I can do something else like swinging burgers at McDonalds, so unless you have something else important to discuss I'm going home. And you have made me feel so crappy I might just call-in sick tomorrow and you can do your meeting stand alone."

Sally Fairbanks stood up, and walked out the room. She was done working for this prick.

The USA, Russia, and China lost track of the Zhrakzhong transport very quickly, though an hour later spliced video was able to figure out a general direction of where it went, but it wasn't logical because it wasn't heading for Mars and in fact almost the opposite direction it needed to go to head for Mars.

The reason was it went out 100,000 miles and docked on a Zhrakzhongs major space combatant. The shuttle could not go 245 million miles to Mars and back in a reasonable amount of time, and General Níngsī needed to go there and fulfill his promise to Doctor Brandenhagen and get back right away to deal with any potential issues that could arise. The Military craft could get them there and back in a few hours.

After the shuttle landed on the Space Warship, General Níngsī was met by the Zhrakzhongs Space Warship's commanding officer Captain Luōjiàn who offered:

"General Níngsī, I would like to invite you and your guest to my Space Cabin for some refreshments."

"Thank you, Captain Luōjiàn, but first I would like you to take us to the control room and give my guest here a tour."

"As you wish General Níngsī, this way please."

Zhrakzhong Space Warship shuttlecraft are critical devices as there is often flow of people during battles for purposes of picking up stranded and wounded warriors. As such the need to have the shuttle bay near the control room is very important as in some battles there is little time to escape a damaged ship before it blows up. Because of that design philosophy, the walk from the shuttle bay to the control room was quick.

Once inside the control room Captain Luōjiàn explained a few things. There were no drivers or pilots. It was all computer controlled with Artificial Intelligence. The main purpose of the control room party is to plan strategy with the help of Artificial Intelligence, give orders and initiate weapons launching and firing.

As Captain Luōjiàn explained things, Doctor Brandenhagen surmised they probably only needed one person in the control room and not the 15 that were there out of tradition. The displays were huge. There were no windows on the spacecraft, but they had holographic video that appeared like looking out windows provided by numerous video camera's imbedded in the hull and other sensors.

Those 12-foot-tall displays gave the appearance a person was looking outside the ship into space. And every bright spot had a label, they knew what it was. Their astronomical expertise was immense. Doctor Brandenhagen didn't know he was looking at magnified information. Those objects were a lot further away than what they seemed.

It didn't take long to zip past the far side of the moon. And soon they were pointing a bright planet or star. All Doctor Brandenhagen could see was white light and no images. One thing he did sense based on the external images; they were speeding up even though there was no sound to indicate so.

General Níngsī could see Doctor Brandenhagen was super animated observing all this and decided they could wait until the return leg to go to Captain Luōjiàn's Cabin and have refreshments.

Doctor Brandenhagen had never seen near light speed velocity before. The only reason why they didn't go faster was: the slow down sickness it could cause.

General Níngsī said, "Doctor Brandenhagen, you

will start to see that white dot grow."

Doctor Brandenhagen watched and just like General Níngsī stated, the dot was growing in size. By the time the dot was an inch in diameter on the main surveillance display, it was already turning red. And then it grew and the ship pointed right at it. Soon on the big holographic display, Mars appeared 3 feet in diameter.

"Doctor Brandenhagen, don't be too concerned about us colliding with Mars, what you are observing has been greatly magnified. We have not reached the point to slow down."

"General Níngsī, from what I've observed thus far, I know the Zhrakzhongs and you know what you are doing."

"Thank you for your confidence."

General Níngsī then looked at the Zhrakzhongs Space Warship Captain Luōjiàn and asked, "When did you get the Archeologists to Mars?"

"General Níngsī, they arrived at Cydonia, 18 Martian hours ago."

"Good. Doctor Brandenhagen and I will shuttle down to Cydonia when we arrive."

Martian days are 24 hours and 40 minutes long, hence the time is not too different.

When Doctor Brandenhagen was informed in English what the Space Warship's Captain Luōjiàn said, he was suddenly animated because to have an opportunity to go to Cydonia of all places. This sudden realization prompted Doctor Brandenhagen to say:

"This is an incredible opportunity for an Earth person when no Space Travel to Mars was scheduled for probably five years at the earliest."

"Doctor Brandenhagen you earned this trip by being an honest scientist and taking a lot of ridicule when you maintained your perseverance to your theory."

"It's a shame I didn't bring some equipment along to get some soil samples," Doctor Brandenhagen said.

"Not to worry Doctor Brandenhagen, our Archeologists have all the tools you need including sample packaging. I know you probably want to do checks for Xeon 129. Our scientists on Mars now with the Archeologists are analyzing the soil for you. You can take samples back if you desire, but we will provide you all the details so there is no need to sample them on Earth."

General Níngsī with the help of his Artificial Intelligence had detected the SAC Director had already taken legal action against Doctor Brandenhagen, but General Níngsī had already decided to intervene. *The prick will get a dose of humility when they all got back and figured things out.* He was also saddening to learn Sally Fairbanks had submitted her resignation and didn't plan to go back to work. He liked dealing with these people. They were genuine and honest. The Earth people didn't know they had advanced Photonics to measure their faces and their body in very sophisticated manners to determine whether or not they were lying. This is very important when dealing with foreigners or Aliens such as the Earth people.

General Níngsī would soon inform the two security guys guarding Doctor Brandenhagen's home that *people higher up will be hearing from him soon.*

The vision of Mars magnified was quite impressive as they got closer. Suddenly General Níngsī was informed, "We are slowing down now to approach orbit of the planet."

Doctor Brandenhagen felt and enormous rush as they slid into orbit about the same altitude as the many Space Shuttles that circled Earth.

"We will do a complete orbit as we are slowing down so that people feel comfortable by not breaking too quickly."

The crew was happy that General Níngsī was aboard to receive the special treatment, otherwise they would have braked a lot harder and not made an orbit before they launched the shuttle down to the planet surface.

Because he was first and foremost a scientist, Doctor Brandenhagen watched intently the holographic video, taking it all in, this special treat. Halfway through the orbit he spotted Olympus Mons, the tallest planetary mountain and volcano in the Solar System. This 13.6-mile-tall dormant volcano is the subject of a few science-fiction novels Roger Brandenhagen read in the past. Olympus Mons is an incredible sight from space since it's about two and a half times Mount Everest's height above sea level.

This was really Doctor Brandenhagen's reward for the many years of taking abuse from the scientific community for writing his theory about Mars being wiped out. In a way it was kind of sad to know that Aliens know more about Earth and Mars history than Earth's Scientific Community. And Roger Brandenhagen now knew had he not developed the theory and taken all the abuse over the years, he would not be taking this trip now. General Níngsī knew about all the abuse because his Artificial Intelligence found most of the published sources of ridicule.

There would be more interesting discoveries on Mars since the galaxies premier Archeology team was down on the planet Mars using sophisticated technology to find buried remains of a once prosperous society.

They were not going to do a vast study; they were only going to give Doctor Brandenhagen a lot of discovery he would spend a lot of time writing about in the future.

In forty-five minutes, the Zhrakzhongs Space Warship had slowed down considerably. The Zhrakzhongs Space Warship's Warship Captain Luōjiàn looking at the navigation holograph said, "General Níngsī, we'll be in position to launch the shuttle down to Mars in about fifteen minutes. I suggest you and your landing party proceed to the Shuttle now and get ready for launch."

General Níngsī gestured towards Doctor Brandenhagen and said, "Shall we Doctor?"

Doctor Roger Brandenhagen just about the most thrilled in his lifetime nodded and promptly followed

General Níngsī back to the shuttle.

In what seemed to be about fifteen minutes after everyone going to the planet were aboard the shuttle, the Zhrakzhongs Space Warship's Captain called via the communication network to the Shuttle stating: "General Níngsī, the Shuttle Bay is depressurized and the Shuttle Bay hatches are open and ready for your launch."

"Thank you, Captain, we are departing now."

The Shuttle pilot turned back towards General Níngsī to observe his next action he anticipated.

"Launch the shuttle and proceed to Cydonia where the Archeology team is working."

"Launching the shuttle," the pilot reported back to General Níngsī.

It didn't seem like a lot of movement, but the numerous flat screens showed what appeared like observation windows, but the shuttle only had a hatch, one small window on the door, and all the images were holographs provided by numerous cameras.

The Shuttle moved above the Space Warship, then peeled off to the right. The shuttle occupants were now feeling weightlessness as they were no longer in the gravity field of the Zhrakzhong Space Warship providing artificial gravity.

In about 5 minutes as the speed built up, the Shuttle definitely approached the planet in the exact area they wanted. Dr. Brandenhagen was very familiar with the Cydonia area of Mars and was utterly astonished as he was seeing the image often stated as a face on Mars. Researchers claim this is an optical illusion and nothing more than a psychological phenomenon of pareidolia. When Doctor Brandenhagen looked at the Cydonia region picture taken by the 2006 European Space Agency's satellite Mars Express, it appeared to him he could see a lion's face. Was this also pareidolia?

If they were approaching Earth the shuttle would feel some turbulence. Since Mars does not have much of an atmosphere, the flight felt very smooth. As the shuttle got closer to the landing zone, Roger Brandenhagen could start to make out the appearance of some transports and enclosures. *This must be the Archeologists.*

It did not seem long after that the shuttle was slowing and curving into the landing zone that came up really quick as they slowed.

Moments later they were sitting down on the planet.

Everyone was handed a special mask by the coordinator of the flight and they put on special coveralls with impressive thermal capability but lightweight.

They soon exited the shuttle and were escorted inside one of the enclosures that appeared to have a double airlock. They went in the first door, then shut it behind them which was self-sealing. The enclosure had lit up indicators above the second door with some alien writing that changed colors and the leader opened the internal door.

The enclosure was at least fifty feet long as

Doctor Brandenhagen estimated. He was not too far off the mark. Five men who had soiled clothing stepped forward to greet General Níngsī. Their leader spoke:

"General Níngsī, we feel privileged to meet you and we want to thank you for giving us the opportunity to research this planet and find examples of its past."

"From your earlier reports, I'm very proud of what you Archeologists have achieved here."

"Well sir, knowing the history of Mars helps us to narrow our search and utilizing our cotaiga probes and metastable transducers we found some high probability geometries to explore. In our digs the current readings indicate we are about a foot away from our objective where we think there will be some extensive discovery."

"Don't let me slow you down, go back to work and we'll watch, it shouldn't take long to move a foot of dirt."

"Thank you General Níngsī, the man said, then he and his female assistant turned around and walked back to the trench that appeared to go down like a ramp to 15 or 20 feet below the planet's surface. The dirt excavated was now piled up around the enclosure improving its airtight condition of the enclosure reducing air leaks.

General Níngsī walked over to some technicians who were monitoring some instruments that had two dimensional displays as one would expect with Earth technology, but the image on the devices did seem three dimensional.

The process was dig, monitor, dig. They didn't want to tear up substantial evidence of a civilization wiped out 900,000 years ago. All they knew at this point in time there was about a 10-foot area that was amazingly symmetrical and had metallic properties that made the super sensitive metastable transducers very efficient at imaging the find.

A few minutes later one of the archeologists yelled, "We hit something solid!"

Tension really mounted now. Doctor Brandenhagen was now more animated than he ever was in his life time. These were expert Archeologist's way ahead of Earth technology. What would probably take Earth 1000 years to find was exposed in 18 hours upon landing on Mars.

The Archeologist quickly exposed it. Then one of them came up and said to General Níngsī, "We have found a door of sorts. It may lead to a hidden access and the possibility exists, there could be pathogens down there when we open it up. I recommend everyone put on their face masks and turn on their air flasks as a precaution."

General Níngsī concurred and ordered, "Everyone put on your face masks and turn on your air flasks. They each had about eight hours of breathing with these devices. As soon as the lead Archeologists observed precautions were set, he gave the signal and they proceeded to open up an inch thick steel door.

There were no signs of corrosion on the steel so whoever manufactured it had advanced steel production ability maybe better than stainless steel, doctor Brandenhagen later recalled.

No explosive gases or anything that precluded entry allowed them to proceed. And now it was a come to Jesus' moment for Doctor Brandenhagen as he followed the Zhrakzhongs down the ancient Martian stairway.

Doctor Brandenhagen now believed General Níngsī account of what happened to the Martians. And now he also knew what most likely happened to Atlantis. Some evil empire laid waste to so many innocent beings. This also seemed to justify what General Níngsī was doing in hiding his civilization from other bastards that had no remorse over killing women and children.

The stairway was over 100 feet long and went deep underground. In some ways it reminded Doctor Brandenhagen about the distance some of the DC Metro escalators went down to the train platforms. When they got to the bottom, they found what they were looking for. The ghosts of a dead planet.

They walked around and looked at all the Artifacts. The deceased beings had long ago decayed.

"They probably had oxygen until it was all used up. The last person living breathed the last bit of air that was left."

"This must have been some kind of Emergency Survival chamber."

"There are no passages to anywhere, it was obviously a shelter."

Doctor Brandenhagen walked over and looked at some of the corpses and some materials they had with them.

"It must have been short notice; they didn't bring much down here with them."

"They didn't have stored food or water; they must have assumed it would shortly be over an they could go back to the surface and pick up their lives again.

"Doctor Brandenhagen, we would not have bothered looking for this had you not impressed me with your theory and your explanation," General Níngsī stated. He also felt for Doctor Roger Brandenhagen knowing all the ridicule and vicious verbal attacks others had done to him over the years because he was vocal about his theory.

"There isn't much here to analyze as they obviously came here in a panic," the lead Archeologist stated.

His assistant, the nice-looking female asked, "What are we going to do now?"

General Níngsī being an extraordinary leader and theorist on *canons of society* knew the obvious answer:

"This is their burial chamber. Even though they didn't anticipate they would die down here, they did. To show them respect we must say a prayer for their souls, then we need to seal this back up and leave."

He then turned towards Doctor Brandenhagen and asked, "What do you think Doctor?"

"General Níngsī, I agree with you completely. I feel deeply for these poor innocent people. We must give them their peace as there is no value in exposing this. It's irrelevant to society today and it happened

900,000 years ago. The descendants of the Jupitorians probably are not even aware they did this."

"Doctor Brandenhagen, I'm beginning to like you more and more every day. We tend to look down at Earth people because you are primative in nature, but you sir, are just as moralistic advanced as Zhrakzhongs."

"Thank you for your kind words General Níngsī, I'm nobody special but I appreciate your thoughts."

"Doctor Brandenhagen, there is a possibility our war with the Xīngguī could end within a year. If you would like I would take you back to the Zhrakzhong Empire as we would quickly evacuate all the Zhrakzhongs as soon as the treaty is signed."

"General Níngsī, thank you for your offer, but I'm getting old now. I'm in my late 60's and I know my time horizon is getting shorter every day. I want to remain here and be buried near those I knew in my lifetime."

"I can understand that Doctor Brandenhagen."

General Níngsī then turned towards the lead Archeologist and said, "Thank you for all your hard work. Restore it to the way you found it. A ship will be standing by to evacuate you off the planet as soon as you wrap things up."

"Understand General Níngsī, all will be taken care of as you instructed. Tomorrow anyone looking at this site will not know we were ever here."

"Exactly the way I like it."

General Níngsī turned to his shuttle pilot and

said, "Us leave now."

Moments later, the group that came down to look at the Martians were in the shuttle and buckled up. The shuttle immediately lifted off the planet and notified the Zhrakzhong Space Warship, "We are on their way back to the ship."

It did not take a lot of time to get back up to the Zhrakzhong Space Warship where they were soon entertained in the Captains Space Cabin.

As Captain Luōjiàn was being charming to his big boss, General Níngsī noticed how Doctor Brandenhagen looked very somber. His greatest achievement in his lifetime turned out to be the saddest experience he could ever imagine.

Being a top General in an advanced force like the Zhrakzhongs who faced off against the toughest Empires in the galaxy, was an expert in body language and social engineering. He understood the paradox of Doctor Brandenhagen. The biggest discover of his lifetime turned out to be the saddest. Thus, it was a Pyrrhic victory.

In the Space Cabin, Captain Luōjiàn had all the holographic technology required to see any tactical display or communicate with the control room. As such he preferred to have the forward scanning video up and where he sat at his captain's table, he could look at the holograph and know where they were going and a second display showed where they came from in case another ship was chasing them for destruction.

Doctor Brandenhagen sat, in a seat not far from

Captain Luōjiàn, where he had a direct vision of the video behind them, showing Mars slowly shrinking as they sped up.

In many of the vast battles that happened in the Galaxy there is often severe remorse and regret from officers carrying out their orders resulting in innocent civilians getting killed just like the Martians. General Níngsī had to deal with this and he found the most effective method was to give those officers exhibiting such a condition a particular type of elixir carried aboard all Zhrakzhong Space Warships.

"Captain, I think Doctor Brandenhagen and I would like a serving of Gěnkóviàn Jiǔyàowù," General Níngsī stated.

The Zhrakzhong Space Warship Captain also had excellent body language interpretation understood General Níngsī was politely requesting the serving for his friend who acted like he had just seen a ghost. He nodded and looked up at his steward who was always standing by especially when a high-ranking person like General Níngsī was standing by. He nodded at the Steward who immediately went about serving the two guests.

As to not appear condescending, Captain Luōjiàn said, "I would like a serving too."

General Níngsī should have warned Doctor Brandenhagen that Gěnkóviàn Jiǔyàowù was a strong substance. It was designed to not taste strong but it sure had strong effects as it was laced with alcohol and an opioid byproduct of a plant that was genetically identical to the opium poppy (Papaver Somniferum) on Earth.

The two Zhrakzhong officers watched Doctor Brandenhagen quickly finish his drink which further clarified his emotional state. They knew better than to offer him another one right away or he would be inebriated when they dropped him off at his home. The Gĕnkóviàn Jiǔyàowù did have immediate affects. In moments he was a lot less tense, smiling and "feeling the buzz."

General Níngsī only engaged in small talk as he knew Doctor Brandenhagen was already overwhelmed with enough psychological stimulus hence deserved some mentally relaxing atmosphere void of any serious conversations.

The Zhrakzhong Space Warship Captain Luōjiàn understood vividly now was the time to say less and let his guest relax because General Níngsī would not have made the Gĕnkóviàn Jiǔyàowù request unless something quite extraordinary happened on the planet. They found what they came looking for and it wasn't a pleasant sight. It most likely rattled Doctor Brandenhagen quite well. He would ask the Archeologist all about it when he and his team were picked up later and all their equipment and shelters were removed to hide the fact they had been there.

As the Zhrakzhong Space Warship retraced its way back to its synchronous deployment zone, Doctor Brandenhagen elapsed into a docile condition the other two men knew would happen. Had he noticed how General Níngsī barely sipped his drink, he would not be in the condition he was in now, partially mentally impaired. The good news is by the time he arrived home he would be back to a normal mental condition.

To some extent the Zhrakzhong Space Warship Captain Luōjiàn was glad it went down like this because it's always a pain to play the politics and fake adornment to entertain the high-ranking officers when everyone knew it was just the way the game was played.

At that moment in time, General Níngsī was glad they could forgo the BS such visits required and just relax. Perhaps he should have downed the Gěnkóviàn Jiǔyàowù like Doctor Brandenhagen did. Unfortunately, his day was not done. When he got back to his command center, he had some unfinished business to attend too.

The Zhrakzhongs arrived at the location to launch the shuttle back down to Earth and take Doctor Brandenhagen home.

As the transport shuttle slipped into the atmosphere the KH-14 parked above Washington DC identified the intruder that had left hours before. SAC's Artificial intelligence was back hacking away, putting out a report and notifying who needed to know such as NORAD and NRO.

NORAD was just about to scramble F22's out of Langley Air Force Base when one of Sally's colleagues put the kibosh on it.

"You stupid son of a bitches, you shoot that craft down probably carrying a Zhrakzhong VIP, we will not have an Airforce in a few hours."

It took utter strong language to force the Air Force Secretary's hands to order the STAND DOWN.

He got his ass chewed by the SAC Director moments later. Instead of the ass chewing he should have got a medal for saving the Air Force and most of America's military.

Just as the SAC people predicted that object flew down on Doctor Brandenhagen's street in front of his house and stopped slightly longer this time.

When Doctor Brandenhagen got out of the transport shuttle, General Níngsī got out with him wearing his uniform and walked up the sidewalk together. Two Eight-Foot-tall body guards were a couple steps behind General Níngsī and Doctor Brandenhagen. The two CIA men were astonished looking at those 8-foot-tall monsters.

As Doctor Brandenhagen got to his front door, General Níngsī reached the old-style covered porch area utilizing his ear bud help from Artificial Intelligence, he informed the two security guys:

"Please inform the SAC Director that if Sally Fairchild isn't at work tomorrow morning, I will personally call the President of the United States and tell him some things I know."

"We will."

"I have copies of every single one of your CIA files. I know all your dirty secrets. You obviously would not want me to hand that stuff over to Vladimir Putin or Xi Jinping."

"Yes, we would appreciate if you didn't"

"The President has asked for a meeting, and I

will be calling him soon. I think it's time he replaces the SAC Director who has such poor computer security that allowed us to hack all of it."

The CIA guys did not respond but did feel the sting.

"Perhaps it would be better if SAC Director was working for Sally Fairbanks?" General Níngsī offered.

"I'm sure he wouldn't want that."

"Also, you can tell the Air Force Secretary I have a lot of Space Assets nearby watching me. They could have got to me long before your F22's out of Langley which I know were alerted. We would have shot them out of the sky just as easy as we did in Arizona. Whoever called them off is a true hero. I want your President informed and if he isn't informed, I will personally inform him with some demands that he fires whoever didn't inform him."

"Yes Sir, we will pass that on."

"Tomorrow Doctor Brandenhagen needs to rest up. He had a very terrible day. Do not let anyone disturb him in any manner. If they do, they will be dealing with me very soon afterwards because this home is not only watched by your inferior KH-14, we have our probes watching it. Send the word keep everyone away."

The two CIA men stood speechless; a lot was said very quickly.

"Comprende?" General Níngsī said as the Zhrakzhongs Artificial Intelligence had selected some colloquialisms portrayed by American entertainment in the past.

"The former Marine standing on the right side, said, "Yes Sir!" just like he was back in the Marine Corp.

General Níngsī and his two 8-foot-tall escorts went back to the transport shuttle and it abruptly took off and was back in Arizona in 30 minutes after triggering several NORAD alarms and Secret Service intervention.

Within five minutes after General Níngsī left, a dozen black SUVs came to a screeching halt in front of Doctor Brandenhagen's home.

One of the first persons out of the car was SAC Director Mark Rebman hot under the color.

SAC Director Mark Rebman marched smartly up the sidewalk and onto the porch and was just about to ring the doorbell when one of the Security men grabbed his hand and said, "We need to talk before you do anything else."

"What's the meaning of this?" SAC Director said with apparent anger.

"Sir, before you disturb Doctor Brandenhagen there are some things you need to know."

"Like what?"

"I have a lot of information to give you, do you have a notetaker with you or have someone record it with their cell phone."

"O.K. wise guy what the fuck do you got to say."

"Sir, with all due respect if you bother Doctor

Brandenhagen, you will no longer be the SAC Director tomorrow morning."

"What's this Bull Shit all about."

"Sir you need to calm down and let me give you the information before you go halfcocked and get yourself fired. And it will probably be in a few hours if my guess is correct."

SAC Director Mark Rebman has NEVER had any of his men talk to him like this before. This was almost maddening. Something in the back of his head told him to lower his flag, cool off a bit and open his ears and hear a few things.

"Okay give it to me."

The very decent CIA man who was well respected by his peers recapitulated everything General Stated with great precision.

Then SAC Director Mark Rebman made the mistake of saying, "There is no way I'm going to take that bitch back."

"It's your choice, but something tells me the Alien General will be talking to the President tomorrow and either you will be fired or you will be working for Sally."

The SAC Director Mark Rebman looked back at a few grinning FBI men who were going to cuff Doctor Brandenhagen and haul his miserable ass in and give him a good going over. They stood back their smiling because privately they thought SAC Director Mark Rebman was a flaming asshole, and in this world it's all about leverage and the SAC director may no longer have any leverage as the arrival of the Zhrakzhongs was changing everything.

"Director Rebman, are we going to make the arrests or not?" The FBI supervisor asked. CIA had to bring the FBI with them because they are not legally allowed to operate inside CONUS concerning anything related to law enforcement because of laws and regulations.

One of the CIA guards looked at the FBI guy and said, "If we let you in the house the director will be fired tomorrow and some of you could end up dead."

"Is that some kind of threat."

"Didn't you hear a god damn thing I informed the director?"

"That's all bullshit."

"You don't know about the F22's they shot down do you because its compartmentalized."

All of a sudden, the FBI guy started looking strange.

Yes, they shot down half of two F22 squadrons like shooting ducks in a barrel. They got this place under observation and if you go in there, bad things will happen."

"You think so?" the FBI guy said in a cocky manner.

"Director, why don't you tell these FBI guys how the F22's at Langley were told to stand down tonight.

Also do you FBI guys even know the Aliens are here?"

"What do you mean about Aliens?"

"There is a lot of shit the Director hasn't informed you of. And if Sally Fairbanks isn't at work in the morning the President is likely to fire his dumb ass."

"That's insubordination Mr."

"Oh, yea tell that to the President tomorrow when he fires your ass if Sally isn't back the job, or are you that dumb of a son of a bitch."

"I'll fire your ass."

"Good, Sally will hire me back after you turn in your badge because something tells me you are a dumb son of a bitch and will not tell these FBI guys to go home and in about five minutes there will be an Alien ship here to inform you will be unemployed in the morning."

Doctor Brandenhagen heard most of the ruckus through the door and decided to intervene to save the man's job. He opened the door and surprised them when he walked out.

"Hello Director Rebman, are you that dumb of a son of a bitch you don't listen to your people?"

"Who the fuck are you asshole," the SAC Director Mark Rebman yelled now super pissed off that a scientist was mouthing off to someone like him way up in the CIA food chain.

"Guess who called me today?"

"Enlighten me asshole."

"That's right, General Níngsī called me. And yes, they have cell phones, my number, your number, the Presidents number and I think you are going to get a phone call real soon, and it might be the President informing you have been fired."

"You think so wise guy?"

"Some of these FBI clowns are walking a tight rope too because if I request General Níngsī will see to it they get fired too."

"That's Bullshit and you know it Brandenhagen."

"And if you are so fucking dumb to not know your computers were hacked by the Aliens then maybe you should be fired."

"What the fuck are you talking about?"

"You don't listen to your men, they informed you just a few minutes ago that General Níngsī is willing to hand over all of your computer files to Vladimir Putin and Xi Jinping. He has copies of it all. You just had the largest data breach in US History on your watch. You should be fired over it."

"I do not believe your bullshit."

"See this button on my cell phone? It's a quick dial to General Níngsī. If you and this circus are not out of here in about five seconds, I will hit it and General Níngsī will have people here waking up Washington DC in probably 15 minutes. Now leave or get ready to have to explain it to the President why you are such a dumb ass."

The FBI guy was starting to figure it out, this

was not a joke and he didn't want to get hit by political shrapnel and immediately turned around and directed all his men, "Clear out of here we are leaving."

In two minutes, it was just the SAC Director Mark Rebman, one of his CIA, support guys and the two guards standing by Doctor Brandenhagen.

The director didn't know what to do, he was pissed off and wanted to punch out Doctor Brandenhagen, who embarrassed him in front of the FBI.

Roger Brandenhagen probably could not defend himself against the SAC Director Mark Rebman, but the two other CIA men didn't want the wrath of the Aliens coming down on them and if the Director surged at the Doctor they would have intervened and it would not be pretty.

The two men stood there staring in each other's eyes. Hate was flowing out of the Director; disdain was flowing out of Doctor Brandenhagen sad to learn that America had such a dumb ass in high places. It's called the peter principal. Government Managers always promote incompetent people below them so they never have to worry about someone trying to get their job.

"You know Director Rebman you are interfering with my sleep and I did have a very bad day, I suggest you leave now."

The two guards nodded at each other and the third guy who all too well knew what to do. They grabbed the Director and escorted him over to the CIA SUV who had a diver the car running and ready to go. They threw the Director's ass in the SUV then told the driver, "Leave now and keep going and don't stop until you get back to Headquarters. Your life may depend on it."

The driver had the window down weapons ready and overheard it all. He knew caution was the better part of Valor and with the assistant in the back seat with the SAC Director keeping him under control it was smooth sailing back to Headquarters.

Brandenhagen observed the two men come back up on his porch and he said, "Perhaps if the SAC Director had seen those 8-foot Giants he might have had a different reaction to the information. You men saved a lot of lives tonight and didn't know it and then he said, "Turn around and take a look."

10 Alien transport shuttles were now on the street and 50 or more eight-foot giants approached Doctor Brandenhagen's home with weapons drawn.

The Zhrakzhong commander walked up to the porch and asked, "Is everything ok now?"

Doctor Brandenhagen smiled and looked at the two CIA men and said, "The SAC Director Mark Rebman was acting in a threatening manner so I pressed the help button."

The two Guards started laughing. It was wild, but at the same time it was funny, even for consummate professionals.

"We saw all those automobiles leave just before we landed so we came down softly."

"Doctor Brandenhagen then told a joke, "I know

what you guys would have done with all the dead bodies."

"What do you think that is," the Zhrakzhong commander asked.

"Barbecued Humans with the right sauce on it, tastes like chicken too."

The two CIA men were rolling in laughter, as soon as the artificial intelligence informed the commander through his ear pod what the colloquialism meant, he laughed a little too.

"Sorry you came all the way for nothing."

"No, problem, this was a good exercise for my men to help them keep poised for when the real thing happens."

"Then I'm glad I called."

"I've already been informed to let you know, General Níngsī is a little upset with the SAC Director Mark Rebman about disturbing you tonight. Things will get better tomorrow.

"Thank you I appreciate that."

"Doctor Brandenhagen, I got a special briefing from General Níngsī about what you went through today with the Archeologists. That's why he knows you need to be rested, he also asked me to give these CIA guys the following information: the next time Doctor Brandenhagen is disturbed again tonight we will be sent down here again and our combat craft you see sitting on the street will be here permanently."

"I will make sure headquarters knows that immediately sir."

"Thank you."

The commander ordered all his men back to their combat craft and quickly they all went back into the sky.

This time because of the number of UFO's landing on Washington Streets, the joint chiefs and the secret service had to wake up the President.

The CIA men called the watch officer and not the SAC Director Mark Rebman as he would have expected because they didn't trust the dumb ass and passed on all the information. The watch officer was smart enough to know to call the DCI and explain it all who was shortly called to the White House to brief the president on all this new information.

The Watch Officer's report taken directly from the agents contradicted the reports in many ways the SAC Director Mark Rebman wrote, and when he failed to disclose to the DCI all his computer files had been hacked, as required by policy and regulations, he was soon in very hot water.

Trying to help the dumb bastard, the DCI personally woke up Sally Fairbanks and said, "I want to personally apologize for the treatment you received from the loose cannon. But I really would like you to come back to work and to rescind your resignation."

"I'll think about it," Sally responded.

"Sally, you are key to all this. We need you now more than ever. After this mess is all cleared up, I'll make sure you can get into a better situation that you will feel more comfortable with and not be in a hostile work environment with that asshole."

"Allright, I'll be in the office in the morning, but I'm very tired and do not think I can make it before 8:00."

"No problem. Get rested up. Tomorrow may be a big day for us. We got a lot of egg on our face tonight because of a loose cannon. I have a lot of damage to clean up because of it. And none of it is your fault."

"I appreciate that."

"Good night, Sally."

"Thank you, sir."

The CIA and the FBI have a long history of back stabbing. During WW2, FBI director J. Edgar Hoover had 120 OSS agents arrested in South America and informed Colonel Donovan they would remain in those squalor jails until the end of the war unless the OSS agreed to stay the hell out of South America which was FBI intelligence jurisdiction by charter.

Bob Woodward's book Veil talks about the CIA director Casey and his adversarial relationship with the NSA director Admiral Enright, a book worth reading.

Taking that to mind, the DCI knew the FBI would most likely make his agents feel like shit next week. Some of them met in various venues after hours and during work for combined task forces.

The SAC Director Mark Rebman will be sent on a company paid vacation for a several weeks to get him out of DC and possibly away from any congressional testimony that was likely to spring up if the data breach became public.

Chapter Nine

Xīnggui Plan and Deployment

In the Xīnggui province of Màichōng, Admiral Aete was summoned to the Emperor's palace. One could say the Xīnggui could pass for Koreans physically. In fact, their dress was remarkably like Koreans 800 years ago. If an Earth person got to see a Xīnggui that watched some of the wonderful Korean Drama's they would see the distinct likeness in mannerisms as well as appearance. It was as if you traveled back through time 800 years ago and went to Korea. Except instead of swords and bows and arrows, they had laser pistols, rifles, and Molecular Disrupter Cannons.

The Molecular Disrupter was one of the most ingenious engineering feats of the era. The only problem was it only worked decently at medium to short ranges and would not be effective at long ranges. In space battles due to the nature of incredible velocities at times, a lot of slugfests occurred at short and medium ranges, especially when fleets of 1000 or more Space Warships converged.

Throughout peacetime and during wartime,

the Xīngguī calibrated their Molecular Disrupters. It worked off the principal of shooting an energy beam that had oscillations at a frequency where the enemy ship's mechanical impedance was the weakest. The trick was to discover those frequencies that mattered the most.

The Xīngguī mastered the technique of getting close to an enemy ship and utilizing Molecular Disrupter Cannons at low power, it would find all the specific frequencies that caused the mechanical impedance to drop down to almost zero. Hence at that point it didn't take a lot of power in the energy beam to punch through the hull and cause an instantaneous rapid decompression event usually killing the crew with Asphyxiation. But also, if it happened to rupture a weapons magazine that stored missiles and space torpedo's, it could cause an instantaneous detonation blowing the Space Warship into millions of fragments.

Molecular Disrupter Cannons evened the odds for the Xīngguī who were now on the offensive instead of usually being on the defense. By now, due to the extended conflict, the Xīngguī had determined all the critical frequency signatures for just about any type of Zhrakzhong Space Warship.

Xīngguī had stunningly beautiful women just like modern day Korea. A lot of Xīngguī women would pass for Korean movie starlets, some of the best-looking women in the entertainment industry.

The Xīngguī were very Xenophobic which may have had some influence on the current conflict.

Just like many ancient disputes in the Galaxy, the current war between the Xīnggui and the Zhrakzhongs was manifested by racism and xenophobia on the part of the Xīnggui. The Zhrakzhongs were very accommodative and reasonable. They only had one flaw which agitated the Xīnggui. They had utter lust for Xīnggui women and before the war many wealthy Zhrakzhongs went to Màichōng to experience Xīnggui women for a price, and many wanted to take them home to Zhrakzhong worlds and make them their spouse. Because of hegemony, the wealthy Zhrakzhong appeared to flaunt their influence over Xīnggui women that added greatly to the emotional negativity Xīnggui men often suffered watching Zhrakzhongs behavior. So, when the first provocation occurred over a disputed planet, the Xīnggui wanted any excuse to humble the Zhrakzhong.

One of the miscalculation any country can make is to go to war when you don't know for sure what the outcome might be. Napoleon learned that at Moscow, Hitler learned that in Austria, Czechoslovakia, Poland, Finland, and later Moscow. North Korea learned that in 1950, America learned that in Vietnam and later Afghanistan.

This wasn't Zhrakzhongs first rodeo so to speak, they had 1000-year long wars with other civilizations in the past.

The Xīnggui, a developing Empire thus did not have any motivation to defend their remote villages. But they did defend their capital at Màichōng and their industrial heartland. Destroying villages with no real military potential wasn't a priority for the Zhrakzhongs.

The industrial areas and the capital were extremely well guarded and enormously difficult targets to hit.

Laser guided gravity bombs and missiles were useless against the Xīnggui because the laser directed Molecular Disrupter Cannons, would destroy those legacy weapons long before they got near any targets of value.

Hence both sides had strong defenses at their home worlds. Therefore, the only real advantage could be made in space with blockades and damage to Interplanetary Space Transports and Space Warships. If either side lost space superiority, they could be starved into submission without risk of closeup ground attack casualties to their fighter bombers now proving to have a high attrition rate.

Admiral Aete landed his personal space scooter at a reserved parking spot reserved for him. The Emperor Shāyú's Guards, a very select group of zealous militarists were there to meet Admiral Aete and escort him to Emperor Shāyú. These hand-picked men came from families with close ties to Emperor Shāyú's family for generations. They received patronage directly from Emperor Shāyú, but the quid pro quo was they had to psychologically prepare their sons to be extremely loyal and brave. There were no chickenshits in the Emperor Shāyú's Guards. For their psychological preparation, they earned their rank when sent off to distant warfighting to prove their bravery in live combat while being observed by patronage officers who measured their willingness to take a laser burn or a beam weapon searing pain for Emperor Shāyú.

This patronage system had worked well over the years repelling coup attempts. Every single Emperor Shāyú's Guardsman was under constant scrutiny and visibility to the Emperor Shāyú's Chief of Security Xié'è de Gōngniú. It was well understood that if any of these young men joined the resistance or assisted in anyway with Emperor Shāyú's enemies, he would put his family at risk.

In the few instances Emperor Shāyú's Guardsmen made the fatal blunder of assisting his enemies, Emperor Shāyú's Chief of Security Xié'è de Gōngniú made sure the family received terrible treatment just like the Roman Emperor Caligula did to those he wanted to kill.

Emperor Shāyú's had no fears and he had full control of his Chief of Security Xié'è de Gōngniú, a pedophile whom he allowed having his way with beautiful young teenage Zhrakzhongs captured during invasions, especially those with green skin, red hair and purple eyes.

Xié'è de Gōngniú had immense power. He spoke for Emperor Shāyú in any matter relating to security of any type, that included military situations.

Admiral Aete, exhibited leadership with an iron fist. Aside from Emperor Shāyú himself, Xié'è de Gōngniú and Admiral Aete were the most revered and hated men in the Xīngguī Empire. There was no in between. You either loved them because you were part of the patronage class or you despised them as the evil bastards they were. One thing was clear, these men were well protected because Emperor Shāyú's Guards protected them and the Xīngguī Security Service that took on the appearance of the CIA, FBI, and NSA combined, always had agents near them at all times. There were always three layers of Security Protection. The Xīnggūi Security Service often referred to as XSS agents were always within eye contact of the three men. The XSS agents had "watchers" who tracked and observed the XSS agents to make sure they were effectively carrying out their assignments and never conspiring. The XSS agents never knew who their watcher was or how he did it. Surveillance Systems were robust and there were many cameras placed anywhere these three men would go including the toilet. And to insure the XSS watchers conducted their missions correctly, they had a watcher. Hence there was a watcher-watcher, triple redundancy to ensure Emperor Shāyú, Xié'è de Gōngniú and Admiral Aete always had adäquate protection.

Emperor Shāyú was highly paranoid because of his history of failed coup attempts so he had a watcher of the watcher of the watcher, four layers of scrutiny. Emperor Shāyú also had Artificial Intelligence that surveyed the entire situation and kept everyone honest.

As Admiral Aete walked through the long hallway of the Emperor's Palace with his escorts of XSS and Emperor Shāyú's Guards, he enjoyed looking at the enate artwork and sculptures, some dating back 20,000 years before the Xīnggūi expanded by conquering worlds in other solar systems.

The war with the Zhrakzhongs had lasted too long. Now that Zhrakzhongs have dispersed their populations towards far off solar systems, they were entering the most dangerous phase of the war. With most of their cities empty, they didn't have to worry about reprisal for using weapons like the Jupitorians did on Mars and wiped it out. *Will it come down to that?*

However, conditions had just swung into their favor by an interesting source of INTEL from the Tytrone Philosophers who desperately want to get their Monks out of that squalor Chŏulòu prison designed for political prisoners. Their lives were a living hell and the Tytrone Philosophers were very sensitive to their plight.

Admiral Aete knew it was just a matter of time before he would receive such a gem of information. Timing could not have been more auspicious.

Smart admirals like Aete always corroborate their information before they act on it. This morning he received reports provided by their probes they sent out to verify General Níngsī's forces were located where the INTEL claimed they were. Admiral Aete had no idea this information was purposely planted. General Níngsī wanted the showdown and if Earth's civilization fell victim because of it, that was just unfortunate. Winning and ending this war that had lasted far too long was more appealing to General Níngsī than the survival of Earth, though he would feel sorry for his three new friends.

General Níngsī couldn't tell Doctor Brandenhagen exactly why he invited him to leave with the Zhrakzhongs to insure he didn't die if one of the Xīnggui squadrons got past his defense force and laid waste to Earth. Soon he would also extend the invitation to Sargent Hawthorne and Sally Fairbanks. Hopefully they would accept his invitations so he could protect their lives.

The planted information and the purposeful exposure of some forces to the Xīnggūi probes to snare Admiral Aete in a sophisticated trap to take away their air superiority once and for all, was the key ingredient to winning the war and not losing a large amount of hegemony.

Anticipating what Admiral Aete was anticipating would be the key to springing the trap on them.

The delay in putting up all the camouflage until confirmation the probe flew by, no doubt created almost an orgy of speculation and over-confidence in Admiral Aete. With their Xīnggūi Molecular Disrupter Cannons, Admiral Aete knew he could hit Zhrakzhongs Armada on the ground before they had a chance to take off. Unfortunately, he didn't know they were not there and some of the interesting camouflage included dummy Space Warships inside the compound far away from any real forces thanks to the fact they had over 20 square miles allowing the decoys to be placed somewhere harmlessly out of the way.

The Decoys also served another purpose. It terrified the Americans and after the F22 debacle they had no testosterone left to attempt another foolish F22 attack.

When Admiral Aete got down to the end of the hallway, a triple door entrance to the conference room opened up long enough for him to enter, then Emperor's Guardsmen closed and locked the door.

Admiral Aete walked over to the long table

toward his seat his escort led him towards which had a placard with his name on it. Emperor Shāyú was at the end of the table to his right and the devil himself who made the Nazi Himmler look like a boy scout, was sitting directly across from his chair.

Admiral Aete bowed to Emperor Shāyú and said those official courtesies expected from the Fleet Commander addressing Emperor Shāyú:

"It is a pleasure to see you, your Excellency."

He then turned and bowed to the Devil himself, Xié'è de Gōngniú.

"Please have a seat Admiral Aete."

Admiral Aete sat down and looked towards Emperor Shāyú's who was going to soon grill him on the upcoming mission.

Before they got started, drinks were served. Whatever Emperor Shāyú's drank so did his guests. There was a method to this, Emperor Shāyú would randomly pick the glass he would drink from and if the drinks were poisoned, he had a better chance of survival because if either Admiral Aete did not drink immediately when Emperor Shāyú's toasted them, it would be assumed the drinks were poisoned and they would then be forced to drink it all down right away.

The Chami Elixir tasted delightful, was costly, and only produced on one Plastras Nostras worlds planet and province Coocomonga, where green skinned women existed and had special arousing techniques for men that made them even more irresistible than women on Màichōng that wealthy Zhrakzhongs sought for generations. Green skin, dark green nipples, purple eyes, and red hair had a psychological effect on plain skinned humanoids. But there was more to it, their vaginas contained some unique hormones that multiplied sexual physical reactions that made men that ever experienced it to want it more just like a narcotic.

The Chami Elixir had some other interesting attributes such as expanding sensual awareness and improving perception until the drug wore off. Because of those properties, many Xīngguī Commanders viewed it as a battle enhancement and drank it just before the shooting started. They could be far more daring and reckless after achieving that Chami high.

"Admiral, I want you to tell me what your strategy is for this upcoming mission that is one of the utmost important deployments you have ever made."

"Your Excellency, I've obtained some critical Intelligence and I know exactly where General Níngsī is with his fleet."

Emperor Shāyú had to play dumb as if this was the first time, he heard that information. Xié'è de Gōngniú had on his poker face and likewise would act astonished even though he and Emperor Shāyú had a secret discussion before Admiral Aete arrived.

"And where would that be, Admiral Aete?"

"Your excellency, you need to clear the room of everyone except Xié'è de Gōngniú because this is very critical information, and we do not want a well-placed mole informing General Níngsī we know where he's at, otherwise he could engineer a very damaging trap for us."

Emperor Shāyú knew every person in the room was actually an XSS agent and they already knew of the INTEL, but Emperor Shāyú had to go through the subterfuge otherwise Admiral Aete might lose his nerve attacking the Zhrakzhongs for fear, their plan had already been compromised. Only the men in the room actually knew the details, therefore the information was safe for now. At least that's what the XSS believed.

"Everyone, please leave the room for a few minutes except Xié'è de Gōngniú and Admiral Aete."

When everyone exited the door in direct view of Admiral Aete and shut the door behind them, Admiral Aete pulled out a star chart of 15% of the Milky Way and laid it on the table. There were no markings on the chart to indicate which star they were interested in. The sheet of paper unfolded was approximately 12 by 18 inches in length allowing a great deal of resolution.

Admiral Aete was very familiar with the Gamulin Solar System and pointed to the star.

"This is the Gamulin Solar System star. The fourth planet of this star system is planet Earth. That's where General Níngsī has hidden his fleet and with the number of transports there, most likely brought a large civilian population with him to get them out of harm's way."

"Is it possible he may move his fleet and not be in position to attack?"

"As to not give away our knowledge of his presence we are using probes very sparingly. Also, we have put probes outside that solar system to give us warning they are leaving."

"How would you know they are leaving?"

"Your Excellency, when space craft transit at high speeds, the energy required becomes exponentially high. As such they have to run their power generators at such high-power levels, they give off X-Ray signatures we can track. Also, even though space is more or less a vacuum, there is about one or two hydrogen atoms per cubic meter, hence a large Armada traveling at high speeds gives off a large ion wake we can also track. When we get the combination of the X-Ray signature with the ion wake, we know it's a space craft and a large force."

"What does that all add up too," Emperor Shāyú asked.

"Your Excellency, we have that solar system surrounded by highly cloaked probes. General Níngsī will not be able to relocate his fleet without us knowing it. If he does maneuver within a couple days, we will be able to pounce on him. On the otherhand if he keeps his fleet on the ground resting up his troops after a very long ferry operation because those transports can't move as fast as a Space Warship, we will hit him on the ground and right now the disposition of his ships are parked close together, which means our Molecular Disrupter Cannons will have sitting ducks for targets.

"When are you deploying Admiral Aete?"

"Tomorrow."

"You are ready for either scenario, hit them on

the ground or as they maneuver out of the Gamulin Solar System."

"That's correct your Excellency."

"Alright, Admiral Aete. I have one prime directive for you which I'm issuing now and Xié'è de Gōngniú is my witness."

"Yes sir?"

"Do not come back to Màichōng until you have won or lost the war."

"Your Excellency, I will not come back as a loser."

"For your sake, I hope you are right Admiral Aete."

The poker face on Xié'è de Gōngniú turned into a veiled smile as he knew Emperor Shāyú would have him kill Admiral Aete along the lines of some of the evilest Emperors in galactic history had done in the past, and that included the Roman Emperor Caligula.

Emperor Shāyú knew that Admiral Aete had a lot of tasks to do between now and the time they launched the mission, so he stated, "Admiral Aete, if you are leaving tomorrow, I know you have a lot of tasks to perform. Thank you for giving me the briefing and I wish you success."

Admiral Aete knew he was being dismissed, but the buzz he obtained from the Chami Elixir made all his apprehensions dissipate until the drug wore off. He stood up and bowed to Emperor Shāyú then he turned and bowed to the Devil himself, Xié'è de Gōngniú and bowed very respectfully.

Xié'è de Gōngniú had spies who worked closely with Admiral Aete he would be secretly informed of all of Admiral Aete's actions. If he turned coward during the fighting and fled the scene, Xié'è de Gōngniú's spies would report such actions that would cost Admiral Aete his life. He might not even make it off his command ship alive under those conditions since these spies were also trained assassins with various ability to provide lethal attacks in manners that people normally could not avoid.

All of the XSS men and Emperor Shāyú's Guards, remained outside the conference room because they had not been invited back in. Security Cameras watching the room would put out an alarm if Xié'è de Gōngniú made any attempt on Emperor Shāyú, and after Emperor Shāyú's Guards dispatched all the XSS personnel out in the hallway, they would enter the conference room and waste Xié'è de Gōngniú using their powerful laser pistols. Xié'è de Gōngniú knew better than attempt any harm to Emperor Shāyú even though he would prefer he was dead so they could hurry up and sign and Armistice for this war that had drug on all too long making everyone miserable.

Wars have a way of making strange bedfellows. When Xié'è de Gōngniú fulfilled his promise of releasing the jailed Tytrone Philosopher Monks without the Emperor Shāyú's knowledge, there was a discussion that occurred between him and the Abbot, *Kāiwù de Sēngrén.*

"Your information is very auspicious."

"Arranging to get our Monks out of Màichōng's

Chǒulòu prison was a huge priority."

"Emperor Shāyú could easily have them re-arrested and put back in."

Knowing what kind of snake Xié'è de Gōngniú was, Abbot *Kāiwù de Sēngrén* had some discomfort in his thoughts. He smelled a quid pro quo coming up.

"Abbot, *Kāiwù de Sēngrén* I think we have the same goals in mind, end the war and prevent the next one by ridding ourselves of a Tyrant.

Abbot, *Kāiwù de Sēngrén* was very fearful now because Xié'è de Gōngniú had just crossed the line and if this conversation was secretly recorded, he could find himself bound at the stake in front of a dozen infantry laser rifles that would all be fired simultaneously so that none of the shooters would feel responsible for killing him. It was a shared plausible deniability, that made it a lot easier for individual *lasermen* to pull the trigger.

Xié'è de Gōngniú knew he had *Kāiwù de Sēngrén* trapped in a treasonous collusion which he couldn't wiggle out of. He knew if he outright rejected Xié'è de Gōngniú's quid pro quo, that most likely all the recently freed Tytrone Philosophers would get rearrested and not see daylight possibly for the rest of their lives.

The Tytrone Tytrone Philosophers knew the Xīngguī would all be much better off if somehow Emperor Shāyú was no longer in power.

"What do you expect from us, Xié'è de Gōngniú?"

"*Kāiwù de Sēngrén*, when the time comes, I will put one of your men in position to kill Emperor

Shāyú. He of course will be arrested, tried, convicted, and scheduled for execution. Just before the Tytrone Philosopher Monk is led out to the laser rifle firing squad, he will be swapped with a low life information peddler we arrested. I'll then make sure your Tytrone Philosopher Monk's identity is changed so that nobody can identify him."

"How can you swap these people like that?"

"When we execute people, they are bound up, mouth taped over in such a way they can't utter a sound because their mouths are stuffed with Scadle Berries that prevents their vocal cords from working while the Scadle chemicals are in their throat. The executioners can't see the face, they really do not know who they are killing, and the laser rifles are set up for an automatic twenty-second-long firing by the group which does a fantastic job of destroying the body to the point it cannot be identified. Graves registration people are there to pick up the remains and place them in the incinerator which is a few feet away from the execution cube and does a complete destruction of any remaining body parts.

"That sounds sick. Do the executed suffer long?"

"Xīngguī rights councilors have hooked up monitors to the convicted and determined their cognitive functions end in less than a half second."

"Then why shoot them for 20 seconds?"

"It destroys most of the tissues, less mess to clean up afterwards."

Kāiwù de Sēngrén knew he was trapped. If he didn't

agree to this plan a lot of good Tytrone Philosophers would be re-arrested and their lives put through utter hell for probably the rest of their miserable lives. He also assumed a person like Xié'è de Gōngniú would arrange for him very unpleasantness if he said no.

"How soon do we need to do this?"

"It needs to be completed before Admiral Aete returns from the battle."

"Why?"

"I seriously doubt he will have a significant victory. General Níngsī is a shrewd Commander and as much as Admiral Aete may wish he has the element of surprise on his side, there are so many Zhrakzhongs spread all over that part of the Galaxy, he is unlikely unable to move such a large force at battle speeds to get to a potential war zone around Earth without other entities detecting their transit and warning General Níngsī in time to execute his exit strategy.

"Which means the war continues and everyone stays miserable."

"That's how I see it."

"If you come to my temple, I will give you the answer."

"When?"

"Tomorrow, about this time. If anyone asks you, you came for consultations on the afterlife."

"You honestly think they would believe that?"

"Sure, as people get older, they start worrying

about their Karma and seek us out. No doubt you have killed a lot of men in your life and you have bad Karma which we can help fix."

"You honestly believe that crap?"

"When you arrive, we will teach you how to meditate so that you can start finding the answers you are looking for. There may be solutions you never thought of. With our help we can start to restore your Karma, so that your afterlife will not take on the pleasantness of something like the Chǒulòu prison."

"When you arrive for your answer, you might as well enjoy our other services that might quickly make you feel, you made good use of your time by taking care of two issues on the same visit."

"I'll be there for your answer, but I seriously doubt your other offer will benefit me."

Xié'è de Gōngniú went out the back door of the safe house they used to shuttle the Tytrone Philosopher Monks threw when they returned them to *Kāiwù de Sēngrén's* Temple.

His assistant was in the skycar patiently waiting. Moments later another skycar would come by and men would escort *Kāiwù de Sēngrén* to it and return him to a convenient location a couple blocks from his Temple where it appeared he was returning after a nice walk for his daily exercise routine. He himself would soon start meditation in a manner not too different than Zen Buddhist meditation on Earth.

Somethings are universal to a humanoid type brain. By a quirk of nature, two highly developed societies far from each other developed the meditation techniques the Zen Buddhists on Earth also learned.

Then to make things even more interesting, when the CIA was developing the hemi-sync techniques for their spies, they sent behind enemy lines, they taught them Zen Buddhist Meditation techniques because to get into hemi-sync is very difficult until you master it. Zen Buddhist Meditation was a huge step ladder of sort to allow novices to reach that final step when the two sides of their brain synchronized and information appeared to stop flowing through the photo receptors in the very center of the brain developed by God in his intelligent design. Were the photo receptors placed in the center of the brain for future telepathic communications? Or was it simply a bandwidth issue requiring light speed travel? The theory is those photo receptors are the conduit to the Universe you can reach upon hemi-sync.

Kāiwù de Sēngrén in a few hours tomorrow was going to attempt advancing Xié'è de Gōngniú's mind in just one session to reach that hemi-sync condition as he might in that altered state traveling through the Universe faster than light speed discover an alternative to assassinating Emperor Shāyú. *Kāiwù de Sēngrén* didn't readily know what alternatives Xié'è de Gōngniú had, but he knew he would discover it if he could get him in the altered state. He was also hoping that an alternative method to obtain the results Xié'è de Gōngniú wanted to end the war would manifest and he then be told the plan is canceled, *he had a better idea.*

Tytrone Philosopher Monks did not like the idea of killing any beings no matter how dastardly they were. They preferred the conversion through prayers and meditation and hemi-sync illumination.

Chapter Ten

The Concert

Like good soldier, Sally Fairbanks reported to work the next day. She knew she would instantly feel agitated the minute she saw the SAC Director Mark Rebman. Her morning was starting out well, he wasn't in yet for another confrontation. She sat down at her desk and quickly started looking through her high side emails. She had a switch that selected which computer she looked at, low side or high side. There wasn't much of a reason to go to the low side since almost none of it was used in their work, but she looked at it once a week in case something came in, she should read. If it was important, she would have a high side email or instant message.

In a few minutes the SAC Director's deputy came up to her and said, "The DCI will be here in a couple minutes and wants to meet the task force assigned to our visitors to meet him in the conference room."

"Alright." Sally Fairbanks stood up and followed the deputy into the conference room where soon a dozen task force members were sitting down wondering what the meeting is about.

Just like they were warned, in a couple of minutes the DCI strolled into the room. He didn't look happy but he did look professional. It was assumed he would sit at the end of the table in the SAC Directors seat, which he did.

"Thank you all for attending this meeting. This only concerns the task force personnel. In case you haven't heard the SAC Director has taken leave and will not be back for a few weeks. Since he's not here to write a delegation of Authority, I've already sent one out you will see is in your email. Mike Barnes will be acting SAC Director until further notice.

Sally Fairbanks an expert at body language like most of those in the room, could see some sort of relief on everyone's face. Working for that son of a bitch didn't please any of them. Maybe after cooling his heels on a beach somewhere for a few weeks, he might come back with a different disposition and not be such a prick.

There was some meaningless discussion that followed for a few minutes then the DCI noted the meeting is adjourned and everyone can go back to their tasks, but asked Sally to remain for a couple of minutes.

After everyone else had left the room and the DCI nodded at Mike Barnes he stepped out of the room, leaving the two alone.

"Now that you are back on the team, we will be doing some more interface with our friends out west. You have gone through a lot over the past week, and I read your reports and carved out portions I thought the President should see and briefed him on them. Your report was excellent and I know you need a rest so we can work you hard in a couple more days. I'm giving you a couple days of administrative leave. Turn off your cell phone, nobody will be calling you. Just like General Níngsī said, he didn't want Doctor Brandenhagen disturbed, I do not want the agency disturbing you for a couple days. I've already directed Mike Barnes to make sure everyone leaves you alone. We can manage for a couple days without you. Get rested up and then when you get back, I might have a tough assignment for you, which I know you are fully capable of achieving."

"Alright sir. Thank you for your consideration."

"Thank you Sally. When you went to the Zhrakzhongs the first time, that was extremely high risk since your visit was right after the F22 incident. We are glad it turned out the way it did. But make no mistake about it, we could have been sending you to your death, because we had absolutely no way of knowing how they would react when you approached them. That took a great deal of courage and composure."

"Thank you, sir."

"When you get back in a couple days rested up, Mike Barnes will have a task for you. We are now dealing with probably the biggest event in human history on planet Earth. The public has been shielded from most of it, but we project in about a week or less, we will not be able to contain this story, and the chaos will begin. We also do not know what's in store for us with the Zhrakzhongs."

"I wish we had the answers, but at least they are

friendly towards us," Sally replied.

"You will probably be communicating with them again since it appears you have a good relationship with General Níngsī."

"What is it we need to learn?"

"Is Earth now vulnerable? Their enemies might not be so benevolent. The fact they moved a billion people here to hide them shows, those are probably capable of some heinous acts."

"Yes, most likely."

"You can take off now. Your emails and everything else can wait."

"Alright, thank you. See you in a couple days."

"Stay safe."

"I will."

Sally walked out of the office and it was apparent everyone was looking at her. Rumors were probably going around she got the SAC Director canned. Unfortunately, the dickhead would be back in a few weeks and they would have to learn how to exist with the loose cannon.

Sally's biggest problem now was she wasn't planning for two days off and didn't quite know what she wanted to do. Maybe read a couple books, take in a movie. She sure as hell wasn't going to divulge her mini-vacation to her mother who would be insisting she come over for a visit, a little over an hour's drive down in Chesapeake Bay.

She would go home, scrub off the makeup, put on jeans and a tee shirt and chill out until she decided exactly what she wanted to do. Starbucks on the way home was essential.

In due time Sally was enjoying her Starbucks, washed her face, and had a new Novel she would dig into. The luxury of reading a book all day long seemed so remote these days.

Sally read nonstop for three hours. The book was a page turner. Then she had to get a snack and had some jet lag and laid back on her couch to relax and fell asleep. She didn't want to wake up she didn't care if she slept the rest of the day. This really felt good as she had some sleep deprivation she needed to work out. She probably would have kept sleeping had her phone not rang. She looked at the caller I.D. which had none, but the person calling had an Arizona area code. She answered the phone.

"Hello."

"How are you doing today, Sally?"

The voice was clearly General Níngsī.

"Is this General Níngsī?"

"Yes Sally, its me."

"You have a cell phone now?"

"Sally, I have the best intelligence officers in the Galaxy, they can provide me anything I want."

"What can I do for you General Níngsī?"

"At 7:00 p.m. a Limo as you Earth people call

them, will arrive in front of your home. That will be my people. Have on a nice dress, I'm taking you to Carnegie Hall tonight to hear this lovely Pianist Yuja Wang perform a Tchaikovsky Piano Concerto."

"I have no doubt your intelligence officers know a lot about American Culture and entertainment."

"They do."

"How did you discover this musical performance?"

"The last couple days my Artificial Intelligence has been presenting me with music your planet produces, a lot of it does not make sense to me, but your classical music is not too different than our own. We have similar sounds."

"I see."

"I checked out a few samples and found some that pleased me and Artificial Intelligence found live performances and set up a plan to get you and I there so that we can enjoy the performance."

"You are kind of tall, I would think you would not be able to hide your height."

"That's already been taken care of. We'll be seated in balcony seats after the lights are dimmed for the start of the performance, my agents will arrange a VIP escort to our seats. We'll leave shortly before the performance is concluded to avoid being seen by most of the crowd."

Sally really hated the predicament she was in. She was smart enough to know she could not turn down this request from a man who could raise Earth in 15 minutes if he wanted. But she would have to report the incident. Since she was on orders to enjoy her time off, she felt there was no compelling reason to make that report until she went back to work in a couple days.

She also understood this might help her wrangle more information out of General Níngsī since it appeared he had some kind of interest in her. Was it simply his little head thinking? Or do Aliens have heads or snakes? She didn't want to find that out anytime soon. However, she also knew female spies use all the tools they have available and the honeypot trap worked quite well for the Russians and the Chinese.

She also knew that as more female agents worked for the CIA, there were cases of some extraordinary activity that some of them had done. And more and more women were showing up as stars on the wall of the headquarters entrance signifying there were killed in the line of duty.

She also knew one fact about spies when they die after being captured. They always die a painful death.

The way those women died wasn't pleasant. In some cases, they discovered by defectors. In other cases, they found out how the women died because they learned of their fate through a third party such as British, French, Germans, etc.

One of her motivations to go was to discover how General Níngsī was going to pull it off. There are not many eight feet tall humans. General Níngsī would stand out like a freak. It will also be interesting to see how he dressed.

General Níngsī knew he only had a few days to enjoy casualness because he had been alerted today the Xīngguī had deployed. Through their deep space neutrino communications system.

General Níngsī was ready for the Xīngguī Commander Admiral Aete. However, he would spend the remaining spare time entertaining this lovely woman Sally Fairbanks, since everything was prepared and his artificial intelligence was ready to execute the snare when Admiral Aete drove his fleet into one of the most elaborate traps in Galactic History. Once again history is written by the actions of spies.

Sally Fairbanks knew how to dress for success as she knew the axioms of the honey pot theme, desire was always more stimulating than gratification. *Perhaps that's why I never married*, Sally asked herself?

Dressing up for events at the Kennedy Center in Washington DC was nothing new for Sally Fairbanks. Even though she had no designs for General Níngsī, she knew that his apparent affection towards her by his conduct the times she met him in the past, and not this invitation.

To Sally Fairbanks this was part of her mission because if General Níngsī can sneak into Carnegie Hall without American Intelligence apparatus knowing about it, that also means he could sneak in anywhere including the Kremlin or Zhongnanhai [Zhongnanhai - Wikipedia]

Zhongnanhai houses the office of the General Secretary of the Chinese Communist Party (paramount leader) and Premier of the People's

Republic of China. General Secretary of the Chinese Communist Party, President of the People's Republic of China, Premier of the People's Republic of China, Politburo Standing Committee, Politburo of the Chinese Communist Party, State Council of the People's Republic of China, Secretariat of the Chinese Communist Party, Central Committee General Office, Vice President of China.

Sally Fairbanks always applied risk management to every move she made even though in some cases like being around the Aliens there wasn't much she could do to protect herself. However, knowing she was an attractive female based on all the comments she heard from men and women over the years, there was some risk associated with *desire*. One of the last things she did was take a day after pill to prevent pregnancy in the event she was raped by General Níngsī whose body language and stares gave rise to the possibility he had not been with a woman in quite some time. He might have been one of those in suspended animation for a while during the trip.

Sally Fairbanks assumed she was probably watched by the CIA and a few minutes after she walked out her home exactly at 7:00 P.M. a Limo pulled up as designed, as she walked out her front door and towards the public sidewalk. The Limo driver got out of the Limo and walked around to the rear passenger side door and opened it for Sally Fairbanks. Sally stepped into the Limo and found she was all by herself. Anyone looking in from a distance would also see the Limo was empty except the driver and Sally.

Even though tonight there was an event going on

at the Kennedy Center they drove past it and went into the parking garage, made a circuitous loop, came back out on the street and went in the opposite direction they were heading. No doubt this was a security sweep to ward off and detect followers. The driver had an ear bud on and was in fact a shorter Zhrakzhong male part of the Intelligence Directorate.

The limo made its way to Washington DC Union Station and Amtrak parking. At 7:00 P.M. the lot was almost deserted with just a few cars left. The Limo pulled into the middle-abandoned area that had ample room. The driver stopped the car, got out and walked around to the rear passenger side of the Limo and opened the door and informed Sally Fairbanks, "Your ride is here."

As soon as Sally stepped out of the Limo, about 10 feet in front of her, a Zhrakzhong Shuttle/Transport touched down in front of her. The side hatch of the Shuttle/Transport lifted up and General Níngsī stepped down the ramp that instantly appeared, wearing what would pass as a well-dressed New Yorker out to see a Concert at Carnegie Hall sitting in the most expensive balcony seats.

"Hello Sally Fairbanks, I must say you look exquisitely beautiful tonight."

"Thank you General Níngsī for taking me to the concert."

"The pleasure is all mine Sally."

"Shall we go?"

"Certainly."

The two entered the Shuttle/Transport and the Limo driver shut the passenger door and got back in the Limo and drove off to his designated parking in a covered parking garage where he abandoned it, went to the DC Metro and bought a ticket to take the commuter train to Farragut Court, where he went to a nude dancing bar to wait for his next ride.

Meanwhile, the Zhrakzhong Shuttle/Transport made its way to New York City a lot faster than any Airline. In a similar operation, the Zhrakzhong sat the shuttle down on a semi abandoned uncovered top floor of a parking garage to a waiting Limo. Moments later they pulled up to Carnegie Hall that had very few people arriving since the performance was starting momentarily and all the audience and attendees were already inside.

One of the Zhrakzhong Intelligence men approached General Níngsī and said, "This way General."

The security man led him and Sally Fairbanks inside followed by six others all toting sophisticated laser pistols. The Intel people had already set up a security corridor all the way to the Balcony seats and had purchased the entire section. Within approximately one minute after General Níngsī and Sally Fairbanks sat down in the middle of the Zhrakzhong security detachment, the beautiful and alluring super star performer Yuja Wang walked out onto the stage in perhaps the sexiest attire any concert pianist had ever wore in this building. The orchestra looked very large and nice. The applause was terrific. Anyone who had any doubt the audience didn't love Yuja Wang, they were simply ignoring the very loud cheers. Even Yuja Wang was enjoying the reception. She lived in New York so she was viewed now as a home town girl and stunningly beautiful.

Yuja sat down at the piano and there were a few signals between her and the conductor as the audience quieted down in expectation of the concert beginning.

Tchaikovsky's piano concerto is often played in concert halls around the world because of its rather remarkable beginning. Yuja Wang is a genius. Her repertoire is extremely broad as she has performed all the top piano concertos in the most exquisite concert halls around the world. Composers like Bartok had a new lease on life because Yuja performed the three Bartok piano concertos and made the public appreciate the composer because of her extraordinary performance.

Tonight, there was magic in the air as General Níngsī, one of the most powerful men in this half of the Galaxy which had been thoroughly explored, felt that strong attraction to the performer as well as that glamorous lady sitting next to him. Sally's perfume was rare for scents in New York, because it came from one of the most obscure places that created the essence in a vert labor-intensive manual operation. She obtained her very special perfume only because she was on a team that had to go through this town in order to make contact with some bad amigos, they had to do business with. In the few spare moments, they happened to be in this third world shopping plaza only to obtain something to eat, she acquired the perfume as she was walking into to Plaza with her CIA colleagues. After smelling the perfume and discovering its very interesting scent she purchased it for what is equivalent of around $7.00 in the local currency.

It was rare she used that perfume she had now for a couple years and because of its unusual fragrance, she thought it might have an influence on General Níngsī. She had no idea how much it worked. General Níngsī was more than effected and if it wasn't for the fact, he had respect for her and her position as the defacto spokesperson for planet Earth, he would take her back to his command center and have sex with her all night long whether she desired it or not. The visual of Yuja and the scent of Sally really did please General Níngsī more than he had been in a long time.

As General Níngsī watched Yuja light up the keyboard with her interpretation of Tchaikovsky's piano concerto, he made the mental comparison to her and Xīnguī women in Màichōng. He had traveled to Màichōng posing as a business man a few times like other blockade runners engaged in black markets when he was a junior officer and tasted the forbidden fruit of those alluring female Xīnguī. Something told him in the back of his mind, if he had Yuja alone, she too would provide the exquisite gratification those Màichōng women did. The notion of mingling with a stunning performer like Yuja gave General Níngsī wild speculation of how the transcendence would turn out in a real scenario.

Others watching the performance could not help but notice the attractive female sitting in the middle of a section that was made up of an all-male group. That included one of the cameramen as this was a recorded event and most likely would show up on YouTube real

Paul D. Escudero

soon and on live streaming video of a few networks.

The performance lasted almost 40 minutes. In the very last minute of the performance the security detachment had melted away and were lining the egress route and the last Zhrakzhong agent notified General Níngsī, "Sir we have to leave now. He in turn informed Sally who understood the practicality of leaving before the applauses started and people began exiting the venue.

Zhrakzhong security had this planned out with utter perfection. As soon as they walked out of the Carnegie Hall a Limo pulled up in front of them beating the crowd of 5 other Limo's stacked up in back of them.

Another security man stood exactly where the rear passenger door handle existed, when the car came to a stop. General Níngsī gestured to Sally Fairbanks to get in the Limo and he followed her in and within about 15 seconds the door was shut, and the Limo drove off with an unsuspected group of Zhrakzhongs in other cars now driving down that same street escorting them back to the parking garage.

All the owners of the automobiles in use were removed in a docile condition from the shuttle/transport as their Limo's pulled up and the Zhrakzhongs got out and quickly entered the shuttle/transport with General Níngsī and Sally Fairbanks. The owners would snap out of their trances in about 15 minutes and discover their automobiles parked directly in front of them with the engines still running and keys in the ignition, experiencing a lost time event wondering how they got there and why they were standing there.

Sally's fantastic evening was far from over. In about an hour because of the time difference she and General Níngsī were walking through the forbidden city taking it all in. The group got some big stares as the group was very well dressed and there were giants among them. One of the Chinese security men went searching for a possible basketball game planned and these obviously had to be NBA players except they were all Caucasian. By the time he concluded he didn't discover any possible games and was wondering who the hell these giants were, they were long gone.

General then showed his daring as they were soon walking around inside the fabulous gardens of Zhongnanhai. When Xi Jinping stepped out of his office building with a half dozen of his security detail, they came abruptly in front of General Níngsī and the group of giants escorting the princess.

Kind of startled to see these giants inside the most secure compound on the planet, Xi Jinping asked, "Who are you?"

In perfect Mandarin with the help of Artificial Intelligence, General Níngsī said, "President Xi Jinping, I'm General Níngsī the supreme commander of the Zhrakzhongs. I'm here admiring your beautiful park and gardens.

"习近平总统，我是宁思将军，日罗中军的最高统帅。我在这里欣赏你美丽的公园和花园。"[**Xíjìnpíng Zǒngtǒng, wǒ shì níng sī jiāngjūn, rì luōzhōngjūn de zuìgāo tǒngshuài. Wǒ zài zhèlǐ xīnshǎng nǐ měilì de gōngyuán hé huāyuán.**]

"How did you get here?" "你是怎么来到这里？"

["Nǐ shì zěnme lái dào zhèlǐ?"]

"The same way we will be leaving in a few minutes." "就像我们几分钟后离开一样。" "Jiù xiàng wǒmen jǐ **fēnzhōng hòu líkāi yīyàng.**"

The Chinese security men had been talking into their suit sleeves, no doubt a microphone.

"This is rather unsatisfactory for someone to come in here uninvited."

"一个不请自来的人进来，这可真是令人不快。"
["Yīgè bù qǐng zì lái de rén jìnlái, zhè kě zhēnshi lìng rén bùkuài."]

"President Xi Jinping, in the days to come you will discover I can go anywhere on this planet I wish. But before I leave, I want to introduce you to my lovely friend Sally Fairbanks."

"习近平主席，在未来的日子里，你会发现我可以去这个星球上任何我想去的地方。但在我离开之前，我想把你介绍给我可爱的朋友莎莉·费尔班克斯。"["Xíjìnpíng zhǔxí, zài wèilái de rìzi lǐ, nǐ huì fāxiàn wǒ **kěyǐ qù zhège xīngqiú shàng rènhé w**ǒ xiǎng qù dì dìfāng. Dàn zài wǒ **líkāi zhīqián, w**ǒ xiǎng bǎ nǐ jièshào gěi wǒ **kě›ài de péngy**ǒu Shālì Fèiěrbānkèsī."]

Xi Jinping and his entire security team began their lost time event.

The Zhrakzhong shuttle/transport came down vertically from 100,000 feet in the span of 10 seconds and gently stopped directly behind General Níngsī and the group. About 15 minutes later Xi Jinping and his security men came to and looked around. To say they were a bit spooked was apparent."

In about 30 minutes Xi Jinping was looking at surveillance video with his chief of security and they immediately started trying to figure out who that alluring woman Sally Fairbanks was.

"She did smell amazingly refreshing," Xi Jinping noted.

Chinese supercomputers on the line of Cray XMP's were searching for every Sally Fairbanks on the planet. Because who she was and where she worked it did not take long to narrow down the search and with facial recognition software nailed it. Sally Fairbanks was a high-level CIA employee working in the SAC. Xi Jinping was pissed. He looked at the pictures and in fact knew it was her.

The MSS (Ministry of State Security) General Chen Wenqing asked the most appropriate question: "Do you think the Aliens have sided with the Americans?"

"We need to find that out as quickly as possible."

"Are you willing to risk burning one of our top spies in the Pentagon?"

"I know you know what you are doing. Do whatever it takes. We need to know if the Aliens have some kind of arrangement with the CIA."

The MSS was now looking at this in a totally different light. Aliens aligned with the USA just made the game slightly more complicated.

By the time President Xi was eye balling Sally Fairchild's picture and unraveling his lost time incident, General Níngsī was escorting Sally Fairbanks through GUM stores in Moscow after briefly admiring the imagery of The Cathedral of Vasily the Blessed (Собо́р Васи́лия Блаже́нного, tr. Sobór Vasíliya Blazhénnogo), [Saint Basil's Cathedral]. After about 15 minutes, Sally who had been here before said, "I think I've seen enough."

"Anywhere else you want to go?"

"Yes, how about the Hermitage, one of the grandest places on this planet with about the very best artwork."

In 15 minutes, they were walking through the Hermitage where they stayed for about 30 minutes when artificial intelligence suggested General Níngsī leave because Moscow's Air Defense Center had just scrambled 100 fighter jets.

Because of the recommendations General Níngsī received, they landed the transporter/shuttle down right next to the Hermitage and in less than 5 minutes were gaining altitude abruptly. By the time the 100 Jet Fighters flew over St. Petersburg Russia, there was nothing left but empty space.

"I think we have enough time left for one more stop, where would you like to go?"

"How about the Louvre in Paris?"

In due time thanks to easier penetrations and egress, they were calmly walking around the Lourve taking it all in. One thing Sally did by suggesting all these stops was, General Níngsī was starting to develop a greater appreciation for Planet Earth. Sally Fairbanks at the time didn't know she just saved planet Earth because now, it was taken of the list as collateral damage they would not care about if they won this battle. In the end it didn't hurt the Zhrakzhongs because the directive that said, "Under no conditions will the Xīngguī be allowed to strike Earth, caused the Artificial Intelligence to reprogram its trap and resequencing everything to comply with General Níngsī's orders.

The FSB (formerly KGB) were also pouring over surveillance video and video's some Russian tourists took of the Alien space craft. They also came up with a match to Sally Fairbanks.

Sally Fairbanks was now the most investigated woman on planet Earth because the British MI6 who had hacked Russian computers were also interested in knowing "who the hell is Sally Fairbanks."

As soon as they got their match, they were also astonished the Americans had spoofed them and kept an incredible secret from them. They could feel the burn of the SAC just like the SAC boys felt the burn of the FBI agents who now gave them their just due in their social circles.

None of this got back to the DCI until Sally returned from her well-earned two day vacation.

By the time they made it back to Washington DC it was around midnight. Sally was already looking sleepy so General Níngsī decided it would be best if he just got Sally home so she could rest. As to not complicate her life any more than he already did in China, he had the transport/shuttle go to the preplanned rendezvous at an empty car parking structure that had minimal activity. This was determined by his Artificial Intelligence using a number of probes sent out.

The Limo driver picked up his rides at Farragut Court in front of the strip club. They were well dressed and appeared to have money.

"Where to gentlemen?"

"Hilton Hotel up on Connecticut Avenue. He's staying at the hotel and my car is parked there."

"Alright."

When they arrived at the hotel, the Zhrakzhong Intelligence Agent doing the talking via the help of Artificial Intelligence said, over the Limo intercom, "We are going to take him to his car first."

"No problem." The driver answered."

At quite a distance from the Hotel main entrance, the Zhrakzhong Intelligence Agent picked a random car and said stop here."

The Limo Driver got out of the car and opened the passenger door. The two men got out, out of them pulled out a billfold with lots of cash in it and handed the driver $100.00 bill and said, "Keep the change."

The driver grabbed the bill and said, "Thank you man that is quite generous."

He too soon had a lost time event. The two Zhrakzhong agents leaned him against the car they pointed out and took off with his still running

Limo. They found an empty parking lot at a halfway abandoned shopping mall that Amazon had killed and gave the notifications via communication links to Artificial Intelligence at General Níngsī's command center, and the transport/shuttle was landed in the shopping mall parkinglot exhibiting nobody around since all the stores were closed.

General Níngsī informed Sally Fairbanks, "Your ride back to your home is here."

He got out of the transport/shuttle and she followed him to the Limo where they shook hands and parted company.

The Limo driver took Sally Fairbanks home, then drove back to the Hilton Hotel and stopped the car next to the Limo driver standing and leaning against a parked car where they left him still minutes away from recovering from his lost time event holding the $100.00 note.

His car was still running with the doors unlocked and he possibly would have stayed there quite a while longer, except a couple going to their car after partying at the Hotel confronted him, "Hey dude how's come you are leaning up against my car."

They noticed he was staring into space holding money and he suddenly snapped out of it and looked around wondering, *where the hell am I?*

He looked at the perturbed couple and responded, "I'm very sorry." Then he immediately went over and got into his car and drove away with the couple standing there staring at his car as he drove off wondering, *WTF was that guy doing?*

The following day, the DCI was getting some strange calls from the embassies in London, Moscow, and Beijing. He knew these were strange times. Just as he was going home for the day, his London station chief called and informed him SIS was making inquiries about "who is Sally Fairbanks."

Nobody seemed to know the origin of the inquiry, so it lay resting on his chest until work the next day. He had more pressing issues as the agents sent out to keep an eye on the former SAC Director Mark Rebman had informed him *the guy was crying in his beers and acting suicidal.*

General Níngsī was not able to entertain his new flame Sally Fairbanks the next day because he was busy digging through intelligence reports and tweaking his battle plans as it was apparent Admiral Aete was on his way for the big showdown.

Chapter Eleven

Departure

Admiral Aete slowly with subtlety launched his fleet. There would be no spectacle of numerous ships leaving all at once heading in the same direction to alert his enemies. They would sequentially leave over a several days period, fly to their point Q in space and turn and head to point Y where the fleet would combine. These ships would all think they are going out on training exercises or interdiction patrols.

The **Xīngguī Captains** would not know they were heading for a rendezvous until they were halfway to point Y and then would be informed, they are converging on the Fleet and expected rendezvous time calculated by Artificial Intelligence. The crews had no fear or concern. A gigantic space battle was the last thing on their mind and none of them considered that a possibility since they left the space anchorages of several planets randomly and individually.

But when spies see the anchorages are empty, and the enemy was spoon fed a scenario, it was obvious to the Zhrakzhong spies General Aete was on his way.

There were multiple backups to get this vital

information off Màichōng. The Zhrakzhongs had the best souped up space scooters. As soon as they got the laser communications signals, the Zhrakzhongs would send in several Mosquito's their super sophisticated ultra-high speed spy rescue ships. These light weight technological marvels had no armor or much protection all they had was speed. The spy would leave his space scooter with rocket packs, fly to the Mosquito and get inside as quickly as possible and the automated one-man Mosquito would head for a rendezvous point with a Zhrakzhong Space Warship that would take the spy and his Mosquito back to Zhrakzhong Empire worlds. The fact the several independent spies were being evacuated is because their signals had already alerted Zhrakzhong General Níngsī, the expected attack was already on its way. They were being evacuated to save their lives because they knew the Xīngguī would soon figure out the espionage that just happened and Emperor Shāyú's Chief of Security Xié'è de Gōngniú would torture them to death if he captured them, which was figured a 50% probability. In reality it was more like 75% because Xié'è de Gōngniú had one thing the spies didn't have: time on his side.

In the spy business there are usually so many points of potential compromise, you might as well call a Zhrakzhong spies' landscape on Màichōng, Swiss Cheese since there were so many holes in it and points of penetration.

One of the major issues of spy penetration on Màichōng is ethnicity. Most Zhrakzhongs would stand out due to height and the round eyes and complexion.

The only practical source of spies was in areas

the Zhrakzhongs captured many eons before the current war, where the local population had converted to Zhrakzhong philosophy and canons of governance. Even with the correct DNA, the linguistics and the skills necessary to successfully plant at Màichōng resulted in the need to take children away from their parents at an early age and start the preparation. To develop one good successful spy required training at least 100 children because only 10% of those that began the training, proved to have the intelligence and the intuition needed. And of course, the possibility of capture and double spies always kept Zhrakzhong Intelligence on their toes. Most Zhrakzhong spies sent against the Xīngguī began their journey at the age of three. They were taken off the planet and relocated to Plastras Nostras where they were isolated and their handlers were motivated to train them well since they enjoyed the benefit of being detailed to this incredible planet, where only the very rich could afford to go play.

Those spies recovered in the Mosquitos would never go back to Màichōng. They had other opportunities such as participating in the training programs on Plastras Nostras, they could act as battlefield translators to laser companies in infantry battalions, and they certainly knew if the war ended and a peace treaty was signed, they could engage in intergalactic trade and banking.

Zhrakzhong Intelligence could not afford to allow those Mosquitos get captured. The souped-up space scooters had time delayed self-destruction so they were not going to be of much use to anyone. The Mosquito had a preprogrammed flight plan in it. If for some reason the Navigation System discovered the

Mosquito was being slowed down by some forces such as electromagnetic grabbers or sensors detected enemy warships were near, self-destruction would occur. This was one of the minor points the spies were never notified about in their training programs.

Just like they planned, as soon as the three spies who didn't know the others existed, executed their exit strategy by sending the report and hopping on their space scooters, they went out to space in a relatively quick manner. That is precisely why Admiral Aeta used a space scooter instead of a shuttle.

Only one of the three had been turned and it was advantageous he was going in a direction in quite a different direction than the other two. The Spy more or less didn't stand a chance. The Xīnguī were hot on his tail all the way to his Mosquito. He had barely enough time to get inside and secure the hatch before the enemy was close up on him. The Mosquito did its maximum acceleration which caused the Spy to black out at 20 Gs. This fast start bought him enough time to get out of Xīnguī Molecular Disrupter Cannons effective range.

Xié'è de Gōngniú was extremely agitated and wanted to know exactly what the Zhrakzhong Spy transmitted to Zhrakzhong Intelligence. He ordered the chasing Xīnguī Space Warships to not damage the Mosquito but send their fastest ship with an electromagnetic grabber and capture and retrieve the Zhrakzhong Spy alive.

The chase was on the way and the Mosquito with plenty of fuel left had been traveling with low acceleration after the initial sprint at a super-fast velocity.

The Artificial Intelligence in the Mosquito attempted a series of sophisticated maneuvers, no different than what you see with two birds fighting in the air, such as a hawk verses a dozen blackbirds.

The artificial intelligence that sent out MAY DAY signals could only delay the inevitable. Even though the Mosquito was traveling at approximately the same speed as the chasing Xīngguī Space Warships it was systematically maneuvering and after it determined the enemy ships had stopped its ability to further maneuver as the G forces indicated lock on with a magnetic grabber, a self-detonation sequence started. Sensors indicated the Mosquito was soon in the belly of the Xīngguī Space Warship, so the countdown to self-destruct now crossed the trip wire and the Mosquito Artificial Intelligence informed the Spy to say his last prayers. Ten seconds later was all the Artificial Intelligence would allow the Spy to pray. Self-destruct command was issued and the explosives in the Mosquito detonated in a horrific explosion that not only caused the Mosquito to blow into a million fragments, the Xīngguī Space Warship also ceased to exist. This would be the last attempted capture. Based on the reports of the other Xīngguī Space Warships, in the future if they were in range of Mosquito, they were to zap it with a Molecular Disrupter Cannons.

The other two Zhrakzhong Mosquitos were sent into completely different sectors of space so one had no knowledge of the other nor did any of the crew members on the Zhrakzhong Space Warships sent out to retrieve them and deliver them to entirely different planets.

This was a moment of jubilee for the two spies. Their covers were blown and they could never be sent back to Xīnguī areas while the war was still in progress.

The Zhrakzhong Mosquitos landed in the empty shuttle bays of the Zhrakzhong Space Warships that retrieved them in a fully automatic operation with Artificial Intelligence of the Mosquito linked up to the Space Warship's networks. The two spies were soon back on land in friendly territory, and soon to be enjoying an extended time off while they spend a couple hours a day in debriefing at the resorts they were taken. After years of fear, they would end up in some of the most horrific torture chambers Xié'è de Gōngniú operated, they now had nothing to do for a while but to heal their wounded psyche that years of fear created and came to an abrupt end when their most important contribution to the war transpired.

Admiral Aete received a few escort ships twelve hours after departure and felt slightly safer as he knew they would help his getaway if they somehow stumbled into a Zhrakzhong force. He of course would feal a lot better in another day after more of them started showing up sequentially so they would not assume this was a gathering of forces. Several days later as all participants were present and locked on formations via sophisticated laser transponders that provided all course and speed modifications to each individual ship to lock it in formation. They would also be controlled in battle for maximum power projection at the point of the spear that Admiral Aete would crush the center of the expected weak Zhrakzhong force protecting their entry point into the Gamulin solar system and pass by Mars on their way to Earth to finally finish off General Níngsī and his top Generals who were trapped on Earth and didn't know it. At least that is what he truly believed.

By the time Xié'è de Gōngniú figured out Admiral Aete had lost the element of surprise, he had maneuvered on a new course they would not know of because it was such an ultra-secret, that even Emperor Shāyú would not know where they went for fear of compromise from a well-placed Zhrakzhong spy. Hence the Xīnggui had no way of warning Admiral Aete he may have lost the element of surprise; hence he could be traveling into a trap. This random course they took was well established in the plans that now sat mostly ignored on Màichōng, because they had reached the point where the Fleet was at the mercy of Admiral Aete's judgement and leadership.

One thing that Xié'è de Gōngniú felt was, win or lose this was the pathway to the end of war.

As he sat there smolderingly mad about this Intelligence failure, he realized he needed to go to the Tytrone Philosophers Temple and meet *Kāiwù de Sēngrén* and go through this meditation training as it seemed to him that was the only way he was going to get his buy-in to provide an assassin to kill Emperor Shāyú and allow them to sign an Armistice and immediately end the war.

Xié'è de Gōngniú didn't want to leave his sky car parked at the Tytrone Philosophers Temple where it might draw some attention, so he had one of his most trusted subordinates XSS men drop him off near the entrance. This was not a location he would normally go.

Shortly after entering the temple, *Kāiwù de Sēngrén* who was expecting him was informed by the senior Tytrone Philosopher that Xié'è de Gōngniú had arrived. *Kāiwù de Sēngrén* immediately left his office and walked about 50 yards to the Temple to greet Xié'è de Gōngniú.

"Thank you for coming, Xié'è de Gōngniú," Abbot *Kāiwù de Sēngrén* sincerely stated.

"I'm ready to start the training. You said you think I could reach the realization in just one training session?"

"Yes, you can if you fully cooperate and listen to your instructor. Let me introduce him to you."

"Rawwel, this is Xié'è de Gōngniú the head of security for Emperor Shāyú."

"Good afternoon, Xié'è de Gōngniú. If you are ready to start the training, please come with me."

Xié'è de Gōngniú nodded and the Tytrone Philosopher Monk Rawwel led him to an adjacent building that appeared to be a miniature Temple.

Inside, Xié'è de Gōngniú quickly noticed there were a few other Tytrone Philosopher Monks scattered around the room next to various instruments. One Monk was standing by a large gold disk shaped device holding a tool that could pass on earth as a type of maillot. In a few minutes when Xié'è de Gōngniú heard the sound it made when the Monk struck it with the hammering device, the sounds it created would be equivalent to a Chinese Gong.

Another man stood by a device that had several

objects hanging from strings. When the man struck that instrument, it gave off the sounds of orchestral chimes. There was another man standing by a series of bells. There were other men standing by light sources that put out a variety of colors and patterns.

The lectures began and the techniques of meditation were discussed, both silent and orally:

"Each had its own characteristics and the silent meditation is essential to learn as there could be times and situations, where oral chants for meditation could not be allowed such in a public setting or among many passengers aboard an interplanetary transport where people didn't wish to hear other people's noise."

Xié'è de Gōngniú simply nodded and continued listening.

"Xié'è de Gōngniú, the oral chants required to induce meditation are the first phase of the training because they are the easiest to achieve. Eventually after we teach you, then you will successfully achieve the silent meditation which is most likely the type you will do during a crisis in your life."

As the training continued Tytrone Philosopher Monk Rawwel said, "You will just say these words each time you hear a chime struck: Yǎngwàng Xīngxīng."

The Tytrone Philosopher Monk struck the Chime and Xié'è de Gōngniú uttered the words: "Yǎngwàng Xīngxīng."

About that same time all the Tytrone Philosopher Monks all started humming a low frequency and in unison then said: "Yǎngwàng Xīngxīng."

Xié'è de Gōngniú didn't quite figure it out, this chant on Earth dealt with Chakras and the combination of the chanting and humming cleared the evil spirits out of the room and disgorged them from his soul.

When people first take this training, they are always skeptical at first and Xié'è de Gōngniú was no exception. This sequence seemed to repeat over and over again for about maybe five minutes. It did a good job of removing Xié'è de Gōngniú's consciousness of time. There was a pattern to it and in some ways, it sounded beautiful and was almost like a narcotic. Then one of the multiple Chimes of a different frequency was played and at that exact moment the humming sound the Tytrone Philosopher Monks were doing shifted key and created a different resonance, and just when he would never expect it, the other Monk hit the Gong which modulated the sound and had an eerie psychological effect on Xié'è de Gōngniú. As this continued, Xié'è de Gōngniú's thoughts went somewhere else. He felt the world spinning around him but he was able to keep the chant going. He had to struggle as it was now getting complicated, and the harder he struggled the more he wanted to say: "Yǎngwàng Xīngxīng."

Xié'è de Gōngniú didn't know it nor did the Monks because the mental pathways are able to flow in different ways as the Chakras melt and slip away from the soul and a new reality is formed. Soon there was a flowing red and blue clouds traveling towards an orange symbol in his thoughts. Xié'è de Gōngniú reached a Hemi-Sync condition. The photo receptors at the very center of his brain were now receiving those clouds traveling in his thoughts.

The Tytrone Philosopher Monks continued the sequences until Tytrone Philosopher Monk Rawwel reached 1000 in his count. He looked at the Chimes player who now hit a third frequency, the monks shifted the tone of their humming and the Gong Monk hit the gong hard and it resonated for about a minute. Then it was total quiet.

When Xié'è de Gōngniú reached a Hemi-Sync condition he became silent. There was now total silence in the room. Traveled through the Universe. In the Hemi-Sync condition time references change. A person can live several complete lifes in this state before they wake up and face reality again. It is a bitter sweet moment when that occurs because the person doesn't want to leave and come back. A strange action happens as if God himself is intervening. The Photoreceptors are reorientated and suddenly vast thoughts rush through it going to both hemispheres of the brain. The person regains consciousness at that time.

Xié'è de Gōngniú looked at Tytrone Philosopher Monk Rawwel in the most focused manner without saying a word.

Monk Rawwel knew Xié'è de Gōngniú's mind had traveled somewhere and experienced what no other had because everyone has their own unique trip.

Xié'è de Gōngniú looked down at his wristband and saw the chronometer portion of it indicated he had just experienced a three-hour period of lost time. He then said, "I have things to do, I'm very busy now. I must leave, but I would like to come back tomorrow to continue training."

"Xié'è de Gōngniú let me escort you to the temple and you can leave from the front entrance."

"I appreciate that Monk Rawwel."

As they were walking through the Temple, Abbot *Kāiwù de Sēngrén* met them because he knew when the last gong was hit, they would soon be finished with the training session.

What *Kāiwù de Sēngrén* witnessed was a changed man. He didn't know at that time, Xié'è de Gōngniú had achieved far more than they hoped for. Even Monks training for 20 years had not achieved a ride through the Universe as inquisitively as Xié'è de Gōngniú just experienced.

"Did you achieve any benefit from the meditation, Xié'è de Gōngniú?"

"I did experience something I need some time to think about. I'll come back tomorrow and we can continue the training. I know I have more to learn."

"You will be most welcome when you arrive."

"Thank you *Kāiwù de Sēngrén*. I now feel even better that I was able to get all of your Monks out of Chǒulòu prison."

"We appreciate what you did."

Xié'è de Gōngniú walked outside the Temple and called his trusted assistant on his communicator that was part of his wrist band. In five minutes, he was flown home in the skycar where he would spend the rest of the evening contemplating his experience today.

Xié'è de Gōngniú had superior perceptive abilities from a lot of specialized training with the XSS. He now had to take that internal mental holograph in his mind and figure out exactly what happened and how he knew of all these experiences he had in 4 or 5 lifetimes throughout the Universe.

Tytrone *Kāiwù de Sēngrén* and Tytrone Philosopher Monk Rawwel were in his office looking over the recorded hidden video. Just like businesses on earth tell you the phone call is being recorded for training purposes, the Monks also recorded the training sessions to learn more about their subjects and how the experience affected them.

The Tytrone Philosopher Monks enjoyed doing these chants and conducting the training as it was the beginning to the pathway to enlightenment for the individuals they trained. *Kāiwù de Sēngrén* had seen remarkable changes in individuals in the past, so to observe Xié'è de Gōngniú transcend from a skeptic to one of their fastest learners did create a sense of accomplishment.

Once Xié'è de Gōngniú learned how to achieve the same effects silently, then he would be able to cope with just about every situation he found himself in short of being tortured and killed.

Chapter Twelve

The Calm Before the Storm

General Níngsī could not make his move until Admiral Aete hit the trip wires. If he did, he might spook his quarry and 10 years would have been wasted. Since the outer markers had not been passed, that means Admiral Aeta was too far away to attack today.

General Níngsī decided since could not afford to get involved in activities occurring around the planet because of the pending combat, he filled his morning looking at the *Béésh Łigaii Atsu* (Silver Eagle) Native American Tribe on security monitors.

Sargent Hawthorne arrived with some ranch hands and materials. They were going to be industrious today. The first ordered of business was to build fences to keep the cattle out of their Village yards and a vegetable garden they were going to start today.

By noon all the fences were built and the Villagers were happy because in recent days those steers had been a pain in the butt and obnoxious until hauled away to the Aliens.

After the Tribal women cooked up a meal for the

ranch hands, they all sat down to eat on tribal picnic tables that were recently brought in. The Ranch Hands were mostly Native American guys, were quite pleased at the very tasty meal these women made for them. With Sargent Hawthorne bringing in more and more goodies every day they had quite a bit more to work with.

Once the men soaked up the last bit of gravy with that fresh baked bread and washed down with nice and cool ice tea, it was time to get back to work on the final project of the day for the nice man they all liked, Sargent Hawthorne who also by the way was actually giving them some decent pay to do all this work.

The General felt like he was looking through a looking glass in time and space as he observed these Native Americans slowly evolve. In many ways he was the source of their evolution. Because these Native Americans saw the aliens first hand, they were also feeling spiritual because now they knew they could trust all that information handed down by their ancestors. There was no longer and skeptics or disbelief. Some of them felt real crappy now for their behavior towards their grandparents when they argued telling them simply, they were crazy for talking this people coming from the star's nonsense. Because it's perfectly clear, it was all probably true back then as it is now.

In one of the pickup trucks the ranch hands arrived in was a rotor tiller that many Americans use to plow up garden patches in their back yards.

A couple of those big strong ranch hands lifted the rotor tiller off the back of the truck and they had a gas can with them in case they needed to fill her up.

While they were all eating, Sargent Hawthorn came out and using a shovel marked off the areas he wanted plowed. He had seeds, fertilizer and in some cases a few potted plants like tomatoes.

They fired up ole Betsy (the rotor tiller) and got to work with Sargent Hawthorne directing them every step of the way. One of the items Sargent Hawthorn picked up with the shovel was a lot of cattle dung and had it piled up in the middle of the plowed areas they were working on, mixing it into the soil at the same time they were plowing down really well. This area had been recently soaked by sprinklers so it wasn't too tough for the rotor tiller to chew into it.

In the span of two hours, it all got plowed and shaped to promote plant growth. The potted plants were planted into the ground which immediately gave green cover to almost one third of the area. Everyone seemed excited in the tribe. General Níngsī benefitted immensely watching all this because it helped him not to over plan the battle and strangle his forces with excessive commands. He realized that as he reflected about the distinct possibility the trip wires may get hit any moment.

General Níngsī knew his men were professionals and sick of this war and if they could end it now, they would do everything they could. They would maintain strict discipline and the Artificial Intelligence would help them figure out to win.

The Xīngguī had another disadvantage. In the time that General Níngsī had been on Earth, Artificial Intelligence had studied vast amounts of Earth History and Culture. One of the things they stumbled across was: Sun Tzu Art of War. They studied it and came up with numerous new ideas.

Then Artificial Intelligence discovered another source of information, Carl von Clausewitz: *On War*.

Artificial Intelligence quickly analyzed Earth people were far better tacticians, they just didn't have the hardware!

As General Níngsī was cooling his heels today, enjoying all the events observed at the *Béésh Łigaii Atsu* (Silver Eagle) Native American Tribe, Artificial Intelligence was reprogramming the battle plan which clearly exposed many flaws in their plans. Instead of just six probes they now knew they needed 12 to 20 because Sun Tzu taught them the art of penetrating enemy defenses. It also exposed gaping holes in their plans Admiral Aete could exploit. Admiral Aeta's plan would have worked far better than General Níngsī realized had Artificial Intelligence not discovered the flaws with the help of Sun Tzu.

Wars are won or lost by auspicious moments like this. When General Nye at Waterloo showed up at the battle very late and mis-used his Calvary, he guaranteed Napoleon would lose the battle and his country.

Nye was being insubordinate that day, but it did not save him from a Hang Man's noose.

Sargent Hawthorne explained to the medicine man that over the next two weeks they needed to keep the garden wet so the seeds would germinate. He demonstrated how to water it by hand and explained he would be back in the morning to look at it and advise him further as the seeds were planted.

But would there be a tomorrow for them?

Nobody knew for sure because until they found Admiral Aete the situation had a lot of variables in it.

One thing for certain, the new red barn, fences, garden, trees, and green grass was starting to give the place quite a big change in appearance.

The following morning, as the medicine man *Binii 'łigaii* (screeching owl) woke up and took a cup of coffee outside he was startled. There was a 5-point buck deer out eating his grass. It was a fairly young buck and it didn't see *Binii 'łigaii* for a while, but when it did, jumped over the fence and ran down the canyon below. The water vapor and the smell of grass and freshly plowed garden probably attracted it.

General Níngsī was awake and alert as he felt today would be the day Admiral Aete would hit the trip wires. He had watched the deer for about half an hour and *Binii 'łigaii* with a drink in his hand and spook the splendid animal.

Thanks to Artificial Intelligence using audio to inform General Níngsī about the deer, General Níngsī didn't have to take his eyes and focus off the animal to read research reports.

The sprinklers set out to water the grazing grass for the cattle was also dumping water down the dry canyon as part of the process, allowing it to spring back to life even though the short rainy season was several months from now.

General Níngsī would look back on this special moment recorded in their Artificial Intelligence Data Files as that refreshing moment Great Leaders always wished they had before a slug fest.

Binii 'tigaii drank his coffee then went back inside his home and turned on the A.M. radio and listened to the nearest station and got the morning news report. Nothing new, Central and Northeast Arizona is all he was concerned about.

Around 8:00 in the morning before it got too hot, Sargent Hawthorne showed up in his Jeep with a few more goodies from all the extra gold the Zhrakzhongs paid him. What's this hay for? We will not be getting any more steers for a week?

We are going to spread this hay around some of your plants to help them retain the moisture. Soon all the potted plants that were transferred to the garden had hay around them.

Sargent Hawthorne and *Binii 'tigaii* then started watering everything watering to keep the soil moist.

General Níngsī was watching all this when all of a sudden, Admiral Aete's combined forces hit the trip wire. Thanks to Sun Tzu they got a substantial warning they would not otherwise have placed Earth in danger.

Now that the enemy was in this set piece trap, other forces were re-deployed since they were hopelessly out of position. It was now coming to a head. General Níngsī turned away from the security monitors and put all his attention on the situation at hand.

In all Fleet movements there are always stragglers

going slower due to mechanical failure. Artificial intelligence went after them first to make sure that when forces assembling for the power wedge coming at them from their rears and flanks gave them no wiggle room when they were hit with severe enfilading fire that would sweep away the power concentration at the tip of their formation.

For each Xīnggui̇̄ straggler there were at least three Zhrakzhongs Space Warships. The attacks were so quick and devastating that Admiral Aete received no warnings or casualty reports.

Admiral Aeta was a brave commander leading from the front of the formation. His command ship was in fact the tip of the sword so to speak.

One by one the stragglers were wiped out. At close quarters ranges the Xīnggui̇̄ Molecular Disrupter Cannons should have made a better showing. Part of the issue was each straggler who was commanded by a reluctant captain resulting in poor station keeping almost cowardly in all respects were in such a state of shock when they were attacked, they didn't even get off a single Molecular Disrupter Cannon shot before they were severely crippled and, in some cases, lost power. Therefore, the Molecular Disrupter Cannon were out of commission so quickly in a reduced power situation, they were useless. Those Captains that were stragglers over cowardice learned the error in their ways moments before thy ceased to exist in a gigantic explosion and sparkling debris scattering for hundreds or thousands of miles when the Zhrakzhongs Plasma Debilitater weaponry cooked their cowardly-asses alive.

One straggler by itself would not amount to much of a loss in the overall scheme of things. But after all fifteen stragglers were destroyed without a single Zhrakzhong Space Warship casualty, the Xīngguī assault force battlefield density function received an initial blow of irreplaceable ships in one of the most important confrontations in the history of the Zhrakzhong – Xīngguī conflict. What also had a remarkable impact on the outcome was it also deprived Admiral Aete a set of rear-view reconnaissance which allowed the Zhrakzhong to get to the rears of their main formation with substantial fire power.

As part of the strategy and also to slow down the Xīngguī so they didn't simply fly in mass past the Zhrakzhong defenders and hit Earth real hard, a token force was placed in front of this Incredible Xīngguī Armada. Very few of those Zhrakzhong Space Warships survived and the onrush of concentrated Xīngguī Force that produced the steam roller effect, smashing up and destroying everything in their path when the enemy ships got within range of the Xīngguī Molecular Disrupter Cannons.

Even though they were successful in breaking up the resistance in front of them, they could not fly in straight line course and risk damage to themselves, so there was a lot of maneuvering, twists, turns loops, and other geometries executed as the dog fight continued. The net effect was the frontal velocity was almost cut in half. The trailing Zhrakzhong Space Warships free of rear guards could now accelerate to flank speed and close the gap rapidly.

At the same time the token force in front of the

massive Xīngguī formations was getting sliced up and extinguished forever, Artificial Intelligence sprung the trap. The Xīngguī were now hit with everything the Zhrakzhong had along their flanks as the moved out from behind a number of planets they hid from and adjusted their positions in the early phases to keep the concealment in place.

Admiral Aete was starting to feel good as there were not many more Zhrakzhong in front of them, meaning Earth lay wide open for attack and it appeared they would catch most of the Zhrakzhong on the ground or at low altitudes slowly rising to get out into space as quick as they could to maneuver and gain battle velocities. To help cause Admiral Aete believe most of the Zhrakzhong ships remained on the planet, General Níngsī had a few ships parked on the planet in Mexico and in Arizona he could launch sequentially to help convince Admiral Aete he caught the Zhrakzhong with their pants down in a highly vulnerable state.

Admiral Aete expected a few attacks from his flanks so at the initial enfilade attacks by Xīngguī Molecular Disrupter Cannons, he wasn't concerned and did not react and continued with his plan and put great effort in getting his formations back together to speed up to attack velocities they wanted when they pounced on Earth.

His formations were nearly put back together and speeding up for the dramatic attack on Earth when the withering fire from the savage enfilade fire finally caused him to suddenly re-evaluate everything. In three-dimensional space warfare the flanks are usually two dimensional as commanders like to fly large wing like formations which in essence creates a series of wing men protecting the six o'clock of most of his assets.

An emergency maneuver thus is a loop to the vertical to escape the attack temporarily and get better angles and determination of enemy disposition. There is one particular issue with the emergency loops when you are dealing with flanking enfilade fire, if there is another formation in your rears, you are turning into the jaws of hell.

Admiral Aete assuming the straggler force would have reported sightings of enemy in his rears and since he received no report, he flew caution to the wind doing that looping maneuver with his entire force placing almost every ship in the formation perpendicular to the coming wedge. The enemy has a very small silhouette, but the looping craft are exposing the entire length of their Space Warships making them extremely easy targets for good Zhrakzhong gunners.

The carnage began and Admiral Aeta suddenly realized he had blundered into a gigantic trap now being shot at from 4 directions. He could not complete the loop or the enemy could possibly wipe out his entire force. Therefore, halfway through the loop while he was traveling perpendicular to his original track, he gave out emergency commands directing ships to follow him instead of completing the loop and to accelerate to emergency speeds. They would soon be pulling every ounce of energy from their power plants to propulsion to get out of this trap fast.

Admiral Aeta was lucky to have escaped with half his force and as they continued accelerating heading on the current course Admiral Aete selected all ships started sending status reports so that Admiral Aeta could figure out where he stood. The mission was thus aborted as it was hopeless now to continue as the status reports received from his fleets started showing an attrition he barely could stomach.

One thing he knew was that he was no longer at enough battle strength to fight the Zhrakzhongs because he lost the numerical advantage. As soon as he started getting all the battle reports in one by one with the remainder of his scrambling Space Warships, he slowly pieced together exactly how much attrition he had and a preliminary view of how many Zhrakzhongs Space Warships involved in the attack.

Sensor readings, photonics, and electronic warfare intercepts slowly built Admiral Aeta a time sliced three-dimensional picture. Artificial Intelligence was working at a very high bandwidth carving out three-dimensional video that could be analyzed to gain a better picture of what just transpired.

He also understood the axioms of war. When the enemy knows you are weakened in a battle and they maintained their strength, they will pursue and attack since the momentum is in their advantage and friendly forces psychology is ruptured leaving fear and self-doubt.

He didn't know exactly how General Níngsī was going to attack, but he knew he was coming.

Admiral Aeta knew Emperor Shāyú does not mince words. His instructions, if you lose do not bring the fleet back, was in his thoughts. But to save the fleet he had to go back to home worlds. He would have to sacrifice a few more of his ships acting as rear guards as they continued to speed up to maximum to clear the battlefield area. If necessary, he would commit suicide, but he would get his fleet home so at least half of them could survive and be available at a future date after they recoiled from this disaster, he created by underestimating General Níngsī.

In the heat of the battle, General Níngsī needed to get to his command ship and be with his fleet in the event he had to provide some on site leadership to a few feckless captains he knew existed. His command ship hidden behind Jupiter was on its way. It would be about 15 minutes before he would launch in his personal transport/shuttle. Looking at the surveillance video he saw Sargent Hawthorne standing besides *Binii'łigaii* (screeching owl) Medicine Man. He knew what he had to do and ordered his assistant to go out and bring Sargent Hawthorne to his transport/shuttle and he was taking him with him in fifteen minutes.

Five minutes later on of the security transports flew out the gate of the Alien Compound and landed 10 feet away from Sargent Hawthorne utterly shocking *Binii'łigaii* who was enjoying looking at his new garden.

The eight-foot tall very senior general walked out of the transport and approached Sargent Hawthorne and said, "Sargent Hawthorne, General Níngsī requests your presence right away. I think he has something to show you."

"Would it be ok to bring my friend *Binii'łigaii* with me?"

"I see why not. I think General Níngsī would like to see him as well."

Binii 'łigaii looked back at his wife and said, "I'm going with Sargent Hawthorne to visit General Níngsī."

They were soon inside and heading towards General Níngsī's underground command center and parked a few feet from the entrance. Almost coincidentally General Níngsī stepped out of the command center entrance and boarded the transport/shuttle that his assistant now escorted Sargent Hawthorne and *Binii 'łigaii* towards.

"General Níngsī, Sargent Hawthorne request his friend *Binii 'łigaii* come with him."

"Not a problem, hop on board."

Two minutes later everyone was seated and buckled up and the transport/shuttle took off and went vertical.

Looking at the holograph that gave the appearance of a window looking out to space, *Binii 'łigaii* watched day turn into night and as the transport/shuttle maneuvered to dock into the shuttle bay of General Níngsī's command ship for about a minute they could see Earth below them."

About that time when Sargent Hawthorne was taking it all in he knew they were in space and he offered, "*Binii 'łigaii,* you are the first native American Medicine Man to go into space."

General Níngsī then stated, "Sargent Hawthorne, you are the first Marine Corp Sargent to go into space."

Shortly after docking was complete, General Níngsī led Sargent Hawthorne and *Binii'ligaii* into the command center and up the circular staircase to his command platform.

General Níngsī then announced and artificial intelligence registered his command, "Join the fleet and direct all ships to pursue the Xīnggui. This is their combined fleet and we must crush them to end this war."

The command ship had artificial gravity, therefore Sargent Hawthorne and *Binii'ligaii* could stand next to General Níngsī and view the numerous display panels showing all kinds of tactical information. Sargent Hawthorne looked out at the sprawling Combat Information Center and could see at least 400 Zhrakzhongs monitoring and operating numerous consoles. It was an incredible sight.

The Zhrakzhongs command ship didn't need much protection as it had massive firepower. However, conditions sometimes happen that you least expect, so General Níngsī always had an escort with his command ship whether he was aboard or not. As they traveled at extreme speeds watching the planets go past as they flew to catch up with the Fleet, Sargent Hawthorne could see on some of the viewer screens the images of all the Zhrakzhongs escort Space Warships. The sight was impressive.

If the truth be told General Níngsī and his escorts alone made a very powerful striking force. He also had the fastest ships in the fleet as part of his escorts for moments like this where they could catch up to the rest of the fleet already traveling balls to the wall.

General Níngsī was able to catch up to the fleet sooner than he realized.

A few of the rear-guard ships Admiral Aete left behind were doing Kamikaze like attacks, flying into the frontal wedge of the Zhrakzhongs formations.

In addition to the damage the Xīngguī Molecular Disrupter Cannons caused as the ship converged with the Zhrakzhongs, they intentionally attempt to ram the biggest Space Warships at the tip of the charge.

In practical terms all these Kamikaze style Xīngguī attacks did was delay the inevitable.

Zhrakzhongs had learned how to deal with such attacks, therefore chased in a formation that created an image like an arrow. Knowing the obvious tactic, the Zhrakzhongs did random course changes and the image of the side of the arrow firing Zhrakzhongs Plasma Debilitater weaponry with a Time on Target (TOT), the Xīngguī control room personnel were usually fried upwards to a minute before the collision would occur giving the Zhrakzhongs just enough time to maneuver knowing the Xīngguī and their onboard Artificial intelligence would be incapacitated and not be able to make further course changes allowing collision avoidance. It also made it impossible for Xīngguī Molecular Disrupter Cannons to do their damage.

The plan had a huge flaw in it. Had Admiral Aete sent 10 ships instead of one at each Kamikaze attack, the results would have had more successful and some of them would be able to hit Zhrakzhongs and take out high valued targets. Such a plan could have slowed down the Zhrakzhongs so severely, it would have allowed the remainder of the Xīngguī fleet to high tail it back to their home worlds with little or no more destruction.

Thanks to these mild skirmishes slowing down the fleet, two things happened. General Níngsī was able to catch up with the fleet quicker and his two guests, Sargent Hawthorne and *Binii'łigaii* got to see Space Warships larger than American Aircraft Carriers have horrific explosions with incredible pyro-techniques effect.

The Earth people had no idea how much the images were magnified. The surreal manifestation of the imagery with the magnification made this all appear as if it were close up, but in reality, it was quite a distance off. With the Zhrakzhongs technology, the imagery had real time removal of Doppler effect and other image blurring issues. The resulting images were crisp and clear and terrifying. In the matter of a few minutes the Native American Medicine Man *Binii'łigaii* got to see events that would be 200,000 years into the future for any Earth descendants. Nobody from Earth had traveled this far out into space before or ever participated in an epic space battle. The effects of watching all this unfold was stunning to say the least.

The fleet knew General Níngsī's command ship was rapidly approaching. Already his artificial intelligence beamed aboard at the same time he arrived was taking control of the battle. The force commander did not reorganize correctly for those pin prick attacks by single ships, but Artificial Intelligence already reformulating new policy and tactics based on Sun Tzu and Clausewitz theories and experiences repositioned the fleet.

As most of the fleet slowed for a brief period, two ships were seen ahead as sacrificial lambs. They were positioned like American fighter jets with one ship out in front and a wingman offset to the side. Compiling video available on the internet of numerous WW2 air combat events, this formation once employed had dramatic effects in eliminating the fleet's forward advance speed. As the Xīngguī Kamikaze attacks came in the fleet was far enough behind to experience any type of damage, so the formations were maintained with precision.

The Xīngguī Kamikaze could not run between the two ships or it would receive flanking full broadside enfilade fire. This new technique had amazing results as the Xīngguī Space Warship got into position to fire its Molecular Disrupter Cannons, Zhrakzhongs Plasma Debilitater weaponry which had a range advantage was already firing from both Zhrakzhong Space Warships and the Zhrakzhong further offset because the Xīngguī Kamikaze had to point the ship it planned to ram. That meant about a minute and a half before the Xīngguī Kamikaze reached the impact zone, it was receiving a full lethal full broadside Plasma Debilitater kill shot from the flanks.

Every Plasma Debilitater weapon on the side of the Zhrakzhong effectively wingman shooting at the Xīngguī Space Warship was automatically tracking and attacking with terrifying accuracy and effectiveness killing the crew and disabling its internal Artificial

Intelligence which prevented further steering allowing the Zhrakzhongs to maneuver out of the collision with a few seconds to spare. However, the Zhrakzhongs did feel the shockwaves created from the immense explosion of the dying ship.

With this new method of minimizing Xīngguī Kamikaze effectiveness, General Níngsī having caught up with the fleet were now slowly catching up with Admiral Aeta.

Admiral Aeta's greatest fear now materialized. He had escaped the jaws of hell in a set piece trap, only to be confronted in open space with no planets to maneuver around to circumvent a superior force chasing him like the one now in his rears. Admiral Aeta was operating within the guidelines that most modern space-based Empires dictated. He thought his worst nightmare was behind him. He was wrong. The biggest ruse in the history of the Galaxy was now unfolding.

The Zhrakzhongs did relocate a lot of their population to hundreds of planets to protect them in the event their planets were destroyed, but there was another reason. To scatter fleet components without exposing the real intent.

Those scattered fleet components through some very sophisticated communications methods were slowly mobilizing and heading to a projected point in space that running from Earth would most likely put Admiral Aete in a panic move back towards Xīngguī province Màichōng.

Up to this very moment Artificial Intelligence on General Níngsī's command ship estimated Admiral

Aeta's Xīngguī Fleet was geometrically aligned on a projected track that would put it in position to get smacked by the previously distributed fleet components now aligning for the final showdown.

Back at the NRO building next to Dulles International Airport, KH-14 and Hubble cameras were now pointing at the ongoing space battle that had intermittent explosions as the Zhrakzhongs ripped apart Xīngguī Kamikaze attackers one by one.

Chapter Thirteen

It Was Bigger Than a Typhoon

Sally Fairbanks reported back to work fully refreshed after her little sojourn with General Níngsī and finishing the book she intended to complete during that period.

Sally Fairbanks knew General Níngsī had blown her cover with the statement to Xi Jinping. What she didn't know her morning would get a little complicated because of the British.

CIA people have to report all foreign contact, intentionally or otherwise. Those who forget to do this end up polygraphed and, in the shits, and in a job, they really do not like. Sally Fairbanks understood all this is how it is, so like a smart employee should she had her foreign contact report all filled out. She was going to wait until later that morning when she expected to get called into a meeting concerning the Zhrakzhongs.

While Sally Fairbanks was getting caught up on her email, Mike Barnes walked up to her an asked, "Could you please come with me into the conference room. Sally followed Mike Barnes in and there was the DCI sitting not looking to happy.

Sally Fairbanks sat down and the DCI started in on her.

"Sally, this morning I've had some conversations with the British SIS, Richard Moore. I was mildly disturbed in what he informed me of."

Sally didn't say anything, she just sat there waiting to hear what it was all about.

"I can't tell you how the British know this because it's a closely guarded secret, but apparently you were in Russia a couple days ago."

Sally knew her goose was cooked so she got professional really quick and said, "Sir I have my foreign contact report filled out at my desk, may I please go get it and provide it to you. I can email Mike Barnes a copy after the meeting."

"Sure, go get it."

The DCI was mildly interested to see if it matched what the British claimed, "The Russians scrambled over 100 SU-57 jet fighters."

That wasn't that big a deal, what the big deal was, "The Russians Identified Sally Fairbanks and she was with the Aliens when they scrambled the jets."

Sally might be that meek looking CIA spy but if everything the British reported was true, the DCI had a problem on his hands.

Sally returned with the official copy already signed with a CIA serial number on it. That means she had gone through administrative procedures and that serialized copy that included the date she electronically signed it was on file as of YESTERDAY.

The DCI shook his head and looked up towards the ceiling with that grim WTF look on his face.

"Sally, this puts me in a difficult position."

"I signed it yesterday, you need to speak with the admin people who sit on their asses and don't do their jobs quick enough to inform you."

The DCI knew Sally was probably safe on this one, she was just along for the ride with the Aliens being a good interface for America. But when he looked down and saw Xi Jinping on the paper, he just shook his head. No doubt the MSS have also already tagged Sally Fairbanks.

The DCI was all twisted up inside. These recent days had been rough on him. First, he had to send the head of SAC out on a vacation and now Sally Fairbanks just had a phenomenal day with the Aliens that will take time to explain to the President which he had to do before Xi Jinping personally called the president and asked him why he had one of his CIA people in a secret controlled area of China without his permission.

And they think Watergate was a big deal……

As the DCI was thinking about what to do next, his assistant came in the room and asked him, Director, I recommend you look at the KH-14 video and we have Hubble video from it being repositioned this morning.

The DCI handed the remote control to Sally and asked her, "Sally could you please select all the appropriate channels."

Sally turned them on one by one and soon it was rather intense in the room.

No Americans had ever observed a real space battle like this before. It was unimaginable.

The real time imagery of the KH-14 was rather incredible. Soon Hubble pictures started flashing up with delays. Artificial Intelligence selected which frames to show and gave the viewer enough time to focus in on the image of the explosions.

It was a scary time for everyone in the room, especially Shelly Fairbanks who knew vividly that if General Níngsī didn't win this battle they would all be wiped out in a few hours as the Xīnggui extinguished this planet just to make sure they killed all the Zhrakzhongs in Arizona and Mexico.

In one respect, timing was perfect. It was unlikely anyone would be concerned about Sally Fairbanks today as all this unfolded. If there had been any reason to proceed with disciplinary actions that quickly faded as the DCI now had bigger fish to fry.

"Mike, put together a task force immediately, I'll probably be requested to brief the President within a couple of hours."

Mike Barnes named six names off the top of his head and asked Sally, could you please go grab them and bring them in here for a quick meeting."

"Yes, sir."

Sally went out to all the offices and notified each of them which were in the office at that time to report to the conference room.

The group was soon gathered and a few of them were surprised to see the DCI. He usually only came here for personnel problems or administrative SNAFUs.

The DCI started right in and said, "I need to have a report ready in about two hours. I suspect Sally may know more about this than we realize so she may help fill in the blanks."

The group watched the satellite monitors and the series of Hubble pictures that were rather incredible and scared the crap out of some of them.

"Is this a space war?"

"Sally, since you know General Níngsī and was with him a couple days ago, can you elaborate?" the DCI asked.

"The Zhrakzhongs have been in a long-protracted war with the Xīngguī that exist a great distance from here. The Zhrakzhongs recently brought one billion of their population here and settled half in Arizona and the other half in Mexico to protect them with distance. I've had several discussions with their leader General Níngsī about the possibility the Xīngguī may have followed them here putting this planet at risk. No country on this planet has the ability to defend ourselves from the Zhrakzhongs or the Xīngguī. It's sad to say Earth might become collateral damage as it appears the warzone has come our way."

Watching all those intermittent incredible explosions, one of the Analysts asked, "Is there any way we know the identity of any of those space craft?"

Sally Fairbanks offered, "I've seen the front of General Níngsī's command ship. If they turn around and start coming back this direction, I can give you some identification of the Zhrakzhongs. I've also seen video of fighting between the Zhrakzhongs and the Xīngguī that occurred approximately 10 years ago, so if they have not radically changed their design, I think I can identify them."

The DCI quickly figured out what he needed to do and called the NRO.

"Hey Christopher, this is the DCI. I'm in the SAC conference room looking at the video on channels 4, 6, 7, 8 , and 9. Can you do a rewind and send us the video of when you first started recording with KH-14?

"Sure, no problem."

"Link it up on channel 5."

"It will take a few minutes, and we'll start playing channel 5."

The group waited patiently with some trepidation as the NRO diligently went to work getting a video feed set up on channel-5. These were internal video channels with fiberoptics controllers good for top secret with no ability to break into it. When a user requested the video, the sender's system did a wrap checking hardware serial numbers in the fiberoptic transmitter and receivers to make sure it matched the firmware registration. If not, the link was shut down and no video was sent. By all appearances if that happened it looks as if the video channel is dead, no laser light on the fiberoptics.

By the time the KH-14 started recording the

battle, explosions had already occurred while the Zhrakzhongs were knocking off the Xīnggui stragglers.

Common sense was the Xīnggui would be the major force coming this way for the attack, all bets were on that.

You really can't see a space ship traveling fast without light in the dark of space. The Xīnggui had a force of over one thousand Space Warships. It was an incredible force. Had Admiral Aete not reacted to the piece meal small force in front of him and did the loop when the flank shooters began and simply just increased speed, they could have made it to Earth and wiped it out. They would have caught General and a number of his Generals in the command center and killed them creating a material deficiency in the Zhrakzhongs top level leadership ranks and possibly created a situation that would make the Zhrakzhongs an inferior fighting force for the near future.

It was hard to see who was who in the zoo until the flankers started that enfilade attack.

The combination of lasers, Xīnggui Molecular Disrupter Cannons, and Zhrakzhongs Plasma Debilitater weaponry lit the space up like it was daylight. Now the ships images could easily be discerned.

"Those are Xīnggui Space Warships coming right at us!" Sally Fairbanks exclaimed.

"You sure about that?" the DCI asked.

"Yes. But I recommend you bring in Doctor Brandenhagen who also watched the video to get a second opinion."

The DCI looked at Mike Barnes and said, "Get Doctor Brandenhagen in here right away. Have a nondisclosure sheet ready for him to sign. He's not cleared for half this crap."

"Right away boss."

Roger Brandenhagen was sitting back in his recliner meditating and listening to Hanns Wolf piano concerto when that pesky cell phone lit up.

The caller I.D. was Mike Barnes. He met Mike at the SAC. Roger wasn't expecting this phone call and was mildly perturbed, but he answered anyway.

"Hello Mike, what can I do for you?"

"Doctor Brandenhagen we need your assistance immediately. This request is coming personally from the DCI. There will be a car pulling up in front of your home in about 15 minutes to bring you here. The guys guarding your front door will be notified momentarily. And come as you are, don't waste time changing your clothes."

"What if I am in my pajamas?"

"Ok then put on some street clothes."

"I'll be ready in 15 minutes."

"Thank you, I highly appreciate your help."

"Okay see you soon."

Mike Barnes hung up. He didn't even have enough time to say good bye as he had several calls to make.

Roger got out of his recliner, went upstairs and took off his pajamas and put on blue jeans and a Hawaiian shirt of the type he liked to wear. He was growing his hair out longer now and his beard was slowly taking shape. It appeared he had "checked out."

Knowing how these CIA people operated, he could be stuck in that conference room a long time and getting hungry, so he stopped by the kitchen poured a cup of coffee out of his coffee maker into a traveling cup with a lid on it and grabbed several of those donuts he was getting ready to eat and put them back in the paper bag they came in and walked to his front door. As soon as Roger stepped outside, he turned to the agent he liked who helped stop the BS a few nights before and handed him the bag and asked, "Would you like a donut?"

"Sure, why not?"

Roger then turned to the other CIA guy and handed him the paper bag and asked, "Would you like a donut sir?"

"Sure, I don't mind if I do."

Roger then said, "I have a coffee pot full of coffee in my kitchen, the door is unlocked so if you want coffee, feel free to get yourself a cup. There are numerous cups in the cabinet just above the coffee maker."

"Thank you Doctor Brandenhagen."

"Also, I know it gets tough waiting out here so instead of peeing on my bushes, feel free to use the restroom."

"We appreciate your concern Doctor Brandenhagen."

"I'm more concerned about you killing my bushes with all that extra CIA coffee."

"No problem, sir. It looks like your ride is here."

"That was quick."

Roger was soon in the car in the back seat next to one of those evil looking guys who would probably snap the head of a kiten off if they had the chance.

"Would you like a donut?"

"No thanks."

Roger then asked the driver "Would you like a donut?"

"Sure, why not."

The driver was going extra fast up I-66 in the fast lane and ignored the Hiway Patrol motorcycle that soon was behind him. Before long the driver pulled into the front of the commercial office building to drop off his ride, then walked back to the Hiway Patrolman on his motorcycle. They knew Roger knew where to go, so they said, "Go on up to the 14th floor, they are expecting you."

The driver and his assistant were each about six foot five, wearing suits and the Hiway Patrolman could see what was probably pistol holsters.

"Did you notice the Government license plates?"

"Yes sir, but you were speeding."

"This is official U.S. Government business and you are on Federal Property now, I suggest you take your motorcycle out of here now before we have a couple FBI agents take you downtown and tickle you all night long."

"Can I at least see a badge or something?"

The driver thought it would only be decent of him to do so, therefore he pulled out his FBI badge given him for combined task force operations. The Hiway patrolman just about shit himself because he had heard about the "tickle" torture techniques. People think waterboarding is bad, they have no idea.

"Have a nice day, sir."

"You too patrolman, now get out there and write a bunch of tickets. We are counting on you."

The Hiway Patrolman had no idea this was a government complex but as he was driving off, he noticed some of the placards on the reserve parking. Almost as dumb as the black SUV's they drive around in, they tell the world who their visitors are just because some jack ass SES wants to be treated like a dignitary.

By the time Doctor Brandenhagen arrived at the conference room, the group had seen the entire video and most of them were frightened because Sally Fairbanks analysis was always spot on, if the Zhrakzhongs lose this battle, the Earth would be laid to waste.

Their personal psychology would get a huge boost if Doctor Brandenhagen confirmed those were Xīnguǐ who looped around and bugged out.

"Thank you for coming right away, Doctor Brandenhagen."

"It was all good we made good time with the police escort."

The DCI didn't know that was a smart-ass remark but he would find out later when the Virginia Hiway Patrol complained a couple of their agents threatened to tickle their patrolman.

"Doctor Brandenhagen, all this of course is highly classified and you will be required to sign this non-disclosure form, then we have a video for you to watch and we want your inputs on it."

"Sure."

Roger Brandenhagen signed the forms and the video began.

Take a good look Doctor Brandenhagen. When General Níngsī showed you and Sally Fairbanks the space war holographs can you help us identify whose ships are in these videos from that experience?"

"Sure, no problem."

When the video got to the point the flanking enfilade fire began and the space was lit up nicely, Doctor Brandenhagen immediately said, "Those are Xīngguī Space Warships coming right at us."

"You are absolutely sure about that?"

"Yes. During the video that General Níngsī showed us, we had a lot of time to stare at those ships."

"Do you recognize the ships that are apparently

attacking the Xīnguī Space Warships?"

"Yes, those look identical to some I saw parked with General Níngsī's command ship the first day we met him."

"Do you see his command ship in any of that video?"

"No."

Within moments of that statement the DCI got a phone call from NRO and he asked, "Sally, can you turn on channel 2, NRO has some new video to show us."

In the time they were watching all that, NRO stitched together some videos from KH-14 and KH-11 video which showed a shuttle type craft go up and land on a Space Warship.

"Do you recognize that ship?"

"Yes, that's General Níngsī's command ship."

Over the next hour they watched General Níngsī's command ship and its escort chase after his fleet and rejoin it. They were going at such high speeds now there was Doppler modulation of the ship images NRO could not correct so it appeared the images were coming in and out of focus at the same time the size of the images were shrinking. Eventually they could no longer make out the ships but they did see incidental explosions when ships blew up.

"Looks like the good news is they are taking the war away from his planet."

"Yes, but we still have one billion Zhrakzhongs in Arizona and Mexico.

"What kind of military presence is still left?"

"We do not know but we are going to have an SR-72 fly over today."

"Any fear the Zhrakzhongs will shoot it down?"

"As long as they do not show any threatening behavior, they may allow it to pass over."

As soon as the SR-72 flying in from the ISR base in Eastern New Mexico got to the Eastern Perimeter it was suddenly met by some Alien ships who took control of the plane and turned it around. The only good news was during the banking in the course change maneuver, the cameras that were already rolling got a look into the compound. From this distance and altitude, the decoys looked real. As soon as the SR-72 was about 100 miles East from his point the aliens notified the pilot, "We have returned control of your aircraft to you. Please do not come back."

The SR-72 could fly as fast as 4,000 miles per hour in an emergency. Its cruise speed was 3,000 miles per hour. It took very little time to get back to Clovis, New Mexico.

After the plane landed the duplicate hard drives that recorded the imagery were taken to the TOP SECRET lab and Air Force Technicians immediately started the file transfer on a fixed land line fiber optics, they had on lease for the next 10 years. This was a point-to-point network isolated from all other sources. Cisco who built the hardware had a bandwidth of 400

Giga Bytes, but the servers processing the data could not operate that quick. So, the effective bandwidth was only fourteen Gigabytes per second.

It took 15 minutes to send the files to their customer: NRO.

In 15 minutes, the task force was looking at the little bit of video the SR-72 recorded before the Aliens took control of the ship and turned it around.

When the task force was looking at the imagery one of them said out loud, "Holy Shit."

The NRO is able to take the raw data and magnify it upwards 100 times using Wavelets and Stochastic Resonance.

"Any comments?"

"The ships on the ground look identical to the ones they just observed fighting in space."

"There is still an impressive force left on this planet."

"I wonder why the Zhrakzhongs didn't send them up in the battle?"

"They are probably the reserve force and felt they didn't need them."

Little did the group know General Níngsī threw at them everything he had in this *win all* space battle. Earth people had no idea what was at stake here and the implications if General Níngsī lost this battle. The Xīngguī Emperor is utterly ruthless. One might say he makes the Jupitorians who wiped out Mars look like boy scouts.

"How soon can you put this report together?" the DCI asked.

The rest of the CIA employees in the room were chickenshits when it came to power politics and didn't want to say it. Sally Fairbanks knew it was time to put their office back together since the Tyrant SAC Director Mark Rebman was on leave and a reasonable man like Mike Barnes was in Charge.

"Director, it used to be we put out a quick look report. If you allow us to put out a quick look report, we can have it on your desk in 30 minutes."

"Do it!"

"Yes sir."

The DCI got up and said as he was leaving, "I'll be in my office waiting for that report, I have some important phone calls to make."

The DCI then turned towards Doctor Brandenhagen and Sally Fairbanks, "I know you will probably feel unsafe because the Alien Compound is a War Zone now, but after I read the report, I think I will have you two, return to Arizona and meet with the Zhrakzhongs. You are otherized to inform them we watched the Space Battle with our photonics and would like to get a feel for how things stand and what kind of immediate threats this planet we should be aware of.

The DCI departed and Sally who had a laptop in a docking station said, "I can bring my laptop in here and we can work on it and request more video if we need it to fill in the blanks."

Mike Barnes said, "Good idea."

Sally also had some old quick look reports she could simply edit, change the serial number and date on them and not waste half a day doing it the way the SAC Director on Vacation insisted was *absolutely necessary.*

As they brain stormed and glued this thing together with Sally Fairchild typing at about 120 words per minute, just like they promised in 30 minutes it was ready to present to the DCI.

"I'll go to my docking station and email this to the DCI. All of you except Doctor Brandenhagen will be on distribution."

Sally abruptly stood up, went to her office, plugged the laptop into the docking station and in the span of two minutes hit the send button. She then bent over with her hands together on her forehead and attempted to do some silent meditation as she now felt the enormous pressure.

Sally also knew one other harsh reality. Americans are not the only people with fancy equipment to scan the universe.

Khabibullo Abdussamatov, a Russian astrophysicist of Uzbek descent. who was the new voice in global cooling mini-ice age theory, was also a brilliant scientist and a man of impecable morals, headed Space research laboratory at the Saint Petersburg-based Pulkovo Observatory and the Russian Academy of Sciences.

Because of scientific collaboration that exists because of the International Space Station and other areas of space research, the CIA knew a lot about the toys that the brilliant scientist Khabibullo Abdussamatov had at his disposal. She also knew the extensive hacking of American Intel by Russia and China and had no doubt either through computer resources or HUMINT that Khabibullo Abdussamatov knew a Space War between the Zhrakzhongs and the Xīnggui created those massive explosions and that he had his eyes in the sky looking at it.

The Chinese usually keep their INTEL to themselves and are just as subtle as the British when it comes to spying, so it's expected they would not show any reaction unless somehow, they felt it was in their best interest. She also knew President Xi knew she had some kind of connection to General Níngsī just two days before this Space War started. She's already burned by the British, and it's quite possible she would soon get burned by the Chinese and the Russians as this drama all unfolded.

To some extent Sally Fairbanks felt actually relieved to be sent out to the War Zone in Arizona to escape the dirty politics that might soon start as soon as the President is informed, she visited President Xi with the Aliens and the Russians scrambled 100 SU-57 fighter jets to chase her and the Aliens down.

The SAC director now enjoying Matai's on the beach would probably rejoice in firing me, Sally Fairbanks was thinking as she was suddenly called back into the conference room and the DCI was there for a couple remarks and probably a critique of their quick look report.

"Allright gang, I know you didn't have the luxury of time to put this report together, so it has to go as is. I'm personally heading over to the White House now to brief the President. Mike, I want Doctor Brandenhagen and Sally Fairbanks taken to Andrews immediately and flown out to Tucson. They need to go interface with the Aliens and find out what's going on.

Doctor Brandenhagen, then said, "Doctor, I'm not dressed for success and all I had to eat this morning was a donut and a cup of coffee."

"We have snacks on the Gulfstream 700 you will fly in today. I'll call ahead and have meals waiting for you that you can eat on the helicopter ride going North."

"What happened to the GS650, I thought it was a good enough plane."

"Don't ask."

Those kinds of statements usually meant bad things happened and not to go there.

Roger Brandenhagen knew from what he's read that every now and then when agents are extracted in enemy territory, something like a stinger missile or enemy jet fighters bring it down. Some of the stars on the wall at CIA headquarters are for personnel killed in plane crashes while performing missions. *Some poor bastard who thought he was making it out alive lay dead in a smoldering heap.*

Roger Brandenhagen had not shaved yet and

he would normally not like to be seen in public in the manner he appeared, but he knew this was serious business and he would take a long hot bath tomorrow if he managed to get home.

As Roger Brandenhagen set there just taking it all in, Mike Barnes suddenly said, "The helicopter is here to take you both to Andrews."

Sally had a girl's billfold and her cell phone. That's all she needed. Roger had a cell phone with him as well, but assumed he would not be needing it.

Sally and Roger stood up and Roger followed Sally out the conference room past her office and to a hallway that went to the elevator. A few minutes later they were walking out the elevator on the roof of the building and climbed into the CIA Sikorsky-97.

This sleek fast baby would get them to Andrews while cruising at 250 miles per hour. Roger said on the helicopter, "I wish I brought a book along to read."

Sally smiled knowing Roger was full of shit, there is no way he could concentrate now to read a book. His mind had to be transfixed on the current events.

Sally was right about one thing it was good for her to get the hell out of Washington DC right away because phone calls from Russia, China, and Great Britain ushered in some dirty politics and when she was invited to go somewhere to do some explaining to administrative officials and the State Department, the DCI had the easy way out by saying, "I'm afraid she's not available."

"What do you mean she's not available?"

"She's deployed on a mission."

"What kind of mission?"

"Top Secret SCI we are not in a SKIF, I'm sorry can't discuss it."

"We would like to set up a meeting and get to the bottom of these concerns the Russians and the Chinese have. Our partners the British are perturbed as they feel you sand bagged them and kept them in the dark."

"They were not cleared to know about her mission."

"That appearance in China was some sort of mission?"

"I'm sorry sir, but I must end this call you have just violated security protocols."

The DCI then hung up on the State Department Agent and had a smile on his face. *This may just work out afterall*, he thought.

When they arrived at Andrews, Mable Potter was standing by the GS700 all smiles she was happy to fly with her favorite passengers again.

"Welcome back."

"Thank you."

Mable followed the two up into the aircraft and noted Doctor Brandenhagen looked a little rough and unshaven. But she had just what he needed.

Mable went up to the cockpit and informed the pilots who already saw the door locked signal, and said, "Passengers are onboard we are ready to leave."

Today the GS700 would take off on runway 01R because 01L was temporarily shut down, which is the case when Air Force One has that runway reserved.

The GS700 was fully fueled, extra light thanks to lack of passengers and cargo. The Jet Jockies in the cockpit were very happy their climb would be quick. Their initial course was 240 degrees traveling at Mach 0.9 approximately 666 miles per hour.

Almost like before, they arrived at Tucson 3 and a half hours later, before lunch time in Tucson Davis-Monthan Air Force Base.

The Army's Sikorsky UH-60 Black Hawk helicopter was already for takeoff. The GS700 pulled up 50 feet away from the Blackhawk and disgorged its passengers. Two minutes later Sally and Roger were in the Helicopter that had permission to take off vertically from where it was since there was no inbound or outbound traffic at the moment.

The same helicopter had been used on all these missions to the Alien Compound. The Zhrakzhongs assumed someone would show up inquiring about the SR-72 incident as well as the ongoing Space Battle they knew had been detected by the American's KH-14 satellite. That video stream also helped the Zhrakzhongs who used it to monitor the space battle from a different angle.

Fifty miles North of Tucson two Alien UFOs came alongside the Helicopter they were well acquainted and the pilots were informed, "For security reasons, we have control of your aircraft. Do you wish to land by the *Béésh Łigaii Atsu* (Silver Eagle) Native American Tribe?"

"Yes, that is our destination." The pilot responded.

The pilots then sat back and enjoyed the ride. The possibility of running into another aircraft was minimum because, the aliens had good sensors.

The flight went straight to the *Béésh Łigaii Atsu* Tribe which cut off a lot of flying time since they could avoid taking the long way around for safety and fear of being shot down.

While on the GS700, Mable who comes prepared for a lot of issues including razors, shaving lotion, tooth brushes, tooth paste, etc. The snacks she served hit the spot too. And now Sally and Roger munched on some Colonel Sanders the pilot picked up for them before they got there. Mable reimbursed the pilot with some CIA money they gave her for events like this when traditional practices were not going to provide what they needed.

Roger Brandenhagen kind of got a cheap thrill throwing the chicken bones out of the side door that was open to help keep them cool in the hot Arizona weather which felt good at this altitude. However, it probably cost them a few miles per gallon in fuel.

The time passed quickly. The KFC and the Pepsi really made a miserable day feel a little better.

By the time they landed at the dirt road leading down to the *Béésh Łigaii Atsu* Village, it was now getting close to 2:00 P.M. Oddly Sargent Hawthorne was not there to meet them, but coming in they could see his jeep parked over at the Village. Nobody including the General was able to reach Sargent Hawthorne and so the General called Sally Fairbanks.

"Sally?"

"Yes," Sally replied as she recognized the Generals voice.

"Hi, this is General Short. I've been trying to reach Sargent Hawthorne to meet you and give you a ride, but have not been able to reach him and the phone answer says the customer is not available. Can you look into the matter and call me back after you find out what's going on?"

"Yes General, I would be happy to. We see his Jeep parked in the village, and I'm sure he can hear this helicopter. I'll call you back after I find out what's going on."

"Thank you Sally, I appreciate that."

The General hung up; he was a busy man at the

time while the Pentagon was starting to mobilize troops for reasons nobody knew.

It did not bother Sally and Roger to walk down the hill to the *Béésh Łigaii Atsu* Village after sitting for hours.

Zhrakzhongs security surveillance video spotted and identified Sally Fairbanks. Another General-on-General **Níngsī's staff decided to go pay a visit to Sally** to explain a few things she was unaware of because he knew his boss had a distinct interest in this woman.

They got to the village before the Zhrakzhong General arrived they didn't expect. *Nizhóní Ch'ilátah Hózhóón (beautiful flower)* who is *Binii'łigaii* (screeching owl) medicine man's wife saw Roger and Sally out her window and came out abruptly to talk to her.

"Where is your husband and Sargent Hawthorne?"

"They went to go see General Níngsī first thing this morning just after sunrise and have not returned."

Knowing General Níngsī was heading deep out into space and these guys were gone told Sally Fairbanks in her thinking, one huge possibility exists: they went with General Níngsī.

Sally and Roger stood there for a while having a minor conversation with *Nizhóní Ch'ilátah Hózhóón*.

"I suppose we should walk over to the Zhrakzhong compound gate and ask to talk with an officer," Sally Fairbanks said.

No sooner than she got the words out she observed the Zhrakzhong compound gate opening and a Hovercraft immediately came out and traveled up to near where she was standing and stopped. The whining turbos shut down and the door opened followed by a Zhrakzhong walking out of the Hovercraft over directly to Sally Fairbanks.

"Hello Sally Fairbanks," the General stated.

"Thanks for coming here, I wanted to talk with General Níngsī about a few things."

"He's not here at this time, but if you would like to come to the command center, I can provide a lot of information for you."

"Yes, that would be helpful."

Sally knowing all the possibilities didn't want to discuss it in front of *Nizhóní Ch'ilátah Hózhóón.*

Moments later the Hovercraft was inside the Zhrakzhong, and like before, they transferred to a flying box and made their way to the Command Center.

Down deep underground in a very complicated command center the General started the conversation, "We know you know about the Space War ongoing."

"That would not surprise me, we have a hard time keeping secrets."

"We actually found the KH-14 video highly useful as it gave us a better look at the battle from a different angle."

"General, can you tell me where Sargent Hawthorne and *Binii 'ligaii* are at this moment?"

"Sally Fairbanks, General Níngsī has requested I send you some pictures he took with his cell phone he knows works on your system and we have your phone number so those photographs have been sent to your private phone number. If you turn on your cell phone now, you will see what we sent in case there are any questions."

Sally pulled her cell phone out of her pocket and turned it on. It booted up quickly and she actually had good reception and four bars so signal strength was good. She checked her inbox and sure enough was a number of new mails from XYZ who she assumed was General Níngsī. She opened up the first email and sure enough the Medicine Man and Sargent Hawthorne were standing by General Níngsī on his battle bridge with all the displays showing information and the huge room of his Command Ship fully exposed. She said to herself, "Oh my god, CIA analysts will have some fun with this picture.

It was clear to her the historical significance of all this: Sargent Hawthorne and *Binii 'ligaii* (screeching owl) from the *Béésh Łigaii Atsu* (Silver Eagle) Native American Tribe and their medicine man were the first two humans from planet Earth to participate in a Space War.

Another factor that Sally would discover later, during a lunch break discussion, General Níngsī while having a conversation with *Binii 'ligaii* heard some of the supposed ancient tribal history that included interactions with Aliens and stories how they defeated the great Evil Alien invaders.

General Níngsī and his Artificial Intelligence quickly analyzed the Ancient Tribal folklore and came to the realization it was actually a great strategy. At this moment just before the next critical phase of the battle, the Zhrakzhongs had Sun Tzu, Clausewitz, and Tribal Warfare techniques that were easily converted to three dimensional. The Xīnggui knew none of this and soon Admiral Aete would do some soul searching to figure out why General Níngsī seemed to know in advance every move he was making. His crews were starting to unravel. That is the mental mindset he witnessed before when they were greatly hurt in battles such as during the Battle of Huátiělú. Will this turn into another Battle of Huátiělú? Will he ever see his home again? Was he starting to have self-doubt like those seemed to have around him as well? Admiral Aete knew the first Axiom of War: *If you expect failure, you will fail.*

Admiral Aete could not do what General Níngsī could, "Request reserves, because another one of his blunders is he took them all with him. He was so convinced in the INTEL that he would catch General Níngsī with his pants down on Earth, the thought of a protracted campaign with potentially devastating losses just didn't seem possible. And here he was facing exactly that, but the worst was just about ready to happen.

After reviewing all the images, they sent Sally Fairbanks, she said, *"Binii'łigaii* (screeching owl) medicine man's wife *Nizhóní Ch'ilátah Hózhóón (beautiful flower)* will be asking us when we return to the village without her husband, "Where is he?"

The General realizing the situation Sally was in knew he had to answer this question with the only plausible statement.

"Show her the pictures on your cell phone and tell her, he is with General Níngsī doing very important work, and the General has stated, some ideas and information that *Binii 'łigaii* has provided is very valuable and when he gets back in a few days he will be rewarded for this."

"I'm not too sure how *Nizhóní Ch 'ilátah Hózhóón* will handle this."

"The Zhrakzhongs were very fortunate for the assistance that *Binii 'łigaii* and Sargent Hawthorne had provided. Another nice piece of information: never in the history of such an important Space Battle has people from a far-off civilization been invited aboard to participate and watch firsthand the entire battle. *Binii 'łigaii* and Sargent Hawthorne are thus now historical figures in Zhrakzhong History."

"General, I'm supposed to hop on that helicopter and go back to Washington and give them a report in all this. However, what you have just informed me of, leads me to believe *Nizhóní Ch 'ilátah Hózhóón* will be having a rough night. Someone needs to stay with her until her husband comes back. She will take it very hard if *Binii 'łigaii* is killed in this Space Battle. Since I'll be staying with her, have one of your men come and update me a couple times a day until this is all over."

"Sally Fairbanks, I'm absolutely sure General

Níngsī will be pleased to learn of your actions."

"I appreciate your kind words General."

On behalf of all the Zhrakzhongs I want to personally thank you because the time you spent with General Níngsī before he departed helped his psychology immensely."

"I'm glad he enjoyed the time. I certainly did."

"He left here to go into battle pleased and informed me personally that he will go off to battle feeling very positive for being around you and enjoying time with you just before he had to deploy."

"Well thank you for all that. But I would like to go back to the Village now and be with *Nizhóní Ch'ilátah Hózhóón* until her husband returns."

"I'll take you there now."

Sally Fairbanks and Doctor Brandenhagen were taken back to the *Béésh Łigaii Atsu* village where Sally met Nizhóní *Ch'ilátah Hózhóón* standing by her home.

"Hello *Nizhóní Ch'ilátah Hózhóón*, I want to talk to you but first I need to give Doctor Brandenhagen some information as he needs to fly back to Washington right away."

"You are not going with him?"

"I'm going to stay here until your husband returns with Sargent Hawthorne."

"You certainly are welcome if you can handle living in our village."

"Nizhóní Ch'ilátah Hózhóón if I told you where I've had to sleep sometimes in the past you would know I will have it pretty good here in comparison.

"Sally, what did you want to say to me?" Roger Brandenhagen asked acting slightly impatient.

"Roger us walk up to the Helicopter I will tell you on the way."

After they were far enough away from the village as to not have anyone there hearing their conversations, Sally said, "You will have to go back and brief the DCI. With all the crap going down about my little joy ride with General Níngsī, it's probably best I stay out of DC for a few days anyway."

"Okay, what do you want me to tell them?"

"When we get up to the helicopter, I'll forward all those pictures to you. Do not give them to anyone but Mike Barnes. Do not even let anyone know you got them or your life could easily become a living hell."

"Gotcha."

"Ask for a private meeting with Mike Barnes, he's a reasonable person. He has an internet address where you can send those low side pictures up to the High Side where they will go into a protected environment. As soon as you send the pictures, erase them from your cell phone. You do not want to be in possession of any of those pictures because if the bad guys discover it, you could come up missing."

"I understand."

"After you brief Mike Barnes tell him you need

to talk with the DCI on another matter. He will be confused as to why I'm still here. While you are with the DCI and Mike Barnes together inform them about *Binii'łigaii* and Sargent Hawthorne. Ask the DCI to call General Short to inform him where Sargent Hawthorne is due to the sensitivity of all this."

As they continued walking towards the Helicopter Sally started forwarding all the emails with the photographs to Roger Brandenhagen so by the time, they got to the helicopter she was able to turn off her cell phone and save the battery. Perhaps she would ask the Army guys if they had a charger with them since they usually had everything including portable generators.

Nizhóní Ch'ilátah Hózhóón watched Sally Fairbanks walk down the hill in a very cheerful manner. The thought she would be out of reach of the DCI and the SAC for a few days pleased her.

When Sally approached *Nizhóní Ch'ilátah Hózhóón* she could hear the helicopter revving up its two General Electric T700 turboshaft engines behind her.

A turboshaft engine is a form of gas turbine that is optimized to produce shaft horse power rather than jet thrust. Turboshaft engines have high power output, high reliability, small size, and light weight. A moment later the helicopter was in the sky heading South to Tucson.

Just like in the past the Zhrakzhong escorts arrived and flew the helicopter down to almost 50 miles from Tucson. It did not take the Blackhawk long to cover the distance to Davis-Monthan Air Force where air traffic controllers directed it to its favorite landing spot, exactly where it would be tied down for the night and refueled.

The CIA's GS700 Corporate Jet stood by at the ready with Mable Potter standing by the ladder. Mable was surprised not to see Sally Fairbanks.

As soon as Doctor Brandenhagen got near the ladder for the GS700 he informed Mable Potter, "Sally is staying with the *Béésh Łigaii Atsu* (Silver Eagle) Native American Tribe, we had some new developments.

"When will she fly back to DC?"

"My guess is when she damn well feels like it. Sally has a way with her."

"That she does, but there are not many women in the CIA who work as hard as she does."

"I've seen her in action. I know what you mean."

"Alright, hop aboard so we can get out of here."

"My pleasure," Roger Brandenhagen said as he was also thinking about that nice long hot bath when he got home. He had several of those Epsom Salt bags at home for when he wanted an extra-long bath to sooth his muscles after a tough day.

Five minutes later they were airborne and climbing rapidly with an extra light aircraft because the pilots decided they could wait and have the plane refueled back at Andrews so they could enjoy this fast takeoff almost straight up to 50,000 feet. Within moments after getting to 50,000 feet where they didn't have to worry about traffic except possibly an SR-72 or a TR-3B, they hit Mach 0.9 right where the autopilot and auto throttles were set.

Thanks to the wonderful tail winds pushing them along as the jet stream was heading in the exact same direction they were, they touched down at Andrews in just three hours. It was only 10:00 P.M. so Roger was enthused he would get a nice long sleep after he had his bath and popped his melatonin pills.

The Limo driver was slightly confused that Sally Fairbanks wasn't with Roger since she was on the itinerary of who to take home.

Roger explained it and said, "Do us a favor and do not let anyone know I came home alone because I want a good night sleep and because of events that happened today, Sally doesn't want to be disturbed and she has her phone turned off."

"Allright Roger, I usually send in my rider list late at night when I'm done, but I'm off the clock at that time and nobody looks at it anyway. I'll submit it first thing in the morning. If they bitch about it, I will say I wasn't authorized overtime."

"Good plan."

Sally made a good choice because had she came back with Roger Brandenhagen its likely she would have got snakebit by some of the State Department dickheads that were making a big deal over what she did in order to promote themselves in the eyes of their supervisors to climb the ladder of success. Her delay in returning worked out best for everyone.

Back at the *Béésh Łigaii Atsu* (Silver Eagle) Native American Tribe Village, Sally and *Nizhóní Ch'ilátah*

Hózhóón (beautiful flower) medicine man's wife had gone inside her home because she figured Sally was hungry and something to say she didn't want to say in front of other Tribe members.

"This really tastes good," Sally said.

"I'm glad you like it."

The fresh baked bread with real butter added to an exquisite meal for Sally.

"What kind of meat is this?"

"That's deer meat that *Binii'łigaii* shot. Normally I would not be able to make that for you, but with the money Sargent Hawthorne helped us make selling beef to the Aliens, we got that new refrigerator and a solar system with a battery storage to keep the refrigerator running day and night."

"It's really tasty, that's for sure."

"The sauce I used is a native mixture of urbs and spices. The meat soaked in the special marinade over night. I was planning to make that dish for *Binii'łigaii* but I assumed you were going to tell me he's not coming home tonight."

"I might as well tell you now, he's not coming home tonight and I'm not sure exactly when he and Sargent Hawthorne will come back."

"Is he safe where he's at?"

"*Nizhóní Ch'ilátah Hózhóón*, I'm never going to lie to you or hold the information from you, but in order to protect me, you must not tell anyone what I'm about to tell you."

"Okay, I understand. I have not lived in this village my entire life. I used to live with the Navajo people and I attended college and had good grades, but I fell in love with *Binii 'łigaii* while I was a teenager. After I graduated from college with a degree in the Financial Services, I came home and tried working for Morgan Stanley for a few months but my heart wasn't into handling other people's money. I knew who I loved and I sought him out. He was single and available and the assistant Medicine man for this tribe. The Medicine man he replaced died from old age making him the new Medicine man. I had my friend drive me down here and when I saw *Binii 'łigaii* he saw that look in my eye and knew why I came. He was happy, his heart was overflowing with happiness. We were the perfect couple. I had seen the cruel world and knew down deep inside; I would feel far more spiritualistic with *Binii 'łigaii*. And if you know my people's history, once I was married to *Binii 'łigaii*, my family disowned me.

"That's sad," Sally responded.

"Actually, I'm not sad," I got what I wanted. A wonderful and intelligent and caring husband who has treated almost every single tribe member multiple times. They have faith in him."

Sally had just completed her meal as *Nizhóní Ch'ilátah Hózhóón* finished speaking and thought now might be the time to lay her cards on the table and show *Nizhóní Ch'ilátah Hózhóón* where her husband really was and what he was doing.

"I have some photos and videos of where your

husband is and what he is doing."

"May I see them."

"You may, but I must warn you it may frighten you. If you do not think you can handle the severity of some of these video's you should not look at them, but if you want to see it. Then I will show you."

"I need to see it. If something happens to my husband, I want to know what it was that took him away from me."

"Alright but I do not recommend letting your kids see this."

"Sure, give me a minute."

Nizhóní Ch'ilátah Hózhóón stood up and instructed her children to go into their bedroom, read some books and stay there until they were told they could come out. She walked with them to the door to their bedroom and shut it after she saw each kid had a book in their hands.

"Okay Shelly, let me see what you got."

Shelly then showed all the pictures first, then the spectacular video. *Nizhóní Ch'ilátah Hózhóón* was suddenly a changed person. While in college she had seen Star Wars movies and other science fiction thrillers, and here was *Binii'ligaii*, just as if he were on the Battlestar Galactica in a major space battle. It was rather astonishing. *Nizhóní Ch'ilátah Hózhóón* would say a lot of prayers tonight because the Tribe could ill afford to lose their one and only medicine man. He had not chosen or started training his replacement. That was years into the future. She also did not want to lose her precious love, a man who captivated her like no other with his kindness, sweetness, and deep and sensitive thoughts.

Nizhóní Ch'ilátah Hózhóón then surprised Sally as she walked over and grabbed a cell phone off the top of the new refrigerator and came back to the kitchen table and asked, "Could you please send me those files. One day *Binii'łigaii* may want to look at them or show his grandkids."

"I will, but do yourself a favor and do not show it to anyone because it could cause you a lot of trouble when people discover what your husband had done. He will have to keep this to himself for the rest of his life."

"I understand completely. As a student studying the financial services industry, I had to look at a lot of news reports and see how that impacted the movement of securities. I know people can be vicious. This is for our consumption only."

Sally was feeling a lot better knowing she was talking with a sophisticated woman who had seen the modern world at the same time had not given up her native American roots where she chose to live in her Husband's tribe.

Sally was also grateful for another matter and asked, "*Nizhóní Ch'ilátah Hózhóón*, would it be possible to use your cell phone charger, I didn't bring one with me, and I plan on staying until your husband returns."

"Sally, the charger cable is up on top of the refrigerator, feel free to hook up your cell phone anytime. It's hooked to the same power that provides the refrigerator."

"Thank you I really appreciate that. I'm afraid some of the people I work for will be calling me tomorrow and my cell phone battery would run down."

The women continued talking casually about irrelevant things as the evening slipped into night and Sally later suggested she sleep on the sofa in case someone called her from work, she didn't want to disturb the family. She also placed her phone on silent ringing where she would feel the vibration, then go outside and talk if necessary.

The Limo dropped Roger Brandenhagen off in front of his home. He walked up the sidewalk and saw the second shift guys were there and the Television Trucks were long gone. *Perhaps they gave up on me?*

The first shift CIA guys informed the second shift, "Roger said its okay to use his bathroom and to stop peeing on the bushes."

As Roger reached his porch, one of the second shift guys said, "Your bushes are safe tonight and we put in a couple extra rolls of toilet paper in your house just in case."

"Thank you."

Roger was getting kind of hungry so he went in the Kitchen and noticed the coffee pot had fresh coffee smell like it was freshly brewed. He also noticed several bags of Starbucks coffee bags.

"These are decent guys, Roger thought.

After putting together a snack and a drink that hit the spot, Roger went upstairs and made his way to the master bedroom and started the water running and poured in his Epsom Salt then undressed and hopped in. *Man does this feel good!* Roger thought.

After the bath and some melatonin, Roger laid down in his bed with a book about the Space Force, Project Jupiter and began reading where he last left off where the book marker was. After about an hour when he knew, he was starting to feel drowsy thanks to the melatonin, he sat the book aside and turned out the reading light and shut his eyes as he attempted some silent meditation and before he knew it, it was morning. He woke up and could smell what appeared to be fresh coffee. There was another odor that was pleasing: Bacon!

Roger put on his robe and walked down into the Kitchen and there was one of the first shift guys cooking the bacon.

"How do you like your eggs and toast?"

"Sunny side up and the toast not too burnt."

"Have a seat Roger, I'll be serving your breakfast in about five minutes. Would you care for some orange juice?"

"Sure."

The CIA man pulled a new orange juice container out of the refrigerator and poured a glass for Roger.

"Roger suddenly realized he didn't know the spook's name. Say buddy what's your name?"

"Kevin."

"Pleased to meet you, Kevin."

"Likewise."

"Kevin, you made one huge mistake."

"What's that boss?"

"There is only one place setting at this table, there needs to be two, so you can sit down with and have some of that great smelling coffee and bacon too."

"That's very kind of you Roger."

Roger stood up and said, "I'll take care of it. You just keep cooking and make some for your three Amigos."

"That's what we are talking about boss."

"I'm sure one of the guys in the back can come in at a time and you can relieve your buddy out front later so he can get something to eat."

"I'm sure he'll appreciate it."

After all the food was set out and the two men started munching down, and enjoying that wonderful coffee that made such a fantastic aroma, Roger asked a few questions.

"Tell me Kevin about your journey, how did you get tied up with the CIA?"

"Roger, I started out in the Marine Corps after I finished college and the ROTC. After six years in the Marine Corps where I became the company commander of a drone squadron, the agency recruited me."

"So' you left the Marine Corps and went CIA?"

"They recruited me while on active duty and put me in some paramilitary operations. Once they decided they needed me more that the Marine Corps did, they pulled some administrative prank and in a days' time I was out of the Marine Corps and suddenly an intelligence officer in the CIA."

"I don't want to offend you Kevin, but how can guarding someone's home be exciting?"

"Roger, its more complicated than you realize."

"How's that?"

"Not only do we have to worry about those News Media trucks out there every day, but you are a person of interest, not only to the CIA, but also MSS, FSB (KGB), MI6, PSIA, and a few others."

"Who's the PSIA?"

"Public Security Intelligence Agency of Japan." [(公安調査庁, *kōanchōsa-chō*)]

"Are they like the CIA that does foreign espionage?"

"Theoretically they only do domestic spying to detect espionage and sabotage, and other crimes."

"Why would they come here?"

"Normally the Naikaku Jōhō Chōsashitsu [Naichō (内調)] would do this kind of spying, but to give the Prime Minister deniability, the have the PSIA do it."

"Why would the Japanese be interested in me?"

"For the same reason the Chinese MSS are."

"Because I did a TV show?"

"Roger, I hate to be the bearer of bad news, but China, Russia, Japan, and Great Britain know you have spent some time with the Aliens."

"What would they do with me?"

"Kidnap you and take you some place and give you an interrogation like you never had before."

Suddenly Roger got the big picture, he was basically a sitting duck and these four CIA men were here for far more than keeping those pesky news people away from his house. Which means they are experts of detecting surveillance and attempts to get Roger. He might as well sign up for the witness protection program now!

Roger then thought of something he would do that would probably give this CIA man something to think about.

"Kevin, I have something I'm going to show you now. Most of America and the rest of the world probably do not know what's going on. I have some videos and pictures I will be giving to the DCI later today as I'm sure they will be picking me up in a while to attend a meeting."

Roger pulled his cell phone out of his robe and typed in the passcode and selected some pictures and handed his cell phone to Kevin who took a look. The 8-foot-tall alien in the picture looked exactly like the person who came here with Roger the other day.

Kevin suddenly was unhappy because he knew he was probably going to get polygraphed for looking at these photo's but suddenly he didn't give a shit. He was glad to see what inside a huge Alien Space ship looked like. He also knew the two others standing by the Alien did not look Alien and could pass for Mexicans.

"Who's the other two guys?"

"One of them is a medicine man for a native American Tribe. The other is retired Marine Corp Sargent Hawthorne."

"What are they doing on the Alien ship?"

"They are participating in the Space Battle."

"There is a Space Battle going on?"

Roger said, "Sure is let me pull up a video for you."

Moments later Kevin was watching and astonished.

"This is fucking insane," Kevin said after a while.

"Now you know why I will be getting a ride in a while. I expect to get my wakeup call any moment."

Kevin knew there was more to the story, and he didn't want to know anymore. All this was challenging his religious beliefs. Faith was having a huge problem this morning.

Roger then said, "I'm done eating, cycle the guys in I want them to have some of this. He then got up and walked over to the dish washer and put the dirty dishes in it. When he left home to fly out West, his dish washer was full of dirty dishes. Now it was empty and there was soap in there ready to go. Roger was impressed what these guys were doing, plus it would save his bushes!

Roger went upstairs to dress decently and as predicted, he got his phone call and was out in front of his home thirty minutes later getting into a company black SUV.

In a brief period of time Roger was back in the conference room after others had just left with their marching orders: *Locate Sally Fairbanks who was missing in action.*

Mike Barnes wasted little time before he asked, "Do you know where Sally Fairbanks is?"

"Yes, she's at the *Béésh Łigaii Atsu* (Silver Eagle) Native American Tribe."

"Why did she stay there?"

"I probably should not have brought my cell phone in here, but I have some pictures and videos to give to you and after you look at them we can discuss why she remained behind."

"You should not have brought that cell phone in here."

"Where do you want me to send these videos and pictures."

"Give me a minute I have a special laptop with a cable you can transfer the files to."

Moments later Greg was spitting the pictures and videos to the laptop that had special software to suck in data from cell phones so that spies could take such information and promptly email it to a special address without actually going to the internet.

Because of file sizes it took 15 minutes to do all the transfers, then Mike Barnes started looking at all the pictures first then moments later he started playing the videos.

It's one thing to see a space battle from far away via a KH-14 satellite. It was another thing to see it from the sensors of the alien ships up close. Mike Barnes was captivated in what he watched. It also scared the living dog crap out of him because he saw first-hand the horrific ability these huge ships had. Earth had no way to protect itself. We were at the mercy of the Aliens.

Even though some of the ships were thousands of miles apart, because of the loop that Admiral Aete was attempting, they got really close in some cases only a few miles apart. Watching those Xīngguī Molecular Disrupter Cannons and Zhrakzhongs Plasma Debilitater weaponry tear each other's ships up with those massive beams was very sobering.

After Mike Barnes finished looking at the last video, he turned towards one of the SAC agents and said, "Go get Mr. Bissonnette."

About 5 minutes later the SAC agent returned with another gentleman who ostensibly was Mr. Bissonnette.

"What do you need Mr. Barnes?"

Mike Barnes turned and looked at Doctor Brandenhagen and said, "Roger, these photographs and videos have been just now classified as TS-SCI with -V, Q, and T tags. They are now extremely highly classified which means you can no longer be in possession of them. With the possibility of us forcibly giving you a polygraph, have you sent copies of these pictures and videos anywhere?"

"Absolutely not."

"Alright, how did you get them?"

"The Aliens gave them to us. Sally wanted me to make sure I gave them to you and nobody else. Her instructions were quite explicit in that she only felt safe to give them to you and the DCI. She wants the DCI to see all this."

"Roger we are going to have to clean your phone. Mr. Bissonnette is not only a technologist; he is also a forensics expert and will make sure your phone has no traces of those photos or videos left."

"Sure, I'll let you do that as soon as the DCI sees the pictures."

"You might have to wait a while, he's a busy man."

"Sally has earned my trust. I will wait however long required. But I will not let Mr. Bissonnette touch my cell phone until the DCI sees the pictures and videos."

"All right I will contact him and explain this to him and see when he can come here to view all this."

"Thank you I appreciate it."

"You're welcome."

Mike Barnes then looked at Mr. Bissonnette and said, "Please have a seat. I'm going to find out when the DCI can see us."

Five minutes after Mike Barnes left the room, he returned and said, "Roger you are in luck, the DCI will be here in a few minutes."

Within another five minutes or so the DCI marched smartly in the room and Mike Barnes said, "It might be better if you look at this on the laptop instead of his phone."

"Can you just hook the laptop up to one of those video monitors?"

"Sure."

Mike Barnes walked over to one of the blank video monitors and grabbed the coiled-up video cable and undid the Velcro so he could unwind it and hook it up to the laptop.

Moments later the large flat screen was showing all the pictures and videos. Roger could see that observing these videos had a big effect on the DCI.

After the video finished, the DCI looked at Mike Barnes and said, "If those two Americans come back alive, I want them brought here for debriefings so they can tell us their stories and fill in the blanks."

The DCI looked at Roger and asked, "Tell me why Sally didn't come back with you."

"Sir, it's quite apparent she wanted to stay with *Nizhóní Ch'ilátah Hózhóón (beautiful flower)*, the medicine man's wife in case he dies in this space battle. She knows *Nizhóní Ch'ilátah Hózhóón* will take it really hard. Also, the Zhrakzhongs promised her they would send out a representative every day to inform her of what is happening so she can prepare *Nizhóní Ch'ilátah Hózhóón* in case there is some really bad news."

Mike Barnes being the consummate professional said, "Doctor Brandenhagen, the DCI has looked at the video and the photographs, may we please have your phone now to remove all the images?"

"Sure, no problem."

The DCI then figured out what he needed to do next. "Roger, I don't like breaking up a good team you helped create. Pack your bags, I'm sending you back to Arizona. Instead of landing at the Airforce Base, you will go to the nearest Airport so you can rent a car, and help Sally with what she needs. You can get a room at a nearby hotel."

"Sir, the nearest hotel is one or two hours away."

"That's okay, I hear Arizona is very scenic. Enjoy the drive."

"How soon do I leave?"

"It shouldn't take you more than 30 minutes to pack what you need for a long stay. When you are all set, the driver will take you some place nearby to hop on a helicopter to fly you over to Andrews. That GS700 is probably ready to fly now. We have new pilots ready every morning for matters like this."

Roger was soon back traveling to Arizona. He then asked Mable Potter to call Sally and inform him he was on the way and anything she needed to order it at a store near where he was landing and he would pick up the package before he drove down to the *Béésh Łigaii Atsu* (Silver Eagle) Native American Tribe village.

Mable made a command decision and on the way to Arizona she redirected the GS700 to Denver because she knew just the store at the Airport that would have everything Sally needed.

After Roger and Mable got into the airport terminal via a gate often used by the CIA for access to their underground facility under the Airport Mable could not divulge to Roger, she said, "Roger, I'm going to go buy Sally all the things she asked for. Here's a couple hundred dollars, go to that steakhouse over there and get yourself, me, and the two pilots a meal. Get them the New York strip. I'll have their lovely shrimp salad; you get whatever you want. I'll meet you back on the airplane."

Mabel had a lot of money. One of her buddies in the CIA who played the stock market and probably got a lot of insider information offered to manage her stock trading account not associated with her retirement. After the huge loss she took in 2008, Mable was more than happy to have someone who knew what they were doing make those trades for her. Her buddy told her, "Never look at your stock account until I let you know its ok, because I do not want you to get nervous and freak out."

As such he did amazingly well and after he did

his exit strategies now and then when her account was flush with cash and a few stocks he informed Mable now is the time she could look at her account.

Mable once asked the friend, "Where's all the stocks?"

"You are now in cash as I see a Black Swan event coming up. This administration has their head's so far up their asses, they will give us this gift."

"What do you mean by a gift?"

"The dude has no clue and we'll be seeing a 25% correction real soon."

"How do you know that?"

"It's baked in the tea leaves, don't ask."

The man was right again!

Mabel had her password; she could look at her stock trading account anytime she wanted. A few days after the big drop in the stock market she was glad she had that huge pile of cash with no risk. The following week the market seemed to stabilize. Wall street personalities were saying now's the time to buy, but a lot of people who just gave an ounce of blood in the stock market drop were not willing to put any more money in the market.

On a hunch Mabel went into her account a week later and looked. She had no cash and a lot of stocks! Her friend played that black swan event perfectly!

$200 was chump change to her now. Just this year alone her stock trading account was up 1667%. She truly hoped one day she didn't have to explain to the Inspector General's office how she came up with all that wealth. She knew she would just tell the investigators, check my stock account, I'm a good stock picker!

Out in the middle of nowhere it seems next to a small town, the Navajo's have an impressive medical facility. What is also amazing is next to the hospital they have a nice paved runway so that Navajo medicine men can fly their patients to this facility for emergency surgery and other critical medical needs because their reservation is quite large. Getting them to the facility via automobile would take too long to save lives of tribe members who suffer a major heart attack, stroke or other pressing medical emergency. That paved runway was perfect for the GS700.

Thanks to the General who not only knew Sargent Hawthorne, he also personally knew other retired Marines who lived nearby who were there to pick up Roger and give him a lift to the *Béésh Łigaii Atsu* (Silver Eagle) Native American Tribe village which allowed him to avoid that helicopter ride from Tucson.

The General informed Roger Brandenhagen in a phone call while he was flying from Denver to the medical facility: "You do not need a rental car. My guys will give you any transportation you need. Plus, it will let you do a lot of sightseeing."

The GS700 landed at the medical facility and the pilot figured the Jeep near the end of the runway was Roger's ride. There were no fences. Anyone could just drive onto the Tarmac. They could do that here because in this part of the country people respect one another and city trash wasn't welcome.

Roger stepped down the ladder nice and full from the steak sandwich Mabel bought him. And since the plane was on the ground waiting for Mable who was in charge to give the two Air Force officers their directions, they had about 15 or 20 minutes to enjoy those New York strips Roger brought them with a little note inside: *Mable bought this for you. Please be nice to her.*

Roger wasn't going to come back anytime soon, so the GS700 flew back to Andrews and was immediately prepped for the next mission.

Roger was starting to think: *it seems like all these Navajo's like Jeeps.*

The landscape around that area had a lot of flat land, but it also had some rough areas too and it helped to have a four-wheel Jeep for many of them. The new Jeeps were just as comfortable as an automobile, so why not?

Roger soon met another retired Marine driving the Jeep parked at the end of the runway, named Gáagii Adakai. Gáagii was named after the crow that was making a lot of noise outside the window of his parent's bedroom while he was born. Gáagii's father said, "I'm going to go get my shotgun and silence that thing."

Gáagii's mother steep in native traditions responded, "You can't shoot that bird. It was sent here from the gods to give our son a name."

Just like Sargent Hawthorne, Gáagii was a brave Marine that most others hoped was near them when the fighting started.

Gáagii was very savvy and had been around Marine Aviation and knew the proper time to pull up to the jet. He pulled up about 15 feet from the ladder of the Jet and got out.

"Are you Sargent Gáagii USMC retired?"

"Marines never retire, we just take a long break, yes that's me."

True to his form, once a Marine, always a Marine.

The pilots helped carry the luggage and packages down and wanted to stretch their legs and smell the fresh air of the Wild West. They too soon met Sargent Gáagii USMC retired (on long vacation). The Air Force officers who respected Marines a great deal because they had protected them flying in and out of Afghanistan and Iraq. It was Marines like Sargent Gáagii Adakai they owed their lives, so the handshakes were respectful and genuine.

Sargent Gáagii Adakai's favorite General made sure he knew this was another real mission and even though he wasn't getting paid, "Make sure and keep up the reputation of the Marine Corp."

"General, with my fat paycheck from my retirement, health care, and good investing I did over the years while I was deployed to the middle east, money is no longer necessary. I welcome these assignments because it gets kind of boring waiting to hear the chickens in the morning."

"Perhaps I need to give you a more difficult assignment, Sargent Adakai."

"General, you know you can count on me any time."

"Sargent Adakai, once again you know I appreciate your services. Its guys like you that make the difference."

"Thank you General, I promise to never let down the Marine Corp."

"Sargent Adakai, I know I can count on you and I do appreciate that."

"Thank you General, it looks like we are loaded up and ready to go. The Airforce Officers flying the plane helped to load up the cargo."

"That's good to hear Sargent Adakai, that's what I like, teamwork."

"I'll let them know General."

"Talk to you again soon Sargent Adakai."

"Take care General."

Mable Potter had been at a few cocktail parties with the General and on the way back to DC will inform the two pilots how the 4 Star General appreciated their great support when she shows them the text message she received.

A number of minutes later after Sargent Adakai and Roger Brandenhagen waved good bye to Mable and the two pilots, they were driving down a well-maintained two-lane U.S. hiway. In about an hour they turned onto the dirt road that led down to the *Béésh Łigaii Atsu* Village.

The Army personnel manning the road-block was expecting them. A second Lieutenant was there to supervise the troops stepped up to the Jeep on the driver's side and said, "You must be Sargent Adakai USMC."

"That's right sir."

"My guys are moving the barrier for you. It will take just a moment."

"No problem."

"Pleased to meet you Sargent Adakai."

"Pleased to meet you also sir. Give my best regards to all these soldiers."

"You can count on that Sargent Adakai. You can now proceed; the barrier is out of your way."

"Thank you, sir."

The officer saluted and Sargent Adakai saluted back."

"The General who talked to that second lieutenant about 30 minutes prior explained to him, the valor this Sargent carried with him. He really was a true American hero an had been through far more hell than the officer could imagine. But as he was taught in the Marine Corp, *what doesn't kill you will help make you a better person.*

The real truth is Sargent Adakai missed being on missions and being with his Marine brothers. He felt lucky Sargent Hawthorne was around these parts.

"That's Sargent Hawthorne's Jeep."

"It is but don't ask any questions."

"Is he here?"

"Sorry, that's what you guys call OPSEC.

Sargent Adakai parked his Jeep next to Sargent Hawthorne's Jeep and at that time, *Nizhóní Ch'ilátah Hózhóón* and Sally Fairbanks walked out of the house to help carry things indoors.

"You sure came back quickly?"

"I was worried about your safety so I came as quick as I could."

"Yea but I bet tonight it will be me protecting you."

"I don't mind having a younger woman protecting me."

"We do not have any hotel rooms here in the village."

"Not a problem. This evening, Sargent Adakai is going to drive me to the town where he lives. His cousin owns a hotel there. I've reserved a room."

"You too scared to stay here?"

"Since a fine-looking woman like yourself is staying here, I need plausible deniability."

"We could make you a bed up in the hayloft."

"It's best we avert any rumors by the distance."

"Thanks for bringing me all these things. Mabel texted me a list of everything I asked for. I really do appreciate it."

"Does that mean you can stay indefinitely?"

"Some of the things I had sent out here are for *Nizhóní Ch'ilátah Hózhóón* to give her husband a lot of pleasure when he returns."

"That's smart planning, but who's going to take care of the kids?"

"The Tribe knows how to handle full moon nights, not to worry."

Chapter Fourteen

Meditation

On the Xīnggui province of Màichōng, Emperor Shāyú's Chief of Security Xié'è de Gōngniú who was now feeling a transcendental moment of surreal manifestations from his first experience with the Tytrone Philosophers silent Meditation methods. While he was sleeping last night at home after the experience, he heard the chimes and the Bong in his dream and the words Yǎngwàng Xīngxīng kept repeating in the midst of flowing colors in his mind. He didn't know how long it lasted, but eventually daylight returned and he was rudely awakened by his wakeup call from his most trusted assistant Bùlǔtúsī.

"I'm sorry to disturb you but Emperor Shāyú wants to see you right away."

"I wonder what he wants?"

"Before I could get a chance to ask him, he ended the communication link."

"Alright, pick me up in front of my home in 30 centons."

"See you then."

Xié'è de Gōngniú hung ended the communications link and went about getting ready. He first drank a vital mineral and energy drink; they used the restroom so he would not have to go again until long after he was finished with the meeting at the Emperor's Palace.

Xié'è de Gōngniú walked into his robotized body scrubber that thoroughly cleaned him and during the process gave verbal guidance like, "Close your eyes and lift up your arms."

The robot-bath took about three minutes, then the automated body blow dryer did its magic including drying his hair so that when he sat down at his personalizer, the automated robotic hair stylist would make him look sharp.

He put on a security suit that had a laser proof vest, and several super battery packs his laser pistol would immediately plug into giving him three or four times the number of laser pistol shots a laser weapon fully charged up normally could do.

His suit looked totally innocuous and he could pass for a banker or a corporate business man with this attire. Most everyone would never guess all the bells and whistles a security suit really had.

Exactly 30 minutes after the phone call he walked out of the front of his home and the skycar came down that his trusted assistant was driving. The door to the skycar lifted up and he stepped inside. Moments later they were in a three-dimensional freeway heading in the direction of the Palace and soon transitioned out of formation of commuter skycars and flew off to the well-hidden Palace.

Since this was controlled airspace, nobody could fly over the Palace. The assistants skycar was vectored by transportation and security services to a parking structure where they landed in a designated parking stall.

They went to Emperor Shāyú's parking lobby they were familiar with that has 7/24 Emperors guards controlling everyone arriving and leaving.

You didn't arrive or leave without Emperor Shāyú's permission. The two men were met with two other XSS men assigned as Xié'è de Gōngniú's body guard to prevent assassination. As they passed by Emperor Guardsmen, one could feel the tension in the air as the two groups despised each other from past history.

Since the Emperor's Guards were recruited from patronage families, they looked down at XSS men who were often recruited from Space Marines and of different social status. The XSS men all thought they had proven themselves in mortal combat before recruited for spy network projects, and they felt the only thing the Emperor Guards could prove is their loyalty to Emperor Shāyú. Hence, they were emotionally and socially miles apart.

Xié'è de Gōngniú was escorted out to a pool where Emperor Shāyú was thrown chunks of meat into the pool filled with fish that had razar sharp teeth and were purposely starved for several days before the Emperor's Guards threw the Emperor Shāyú's enemies in the pool to swim with the fish.

When the pool cleaners drained the pool and

caught all th e fish with nets and put them into an adjacent pool with a lock between them, they removed the remains of the body, which usually was only the skeleton and feet in shoes. The bones were then crushed and added to the fertilizer that kept the surrounding parklike area looking healthy.

Xié'è de Gōngniú never knew for sure when he might have to go take a swim. He hoped today wasn't one of them.

The three other XSS men were held up and asked to remain seated in chairs at a table about 50 feet away from Emperor Shāyú. They were then offered refreshments. The men were always paranoid about being poisoned or worse yet suddenly in need of a toilet, so they declined and sat there observing Emperor Shāyú and their boss.

"Your highness, what did you wish to see me about?"

"Xié'è de Gōngniú, I was just informed you paroled the Tytrone Philosophers."

"That's correct. It was the price we had to pay to get the strategic information of where General Níngsī was hiding with his Generals."

"I want them re-arrested immediately and taken back to Chǒulòu prison."

"Your excellency if we do that, we will jeopardize future INTEL.

"I do not care, I know Admiral Aete will win this huge victory, so we will not be needing much INTEL in the future."

"With all due respect, I advise against taking such actions."

"Xié'è de Gōngniú I gave you an order I expect you to carry out. You know my little fishes here would love to go swimming with you."

Xié'è de Gōngniú received the message loud and clear and responded. "I will have them rearrested immediately."

"Thank you. You are dismissed."

Xié'è de Gōngniú, turned around and walked directly towards his three men and approached them and said, "We have a task to do."

The four men were escorted back to the parking structure by Emperor Guardsmen and returned to their skycars and left. They flew back to Xīngguī Security Service Headquarters where they met in a conference room.

"We have been ordered to rearrest the Tytrone Philosophers"

"How are we going to find them. Many are probably in hiding fearing they would be rearrested."

"I have an idea how we can relocate them. I want each of you to go to individual Tytrone Philosopher Temples spread around Màichōng and have the Monks train you on meditation. After four or five sessions you will know where the Monks are.

"When do we go?" His trusted assistant asked.

"Right now. But I want you to give me a ride back to Kāiwù de Sēngrén's Temple. They can do another meditation training and pick me up in about four hours."

"Yes, sir."

The men stood up and walked back to their skycars to go carry out Xié'è de Gōngniú's instructions.

Kāiwù de Sēngrén was not expecting Xié'è de Gōngniú quite so early and was mildly surprised.

The Tytrone Philosophers were doing meditation training with someone in the special building. Xié'è de Gōngniú could hear the eerie and strange sounds it created even though it was in another building.

"You are very early today."

"We need to talk."

"Us go to my office."

Moments later as Xié'è de Gōngniú was sitting in a visitor's chair facing Kāiwù de Sēngrén at his desk the conversation began:

"What did you want to talk about."

"I just came from Emperor Shāyú. He has ordered me to re-arrest all the Tytrone Philosophers and take them back to Chǒulòu prison.

"What are your plans?"

"You know what I wanted to do. You said as soon as I received this training, I would discover a different method or way to go about dealing with Emperor

Shāyú."

"That's correct and based on yesterday's experiences you will soon discover that realization."

"Us continue with the training; I want to get this done because I'm not enthused to carry out the Emperor Shāyú's latest orders."

The Monk hearing an end to the current training because of no gong sounds since they started talking meant the training was over and they could now enter the sacred building.

"Us go to the Gǔlǎo de Shēngyīn Meditation Center and today you will learn verbal meditation processes."

"I'm ready."

Kāiwù de Sēngrén led Xié'è de Gōngniú to the Gǔlǎo de Shēngyīn Meditation Center not too far away from his office. Inside were five Tytrone Philosopher Monks on their knees sitting and evidently praying together in a low volume chorus that exemplified the nature of their calling.

Kāiwù de Sēngrén quietly motioned to Xié'è de Gōngniú to sit where had been yesterday facing the raised platform where the gong, chimes, and a few other instruments were located.

Kāiwù de Sēngrén quietly walked to each Tytrone Philosopher Monk and for one stanza joined in on the group prayer. That Monk then rose and took his place on the raised platform in front of Xié'è de Gōngniú.

Within a couple minutes, Kāiwù de Sēngrén

repeated the process and the sound slowly died down as each Monk ended his prayer and walked up to the raised platform.

"Today we will do the aural chant for the purpose of obtaining a meditation plateau to enhance your pathway to enlightenment," Kāiwù de Sēngrén stated.

One of the Monks had a flute like instrument, another had the mallet for the Gong, and the other had the hammer like device for the chimes. Another Monk was standing at the table with a variety of bells of different sizes. Their meditative orchestration would soon begin.

One of the Monks began the chant by softly saying, "Yǎngwàng Xīngxīng," followed by a chime of a particular sound.

Kāiwù de Sēngrén then said, "Join the chant and say "Yǎngwàng Xīngxīng," when the others say it.

After Xié'è de Gōngniú joined in for a few minutes, the Monk playing the flute began a series of notes that seemed to articulate the chants.

Kāiwù de Sēngrén sat perpendicular with Xié'è de Gōngniú who faced the other Monks. Mixed in with the flute was intermittent chimes and once in a while as the Flute resonated on certain notes, one of the chimes was struck giving off a surreal resonance that modulated the Flute. After one hundred repeats of "Yǎngwàng Xīngxīng," the Gong was hit and resonated for over half a minute before it died off and could no longer be heard.

Xié'è de Gōngniú slowly slipped into another

mental state. He tried to fight it and the harder his mental struggle the greater the acceleration to that altered state. The music and chants now fully had control of his thoughts. His mind transcended too somewhere else. Bright colors and strange scents permeated his thoughts. His metabolism and breathing slowed. His blood pressure dropped from 120 down to 60 his altered state transfixed his thought processes to new agenda's. His whole personality shifted. He was no longer the cruel bastard he used to be. His ruthless ambitions quickly faded. He was now a cosmic vibration, a butterfly flying into a gentle breeze, total peace was within him. All his demons and fear were gone. He escaped this universe and flew to the heavens watching planets, stars, and galaxies floating past him as he went to that sphere of enlightenment.

Time had no boundaries where Xié'è de Gōngniú went. He easily observed thousands of centuries and the passage of time as those ethereal waves of enlightenment crashed upon him giving him great understanding as each wave passed. He didn't want to leave this palace of enlightenment but something was slowly pulling him back to reality. The sounds slowly decayed until it was utter silence. He opened his eyes and it was darker in the room and all the Monks were gone. He wondered how long he had been gone on this trip to the sphere of enlightenment that somehow, he remembered?

Xié'è de Gōngniú looked down at his arm wrist band that held his communicator, his nuclear clock and a variety of built-in instruments that would enhance his espionage when he conducted it. Over four hours had passed. He wondered, *when did the Monks leave?*

He stood up and knew which way to go to the Temple, figuring that's where they all went. He was wrong. They were all gone, every one of them. Even Kāiwù de Sēngrén was nowhere to be seen. He walked to Kāiwù de Sēngrén's office and the door was open and nobody was present. He walked around the complex, not a soul was there. *Did I jump out into the universe at a different time and place,* he wondered.

There was no use hanging around here. It appeared the Tytrone Philosophers had heeded his warning they would all be arrested in mass and they bugged out.

What can he do now? What can he tell the Tyrant Emperor?

Xié'è de Gōngniú walked out the front of the Temple and looked around. It was definitely later in the day and everything appeared normal. He could see Xīnggui moving about and in the sky, he could see the three-dimensional skycar airways with normal traffic. He looked at the chronometer on his wrist band and it was the same date, just a few hours later.

He called his trusted assistant and requested, "Can you come by the Temple and pick me up?"

"I'll be right there."

Within five minutes the skycar arrived and Xié'è de Gōngniú said, "Take me back to the office."

"Yes, sir."

When he got back to the office, he observed the

other two XSS men sitting in the office. They had arrived thirty minutes earlier.

"How were your experiences?"

"Nothing like I've ever experienced in my life, one of the three said.

Xié'è de Gōngniú could see these were changed men. They were no longer the gung-ho go bust some ribs kind of guys. They too had been transformed.

They all had some transcendental psychological manifestations of conditions they never expected to experience in their lifetimes.

One of the other men offered, "I went into an altered universe and when I woke up, all the Tytrone Philosophers were gone."

"Same here," one of the other men said.

Xié'è de Gōngniú looked at his trusted assistant and asked, "How about you?"

"I know they didn't drug me because I had nothing to eat or drink, but I too slipped into a different universe and when I was awakened, all the Tytrone Philosopher Monks were gone."

"What are we going to tell Emperor Shāyú?" One of the men asked.

"This is our story which is true. We went to visit them to do surveillance and they all disappeared. We'll look at all forms of transportation surveillance videos to see where they went."

Unknown to the Xīngguī Security Service, after

the last roundup of Tytrone Philosopher Monks, they feared the Tyrannical Emperor would send security forces after them, especially when they learned Xié'è de Gōngniú didn't have permission to release them.

The Tytrone Philosopher Monks had numerous loyal Xīngguī who would do anything for them including taking a laser burn through for them. As soon as Kāiwù de Sēngrén knew Xié'è de Gōngniú's mind had entered that deep meditative state and would likely not awaken in hours he stood up walked over to the first Monk and said, "Keep the chant going. We will be leaving soon; we need to escape before all of you are arrested again."

Abbot Kāiwù de Sēngrén went to his office and called one of his volunteers and in their conversation, he said the phrase, "Do you have some new flowers blooming yet?" The volunteer knew that phrase meant: *we will be arrested soon, we are now executing our exit strategy.*

The volunteer answered, "No new flowers today." That phrase meant I understand and *I will contact other followers and your transportation will be arriving soon.*

The most eloquent escape in Xīngguī history now began.

It's quite normal for a number of sky cars to arrive and park at the Temple because groups would come in during the day and experience their meditation and prayers together. Any surveillance would not catch what happened unless they did a series of replays and discovered more people were leaving in certain skycars than what arrived earlier.

Since there were no arrests initiated that morning, there was no surveillance and when the Tytrone Philosophers were evacuated they merely took off their robes and put on street clothes and went to the volunteers skycars and flown out of there. Hence, it would now be a mystery how they avoided the snare.

The Xīnggui Security Service would now start looking for the Monks. Màichōng is a big place with lots of transportation to other planets and provinces. Even though a war was going on out in space a long distance away from Màichōng, life was normal and there had never been any Zhrakzhong attacks on the lesser planets, since they had very little military or commercial value.

People who grew up on those lesser planets and were educated in the finest universities in places like Màichōng often stayed in that province engaged in activities their education prepared them for. However even if they lived in Màichōng, they routinely visited their families back on those remote planets. Before the Xīnggui Security Service started a massive man hunt to discover where the Tytrone Philosophers were, all of them except a couple had already left the planet and were well on their way to worlds and provincial cities on lesser planets scattered across the Xīnggui Empire.

Kāiwù de Sēngrén and his most trusted Monk remained hidden in Màichōng in remote areas that seldom if never saw any Xīnggui Security Service Agents. Some of the Monks made it to Plastras Nostras worlds, the last place Xīnggui Security Service would look for them.

One of the Monks who retired due to age and health moved to Plastras Nostras where there were claims some of the mud baths there, enhanced health and vitality. Even though he's a retired Monk living on a modest pension, he nevertheless remained in contact with Kāiwù de Sēngrén who reached out to him when the Tytrone Philosopher Monks were arrested several years ago. When the Monks were free, the retired Monk was instantly recruited as part of the support structure in the event they had to go into hiding in the future.

Because of the extremely sophisticated exit strategy, the Xīngguī Security Service lost all contact with any Tytrone Philosopher Monk. Xié'è de Gōngniú actually admired the sophistication and daring the Tytrone Philosophers demonstrated when they bugged out.

Members of the Emperor's Guard tipped him off there had been no Tytrone Philosophers arrested. The following day he summoned Xié'è de Gōngniú to his palace for an explanation.

The same four amigos arrived and they were treated more or less the way they had been at their last visit with three of them kept away from Emperor Shāyú.

"How many Tytrone Philosophers arrests have been made?

"None."

"Please explain."

"Someone tipped them off, they all went into hiding."

"With all your toys you should be able to round them up."

"They slipped away with no trace and we have facial recognition recordings of all the Tytrone Philosopher Monks previously arrested, and nobody with those identities has left the planet."

"Then where did they go?"

"We are looking for them."

"The fact Tytrone Philosophers all disappeared demonstrates to a large extent they can't be trusted and are probably engaged in nefarious activities to undermine me."

"I doubt that."

"What makes you say that?"

"They are more interested in souls and not any materialistic or political structure on this planet."

"My spies tell me they are trouble makers."

"I'm your chief spy and I see none of that."

"I have other spies in case you prove to be unreliable and need to take a swim with my fish."

"Your excellency, threatening me is not going to help find the Tytrone Philosophers."

"I might just have to have my spies take over the case and find them."

"Your excellency, as you know with this war going on I'm a busy man working on military intelligence. The Tytrone Philosophers are irrelevant to me, I need to concentrate on more important things like rounding up Zhrakzhong spies."

"You didn't do such a hot job rounding up the three recently."

"They had an ingenious egress plan. One of them was killed."

"At the cost of one of my Space Warships."

"The captain should have been smart enough to realize the craft they call a Mosquito most likely had a booby trap on it. He never should have attempted to capture the spy in the manner he did."

"I want those Tytrone Philosophers rounded up immediately."

"I'll make a bet with you. Have your Spies find the Tytrone Philosophers, if they find them, I'll jump in the pool with your fish. If they can't find them, then after a month I want the honor of tossing them in your pool."

"Go back to work. My spies will find the Tytrone Philosophers."

"As you wish your excellency."

Xié'è de Gōngniú knew the obvious, some idiot in the Emperor's Guards who thinks he's smart feeding the Emperor Intel based on rumor, is going to learn the first lesson in life: *stick to your own talents in your own business and stay out of others.*

After the four made it back to their offices, Xié'è de Gōngniú informed the others: "Emperor Shāyú has some neophyte who thinks he's a spy looking for the Tytrone Philosophers. We are going to sit back and let them do their work. When they fail Emperor Shāyú will be calling us back to his Palace inquiring what we are doing about it."

"What will you say to Emperor Shāyú," His trusted assistant asked.

"I will say, Emperor Shāyú, you told me you had your own spies looking for the Tytrone Philosophers. What's their problem? Why is it they haven't come up with a shred of evidence?"

Chapter Fifteen

The Battle of Wukar

There were a number of directions Admiral Aeta could have taken, but he was so rattled he made the wrong choices as the battle continued at high speed. By pointing Màichōng on the Xīngguī home worlds where he knew Emperor Shāyú's personal defense force remained with lots of ground to space defense systems, he could get his Fleet back to a safe area where they could calm down and figure out their next moves.

Admiral Aeta remembered the Tyrant Emperor Shāyú's threat not to bring the Xīngguī Space Fleet back. Admiral Aeta was willing to sacrifice himself to save the remainder of the Fleet which Xīngguī would desperately need to protect the Empire, even if they lost this battle.

There was no reason for Admiral Aeta to believe the Zhrakzhongs had any sizeable fleet at the Wukar Star System that laid in their path. General Níngsī in his set piece plan had Artificial Intelligence determine all of the most likely courses Admiral Aeta would take if he got blooded and made a run to his home planets to get into their security zone the Zhrakzhongs could ill afford to travel towards.

"If Admiral Aeta travels all the way to the Gamulin Solar System and planet Earth, in a high-speed chase, the most likely course would take them past the Wukar Star System," Artificial Intelligence explained to General Níngsī while at the same time provided graphics in the pre-battle planning.

Admiral Aeta would not travel past Wukar on his way to Earth, but if rattled and making a beeline home after his presence was known, halfway to Màichōng from Earth on the expected high-speed transit, was Wukar.

General Níngsī had his forces well hidden in Wukar and were alerted by high-speed craft that Admiral Aeta had launched his attack and was heading to Earth to wipe out the Zhrakzhongs. The Zhrakzhongs Wukar force sent out probes monitoring the expected approaches assuming this all manifested the way General Níngsī and his Artificial Intelligence expected.

When Admiral Aeta's Xīngguī Fleet approached Wukar the sledge hammer was waiting for him.

"Sir we have detected Zhrakzhong Space Warships ahead of us," The Tactics Supervisor reported looking back towards Admiral Aeta standing on his command platform.

"Can you determine how many?"

"We are still too far away to get good sensor readings to separate out the contacts."

"Is it just a few or is it many?"

"I'm sorry we are still too far away to make that determination."

With General Níngsī hot on his heels he could ill afford to slow down. He had only one choice. Continue on a straight-line course slugging it out with the Zhrakzhongs in front of him, because those behind him would do a lot of damage if they caught up.

"I suppose it really doesn't matter because we have no choice but to fly threw their formations."

"That's bloody suicide," the Tactics Supervisor responded.

"If you look at the rear sensors, you know we can't loop back or do any tactical maneuver's because we know what's behind us. I would rather take my chances with what is in front of me."

"Sir if you must do this, I recommend you put two ships in front of us to take our blows. The fleet cannot afford to lose you at a moment like this."

"Very well position two ships in front of us. If they have to be the battering ram, so be it."

As the drama unfolded, the Sensors operators on the lead ships were now starting to get a better picture and it was ugly no matter how they painted it.

Admiral Aeta thought, *General Níngsī knows every move I'm making, we must have a spy amongst us. I will have to take this to Emperor Shāyú.*

General Níngsī knew the chase would be up as soon as Admiral Aeta got past his Wukar forces. He also knew based Artificial Intelligence, it appeared the

Xīngguī Fleet would simply plow through this force and take any casualties they had. No doubt there would be a lot of survivors due to the closure rate, time on target (TOT) would be cut down and the gut-wrenching close order battles would determine the outcome.

They were now close enough to the Wukar Forces to see them converge with the Xīngguī Fleet on sensor displays. Up until now the space around them was dark because they were not close enough to fire on the Xīngguī and have enough beam shape and TOT to damage the Xīngguī ships. Looking at photonics it was relatively dark with just starlight except for the infrared could see the enemy ships bathed in starlight as they got near any stars.

The battle started when the two converging forces started firing at each other. That lit up the space and General Níngsī could see explosions ahead.

Equal number of ships on both sides were exploding. Admiral Aeta could not tolerate the same level of destruction as the Zhrakzhongs because they still had 95% of their ships intact and Admiral Aeta was down to 600 ships from the original 1000.

He made his choice and he would live with it. The two sacrificial lambs in front of him were destroyed and he made it through the gauntlet unscathed to fight another day.

The Wukar Forces were blooded losing half their ships. However, as Admiral Aeta and the remainder of his fleet got past the Wukar Space Warships, their velocity was such they would never catch up to do any more fighting. It was over for now. To continue the chase would be foolish as in a few more hours the Xīngguī would be close enough to their home worlds to receive substantial reserves if the Emperor Shāyú was willing to commit his personal defense fleet. That question they would never know for sure, so it wasn't worth the gamble.

General Níngsī gathered his fleet together so that Artificial Intelligence could get all their gun camera video the data reduction people could use to splice together a documentary of this huge battle that just happened.

It may not have been a Battle of Huátiělú, but the end results were the same, and now Admiral Aeta was on shaky ground with his Emperor and his highness didn't know Admiral Aeta was by far his best and most experienced Admiral, so if he gave Admiral Aeta to his fish, he would not ever have quite the leader for the future.

By the time the Xīngguī Fleet arrived in orbit of at Màichōng, there were only 500 of the original ships remaining. And of the 500 that remained a lot of them had battle damage and need to go into a space dock and get substantial repairs. If there was a time when the arrogant Emperor Shāyú should have signed the Armistice offered him, it was now.

Since Xié'è de Gōngniú was in charge of all intelligence including military intelligence, his men were overwhelmed with data reduction and documenting the battles. All sensor data recorded was obtained promptly by Xīngguī Security Service personnel who immediately went from ship to ship interviewing all the Captains and Tactical Supervisors. Their qualitative mission reports were gathered with commanding officer endorsement on official inquiry.

A few days later Emperor Shāyú was still arguing with Xié'è de Gōngniú about the disappearance of the Tytrone Philosophers.

"Sir, I do not have time to deal with the Tytrone Philosophers. I have a huge data reduction challenge to give you an accurate picture of what happened to our fleet and the actions Admiral Aeta took."

"I want you to put some priority on rounding up those Tytrone Philosophers."

"With all due respect sir, what's holding up your personal spy A-team? How many leads do they have?"

The emperor knew he had overloaded his asshole with those declarations, but it upset him that Xié'è de Gōngniú was talking to him with such utter disrespect.

"I almost feel like throwing you in with my fish right now."

"Yes, your highness, I know you can do that and there is nothing I could do to prevent it. I serve you. I am your intelligence chief and because your Admiral just bungled this space battle the Empire is at risk. I want you to know that if you did throw me in with your fish, that its possible you would join me soon because that would piss off a lot of my men."

"Are you threatening me Xié'è de Gōngniú?"

"Your highness I serve my Empire with complete dedication. Every day of my life is spent keeping you alive and the Empire safe. If you kill me who's going to protect you? My agents certainly would no longer feel great about foiling any more assassination attempts. They are dedicated to me, see just what your colorful Emperor's Guards can do if they descend upon your palace and kill every one of them. I'm sure that would happen if you kill me. You also need to know you would be helping the Zhrakzhongs if you kill me. Which means your Empire would end sooner than you realize, do you understand?"

"I view your comments as treasonous and insubordination."

"Listen your highness I'm here to keep you alive and the Empire together. Stop being so arrogant and wrecking your own Empire. Every move you make is disastrous. This battle you forced on Admiral Aeta even though he advised you against it just resulted in the loss of half our Fleet. For the sake of the Empire, you need to start listening to those who work for you."

"The Tytrone Philosophers are my enemy. I want them smashed."

"Your excellency, the Tytrone Philosophers are not your enemies. They are merely fleeing your ruthless attacks on them with no basis."

"My spies tell me otherwise."

"The same incompetent spies who can't find them?"

"You do not have the right to talk to me that way."

"Your excellency, there is another way to handle the Tytrone Philosophers."

"What is that?"

"They are obviously still here but in hiding. I know how to arrange a meeting with you and them. I would like to take you to their Temple and experience meditation with them. If you do that, you will quickly discover they are not a threat to you, and I believe the meditation techniques they will teach you will actually help you do a better job maintaining this Empire for future generations."

"Are you sure you are not just setting me up for assassination?"

"Your highness, if I wanted to kill you, then you would have been dead a long time ago. These neophytes that you think protect you cannot stop real assassins. It's only the XSS that keeps you alive."

"What assassination attempts have you thwarted?"

"Your highness, there has been many. But if we tell anyone including you about our success, then it places methods and techniques at risk. To save you we cannot divulge what we do. In reality, your Emperors guards are nothing more than a show piece. Some of the assassins we killed view them as the joke they are."

"They did a good job of keeping them out of the Palace."

"No, they didn't, we killed some of the assassins not too far from where you are sitting."

"I do not believe that."

Alright, I will give you one example and one example only because of your doubt. Come with me over to the flower bed over there I need to show you something we have not had time to clean up."

Emperor Shāyú was now quite animated as he followed Xié'è de Gōngniú over to the flower bed.

"See those yellow flowers?"

"Yes."

"Walk over there and look behind them."

"The emperor did and looked down and said, "I see a huge puddle of a red substance."

"That's about a pint of Xīngguī blood."

"From an assassin?"

"Sir, I really am super busy now with Military Intelligence briefs, I need to get back to work."

Emperor Shāyú looked rather shocked with what he looked at and said, "Sure go back to work, I'll talk to the Emperor's Guards about this."

How the pint of blood ended up behind the flower bed would be a big mystery. Even if it was planted, the Captain of the Emperor's guards had no excuses, why there was that nice puddle of blood only a few feet away from where Emperor Shāyú often reclined enjoying the sunset or watching the stars at night.

The truth is an XSS man attacked the assassin with a knife while he put his hand over his mouth and held him until he knew he was dead. An XSS assistant quickly helped carry the body out of the compound where an electric cart was waiting that hauled the body to a service truck. The electric cart was driven up into the service truck and doors shut. With manipulations of the security system by the XSS, none of this was recorded. Emperor Shāyú's enemies never could figure out what happened to their spy and their insider who belonged to the Emperor's Guards and let the assassin into the courtyard had no idea what happened. The Emperor's Guard Traitor could not be around if Emperor Shāyú was killed.

Meanwhile, General Níngsī gave the Zhrakzhong Fleet their new orders and repositioned them for the next round, which could happen soon if Emperor Shāyú got arrogant and went on the warpath right away.

General Níngsī, his escorts plus a few other Space Warships who exemplified extraordinary valor in the battle turned and made a high speed run back towards Earth. They still had a billion people on that planet that was currently almost defenseless. In the days to come General Níngsī would be ordered to put half of the Zhrakzhong population back on high-speed space craft and take them back to the Zhrakzhongs, home worlds. With the savage destruction the Xīnggui just experienced, it was felt they would no longer be an immediate menace to Zhrakzhong worlds.

General Níngsī figured the best way to do it is abandoning the Mexican complex and disassemble it and send those Zhrakzhongs back first. Then he only needed to defend one location which would make his defenses easier with a smaller force he expected in the days to come as the fighting moved closer to their home worlds.

Roger Brandenburg spent a comfortable night in his hotel in a town that was remarkably nice and low key. Most of the people in the town were Navajo and very polite.

The food at the restaurant was also superb. It was one of America's best kept secrets. People who like to drive U.S. 160 would find this place. During the spring, summer, and fall months, the hotel had high occupancy rates, they had a lot of repeat customers.

Roger took the hint to leave so that Sally could be with the medicine man's wife *Nizhóní Ch'ilátah Hózhóón (beautiful flower)* in her hour of need and not around men such as Roger and Sargent Gáagii Adakai. Women suffering don't want strange men hanging around.

It was a long night for Sally and *Nizhóní Ch'ilátah Hózhóón*. They had no idea when General Níngsī would come back or even if he would. Sally did not rule out the possibility *Binii'łigaii* (screeching owl) the medicine man, was killed in the space battles. If that happened the entire Tribe would be crying because everyone looked favorably upon *Binii'łigaii* who had helped deal with their pain and suffering numerous times. He was friendly and pleasant to be around.

General Níngsī knew he had to get Sargent Hawthorne and *Binii'łigaii* back to Earth. He realized their friends and families were most likely very worried, but he had the decency to send pictures and videos to his hand-picked General he left behind on Earth to handle matters. He hoped that would satisfy their concerns.

Actually, it made things worse.

It was morning the next day when General Níngsī's command ship reached Earth's orbit and set off numerous alarms with NORAD.

The Russian NORAD counterpart, Strategic Missile Troops РВСН – [Ракетные войска стратегического (Raketnyye voyska strategicheskogo)] went on alert. Just as Sally Fairbanks predicted, their scientists had a lot of toys and they too observed the Space War. It was very sobering.

China's space program administrated by CNSA [China National Space Administration] unlike NASA as an independent organization is joined at the hip with PLAN [Peoples Liberation Army Navy]. China uses ground and space-based systems for national security, detecting space craft launches, including ICBM's. Thanks to Ukraine and certain American Corporations making a fast buck, China was also watching the Zhrakzhongs with great fidelity now orbiting the planet. The world was extremely nervous especially Russia, China, America, ESA, and Great Britain who all watched some of the space battle.

The world was changed forever. Our neighbors the Chinese (because of technology we really are now neighbors) and the Russians were no longer super sensitive to Americans and likewise.

It was in the morning right after the Chickens were waking up the Tribe with their obnoxious crowing in the morning, that General Níngsī's transport/shuttle flew down to the Arizona compound. He knew Earth had probably watched the space battle and he certainly sent pictures of it and video down to show *Binii'ligaii's* wife so that she would know he was with him and would be gone for a short time.

There was no big reason to hide the transport/ shuttle any longer so he ordered the shuttle pilot to land at the *Béésh Łigaii Atsu* (Silver Eagle) Native American Tribe.

The Army Second Lieutenant had his field ISR equipment with him and was quickly getting the event recorded for his bosses back at the Pentagon.

Shortly after the transport/shuttle landed, General Níngsī exited the craft with Sargent Hawthorne and *Binii'ligaii*.

Nizhóní Ch'ilátah Hózhóón was cooking breakfast and just happened to look out the window and see the transport/shuttle suddenly come down. She turned off the stove and turned back to Sally who was busy hammering away at her cell phone reporting to assholes that were pissing her off expecting a big report that wasn't going to happen on a cell phone.

In her frustration, Sally said, "I'll file a report I get back to the office. I do not have a computer here to work with."

About that time *Nizhóní Ch'ilátah Hózhóón* said, "Their back!" She then ran out the door swiftly.

Sally was hot on her tail ignoring the last text message from a bozo who did not understand reality: "I DO NOT HAVE A COMPUTER HERE."

Nizhóní Ch'ilátah Hózhóón ran up to *Binii'ligaii* and

threw her arms around him. She was so grateful he came back alive. Sargent Hawthorne stood there giving them space and a tender moment. General Níngsī enjoyed watching this affection and he had a surprise for them as soon as the emotional transcendence dissipated a bit.

They hugged for a small eternity then *Nizhóní Ch'ilátah Hózhóón* realized there were other people around them.

As soon as it appeared that activity had died down, General Níngsī made a statement which was being picked up by the big ears system of the ISR people up on the hill at the roadblock.

"To everyone here, having Sargent Hawthorne and *Binii'łigaii* with me during the battle was very beneficial. *Binii'łigaii* shared with me some ancient Navajo Warrior techniques they used to defeat their enemies which I integrated into my battle plan. Some of my success is partly because in our discussions, it became clear to me the advantages these techniques offered. Sargent Hawthorne who's a hardened battle tested warrior helped to explain what *Binii'łigaii* said and further elaborated so that a fundamental plan could be adopted *insitu*.

I have awards to give to these two courageous men who proved their bravery to me. *Binii'łigaii,* this is for you. The general put the huge pure gold medal attached to a beautiful ribbon around *Binii'łigaii's* neck. Then he took an identical medal and placed it over Sargent Hawthorne's neck just as Roger Brandenhagen and Sargent Gáagii Adakai were pulling up in a Jeep.

General Níngsī smiled as Roger and Sargent

Adakai got out of the Jeep and walked up next to the others.

Sally Fairbanks explained to the two arrivals, "General Níngsī just awarded them each a medal for their participation in the space battle."

"Does that mean they were the first people from Earth to participate in a Space Battle?"

"I'm sorry to inform you Doctor Brandenhagen, the people from Atlantis were the first to fight in space and unfortunately they lost."

Sally looked at Roger and said, "I hoped you checked out of your hotel, we'll be leaving today."

"Actually, I did not rule out the possibility and informed the hotel I would call them before noon if I thought I needed a room for the night."

General Níngsī who was about to leave said, "Doctor Brandenhagen, I would be happy to take you along on the next battle which will occur sometime soon."

"You know where to find me General."

"Yes, I do. Do you think I should kidnap Sally and take her with us?"

"I would not want her to escape all the RED TAPE she has to deal with. I recommend you leave her behind."

"On that note, I must leave. Sargent Hawthorne and *Binii 'łigaii*, never forget, you were my crew members and my advisors to one of the greatest Space Battles in a very long time. I was honored to serve with you."

Sargent Hawthorne gave the General a crisp USMC salute and replied, "Thank you General Níngsī for giving me the ride of my lifetime."

General Níngsī bowed in Zhrakzhong tradition, turned around and stepped into the transport/shuttle that went up in the air and flew almost 10 miles to his command center through a slot in the camouflage that opened for his craft and immediately shut after it was inside and landing.

Sally should have realized they were being watched from above as well as the Army guys up the hill and her cell phone rang with a Mozart piano concerto 21 melody that gives it its distinct sound that most people would recognize but not know it was Mozart.

"Hello."

"Sally this is Mike Barnes. A helicopter will be leaving Tucson momentarily to pick you up. A jet is heading to Tucson and should arrive shortly after your helicopter gets back to Davis-Monthan."

"Understand all."

"One other thing, we want you to bring Sargent Hawthorne with you. Tell him we'll bring him back tomorrow. We need to debrief him and get his comments for the report."

"Allright, I'll let him know, but you realize he's retired and not on the payroll."

"Inform Sargent Hawthorne in about five minutes he will be working for a Beltway Bandit and we will give him back pay and intelligence officer hazardous duty pay 25%."

"If he shows up with us, then he's going, otherwise you may have to send a team out here to talk with him."

"Explain it to him and if I don't hear from you I will assume he's coming."

"Sure thing, Mike."

Sally hung up and walked over to *Nizhóní Ch'ilátah Hózhóón* and said, "A helicopter is coming to get us soon. Plus, I think you want to be alone with your husband for a while."

"Sally, thank you for staying with me. I really appreciate it. I might have broken down had you not been here giving me emotional support."

The two women hugged which made *Binii 'ligaii's* eyes water up slightly as he realized how this adventure put his wife through some troubling times.

Most of the Tribe was over near *Binii 'ligaii's* home and had watched the impromptu award ceremony. The eight-foot-tall giant in that impressive uniform captivated them in one way, but also put fear in them in another. They saw the two huge gold medals on the two men that weighed about a pound each. It had Alien design on it which added greatly to their curiosity of where *Binii 'ligaii* had gone and what he had done. The Alien UFO also made a huge impression on them. It made very little noise.

Nizhóní Ch'ilátah Hózhóón suspected it would be a while before the helicopter arrived and suggested,

"Sally and you guys, come to my house I'm cooking breakfast, I'll make enough for all of us."

In due time, the kids were crawling all over *Binii 'tigaii* and looking at his medal and asking a lot of questions. Sally, Roger, Sargent Hawthorne, and Sargent Adakai were all very happy that this special man made it back alive from a galactic scale space battle because his family was precious.

Sargent Hawthorne and *Binii 'tigaii* were already good friends. But going out into space and participating in a horrific space battle brought them even closer. They had shown their braveness to each other and when lesser men would have coward, General Níngsī recognized a rare trait in these two men. They had no apparent fear and only concern for him. He could never ask for more in anyone including his best warriors.

The two visitors during the space battle standing proudly with General Níngsī also had a calming effect on everyone who casually observed them in the Combat Information Center. He had never seen his warriors this calm before. The effect was quite extraordinary. *Perhaps the reason why we did so well was the effect these two men had on us?*

As the time slowly ticked away there was a sense of dread. The friendly medicine man's family had grown fond of Sally and they would be sad when she left. Breakfast had concluded, the dishes were already washed and that unmistakable sound of a "chopper" arriving gave them all a jolt of reality as it was time to get up the hill and board the aircraft.

Roger's luggage was still in the back of Sargent

Adakai's Jeep so he offered, "I'll give you a ride up the hill so you don't have to carry your luggage."

"We appreciate that."

Sally and Roger shook *Binii 'łigaii's* hand and Roger said, "It's a privilege to know you. If you ever want to visit Washington DC and see the museums, you can stay at my place, I got plenty of room."

"I just might one day do that, *Binii 'łigaii* said."

The group hopped in the Jeep and in a couple, minutes were loaded up into the Blackhawk that went airborne soon after.

"Sargent Hawthorne when we get to Washington, you can stay at my place, I got four CIA goons protecting my home, you will be safe."

"I might need to do a little shopping; I didn't bring anything with me."

"We are about the same size, I got lots of things to wear. In fact, I have an evil Idea, I'll dress you up in some of my clothes and have you run out the front door and as they are chasing you down, I'll sneak out so I can get over to Crystal City Sports Bar and have some beers with the boys."

"Not a problem I'll meet you over there."

"How will you evade the CIA guys?"

"Never underestimate the resourcefulness of a Marine Corp Sargent."

"That I would never do. Especially those who went 15 light years away in a day."

"That's how far we went?"

"At least."

"Now you know why people are interested in you."

The Zhrakzhong UFO escorts were with the helicopter heading south in due time. Sargent Hawthorne who had deployed off many helicopters enjoyed this ride extra special. He didn't mind Army guys flying him around for starters, and the Arizona countryside was even more special since he made it home alive.

Watching those huge ships explode in space was an eye opener for him. He did one operation where the Navy flew him and a bunch of Marines off an Aircraft Carrier operating as a gator freighter. It seemed to him those Alien ships were a hell of a lot larger. He put it all into perspective when General Níngsī's command ship was passing through his fleet getting to the front during the chase. Those were huge monsters and they flew at incredible speeds. *I suppose everything is relative?*

The military and the aircraft manufacturers were quite interested in figuring out how the Aliens were able to take control of the Helicopter and the SR-72. Did they purposely crash some of the F22's? There was a lot to learn. Sally Fairbanks ride with General Níngsī landing in China in one of the most secure places on the planet didn't set well with any of the leading world's power. And over the past couple of days watching the Space War horror show, put them at great fear.

All these years squabbling with each other and

having proxy wars like Korea, Vietnam, Iraq, and Afghanistan diverted their attention which now they paid dearly for. Seventy-five wasted years. But could they really have done something by then to thwart this invasion? After looking at the size of the ships, probably not.

The Aliens today did something different. They took the helicopter ALL THE WAY to Tucson. It was if their instructions of avoiding detection were over. A new paradigm seems to have manifested.

The Aliens got so close to the Air Force Base, that Air Traffic Controllers were able to view them through binoculars. Government coverup was soon to be over. No more Majestic 12 squelching legitimate UFO reports and Alien Contacts.

Sally, Roger, and Sargent Hawthorne climbed aboard the GS700 and were soon airborne. While they were climbing up to their flight plan of 50,000 feed and Mach 0.9, the pilots saw the two UFOs outside their cockpit windows and just about shit their pants. This was real and no BS this time. They snapped some pictures with their cell phones. They then hit the flight attendant call button and Mable Potter immediately came up to the cockpit and asked, "What do you guys need?"

"Look out the windows both sides of the aircraft and snap some photographs you can give to the CIA to back up our claims."

Mabel looked out and was immediately taken back knowing what all this meant.

"Alright boys, I'll take pictures from the cabin windows."

She then went back and sat down and asked Sally, "Do you see anything interesting outside the windows?"

Sally typically didn't look out the windows because she was either taking a nap or talking to some asshole on the phone who got under her skin. She looked and based on the paint type she remembered that was unlike anything we paint our aircraft casually said, "Relax that's just our Zhrakzhong escort. I think General Níngsī likes me and wants to make sure we get there safely. Go warn the pilots the Zhrakzhongs will soon take control of the aircraft and fly us to Washington, and they will violate their flight plan."

"You are calm about all this?"

"I flew around the world with the Zhrakzhongs and I'm in trouble illegally entering Russia and China. I'm surprised they didn't fire me."

"You are pulling my leg."

"Ask Doctor Brandenhagen how he got to Mars."

"Sally, I would feel better if you would start calling me Roger."

"Sure Roger, did you find some goodies on Mars?"

"You know I did."

"But you never put it into the report."

"Sally I will admit what I found was heart

breaking. As General Níngsī said, "May we let them rest in peace."

Mabel was looking at the two wondering if they were some sort of pranksters. She suspected Roger's cell phone had been wiped so she pulled out her cell phone and said, "Sargent Hawthorne participated in the Space Battle with General Níngsī. Take a look at these pictures then I'll show you some video."

Mable was looking at imagery way above her security clearance level, but there was no way she would know the classification on all this.

Then it got real exiting, here she was watching Space Battles on Sally's cell phone and knew two Alien ships were flying wing tip to wing tip with them and the pilots were stunned the Aliens took control of the aircraft from them.

After she finished the videos showing Sargent Hawthorne on the Alien ship standing next to General Níngsī and *Binii 'ligaii,* mixed in with a number of Space Combat scenes, she could not help but look at him in another light. In reality, this man represented the entire world in that epic space battle. Mable Potter had seen a lot in her days. And as bad as it was sometimes hauling half dead spies out of dreaded countries, nothing as terrifying ever existed like she saw on the cell phones. The three Amigos she was taking back to Washington DC were something else. Life stories nobody would ever believe. But half the things the CIA did were unbelievable so it should not have come to a surprise to her.

She suddenly felt a lot better about things

knowing Sally and Roger and Sargent Hawthorne had a lot of dealings with these aliens merely providing them escort service.

She decided she better go up to the cockpit to tell the pilots not to sweat it if the Aliens took control of the aircraft.

"Hi guys."

The pilots appeared to be in a strange mood.

"I just wanted to warn you, the Aliens will probably take control of the Aircraft, don't fear, they are only here safeguarding us. We have people on board the Aliens want to protect."

"The pilot turned back to Mable with that god awful look on his face and said, "They already took control of the Airplane."

"Sorry, I should have warned you earlier."

The pilots felt good about one thing. Since they had Mable onboard, she could vouch for them violating their flight plan which resulted in them getting chewed out by several air traffic controllers.

The pilots didn't really have to worry because they flew under a KH-11 satellite that was being repositioned over Arizona who captured the images of the formation. And even though KH-11 was 1970's technology, its output fed into a 2021 super computer running artificial intelligence who spotted the image and locked on it and immediately started spitting out reports that got the attention of the human controllers. Traveling at Mach 0.9 from the ground view seems like the aircraft is moving along smartly. From 25,000 miles in space its crawling along and easy to follow. However, with a lot of magnification it seems like the ground below is moving fast. This is the same KH-11 that Cosmos 2542 was following until it met its demise taking images of the new moon dark side.

Other than the Aliens flying the aircraft for them, most of the flight was uneventful.

The plane landed and an Air Force Full Colonel met the plane and started chewing out the two pilots because the FAA complained to the Air Force. Mable who was still with the plane as its executive officer walked up to the full bird Colonel and said, "Colonel, I need to have a word with you in private, us go up on the airplane and shut the door so nobody hears the TOP SECRET information.

The Colonel didn't like a civilian getting in his face, CIA or otherwise.

"I do not want to talk to you right now I need to deal with these two pilots."

"Okay hot shot, either you talk to me right the fuck now or my boss will be talking to the Secretary of the Airforce in about fifteen minutes."

The Air Force Colonel looked at Mable and asked, "Just who the fuck are you?"

"Colonel you just dropped an F bomb on me. The Secretary of the Air Force is not going to be too happy with your dumb ass in about fifteen minutes. I really suggest you get your ass up in the airplane so we can have a little TOP SECRET chat if you know what's good for your career."

The Colonel wanted to get to the bottom of this BS with the civilian and said, "Okay us to up into the airplane. This better be good."

Once the door was shut and locked, Mable went over to her special cabinet and pulled out a non-disclosure form and handed it to the Colonel and said, "Sign this asshole because you are going to get a briefing now."

When the Colonel saw it was in fact a TOP SECRET-SCI non-disclosure form, he suddenly got curious and finally shut up.

Mable said, "What I'm going to tell you and show you is really going to make it hard for you to sleep at night, but under the circumstances I need to protect those two pilots who did nothing wrong."

The pilot looked at Mable now starting to think instead of attack, settled in with ears wide open.

"Alien space craft took control of this plane shortly after takeoff. If you talk to the FAA jerks or my buddies at the NRO they will tell you no airplane has ever gone in such a perfect straight line before."

"To show you I'm not bullshitting you, I do have a CIA cell phone cleared for TOP SECRET. Here's some of the images of the UFO I took."

The Colonel was starting to really calm down now as he started to figure out who he was dealing with.

"This is truly Amazing," the Colonel said as he thumbed through the pictures sometimes including shots that had the pilots in the picture.

"I'm going to tell you another thing Colonel, that's why you are signing that none disclosure form and if you don't you will go to a military brig, those three civilians we brought here, have been on those alien craft including trips to Mars, and 15 light years away in a space battle. You really don't know the half of it, so I would really appreciate that after you sign that none disclosure form you go down and apologize to those two pilots who did nothing wrong. I plan on having the CIA brief the Air Force Secretary over this matter. They will be required to go into a special debriefing and will not be available to fly for a few days, so you need to give us another crew."

The colonel who was hot under the collar a few minutes ago, was a changed man.

"I'm very sorry, I was a jerk. I will gladly apologize to the two men. And I'm sorry if I spoke at you in the wrong tone."

"That's ok Colonel, in the heat of the battle we sometimes let our emotions take over. I know this is tough on you, it's tough on all of us and it will challenge our belief systems."

"You can say that again."

"Us go down and see your two men who have given us superb support. I want them on all my flights."

"Allright."

The Colonel went down first in a very determined manner and walked up to the two pilots who were standing near the front of the aircraft.

"Hey guys, forget everything I said before. You guys have done a super job and I'm proud of you. I now know more about the exigencies you faced flying."

"No problem, Colonel," the copilot said as the two pilots knew the Colonel probably got a thorough briefing by Mable Potter.

"Do you guys need a lift anywhere?"

"If you are going by Alexandria, you can drop me off," the pilot said.

The copilot chimed in and said, I live close to him and my car is parked at his house. We got a lift here this morning by his wife so we would not have to leave our cars on base."

"Follow me, us go."

The company sent a Limo to pick the three Amigo's up. The driver explained to Sargent Hawthorne, "We have a reservation for you at the Crystal City Mariotte."

"I do not need the reservation, I'm going to stay with Doctor Brandenhagen."

"The company will pay for your hotel room."

"That's okay, I prefer having four CIA guys outside Roger's house protecting me."

"As you wish."

They all got dropped off and as Roger was

going up the stairs to his porch, he introduced Sargent Hawthorn, "This is my good Buddy, a retired Marine, so if you guys get into a firefight, he'll be here to help you out."

Sargent Hawthorne felt better staying with Roger who he had decided was a friend. They had done a lot together and when General Níngsī informed Sargent Hawthorne what they found on Mars, he knew Roger was a heck of a guy.

Roger was hungry and used to Uber Eats and others delivering food so he asked Sargent Hawthorne, "Would it be ok if I order some Kentucky Fried Chicken?"

"No problem, I like KFC as well.

Roger then said, "I need to find out if my CIA buddies want anything before, I call in the order."

Roger went out the front door and asked the two men, "Hey I'm going to order some KFC Chicken, you guys interested?"

"Sure, I'll have some."

The other nodded his head in affirmative. Roger didn't bother asking the guys out back, he went ahead and ordered for them anyway.

It did not take long to get the delivery. Roger went out the back door and approached one of the two guys and said, "I ordered some Kentucky Fried Chicken, it's in my kitchen if you guys one to take turns and get a snack."

"Thanks, we appreciate that, and oh by the way,

your bushes are safe, but your neighbors are not."

"I don't like them Northeast snobs, so that's ok."

Roger went back inside his home and called in a couple buckets of chicken, one original recipe he liked and the other crispier.

KFC delivered the meals and the CIA men rang the doorbell and his favorite 2nd shift guy handed him the plastic bags of goodies.

"Where's the delivery guy so I can pay him?"

"He already got paid."

Roger was starting to like these CIA guys. Free coffee, free toilet paper, etc. He never used the down stairs bathroom unless he had to urinate, but it was amazing clean all of a sudden.

After the KFC and a few beers, it was time to hit the sack. Sargent Hawthorne was all quickly adjusted to his new surroundings and would much rather hang out with Roger than be stuck in a Crystal City hotel.

Morning came too Early and as expected, Roger got his wakeup call.

"We'll be arriving in 30 minutes to pick you guys up."

Roger could smell the bacon and the coffee and didn't like to rush, as his best hours for pooping were in the morning.

Now just exactly what was the poop deck on the old wooden sailing ships?

Roger walked over to Sargent Hawthorne's temporary bedroom and knocked on the door and said, "Are you awake yet, we will be picked up in 30 minutes."

"Okay, I'll be right down stairs in a minute."

"Meet me in the Kitchen for a fast breakfast."

The CIA came through for Roger once again. One of the first shift front guys was cooking the bacon and eggs. It smelled damn good.

"Roger, would you like some orange juice?"

"Most definitely and pour a glass for Sargent Hawthorne who will be joining us in a minute."

"Alright boss."

The CIA man poured Roger a glass of orange juice, and a fresh cup of coffee made from Starbucks coffee.

There were several pieces of toast piled up on a plate with jams on the table. The eggs were all cooked the same way, sunny side up.

Sargent Hawthorne joined them in a couple of minutes fully dressed in a change of clothes provided by Roger.

"Have a seat, we are going to eat before we go."

"What we going to do when the suits show up?"

"They will have to wait, because I like to use the bathroom after breakfast."

"Me too."

"I'll use my upstairs bathroom when the time comes, you can use the downstairs bathroom. Its super clean because the CIA cleans that bathroom for me every day."

"They must be good guys."

"Yea, just like lawyers we have to bury 12 feet down."

"Why is that?"

"Because down deep, they are not so bad afterall."

The CIA cooking the eggs and bacon and putting butter on the toast was chuckling after that joke.

"Nothing better than a breakfast cooked by high priced CIA Agents."

"Hopefully he didn't put salt peter in your coffee for that stupid joke."

CIA agent: "We would never do anything like that. We got better stuff to put in, like agents that will help you deposit your breakfast a few minutes after you eat to make it nice and fast in case you are constipated."

"Nothing like teamwork."

"You got that right."

Just as soon as Roger Brandenhagen sopped up the last bit of egg yoke with the remainder of his toast and downed that excellent Starbucks Coffee, he said, "I know he must have put some of that extra lube in my coffee, because I really do need to go now!"

Roger made his way upstairs and Sargent

Hawthorne said, "I better use the facilities now so I am prepared for an all-day meeting, just in case."

Sargent Hawthorne went about his business, and like a good marine was ready and at parade rest when the two SUVs pulled in to pick up their rides.

The one remaining front guard opened the door and said, "Your ride is here."

"I'm ready, but unfortunately Doctor Brandenhagen is using the bathroom. Something about the CIA putting some good stuff in his coffee. This may take a while."

"I'll let the driver know."

Finally, fifteen minutes later, the driver approached both CIA men at the front entrance, since breakfast was all cleaned up quickly and asked, "What's the holdup? The dispatcher is on my ass to get those two guys over to Dulles."

"Doctor Brandenhagen is sitting on the shitter, he's an older guy, it takes them longer," one of the front guards replied.

Incidentally two minutes later, Doctor Brandenhagen walked out the front door and said to the CIA man who cooked the breakfast, "I don't know what the hell you put in the coffee, but it did its trick. Thank you."

"My pleasure. Should I double up the dose, tomorrow morning?"

"As long as I don't have to go back to Arizona that would be ok."

The men walked to the two waiting SUVs with a sour look on the driver's face who just got another "nice" phone call from his dispatcher.

"Get in the second SUV."

"Sure."

No VIP treatment today to open the doors to the SUV. The drivers must have been pissed about the poop delay.

Finally, the caravan takes out and makes it way on I-66 on the way to the Dulles turn-off. A motorcycle cop came up behind them and passed them. If this was the same guy they ran into the other day, he obviously got a calibration.

Right up-front door delivery, and five minutes later Doctor Brandenhagen and Sargent Hawthorne were walking into the familiar conference room.

Today was quite a bit different than ever before. The conference room was full. All the seats at the table except two next to Mike Barnes were taken. A few feet away from the long conference table were chairs against the wall, providing a second layer to the bureaucratic onion. Every single bureaucrat in the room had on a suit or business dress attire for the women and number of military personnel had on uniforms in accordance with dress of the day requirements, which specified semi-formal dress uniforms. Hence the room as intensely stuffy for Sargent Hawthorne.

Mike Barnes nodded at his assistant who went over shut and locked the door. There would be no intrusions or interruptions.

"Hello everyone, I'm glad you could all make this on short notice," Mike Barnes said as he stood up at the end of the table so he could see everyone in the room.

Mike Barnes then announced, "My assistant, Mike White will be carrying around an attendance sheet for each to sign into. We need your name, rank, position, agency affiliation, and who here you represent and your agency interest in this matter."

Mike Barnes knew there were CIA, NSA, DIA, AFINT, Space Force, and representatives for the Joint Chiefs. He saw a couple stars on the scrambled eggs these men brought in with them and on their uniforms.

Mike went over a quick description of the agenda which showed behind him on the large flatscreen and said, "In order for us to cover a lot of issues in a brief amount of time because we are busy, there are pads of paper and pencils on the conference table and the desk by the door. If you have questions during the discussions, write them down and we will answer you direct after the meeting because many here may not be interested in your aspect of these proceedings and have other jurisdictions. After the meeting is adjourned, we will take your questions in badge order."

That allowed the Generals and Admirals to get their questions answered first so they could get back to the Pentagon or Fort Meade or elsewhere.

"I want to take the time to introduce a few people to you. When I introduce you, please stand up so the attendees will know who is who."

"First person I want to introduce is Sally Fairbanks. She has been the CIA's main coordinator with the Aliens and has been on site for all interchanges between, our government and the Aliens."

One of the Air Force Generals with three stars on his uniform interrupted and asked, "Mike, I do not see any foreigners in this meeting. Were any invited?"

"Thanks for answering that question General, and I will go ahead and answer that now instead of at the end of the meeting as planned, because it is a very serious question and deserves an immediate response."

Mike Barnes looked at the General with a pair of eyes that looked like they just came out of hell itself. As Mike Barnes pierced the Generals eyes with the look he gave him, the General was suddenly feeling rather uncomfortable because the evil he could feel was immense. He knew the SAC people could leave him floating down the Potamic, just like the former CIA director who ostensibly had a heart attack and fell overboard his boat.

"General, Aliens only exist in Mexico and here in America near the Navajo Indian Reservation in Arizona. As such our sovereign rights gives us exclusive interface with the Aliens, and until the Aliens land in their country they have no basis for being here. Furthermore, our boss the President of the United States has directed us to allow no foreign visits until further notice."

"What about the Aliens visiting China and Russia?"

"General, we'll cover that in a sidebar after the

main presentation is complete and people who have no need to know about that can go about their business and we don't tie them up in this conference room when they have many tasks they must do."

Mike Barnes was about to give the General some simple answers if he kept talking such as, "We'll discuss that in a sidebar." But the truth is he wished he could get away with telling the General to simply shut the fuck up."

"Thank you Sally." Mike Barnes nodded at her and she knew to sit down and zip it until required.

"Next Person I'm going to introduce you is Doctor Brandenhagen. He's a controversial person because his views and theory on Mars. Thanks to the Alien Arrival, we have been able to confirm a lot of Doctor Brandenhagen's theory is backed up by galactic history. We will not be discussing his theory in this meeting but we will discuss his involvement with the Aliens."

Mike Barnes nodded at Doctor Brandenhagen who then sat down, feeling good he didn't dress up for this event because he felt a lot more comfortable dressing casually which also matched what Sargent Hawthorne was wearing.

"Finally, I'm going to introduce you to Sargent Hawthorne, decorated United States Marine Corp, retired. Since he was present during the first topic, I'm going to now reveal what that is."

The room had little idea how he fit into the overall scheme of things, but they certainly were curious how a retired Marine Corp Sargent rose to the level of top management interest about his association with the Aliens.

"Only one fourth of the attendees have seen the video I'm going to show in a minute. But before I roll the tape, I'm going to ask Sargent Hawthorne to give a short version of his journey with the Aliens."

"Thank you, sir, for asking me about what my role was. For starters I was helping my friends the the *Béésh Łigaii Atsu* (Silver Eagle) Native American Tribe. The leader of the Aliens, General Níngsī who took interest in them. I was principally working with *Binii 'łigaii* (screeching owl) the *Béésh Łigaii Atsu* Tribe's medicine man who I know well. *Binii 'łigaii* and I were invited to visit General Níngsī on his command ship and later his underground bunker. General Níngsī said he would like to take me into space, and I indicated the willingness to go on a trip. Therefore, when their enemies, the Xīnguī approached Earth, General Níngsī invited *Binii 'łigaii* and myself to accompany him into space and observe the space battle. We agreed to go and witnessed most of it. He then brought us back to Earth so that we could be with our friends and families."

"Thank you, Sargent Hawthorne, for your excellent description of how you fit into all of this."

Now I want to have Doctor Brandenhagen explain where General Níngsī took him after Sally Fairbanks explains what General Níngsī said to her concerning Doctor Brandenhagen beforehand.

Sally Fairbanks said, "The General who has access to all our computer files worldwide, knew all the issues associated with peers and media who were not very kind to Doctor Brandenhagen, and was pleased how he showed bravery and perseverance in sticking with his theories in spite of all the abuse, and offered to take him to Mars to help prove his point."

"And why did he want to do that?"

"Because he had actual information on Mars being destroyed 900,000 years ago by the Jupitorians, exactly like Doctor Brandenhagen stated in his theory. The only piece of missing information Doctor Brandenhagen didn't have was who did it."

"The Zhrakzhongs know for a fact the Jupitorians wiped out Mars?"

"Yes, they do."

"Thank you Sally."

"Okay Doctor Brandenhagen tell us about your Mars trip.

"I will openly admit that SAC knew I had been invited to Mars. The Director of SAC directed me not to go. I went anyway because I felt the SAC had no legal jurisdiction to stop me from going to Mars, and it was just an opinion the SAC Director assumed he could enforce. The Aliens came to my house, disabled the CIA men guarding the front of it and took me on a transport/ shuttle up in space, where we landed in a hanger bay of a Zhrakzhong Space Warship that could get me to Mars in a few hours. Then we arrived to witness a special event the General arranged for me."

"And what was that?"

"They brought an Archeologist team down to the area of Cydonia and did a dig for me."

"And what did they find?"

"An emergency shelter with a number of dead Martians who died when the planet was wiped out with two huge Hydrogen Bombs."

"What were the bodies like?"

"With very low Oxygen content as the planet lost its atmosphere, they no doubt died from asphyxiation and there was very or no decay. They probably looked similar to the day they died, except their bodies had hardened as if it were mummified."

"Do they look like people on Earth?"

"Identical."

There was some noise in the room. Those comments just struck home.

Mike Barnes then thought it would be appropriate to say, "The SAC Director Mark Rebman is on leave for a couple weeks will not be available for a while, got reports from NRO that tracked the transport/shuttle in space. He knew that based on prior discussion, Doctor Brandenhagen was most likely going to Mars with the Aliens and as such had KH-14 satellite feed track them to Mars and back. So, there is no question Doctor Brandenhagen went to Mars."

"Did you bring back any evidence?"

"I didn't need to, the Zhrakzhongs did all the analysis of the samples on the planet before they left so that I would not have to bring any here to take to a lab and deal with the controversy of bringing biohazard material back to the planet."

"Do you have the results of their samples."

"Since I did it on my own time and not being compensated by my temporary employer, I felt no need to share that information with anyone, because I can't really tell the public what we found. The government would not tolerate it."

"Can you give us an indication of what you found?"

"Besides the dead bodies in an emergency shelter, the Xeon 129 samples were identical to what I previously stated in my books and videos that substantiates Mars was wiped out by two huge Hydrogen Bombs, maybe 5000 Megatons.

"Did it do a lot of physical damage?"

"That's not the problem. When it blew away the atmosphere it killed the planet. Nothing can live there now."

"What about the dead Martians and artifacts?"

"General Níngsī decided and I agreed, this was their burial tomb and we should leave it alone. I agreed. The Archeologist team removed any evidence we were ever there."

"Would you agree to show us where it is?"

"No. For the respect of those beings, I will not invade their space again."

Mike Barnes used that last comment as segue to get the video operating.

"Allright everybody, we will now watch the video and I think Sargent Hawthorne would be willing to hang around after the video to answer some follow-up questions."

The video started and it was better than the movies. Some wished they had popcorn.

Alien video capabilities were incredible. It was almost as if they were in an IMAX studio somewhere.

The composite video taken from all the Zhrakzhong ships spliced together, gave an incredible view of the entire battle. Thanks to the Decoys sitting on the ground in the Alien Compound in Arizona, CIA photonics people were able to make measurements on the decoys they thought were real ships. In a few minutes into the Battle, the three-star Air Force General asked, "Sorry for interrupting the video but can you tell us the size of those ships."

Mike Barnes continued playing the video and didn't stop it because as far as he was concerned, this was all just eye candy for people who would be working on the issues.

"The Aliens have a reserve fleet on the ground in Arizona in their secure compound and from Satellites we were able to measure the larger ones are two miles long. After the video finishes, Sally Fairbanks, Sargent Hawthorne, and Doctor Brandenhagen can discuss the ships they observed on the ground."

Everyone in the room observed a spectacular

space battle with horrific images. Consequently, the room took on an eerie quiet.

The first phase of the Space Battle showing the Zhrakzhongs blasting the Xīnggui stragglers wasn't all that impressive since it was one enemy ship at a time. The Gauntlet force that stood between Admiral Aeta and Earth took on a little more spectacular imagery as the Zhrakzhongs recorded from their surviving ship's a couple of the two-mile-long monsters blowing up.

The Three Star Air Force General who felt the need to be heard suddenly asked, "Did any organization on Earth record any of this? There had to be some large explosions we could detect."

"General, yes. We do have KH-14 and Hubble images, but since they were photographed a good distance away, the resolution is not nearly as good."

What caused the three-star Air Force General to stop yakking his voice was the next sequence when Admiral Aeta's Force was suddenly hit from his flanks and from the rear.

When, Admiral Aeta's Force started the loop sequence because of the encounter of enemies attacking from his flanks and then from the rear of his formation is when the devastation hit home and shook everyone watching for the first time. They knew the large ships were two miles long, about 10 times the length of a Nimitz Class Carrier. As such they suddenly come to grips with the fact Earth is a pushover world, easy to be invaded.

The beam weapons and lasers lit up the sky and

gave an eerie appearance. To some it seemed like huge lightning strikes, except they were super straight and not curving and branching like a lightning strike. Just like how a lightning strike shows the horizon momentarily, so did the beam and laser weapons. As such at times all the ships in view of the video camera were exposed briefly for up to 10 seconds. The Air Force General had seen a lot in his 30 years with the Air Force, and even though he was soon to retire, this hit him extra hard because he quickly understood the scale of destruction was massive. If he only knew how bad Admiral Aeta felt snake bit about this time, then he would understand his concerns were mild compared to what Admiral Aeta was thinking. This was the best set piece plan the Air Force General ever saw.

After General Aeta's Fleet maneuvered to their new course and accelerated to maximum speed, the chase did not start with vigor until General Níngsī caught up with the fleet. By then it was too late to engage the Xīngguī until they flew through the Gauntlet force designed to slow him down for the big kill.

Admiral Aeta for whatever reason risked reckless flight through that Gauntlet force assuming the risk to save the fleet from utter destruction.

Soon the video ended and the lights came back on. The room was subdued.

Mike Barnes observed how everyone was subdued and there were no questions coming so he had one for the three who went on the Alien ships.

"Sally, Sargent Hawthorne or Doctor Brandenhagen, would any of you like to comment on what you saw on the ship?"

Doctor Brandenhagen spoke first and said, "I have something I would like to state. Sargent Hawthorne and *Binii 'tigaii* (screeching owl) the medicine man, were given prestigious awards by General Níngsī for their participation in the Space Battle. *Binii 'tigaii* provided General Níngsī some ancient native American fighting techniques which his artificial intelligence converted to three-dimensional and used them in the battle. They are the first non- Zhrakzhongs to receive those awards. Since it is probably worth a lot of money just for the price of gold, he has it with him and showed it last night."

"How do you know General Níngsī gave him that award?"

Sally Fairbanks abruptly spoke, "I was with them when they received the awards."

Sargent Hawthorn pulled the one-pound gold medal out of his pocket and placed it on the table so Mike Barnes could look at it.

Mike Barnes could see the Alien writing on the front of the medal and looked at the back side that repeated the award in English.

"Interesting Artwork, definitely created by master artists and engravers."

Mike Barnes handed the heavy medal back to Sargent Hawthorne and asked, "What was your impression of the Zhrakzhongs Space Warship's internal sections?"

"Well sir, as you can see in the video, their Combat Information Center is rather huge."

"Yes, that is rather apparent, with at last 400 people in the video. If they have so much artificial intelligence why so many people?"

"Those individuals communicate to the entire fleet."

Doctor Brandenhagen then spoke, "I was on board the command ship with Sally Fairbanks and later was aboard a Zhrakzhongs Space Warship. They are completely different and the Space Warship's Combat Information Center and control room are a lot smaller and operate via Artificial Intelligence. The Zhrakzhongs do not operate their ships. All ship's controls are via Artificial Intelligence. The only reason they have living people in the control room is to have a living person authorize weapons deployment. The Zhrakzhongs informed me they could operate the ship with just one person in the control room."

"It's apparent, when they say something, they mean what they say," Sally Fairbanks said.

"Would there be any benefit to bringing in *Binii'łigaii* to get his statements?" Mike Barnes asked looking directly at Sally Fairbanks.

"Every time *Binii'łigaii* has been with or seen the Zhrakzhongs, Sargent Hawthorne, Doctor Brandenhagen, or myself have been present. We saw everything he saw. His wife is already unhappy he went out in space and participated in the Space Battle. If you take *Binii'łigaii* away, she might have a nervous breakdown," Sally Fairbanks explained.

"Why should that matter, the country comes first?"

"General Níngsī has more or less adopted the *Béésh Łigaii Atsu* (Silver Eagle) Native American Tribe. He would be very upset with you if you did that. Also, remember he knows who you are and everything about you."

"Sally, we cannot get into the data breach as there are uncleared people in the room who do not hold Q, V, and Y clearances to know about that issue."

"Mike, I highly suggest if you want to interview *Binii'łigaii*, you should fly out there. I would be happy to introduce you to General Níngsī."

About that time the three-star Air Force General said, "I would like to go with you and see it myself."

"General, that's a great idea, and maybe you can apologize for sending the F22's after them."

Mike Barnes had the General trapped now. He either went to Arizona or he would be silenced.

Just before the meeting was adjourned, Mike Barnes said, "Sargent Hawthorne, we appreciate all the help you have given us. I'm taking Sally Fairbanks recommendation and flying out to Arizona in the morning. If you would like you can fly back with me and the group I'm taking.

"Thank you, sir, I appreciate it."

The meeting was over and Doctor Brandenhagen

and Sargent Hawthorne were taken back to Doctor Brandenhagen's home where they discussed what they were going to do today.

"I liked your idea of going to the Sports Bar over in Crystal City on 23rd Street near Eads Street."

"How do you think I can break out of my prison?"

"I'll call up a few of my Marine buddies to see if they can help us out."

"Sounds good."

Chapter sixteen

The Fleet Returns

Admiral Aete knew his life was almost over. He defied the Emperor Shāyú and came back without a victory. Death by laser execution was most likely hours away.

Admiral Aete did what he did for the sake of the Xīngguī civilization and if he had to pay the price with his life, that was okay because he preserved the Xīngguī Empire by doing so.

As soon as the fleet obtained orbit over Màichōng, as expected Admiral Aeta was summoned down to the planet by Emperor Shāyú who requested his presence. After giving directions to his executive officer, Admiral Aeta walked to hanger bay number three that had his personal Space Scooter. In many ways it was like a motorcycle with wheels below the small air tight enclosure and a pointed bow that allowed penetrating the ozone layer of the planet at high speed without burning up. His fuel tank was full and topped off, but he wouldn't need that fuel on his way down to the planet. When his business was done on the planet, he would leave Emperor Shāyú's palace and fly back on this personal space scooter if allowed. He also realized the possibility, Emperor Shāyú would have him executed by laser rifles in a few hours.

At the same time, Xié'è de Gōngniú was summoned to the Palace and arrived ahead of Admiral Aeta.

Emperor Shāyú was extremely agitated. Admiral Aeta not only failed in his mission, he lost half of the Xīngguī Space Warships in the process! This was a total disaster. It would take years to recover, rebuild the Fleet and train an adaquate number of personnel to operate them. The Zhrakzhongs didn't need to rebuild existing technology now. Thy had the luxury of pursuing new technology and could take their sweet time building it meaning it would operate with high quality in personnel and more advanced equipment.

The beauty of the Space Scooter is it truly was a hotrod in space and could outrun just about anything. The chances of an enemy space warship in capturing Admiral Aeta were slim at best, though he knew he could not outrun their blasters, lasers, and Zhrakzhongs Plasma Debilitater weaponry if they were in lethal range.

Hanger bay number three was different than most of the other shuttle bay hangers, it opened to the sides of the ship and did not require vertical launch. Admiral Aeta liked this arrangement because as soon as he was inside the capsule of the space scooter and pressurized to fifteen pounds and air tightness check complete, he was ready to go and informed the bridge, "Bridge, this is Admiral Aeta, depressurize shuttle bay number three and open the hatch for my departure to the planet."

"Admiral Aeta, shuttle bay number three is being depressurized for your departure."

Depending on how much reserve air was onboard, often the depressurizing simply dumped the air into space so that it could be completed in a couple minutes or less, which is handy in an emergency. Moments later the bridge reported:

"Admiral Aeta, shuttle bay number three is depressurized. Opening the external access hatch now."

Since the depressurization leaves a small amount of pressure in the shuttle bay to help open the hatch, the electric powered extractor arms did not have to exert too much pressure to get hatch movement open after the locking ring opened.

A minute later, the bridge reported, "Admiral Aeta, shuttle bay number three hatch fully open you may now exit the ship."

Since the Space Scooter was still affected by the command ship's artificial gravity, Admiral Aeta enjoyed when he could use the wheels of the space scooter to catapult him out of the open enclosure. He knew in about five seconds he would probably be a few hundred feet from the command ship and he then lit off his thrusters momentarily to give him added velocity and point downwards to the planet where there was nothing in the way because the rest of the Fleet orbited the planet in distances to prevent collisions and also in a gap where satellites and other space craft were not allowed to orbit because it was restricted for Xīngguī

Fleet operations only. Every other entity had to orbit above the Fleet Zone or would be helped out of the way and most likely blasted into a billion pieces with Xīngguī Molecular Disrupter Cannons if it failed to get relocated by its owner

Since this might be Admiral Aeta's last Rodeo, he decided to ride the Space Scooter down to the planet at maximum design velocity. The recommended speed for planet access was around 18,000 miles per hour which guaranteed approximately 99% success rate. However, at 45,000 miles per hour he had 75% estimated success rate without disintegration by overheating the nose cone and the Space Scooter's fuel tanks and oxygen tank.

Admiral Aeta felt a little juvenile doing what he was doing, but if he was going to be dead in a couple hours, why not enjoy this ride to the limits. He knew he could go even faster, but 45,000 miles per hour gave him acceptable odds.

Slowing down was a problem, but he took care of that as he knew the winglets would allow him to partially glide without having to use his propulsion that included small rockets used to adjust the attitude of the aircraft and keep it stable.

At 10,000 feet he pulled back on the controls that began leveling off the Space Scooter. He was still going at incredible velocity, but with no propulsion and drag caused by the winglets, the velocity bled off smartly. In just a minute he was down to 25,000 miles per hour knowingly leaving behind a sonic boom that would piss off a few people, but he didn't care since he was most likely a dead man in a few hours.

Flying in a long oval pattern before turning to the Emperor Shāyú's palace, bled off a lot of speed and finally the Space Scooter reached 666 miles per hour (Mach 0.9) before making the final turn towards Palace Parking.

It did not take long to get near the Palace and breaking action started. The combination of artificial intelligence and Admiral Aeta's keen piloting skills put the Space Scooter right down on top of the designated parking. As soon as the Space Scooter came to a halt. Vertical supports came down which held it upright sitting on its two wheels now deployed like an aircraft would.

Admiral Aete wore his uniform. Protective clothing was not required because the Space Scooter environmental controls eliminated the need for a space suit.

Admiral Aeta exited the Space Scooter enclosure and walked directly to the Palace entrance where he was met with Emperor Shāyú's security detail along with Xié'è de Gōngniú's XSS detail along to protect him.

Admiral Aeta knew where he was going. The security detail didn't need to help him navigate the complex because they knew he had made many trips to the palace. Just like the previous visit they opened the door to the conference room, and in front of him were the two Devil's: Xié'è de Gōngniú and Emperor Shāyú who didn't look too happy.

Admiral Aeta assumed Xié'è de Gōngniú would

take pleasure in lining him up before a laser firing squad, approached Emperor Shāyú and at seven feet, the distance Emperor Shāyú liked to have between him and anyone else.

"I thought I directed you not to bring the Fleet back here, especially if you lost a horrific space battle."

"I had no choice your Highness. It was either bring them here to save them to fight another day, and protect Màichōng, or get wiped out leaving the Empire fully vulnerable to Zhrakzhongs Plasma Debilitater weaponry. I must add since they moved the bulk of their population to numerous other star systems spread out, they had no fear of our reprisal thus could have laid waste to Màichōng.

"Tell me Admiral Aeta, why did you fail so miserably?"

"Your excellency, the INTEL we received was flawed or planted. We ran into a well-designed trap. I was very lucky to get out of that trap with as many ships as I brought back."

"Xié'è de Gōngniú, I want you to place Admiral Aeta under arrest and take him some place secure where the Space Force is unable to rescue him before I have him executed by my Emperor's Guards."

"Your Excellency, I would be most happy to arrest Admiral Aeta, but I recommend we do not execute him until we have a chance to investigate all the video and sensor files in the fleet and see what actually transpired. Admiral Aeta probably has some good knowledge of the battle. After reviewing all the photonics and sensor information, we will probably have some questions we would like him to answer so we can make determinations of what transpired and what we need to change in the event we have another space battle with the Zhrakzhongs sometime soon."

"Very well, take him away and hide him at a secure location. I'm afraid his fleet would otherwise try to rescue him and do a mutiny against me," Emperor Shāyú stated in the most paranoid manner."

Xié'è de Gōngniú stood up and said, "Please come with me Admiral Aete."

Admiral Aete understood if he resisted in any manner, Xié'è de Gōngniú would enjoy any excuse to zap him with his personal blaster to score points with Emperor Shāyú. He was soon going to discover the "new and improved" Xié'è de Gōngniú.

As soon as the Emperor's Guardsman opened the conference room door, Xié'è de Gōngniú and Admiral stepped out and as they were walking down the corridor to the exit, Admiral Aeta asked, "What's going to become of my personal Space Scooter?"

"Admiral, one of my men will take it to a secure XSS parking structure where it will be available for you in the future."

Admiral Aete didn't know what to think of Xié'è de Gōngniú's statement. It left him with a lot to think about if it implied what he thought it meant.

As soon as Xié'è de Gōngniú and Admiral Aete left the front entrance of the Palace, two skycars were in front waiting for them. Each skycar could carry four passengers but there were only four XSS agents total, hence extra room for Admiral Aete.

"Please get in the rear seat of the first skycar, Admiral Aete."

Admiral Aete was somewhat surprised he didn't have hand or foot restraints, but there were more revelations to follow.

As soon as they were Airborne, the Agent in control of the skycar asked, "Where too Boss?"

I want you to take Admiral Aete and I, to the Tytrone Philosophers Temple and drop us off there and then I want you to go to the safe house and pick up Kāiwù de Sēngrén and five of his Monks and bring them to the Temple so that I may receive more meditation training today. Let Kāiwù de Sēngrén know there will be two of us receiving training including Admiral Aete."

"Sure thing, boss."

In less than 10 minutes the two XSS skycars pulled up in front of the Tytrone Philosophers Temple.

"Please follow me into the Temple Admiral Aete."

Admiral Aeta followed Xié'è de Gōngniú into the Temple, wondering, *what's going on*?

There was nobody in the Temple and it was nice and quiet. Xié'è de Gōngniú walked up near the alter where Tytrone Philosopher Monks provided Tytrone Science lectures to the worshipers.

Admiral Aete, once the most powerful person

besides Emperor Shāyú walked up near Xié'è de Gōngniú who turned around and faced him.

"You had a tough battle didn't you Admiral Aete."

"It was tough and the only way something like this could happen is if the Intelligence was part of an elaborate ruse."

"Admiral, I'm sorry to have to inform you, but you were operating on planted information. The source of that information is no longer living."

"One person can do that much damage."

"That's how it is in the spy business, one good spy is a force multiplier. General Níngsī set you up for this elaborate trap that took more than ten years to fully accomplish."

"Emperor Shāyú is very unhappy, I assume I will be executed sometime today?"

"Admiral, what I'm going to say to you now is only known between you and I. In my humble opinion, the Empire needs you now more than ever and the Empire needs you more than it does Emperor Shāyú."

"Are you suggesting some sort of coup?"

"No that's not necessary. Emperor Shāyú just needs the training that you will receive in a few minutes, then he will change for the better and realize how important you are and he'll adjust his stand on a lot of matters."

"Until we end this war, society will remain in a

troubling period."

"After he receives the training, he will realize continuing this war over ego's is costing the Xīnggui far too much."

"You think he would then sign an Armistice?"

"Yes, I do and even if the Zhrakzhongs militarily defeated us, I doubt they have much interest in occupation. Most of their worlds are intact and their population is scattered and safe. They will be so glad just to get home, we'll have peace for 500 years."

"How will we get Emperor Shāyú here for training?"

"That's where you come in. When the time comes, I will lay out the plan. He will be mad as hell and threaten to execute us both, but after he receives the training, he will calm down and we can get on with business."

"Alright, that gives me high hope. But it's sad we lost so many members of our Space Force in the last battle."

"Admiral, while you are receiving the training, you will know how to deal with it in a far better way. Those people gave up their lives for peace. Right now, it looks like their lives were lost for nothing, but I think when you receive this meditation training, you will realize their lives were not lost for no reason. They made the supreme sacrifice and what they did was put us into position to end this war so it doesn't continue for a few more centuries where in the end, many will have been wiped out over egos."

"Allright, I'm ready for the training when the Tytrone Philosophers arrive."

The two waited with minor small talk and in a brief amount of time the door to the temple opened and Kāiwù de Sēngrén followed by five Tytrone Philosophers walked deliberately up to Xié'è de Gōngniú and Admiral Aeta in his dress uniform since he just finished a meeting with Emperor Shāyú.

"You two want meditation training?" Kāiwù de Sēngrén asked in a friendly manner and a pleasant smile on his face knowing standing before him were two of the most powerful men in the Empire.

"Kāiwù de Sēngrén, yes we want meditation training together. You can give us the same type of training you did for me the first time I was here."

"Alright Xié'è de Gōngniú and Admiral Aeta, will you please follow me."

Kāiwù de Sēngrén led the two men to the special meditation training temple. This room could easily accommodate fifty or more students, but there was rarely more than a handful at any time.

Today Kāiwù de Sēngrén personally gave the training instead of his assistant who was currently off planet hiding like most of the other Tytrone Philosopher Monks. Since this was the verbal training and not the silent which is a more advanced class, the noise level in the room was slightly elevated with the Monks and students humming together. The Chimes, bells, and intermittent gong had an immediate effect on Admiral Aete who was eternally grateful to have his life spared.

A brilliant man like Admiral Aete has a neuron density function of almost double the normal person in Xīngguī society. In a similar manner as Xié'è de Gōngniú experienced his first time, Admiral Aete reached a level of Hemi-Sync in just a few moments. The Monks recognized his behavior as someone who reached such a high level as the dynamics of his humming became almost static. Admiral Aete's mind then went to the Universe as predicted by those who studied and perceived these effects.

And just like Xié'è de Gōngniú experienced before, both men were in that high meditative state for three hours. Similar to how people fall asleep and suddenly wake up in the morning after hours had passed, coming back into a new reality, especially if they achieved a rapid eye movement level of sleep.

Another interested phenomenon unfolded. Some theorize that if two people are physically close together when they reach this high-level meditative state, their new dimensional worlds that manifest in the holograph in their minds can intersect. Some experts think it is in part due to a lost telepathic ability caused by breeding with lower species that they became. Since the physiology is still there including the photoreceptors in the center of the brain, some telepathic interchange is possible to the point abducted people experienced telepathic humanoids. Both men would assume it was merely a dream where they met. However, it wasn't a dream, it was their minds traveling through the Universe through those middle brain photo receptors that radiate in wavelengths many years away from discovery.

As soon as the two men regained full awareness of their surroundings, the Monks were there in front of them waiting for this moment. By observing the two men, the monks themselves gained awareness. Never before had they trained such high intellect physically sitting next to each other. They had no preconceived notions of what the outcome would be, but they did see the dynamic synchronizing of the two men humming almost in an ancient manner.

When Xié'è de Gōngniú was poised to communicate to the Monks he said:

"Admiral Aete will go to your safe house with all you Monks. As soon as he gets there, he is to change into clothes that will not expose who he is. We need to protect him until the Xīngguī Fleet requires his presence."

"I understand," Kāiwù de Sēngrén stated knowing there truly was hope thanks to the willingness of Xié'è de Gōngniú to receive the training.

"Xié'è de Gōngniú, before we depart back to our safe house, may I ask you a question?" Kāiwù de Sēngrén asked.

"Yes, Kāiwù de Sēngrén, what is your question."

"During your meditation did you leave this planet?"

"Yes, I went to the Universe."

"Do you know about how long you were gone?"

"Precisely, I was gone for six lifetimes."

"You entered and lived six lives?"

"Yes, died and was reborn and lived again."

"In your final lifetime, what ended it, why did you come back?"

"Interesting question, your excellency. I came back because I was directed to come back."

"By whom?"

"It was obviously someone spiritually who said I had to return because I had many tasks yet to perform in this lifetime here and now."

"That is what I felt you experienced, but I cannot tell you how I know because I do not know how and why. I just accept it happens."

"Admiral Aete, how about you?"

"I experienced some rather unusual events as if I were drugged. I somehow felt Xié'è de Gōngniú was with me or near me on my journey."

"This is extremely rare. We do not know how or why. Its part of the mysteries of the Universe we attempt to unravel and just as soon as we think we get close to the truth, it escapes us," Kāiwù de Sēngrén said.

"It did not escape me," Admiral Aete stated looking into Kāiwù de Sēngrén's eyes as if he were an evil spirit. One of the possible consequences of tampering with souls and sending them out to the Universe is you do not know what you might be creating. Kāiwù de Sēngrén would meditate all night long to overcome the danger that such a transcendence might have brought on to all of them.

Soon everyone ushered out of the Temple shutting the door behind them and entered the 3 Skycars lined up to take Admiral Aete and the Tytrone Philosophers to their safe house and Xié'è de Gōngniú back to his office where he had to contemplate a few things as well as supervise the battle forensics that he felt were useless, because when you fly into a trap bad things happen.

Nothing of value to this investigation would be discovered because Xié'è de Gōngniú already knew the answers and instead of attempting to lay blame or figure out a new strategy and continue the war, the people would be better served by going to plan B, the Armistice. Now it would just be a matter of how to pull it off. He would certainly need the cooperation of General Níngsī who he knew from his own spies was sick of the war and wanted it ended. *Too bad General Níngsī wasn't in charge of all the* Zhrakzhongs. *It would be far simpler then.*

Chapter Seventeen

Crystal City Rescue

Sargent Hawthorne and Roger Brandenhagen figured out their game plan. At the time Sargent Hawthorne's Marine buddies were ready in their car at the end of the block, the two men would run out the front door and head in opposite directions. They would be dressed up almost identically wearing ball caps so from the rear, the two front door guards would not know who was who. Sargent Hawthorne would be the decoy to get Roger out of the house.

Sargent Hawthorne's cellphone rang. He was lucky one of his Marine buddies stationed in Washington DC over at the Pentagon was a Marine Recon Ranger and as they did their drive by the address verified it with the two CIA guys posted out front which now seemed ridiculous because the TV vans had not been out front for almost a week.

"We are at the end of the block."

"Alright, executing the plan in about two minutes

to the mark. Mark!"

"Ready?"

"I'm not too fast of a runner, I'll be lucky if I hit jogging speed."

"That's ok, you got a fifty-fifty chance because they both will not abandon the post."

"I'll try."

"Thirty seconds get ready.

"Mark 30 seconds."

"I think you were counting in even numbers only that was too quick."

"I will open the door and run out, count to five then follow me.

"Here we go."

Sargent Hawthorne opened the door very silently. The two CIA guys were discussing the upcoming football game with the Dallas team visiting for the season opener and were not paying attention to the door being open. Just like they figured, the first CIA guy would chase and Sargent Hawthorne would not kick in the steam until he got close to make the chase nice and long and tire him out.

"One thousand one, One thousand two...." At five seconds Roger Brandenhagen bolted out the front door and made a right turn running up the sidewalk up the block and the other CIA guy just stood there guarding the perimeter for a while before he decided to give a chase, didn't know if he should chase the second guy. The last person in the world he thought would be running was Doctor Brandenhagen, aka couch potato.

The door to the car was open and the Marine buddies were ready and Doctor Brandenhagen hopped in and they shut the door as the car was screeching away. At the other end of the block another Marine Corps buddy was waiting with a car door open. Being a native American always active and running to stay fit, Sargent Hawthorne kicked in the steam when he heard the car tires screeching in the back of him. He hit the end of the block turned up the street and hopped in the waiting car that also squealed its tires in the big escape.

Inside the cars the two quick getaway artists took off their outer shirts and ball caps and the cars went immediately to a high-rise car parking garage next to some office buildings, parked their cars there and then got on the nearby Metro and rode it to Crystal City, where they got off the train and walked over past Eads Street on 23rd street and a block beyond to the sports bar. This multi-level sports bar with pool tables and lots of craft beers and good things to eat was a great place to gather and watch sports events on many Video screens and large screen TVs hooked up to the internet. There were six people all together and they quickly discovered an empty pool table by a big screen TV where they could kill two birds with one stone. With all his insane beltway bandit income, Roger was floating in doe and said, I got this round as the waitress soon delivered a couple pitchers of beer. Roger then ordered some wings and things to wash down with the fire hose of beers that would be coming.

Marines become brothers but when one separates from the Corps and relocates halfway across the country, it's not practical to have a lot of physical visits, as many end up finding a job and working full time. It was thus a special treat for Sargent Hawthorne to be with four Marines he fought with in live combat. It was better than a family reunion, and the beer, snacks, pool games, and live sports on a big screen TV made it all that much better. The fun lasted a couple hours and the spooks finally found them.

When Roger saw the men in suits including one of the guys, he pissed off by escaping tonight, he had a sudden psychological reaction. He was starting to get really tired of this big brother crap, so he did the one thing he probably shouldn't have. He hit the fast dialer on his cell phone. General Níngsī immediately got the distress call. The spooks didn't have to show any badges, they knew they were bad asses and if these *Gyrenes* wanted to test their combat effectiveness the spooks would show them a thing or two.

"I'm sorry but I've been ordered to place all of you under arrest."

Since they spooks had satellite help finding the cars which enabled them to get the license plates and identify who they were, having those nice and tight haircuts was a dead giveaway they were of the *Gyrenes* persuasion.

And they had handcuffs with them and soon led the six outside the sports bar. The Aliens quickly identified Doctor Brandenhagen and others cuffed being led outside. The Aliens tactical assault craft landed on city streets next to the five SUV's waiting. The CIA guys thought they got an eyeful and stood there almost paralyzed seen UFO's land on Washington DC streets. But the terror was yet to unfold until the eight-foot-tall giants got out of those tactical assault craft and walked up to Doctor Brandenhagen and asked him, are you okay Doctor Brandenhagen?"

"I would be a lot better if I didn't have these handcuffs on me."

The eight-foot tall Zhrakzhong Officer ordered the CIA men, "Take the handcuffs off Doctor Brandenhagen now."

"You are interfering with Federal Business."

"And you are interfering with General Níngsī's desire to protect Doctor Brandenhagen and Sargent

Hawthorne. Unless you want bad things to happen to you and all your men here, I suggest you undo the handcuffs now."

Suddenly surrounded by Fifty-Eight-Foot-Tall Giants with guns bigger than they ever seen in their lives, had an immediate effect on the CIA leader who made a tactical decision on the spot.

"Take the hand cuffs off all of them."

"That was the first smart thing you did tonight," the Zhrakzhong Officer said then he added, "We are going to give these gentlemen a ride home. Please do not disturb them for the rest of the night or we might have to take you on a ride out into space and let you discover what real authority is."

The Zhrakzhongs officer then looked at Doctor Brandenhagen and Sargent Hawthorne and said, "You two will come with me. All you others, will be taken back to your automobiles in the parking garage."

The Marines had no idea the trouble they were in until the next day, but the thrill they got riding in a UFO easily made all the punishment they received, all worth it. Especially when they got transferred to Area 51 for guard duty for punishment, which allowed them to see more spooky things. From there they were able to visit Sargent Hawthorne from time to time.

The Zhrakzhongs tactical assault craft flew up

into space and docked inside the Space Warship that Doctor Brandenhagen rode when they took him to Mars.

The Ship's Captain Luōjiàn escorted them to his space cabin where he gave them the bad news: "General Níngsī intercepted all the CIA's communications surrounding your situation at the *sports bar*. He has ordered me to take Sargent Hawthorne to the *Béésh Łigaii Atsu* (Silver Eagle) Native American Tribe, where his assistance is always required, and Doctor Brandenhagen, he's on a phone call right now informing the President of the United States you are his personal friend, and he is going to take you someplace special and you will be gone for a while. He expects the CIA to continue guarding your home while you are gone."

Of the two men, Sargent Hawthorne was the happiest with his adventure that was almost ready to end. *Too bad I left my Zhrakzhongs medal at Doctor Brandenhagen's home.*

Captain Luōjiàn then had another surprise: "Sargent Hawthorne, you do not know how serious we take our medals for valor. Your award is extremely prestigious even for Zhrakzhongs. The medal has a transponder in it and its being retrieved out of Doctor Brandenhagen's home now by one of our tactical assault ships that delivered the four Marines back to their cars. You will have your medal back in about fifteen minutes."

"Thank you."

"Let's celebrate with a drink I wish to toast you Sargent Hawthorne for your bravery in our recent magnificent Space Battle with the Xīngguī."

"I do not feel like I did anything extraordinary."

As Captain Luōjiàn's steward was pouring each of them a Gĕnkóviàn Jiǔyàowù, he said, "Sargent Hawthorne you had far more impact than you will ever understand. General Níngsī personally informed me that when you and *Binii 'tigaii* calmly and proudly stood next to him in the battle, it gave him far more courage than he normally would have. And the ancient native combat techniques you discussed were immediately converted to three dimensional and utilized during the battle, which helped make a huge difference."

The men were each served their drinks and Captain Luōjiàn said, "This is a toast to both of you since I've gone to space with you under extraordinary circumstances. It was very meaningful to me."

"Thank you, Captain, this is a toast to you and I hope you one day can go home and enjoy some time off," Doctor Brandenhagen said.

"Here's to you Captain," Sargent Hawthorne said.

The Zhrakzhongs Gěnkóviàn Jiǔyàowù Alcohol based medicine spiked with certain psychoactive drugs, quickly had their effect. All three men were in an immediate pleasant state. Moments later, the control room called via holograph, "Captain, Sargent Hawthorne's shuttle is ready to take him back to the planet at the designated landing zone."

"Let me escort you to the shuttle Sargent Hawthorne. They have your medal in the shuttle waiting for you."

"Thank you, sir."

Captain Luōjiàn knew nothing was too good for General Níngsī's three Earth friends he adopted as special to him. Each one of them had a unique influence on his good friend General Níngsī.

Doctor Brandenhagen seemed so cool and relaxed knowing he's being taken out in space somewhere, Captain Luōjiàn thought. *Perhaps it was the scientist in him and the desire for discover?*

Moments later, the control room announced, "Captain the shuttle is on the way to the planet."

Captain Luōjiàn noticed Doctor Brandenhagen had only finished half his drink or he would have offered him another.

The conversation began, "Doctor Brandenhagen, General Níngsī sent me a complete coverage of your career and work. Our nuclear physicists are no more advanced than you are. We just package things differently and have an alternative form of nuclear power because we have more assets available to design and build things with."

"That's very interesting Captain."

"Doctor Brandenhagen, I can tell you why General Níngsī is so pleased with you. He knows how you exceeded all your peers with your analysis and theory on Mars. He was also impressed that you dated the destruction so accurately as 900,000 years ago, and how you stuck with your theory and did not knuckle under pressure to abandon it. It shows you have character, which we Zhrakzhongs by nature, admire."

"Thank you, Captain, for your kind words."

"I can imagine when you went down on Mars and saw the results of your theory first hand it must have had a great effect on you."

"It certainly did and its why we must be cautious in the future in how we reach out to Aliens. We would have no way of knowing who are the good guys and who's the bad guys."

"That is certainly a fine point, almost as astute as your Mars Theory. Earth is blessed to have someone with your insights. Hopefully they will listen to you in the future so you do not go down the wrong path."

"Captain, may I ask, do you have any idea of the timeline where you will abandon Earth and go back to your worlds."

"Doctor Brandenhagen, because the planets aligned for us so to speak, we had a victory far greater than we hoped for. We no longer will need to wait here for one hundred years to move our people back to their home worlds."

"That's interesting to know."

"In anticipation of that move home, the Planetary Transport all the civilians and ground force people arrived in is already starting back for our home worlds. Since we expect and Armistice soon, we'll ferry people from Earth to the Planetary Transport on high-speed Space Warships in a few years so they do not have to spend so much time in suspended animation on the ride home."

"When do you anticipate that beginning?"

"I should probably wait and let General Níngsī give you the details, but I like you and there really is no point in delaying the information to you. The trip you are going on will most likely result in signing the Armistice, so as soon as we bring you back to Earth afterwards, we will start removing all the civilians out of Mexico. The last to leave will be military from Arizona."

"What will you do with all the construction you've done since you arrived?"

"Most of the underground construction to date is General Níngsī's command center and emergency shelters. All other construction is fast, cheap, and innovative construction because of the temperatures and the camouflage above. It will be easy to remove all of it just like we did the Archeologist tents on Mars. Once the command center is empty, its nothing but a concrete shell, it will be filled in with dirt. Nobody will know it exists as we re-terraform over the top of it.

In the matter of moments, the control room called down and said, "Captain, the shuttle is returning from the planet and we anticipate it will arrive in five minutes."

Captain Luōjiàn responded, "Control, as soon as the shuttle is onboard, proceed to the rendezvous point with General Níngsī's command ship."

Captain Luōjiàn noticed Doctor Brandenhagen looking at the monitors. *Was it fear or just simple curiosity,* he wondered?

It didn't seem long before Roger Brandenhagen felt some slight motion, then looking at the video he could see they were speeding up and leaving orbit as the moon appeared to be moving at a distance along their starboard side as indicated by the sophisticated view that would give someone the appearance they were looking forward and to the side of the ship.

Doctor Brandenhagen would not be the first person from Earth to travel outside the solar system. Sargent Hawthorne and *Binii 'ɫigaii* (screeching owl) medicine man had already done that.

The concoction that Doctor Brandenhagen drank was making him feel good and said, "I really enjoyed this drink, may impose on you for another?"

Captain Luōjiàn responded, "I would not mind another one myself." He then nodded at his steward who immediately filled two freshly chilled glasses of Gěnkóviàn Jiǔyàowù walked over, sat the two glasses down in front of each person and collected all the empty glasses and took them back to his pantry and put them into the atomizer cleaner and disinfector.

"Tell me Doctor, back on Earth, what do you like to do in your spare time?"

"Well Captain, I like going to a sports bar about once a week especially during football season. I like going to the symphony, I read a lot of books, watch some video, check out social media and the internet, and go for a lot of walks for exercise."

"Any relationships with females?"

"I have this Japanese girlfriend named Ami."

"In a committed serious relationship?"

"I let Ami call all the shots."

"That is probably the best approach."

"I think so."

"I will suggest that General Níngsī take you to Plastras Nostras."

"What's so special about that place?"

"The Plastras Nostras women have green skin, purple eyes, red hair, and some sexual features that has an amazing effect on Zhrakzhong men."

"Any chance I would catch any deadly pathogens that might kill Ami later?"

"None whatsoever. They have some of the top medical practices in the galaxy. They are germ freaks and would decontaminate you and quarantine you for two weeks before you got near any of their women."

"I think I would pass on the sex part. I like Ami even though I see less and less of her it seems. But I would certainly socialize with them, have friendly conversations and enjoy their company."

Captain Luōjiàn smiled knowing Doctor Brandenhagen would crumble to temptation the minute one of the Plastras Nostras Barracuda's (translated) as they liked to be called had their way with him.

By the time Roger Brandenhagen finished half his drink, Captain Luōjiàn asked: "See that planet we are passing?"

"Yes."

"Look familiar?"

"It does and I'm trying to remember."

"That planet is what you Earth people call Pluto."

"We got there that quick?"

"While you were sipping on your drink and we were discussing those lovely creatures on Plastras Nostras, we went above light speed. We are traveling alone and have full clearance to continue at Battle Speed to the rendezvous point."

"Will it take long?"

"By the time you finish your drink we'll be

slowing down for a personnel transfer."

"What's that about?"

"You will be transferred to General Níngsī's command ship. I will be going with him as this is one of his escort vessels."

"Allright."

Roger Brandenhagen started thinking and asked, "I can play you one of my favorite classical music concerts on my cell phone would you like to hear it?"

"Sure."

Roger pulled out his I-phone and started playing the music and stated, "This is the Kurt Atterberg piano concerto." [Atterberg Piano Concerto in B flat minor - YouTube]

Roger could see in a minute that even though it was poor quality coming from a cell phone he still enjoyed it.

Captain Luōjiàn responded and asked a question in his language that would translate, "Computer, can you see if we have files onboard with that Kurt Atterberg piano concerto music."

"Yes sir, checking now," the Artificial Intelligence

replied.

In about one minute the Artificial Intelligence Reported, "Captain Luōjiàn we have that piano works in high fidelity, would you like me to play it?"

"Computer, Yes please play it now." He then repeated in English what he said to the Artificial Intelligence always listening in the background.

Soon they were hearing the full sound range of the Kurt Atterberg piano concerto orchestration. Captain Luōjiàn was soon wishing he didn't have to send Doctor Brandenhagen to the command ship, there was a lot to learn from this Earthman. His music selection was rather incredible.

As the piano concerto played on, the Zhrakzhong ship's Captain felt an exquisite effect from the music and his drink combining to make an enjoyable experience.

By the time this piano concerto ended, the captain was informed from the control room, "Captain, we are now slowing down for the rendezvous point."

"Control, please inform me when we are ready to do the personnel transfer."

"Captain, we expect in 10 minutes."

The piano concerto ended and Roger

Brandenhagen thought he would give the captain the name of another composer before he left and so he said, "Captain, another performance you might want to hear is Eduard Künneke (1885-1953): Piano Concerto No. 1." [Eduard Künneke (1885-1953) : Piano Concerto No. 1 (1935) **MUST HEAR** - YouTube]

The Zhrakzhong Captain Luōjiàn smiled and said, "Thank you." He then said, "Computer search for that music and see if it is in any of our files."

About 15 seconds later, the Artificial Intelligence reported, "Captain we have that music. Would you like to hear it now?"

"Yes, play it now."

Roger Brandenhagen would not hear the end of the piano concerto, but he could see the Zhrakzhong Captain Luōjiàn was smiling and enjoying it.

Just when the performance was getting to an excellent and memorable moment, the control room reported, "Captain, we are ready to transport personnel. General Níngsī is ready to receive Doctor Brandenhagen."

"Alright Control, I will escort Doctor Brandenhagen to the Shuttle Craft now. Doctor Brandenhagen please come with me."

The men walked to the shuttle bay where the Zhrakzhong Captain Luōjiàn said, "Doctor Brandenhagen, thank you for introducing that music too me."

"My pleasure Captain."

"Hopefully one day, you and I can go to Plastras Nostras together, I would like to introduce you to another form of pleasure."

"It would be interesting to see green women with purple eyes," Roger Brandenhagen responded and added, "I know on your planets you bow. On Earth some countries bow and some shake hands. I'm from a country that shakes hands. Thank you for taking me to Mars which allowed me to see the fulfillment of my lifelong work."

Roger Brandenhagen held out his hand which Captain Luōjiàn having observed such behavior on other planets in the past, shook hands with the shuttle crew observing. To see this very strict Captain Luōjiàn shake the Aliens hand put them into a mild wonder as this voyage to Earth had presented them with countless opportunities for exposure to such a rare and strange culture.

"Good bye Captain."

"Thank you for the music tips, I will explore it

further."

"Have your computer research Beethoven, Brahms, Rachmaninoff, Liszt, Saint Saens, Chopin, and Tchaikovsky"

"I will thank you."

Captain Luōjiàn knew the conversation was being recorded like all others and could later ask the computer to play those composers music as well. Zhrakzhong Captain Luōjiàn was in for a huge treat which left an indelible mark on him, from the transcendence caused by Earth based humanity.

The shuttle pilots gestured to the shuttle craft which Roger Brandenhagen then entered and soon they were off flying a short distance to General Níngsī's command ship.

Looking at the command ship as they approached it from probably five miles, Roger understood how these Zhrakzhongs were a species and a civilization that Earth could not compare too. *How does a cosmic cockroach look upon such magnificent people?*

As they flew closer to the command ship, its size grew to such a huge dimension that it transfixed Roger for a moment and he pulled out his cell phone and took a few pictures as the opportunity arose. He regretted not having a cell phone charger with him. However, after he discussed it with General Níngsī he quickly had Zhrakzhongs Intelligence provide him with a charger and a power converter that allowed him to get ship's power to power up his cell phone.

As soon as the shuttle landed, shuttle bay hatches shut and shuttle bay pressurized, the pilot said, "We can now exit the shuttle and flipped the switch that opened the door they could walk out of standing erect.

As soon as they walked through the shuttle bay hatch into the main compartment, a senior officer was standing there waiting and said, "Doctor Brandenhagen, I will escort you to the Combat Information Center where General Níngsī is waiting for you."

"Thank you, sir."

Roger Brandenhagen followed the officer through the hallway to the short distance to the CIC. Past the blast doors, into the huge CIC fully staffed with Zhrakzhong communications, intelligence, and weapon systems operators. Most of these people were not the eight-foot-tall giants. They were typical height for people living on Earth. They wore spectacular moth-colored uniforms with Red trim and Blue patches. The personnel were about a 50% mix with male and female. One thing Roger did not realize because in the past he only saw most of them from the backside, but today as many were shuffling around doing a variety of tasks related to the expected combat, he could see their face and was soon surprised to see mixed in the middle of them were Green and Blue skinned people that had an interesting look to them. He didn't know what caused the person to make eye contact with him. Roger observed the red head, green skin woman, with the most alluring purple eyes. He was thunderstruck.

Could there be people from the Plastras Nostras worlds fighting with the Zhrakzhongs?

General Nostras knew Roger Brandenhagen was on the way but his back was turned to him. General Nostras a master of body language observed the young *Plastras Nostras* looking at something behind him so he turned and there was no other than Doctor Brandenhagen. *So that's what she was looking at?*

"Greetings Doctor Brandenhagen. How was your trip getting here?"

General Níngsī had a few Plastras Nostras personnel on his ship mainly because within the fleet there were several Plastras Nostras staffed Space Warships where the entire crew were Plastras Nostras Space Force personnel. They were fighting for their independence from the Xīngguī. Unfortunately do to the well-known sexual enhancement these women had, General Níngsī, had to have extra security personnel on board to ensure their safety and their dignity. Normally Plastras Nostras women paid no attention to plain skinners, so to see this woman evidently captivated by Doctor Brandenhagen's presence surprised General Níngsī. *Perhaps I should manifest a meeting of the two after the upcoming battle?* General Níngsī knew medals would not work on Doctor Brandenhagen the same way they did Sargent Hawthorne and *Binii 'łigaii.*

Plastras Nostras women picked their men, not the other way around unless you went to one of the very expensive resorts where the customer got to choose. General Níngsī started thinking of a plan to convince his friend Doctor Brandenhagen to spend time with him. Perhaps if he could create a romance between the two, Doctor Brandenhagen might choose to never go back to Earth. Certainly, deciding to stay on Plastras Nostras instead of returning to Earth would be no different than Chicago people deciding to stay in Hawaii rather than go back to Chicago for the winter.

I will work on this later. For now, I must concentrate on this battle, General Níngsī thought. *Then at a victory party, I will invite that Plastras Nostras woman to be my special guest with Doctor Brandenhagen and see if the natural course of Events would simply run their course. Doctor Brandenhagen is a curious person and if this lovely Plastras Nostras had a spontaneous emotional spike upon seeing Doctor Brandenhagen, she might instigate a Plastras Nostras covalent bonding of the type the dear doctor has never experienced.*

"Doctor Brandenhagen, you will now get to observe the completion of this conflict with the Xīngguī."

"General Níngsī, I will be very happy to learn your war is over and you have found peace, but I would like to offer you my humble opinion."

"What is your opinion Doctor."

"General Níngsī, since we were recently on Mars and saw the results of that horror, I hope that in some way you can find a way to end the war without destroying other planets like the way Mars ended up."

"Doctor Brandenhagen, it's interesting to know that my Artificial Intelligence has studied Sun Tzu art of war, Confucius, and Native American Indian Tribe history.

"That's fascinating to hear."

"Earth has given me a road map to benevolence."

"Tell me General Níngsī, what is your basic roadmap?"

"Doctor Brandenhagen, its clear to me that if I end this war in a vengeful massive destruction and killing of Xīnggui populations, I've really only achieved a Pyrrhic victory just like out of Earth's history. To have a long-lasting peace we must have a treaty that respects each other's borders and allows the free flow of ideas and commerce. I believe there is a way to achieve that without a lot of bloodshed."

"General Níngsī, for the sake of all the

Zhrakzhongs and the Xīnggui, I hope you are able to do that."

"Doctor Brandenhagen, the pathway to peace resides in Admiral Aete now."

Roger Brandenhagen noticed the ships were accelerating. He had seen how fast they could go on the way to Mars, but now, this speed seemed much faster.

"General Níngsī, we are going at an amazing speed. How do you Navigate and avoid running into a planet or a star?"

"Doctor Brandenhagen we have space transit lanes just like your ships on your planet have water routes. Our navigation systems know precisely where we are at all times and since we have accurate steering, we know that if we stay in the middle of those space transit lanes for the distance we want to go, all will be clear ahead of us."

"What about enemy ships that may be waiting ahead in a trap like you sprung on the Xīnggui as they approached our solar system?"

"You are right we would not be able to know, except we sent probes a day ahead of us who have sensors to detect the movement of alien ships, but also in some ways they are like the markers for one of your airport runways. They are a backup to our normal navigation systems we count on to keep us in the middle of the transit lane."

"After a few moments, General Níngsī said, see the large screen directly ahead of you?"

"Yes?"

"That's how we display a space roadmap. In the middle of the display is a fuzzy picture that is a toned-down video of our destination directly ahead. We are too far away to see the final destination, but now and then you see the solid-colored circles that seem to go past us like the planets?"

"Yes, I see those."

"Those are our probes."

"Since the probes have not alerted you to enemy ships, that means it's safe to proceed?"

"Certainly, the probes do one thing for us, they are in essence our early warning receiver and since we currently have no probe alarms, we know it's safe to proceed at very high speeds."

General Níngsī asked, "Doctor Brandenhagen, are you getting hungry?"

"Now that you mention it, I suppose I am."

"Alright we are going to my space cabin in a few moments. But before we do I need to give my Officer on Watch some directions."

"Sure General, I'm at your service."

General Níngsī turned towards the Combat Systems Officer and in standard Zhrakzhong language, *"Have the weapon's operator on station 17 relieved and have her report to my space cabin. Inform her privately, I would like to introduce her to my personal friend, Dr. Brandenhagen. Also mention to her that Doctor Brandenhagen is a distinguished scientist and I would like her assessment of the Doctor she can provide me later."*

"Yes sir, I will do that immediately."

"Thank you. I will proceed now with Doctor Brandenhagen to my space cabin. Please inform me immediately of and enemy sightings or unusual activity."

"Understand all sir."

General Níngsī then turned towards Doctor Brandenhagen and in perfect English thanks to his ear bud said, "Doctor Brandenhagen, us go to my space cabin and enjoy some lunch."

The two men then walked down the circular staircase into the hallway that led to General Níngsī's private space cabin.

Chapter Eighteen

Christiana

Meanwhile the Combat Systems Officer directed his assistant: "Get a relief for the weapons operator at station 17 and ask her to come see me immediately."

"Yes sir," the young officer stated and walked down the circular stairway and about 50 feet where the beautiful woman of Plastras Nostras extraction sat operating the console.

"Excuse me weapons operator, you are being relieved and the Combat Systems Officer wants you to go to him on the bridge, he has a new assignment for you."

The young woman looked at the young officer and responded, "Yes sir." She then stood up walked over to the circular stairway and approached the Combat Systems Officer currently in command of the ship and ostensibly the entire fleet unless overridden by General Níngsī.

The young female had no idea what this was about. Her days were generally seamless and she was well treated. However, she did feel a slight hostile work environment from some of the Zhrakzhong female Space Warriors who stereotyped her as a sex kitten just because she came from the world where many of the galactic salacious stories originated. She knew her watch standing was exemplary because during normal cruising, simulators were thrown at them to check their vigilance. Her measured vigilance factors always posted above average, so to be relieved suddenly left her into a twisted mental state as she wondered, *what is this all about?*

The Combat Systems Officer was always professional and respectful. During the recent space battles, he more than proved his abilities. He was thus golden in the eyes of General Níngsī.

"Sir, you wished to speak with me?"

"Yes, you were relieved because General Níngsī has a VIP guest aboard, his personal friend, and the General wants you to have lunch with them now in his private sea cabin and afterwards, wants you to provide a personal assessment of your observations of this distinguished Alien Scientist."

"Should I go there immediately with my battle dress on?"

"No, since this is a VIP, I think you should take time

to dress in formal attire as you are now a representative of the Zhrakzhongs and General Níngsī."

"How much time do I have to get ready?"

"I would suggest you expedite the change of clothes and go as you are."

"Thank you, sir, I will proceed now with my new assignment."

"Carry on, Weapons Specialist."

Christiana proceeded to her private quarters. Unlike previous Zhrakzhong command ships, she had a desk, a bunk, personal storage and a private toilet and body washer thanks to the technical refresh that got rid of half the volume of computers because of the miniaturization. Command ships were very comfortable, but the rest of the fleet didn't have such extraordinary accommodations.

Plastras Nostras women have an ovulation cycle that dumps pheromones in the air and could create scenarios if they are not careful. Knowing she would be in close confinement with General Níngsī and the Alien VIP, Christiana decided it would be prudent to get into the body washer that would eliminate ninety percent of the pheromones her body was now shedding. She didn't quite appreciate the fact her exquisite beauty would be just as much of an influence to a male's little head.

The entire body washer cycle from start to finish was less than five minutes making Christiana feel a lot more satisfied. She knew the negative ions she inhaled in the body washer would also improve her personal psychology which might help her better adjust to the presence of the Alien.

In just a couple more minutes, Christiana had her dress uniform on usually reserved for pomp and circumstances that Zhrakzhong Space Force personnel often experienced. This was a rush job; she didn't have time to pamper herself as if she were going on a date with a fine gentleman.

Christiana took one look in the mirror and thought, *this will have to do for now.*

Christiana left her private quarters and as soon as she was a mere couple footsteps away, the Artificial Intelligence locked her door for her and would not open it for anyone else because of privacy regulations. Thanks to artificial intelligence she was well protected on this command ship. Rightfully so.

Down the hallway a short distance was an elevator that would take her up to the same level General Níngsī's space cabin was situated. Normally she would not be permitted down this corridor for security reasons. But thanks to Artificial Intelligence her name was on a guest list and she was expected. Facial recognition software confirmed it was Christiana a Plastras Nostran. The green skin, purple eyes, red hair and facial recognition easily allowed Artificial Intelligence to clear her for entrance and had tracked her movement from the Combat Information Center, to her private quarters, then on her trek to the General's Space Cabin.

Even though her dress uniform was in no way designed to beautify or glamorize Christiana, it in fact did so as it contrasted in ways to exemplify her utter beauty. Her fragrance, demure, and sweet disposition made General Níngsī quite pleased. The subtle irritancy he felt from her tardiness as he expected her to march smartly from weapons control station 17 directly to his space cabin, was quickly replaced by resplendence and demure she exhibited in the most alluring fashion. An outsider might think she was personally being over sexy in her attitude and posture, but in reality, she just was as sweet as she seemed. An air of electricity flowed as Artificial Intelligence opened the door for her and invited her in.

General Níngsī knew that it would be impossible to fraternize with one of his crew members. But if there was some possibility his VIP friend Doctor Brandenhagen made inroads to this individual, it would please him, especially if it manifested Doctor Brandenhagen to decide to permanently move to the Zhrakzhong worlds so that his friendship could continue.

"Thank you, Christiana, for giving us your company," General Níngsī said.

General Níngsī had never met Christiana before, but thanks to Artificial Intelligence prompting him with her name and other information in his ear bud, he was ready to make the introduction.

"Doctor Brandenhagen, may I please introduce you to Christiana, one of my crew members that I though you would like to meet who can give you some insights and information about the Zhrakzhong civilization."

Doctor Brandenhagen was totally mesmerized looking at this glamorous alien. Her sex appeal was extraordinary. She was a sight Doctor Brandenhagen would never forget in his lifetime.

"It's a pleasure to meet you, Christiana. I'm actually surprised to meet a Zhrakzhong with a name like Christiana. It seems so Earth like."

Christiana also wearing an ear bud as part of her dress uniform was simultaneously schooled on protocol and things recommended to say to the Alien.

"Thank you Doctor Brandenhagen. I hope your visit thus far has been a pleasant one?"

"It seems I always have interesting times when I'm with General Níngsī."

"And it's about to get more interesting Doctor Brandenhagen," General Níngsī responded.

Christiana had been standing a watch at her weapons control console for nearly six hours before she was relieved and the smell of the food now starting to appear had a surreal effect on her. She was suddenly glad to be called in to give this Alien VIP company as it would soon solve her hunger.

One of the General's stewards approached and said, "Excuse me General Níngsī, we are ready to start serving your meal."

"Thank you. Christiana and Doctor Brandenhagen, will you please join me?"

As they walked over to the table they quickly noticed placards were placed on their seating assignments. Christiana was to be seated to General Níngsī's right and Roger Brandenhagen to his left. Roger and Christiana were facing each other direct.

Roger had never been hit by Plastras Nostras pheromones before. Even though Christiana tried to minimize it by showering before arriving, it would not have much effect on Zhrakzhongs because they had frequent exposure. But for an earth person it was almost an instant shock. Roger didn't quite know how or why the young woman seemed to stimulate him so much. He wasn't sure it was some kind of emotional transcendence, but whatever it was made his sensory overload from Christiana. It was a moment he would never forget. One might say it resembled love at first sight, but Roger had never met this woman before and had no real interchange to foster any types of emotional bonds, and he thought, *"why am I feeling this way?*

General Níngsī an expert I reading body language knew Christiana was somehow drugging Roger's consciousness. It made him even more pleased that he had invited the Plastras Nostras woman knowing that in some way Doctor Brandenhagen seemed to be influenced by Christiana.

The stewards poured the finest wine in the galaxy. Roger having driven around Napa Wine country and tasted the best thought; *this is really good wine!* What Roger didn't know is that during the fermentation process they added some unique enzymes only found on worlds like Plastras Nostras. The results were a wine with psychoactive components that would further pleasantness throughout the meal and long afterwards.

The 24-course meal was something unexpected by Christiana and she enjoyed every moment of it also fortified by the precious wine that one glass alone equaled her yearly salary.

Afterwards, General Níngsī played some holographic entertainment with lovely music. Just like it was on cue, an officer came into General Níngsī's space cabin and whispered something in General Níngsī's ear.

General Níngsī smiled and nodded his head and then said, "Christiana and Doctor Brandenhagen, you will please have to excuse me, but I must go attend to a matter. I want you both to stay here and enjoy more food, drink, video's etcetera. I will be back as soon as I can."

General Níngsī's then abruptly left the room where he immediately proceeded to the bridge and met the Combat Systems Officer to get an update. This was all staged of course. General Níngsī actually wanted Doctor Brandenhagen to spend some time alone with Christiana and hoped that in some way they would start to become friends. He would further that process in all manners he could.

The psychoactive drug in the wine made Christiana far more vulnerable to Roger. There was a kindling of some type of attraction between the two. The staff made themselves scarce on orders from General Níngsī who wanted the privacy to compel further interest between the two.

Doctor Brandenhagen of course enjoyed the eye candy he looked at. Christiana was incredibly beautiful. The green skin and purple eyes were exotic and hypnotic in many ways. Doctor Brandenhagen didn't quite realize he was also now getting hit with a good dose of Plastras Nostras pheromones because the psychoactive drugs in the wine caused Christiana's body to shed far more than she had prior to getting into the body washer.

The conversations flowed almost rhythmically.

Christiana had never had a real lover before. But she had a wise mother who trained her well to keep her powder dry until she met the right man at the right time. This was the wrong man at the worst possible time, but somehow, Christiana slowly became infatuated with Doctor Brandenhagen as they continued their discussions.

"Tell me Christiana, what is your home world like?"

"Well Doctor Brandenhagen," Christiana said just before the interruption:

"Please call me Roger."

"Alright Roger. I come from a world called Plastras Nostras. We are currently under the influence of the Zhrakzhongs, but in our murky past, we have been invaded by the Xīnguī. In the last invasion, the Xīnguī treated my people horribly. We believe in the theory the enemy of your enemy is your friend, thus we formed an alliance with the Zhrakzhongs, who helped us force the Xīnguī off our planet and out of our solar system."

"Is that how you came about as a crewmember for this ship?"

"As part of our alliance, we provide personnel to the Zhrakzhong Space Force. I'm a junior officer and a weapons controller."

"Christiana, you name is so familiar with Earth names. Is there any coincidence?"

"Roger, my name came from visitors to our planet my father met. Perhaps they may have picked it up from your planet in their travels."

"We sure have had a lot of unexplained visitors in the past that ancient folklore suggests came from outer space, so it would not surprise me if they visited Earth."

"Earth has probably had a lot more visitors than you realize."

"Were you part of the last battle?"

"Yes, unfortunately I had to destroy a couple Xīnggui ships as part of my responsibility to defend this command ship. I realize I terminated a lot of Xīnggui in the process. I'm not happy that I killed so many, but the reality is, it was either them or me possibly."

"You did what you had to do."

"I think I can get the Artificial Intelligence to show some recordings of my planet to show you what life is like there."

"I would like that."

Just as if on cue, the Artificial Intelligence in the

background tracking the conversation immediately started showing a three-dimensional video of the Plastras Nostras worlds. Doctor Brandenhagen was interested and realized he was probably the first human from Earth to witness an alien planet with intelligent life and the three-dimensional video and sound looked so real as if you felt you were there.

"Very nice architecture you have in your worlds."

"Thank you. In part is because it's a tourist destination, it receives a lot of development and redevelopment," Christiana said hoping she would not have to get into the reason of what drove so many men from other planets to travel there.

"It looks like you have a lot of water on that planet."

"Yes. About 75% of the surface of the planet is covered by water."

"What is the population of your larger cities?"

"The five largest cities range from thirty to sixty million people."

"Those appear to be very large tall buildings."

"Yes, up to five hundred levels of the taller building which allows our population density."

"With such little land mass, how do you grow enough food to feed everyone?"

"We have ways of growing substantial amounts in green houses spread around the planet, but we also get so many ships coming in for tourism, their cargo holds are half full of imports."

After observing many facets of Plastras Nostras worlds, Christiana asked, "Tell me about your world?"

"Maybe your Artificial Intelligence has videos of Earth to show what it's like."

Before either one of them could think about asking Artificial Intelligence, it started showing intercepted video it took from the internet, microwave, and satellite signals. The video shown was constructed for briefings to General Níngsī and his staff, and took almost two hours to see it all.

"I must say that was very informative," Christiana said.

"What part did you like the most?"

"Watching those people dance really seemed interested."

"You've never danced before?"

"No that is not one of our customs."

"Perhaps I can teach you a few simple dance routines."

"Yes, I would like that."

Artificial Intelligence already knew what General Níngsī's plan was to get this couple involved as a mechanism to convince Doctor Brandenhagen to continue with him to the Zhrakzhong Empire and provide friendship to a lonely General. Therefore, Artificial Intelligence analyzed a series of songs that eventually got to a slow dance it knew would draw them closer. All of this was calculated with astonishing degrees of accuracy.

The timing on the slow dance was perfect because body temperature, pulse, and respiration rate indicated the couple would enjoy a slower movement. Roger was an eager teacher and Cristiana was a willing student and during this slow dance Roger demonstrated and taught, their bodies touched over a large surface area. The feeling of touching the Alien Earth person, excited Cristiana and in the process, she knew she was having a pheromone explosion and other parts of her body were also showing the telltale signs of pre-copulation syndrome that caused Plastras Nostras women to feel a moistness they knew would drive their male partners to the point of insanity wanting the coupling. She wasn't going to inform Roger the condition she was in because she knew it would only cause him more discomfort since they had no ability to act out their motivations on the ship. But one thing it did do was create a secret desire in Christiana so that when the time and place became available, she would carry out her instinct that told her Roger was now developing a romantic proclivity with her. If Roger was willing to commit to a lifelong relationship at that time, she would then unfurl her passions at him in a way he would never regret it for the rest of his life.

Unfortunately for the two potential love birds the fun was going to end in a short while. General Níngsī wanted Doctor Brandenhagen well rested and Christiana would have to go back on watch as a weapon's operator in the equivalent of twelve hours from now and she too needed ample rest because at that time they would be flying into the jaws of hell for the final showdown to end this war, once and for all. And just after the slow dance ended with a growing yearning between the two, one of the stewards came into the room and spoiled the fun.

"I'm sorry to disturb you because I know how enjoyable these moments are, but we have to reconfigure General Níngsī's Space Cabin to a command conference room.

"Not a problem, sir," Roger Brandenhagen responded.

"Doctor Brandenhagen, I'm also to escort you to your assigned state room so that you can get rested and show you all the features."

"Thank you."

"Christiana it's on the way to your private quarters, I'll escort you there as well."

"Thank you."

The three left the stateroom and as part of the ultimate plan General Níngsī wanted Roger to know where Christiana's private quarters were in case, he decided he wanted to visit her and call upon her. If she was interested, she could take him to the crews' recreation center that provided off watch entertainment including thrilling holographic entertainment and music one could enjoy wearing a head piece that cut off all outside noise and allowed two crew members to have total privacy in their conversations.

After the chief steward dropped Christiana off at her privat quarters, he took Roger no more than 50 feet to his which was designed for a mid-level officer with a little more room since they had more responsibility and needed extra storage for all the extra gear they had to carry with them for special tasks and projects that occurred all too often in this bloody gut wrenching war that went on far too long because of all the fire breathers that enjoyed the protections of immense fortifications. The Steward said he had to undress to demonstrate the body washer and the restroom facilities which Roger appreciated as he would never have figured it out on his own.

"In the closet, we have some Space Uniforms and sure grip shoes for you so that you can change out of your street clothes and have the appearance as if you are part of the crew."

"Thank you."

"Your personal holograph which is all part of your desk complex will answer up to any questions you have including advising you on how to properly wear the uniforms."

"What if they do not fit?"

"If for some unexplained reason those uniforms do not fit simply start talking and your personal holograph will answer you. You can inform the holograph in what ways the uniforms do not fit and the Artificial Intelligence will send a tailor right away with other uniforms or make any adjustments required."

"What about those sure grip shoes?"

"Open your closet door, and you will see several pair you can chose that will be the most comfortable for you."

"What if they do not fit?"

"Your sure grip shoes are adjustable for several sizes. Holographic measurement of your street clothes gave our clothing providers all necessary measurements to make these items for you. We fill confident they should all fit and wear comfortably."

"All right I think we covered just about everything."

"Doctor Brandenhagen, you are a special friend of General Níngsī. He cares about your well-being. After I leave one of the ship's doctors will show up soon afterwards to give you a sedative because in about 12 hours, we could be in a combat situation. General Níngsī wants you well rested and not have wasted hours unable to sleep because your mind will be on your destiny."

"Allright."

"One last thing. We are always available to assist you. All you need to do is start talking and ask questions such as, "Can you please contact one of the stewards, I need assistance. We will be immediately notified."

"Thank you."

The steward then turned and left. Since the doctor was probably on the way, Roger saw no point in undressing or doing anything until then so he sat down at the desk.

The Artificial Intelligence was watching everything. Roger had no idea the surveillance he had on him. Artificial intelligence knew it would be about fifteen minutes before the doctor arrived, so it initiated the contact. Roger just about jumped out of his chair frightened when the holograph appeared of a man about two feet tall on his desk who introduced himself.

"Hello Roger, I'm your personal valet Randolph. If you need something you can simply say Randolph or if unsure just start talking and I'll figure out what you want."

"How did you get a name like Randolph?"

"General Níngsī has studied a lot of Earth culture and came across a Randolph who was a very interesting person, therefor he thought it would amuse you. If you want a different name for your personal valet, just let me know and I'll change it."

"No that will be fine."

"Anything you want to know, or assistance with a matter I will be able to help you."

"If I ask you to play me classical music, can you, do it?"

"What would you like to hear?"

"After the doctor administers the sedative to me can you play, Kurt Atterberg Piano Concerto in B flat minor?"

"Let me check my catalog."

In about three seconds Randolph reported, "Doctor Brandenhagen, I have that recording."

A few moments as expected there was a soft knock at the door to Roger's stateroom door and Randolph announced, "The Doctor is here."

Roger stood up to walk over to open the door, but Randolph's artificial intelligence operated the pneumatic powered door and slid it sideways allowing the doctor to enter. The female doctor appeared stunningly attractive walked into the room and the pneumatic door closed behind her. She was carrying a small carrying case, slightly smaller than a lunch box.

"Hello Doctor Brandenhagen, I'm Janxel one of the ship's doctors. You were notified I was coming and the reasons?"

"Yes, Doctor Janxel, I was expecting you. Thank you for coming."

"Doctor Brandenhagen, I know you did not request this medication, but reviewing the records we have for you which includes your trip to Mars, and other events associated with us Zhrakzhongs, you already have experienced a lot of stress. We want you prepared for tomorrow as General Níngsī wants you to be an observer. It will be a long tough day so it's important you are well rested. You will have problems waking up on your own, I will be back after you are rested and give you another treatment that will help you regain all your cognitive awareness."

"Are you going to give me an injection?"

"No, we do not give injections. We use inhalers and other devices."

"Alright, I'm ready."

"Doctor Brandenhagen, in your closet you will see white sleeping clothes. A top and a bottom piece. I want you to take off your street clothes, put on the sleeping attire, then lay down in your bed. I will then administer your sedative."

"Sure thing, doctor."

Roger undressed and put on the sleeping clothes that fit him amazingly well. *These aliens are so crafty they even figured out my sizes.*

Roger walked over to his bed, pulled the sheets back and climbed in. It felt amazingly good. The doctor came to him and put a strap like device around his left arm next to her which had cables going to her lunch box size device that apparently measured his vital signs. She then pulled a device out that appeared like an oxygen mask used on airliners in an emergency or for oxygen at the emergency room in a hospital.

"I'm going to put this breathing apparatus on your face now. Just breath normally and count to 10 audibly for me."

Roger started breathing the sedative Doctor Janxel gave him through the mask. It smelled pleasant. After he counted to seven, he was unconscious. The doctor removed the wrist strap and then took the strap that was part of the bed to hold Roger in place in the event there was a loss of artificial gravity or some sudden maneuver that might create G Forces and throw him out of his bed. He was in the deepest and best sleep he ever experienced. He experienced almost 10 hours of RIM sleep and had more dreams than ever before in his lifetime.

Doctor Janxel then visited Christiana and gave her the same exact treatment and would be back and wake her up just before she went to Roger's stateroom.

Roger went into that drug induced nonconscious state. Randolph true to his word played the Kurt Atterberg piano concerto. The three-dimensional audio that was further processed and filtered by the Artificial Intelligence played through a series of ceramic transducers placed around Roger's bed to provide that splendid three-dimensional audio component that now modulated his dream state.

Ten hours later when Doctor Janxel gave Roger his wakeup air mixture through an oxygen mask like device, he knew he had listened to the Kurt Atterberg piano concerto and other music compositions as Randolph played other selections the Artificial Intelligence deemed highly popular all-around planet Earth including Beethoven, Brahms, Liszt, Saint Saens, Rachmaninoff, Tchaikovsky, Schuman, Bartok, Prokofiev, Hanns Wolf, Eduard Künneke, and George Gershwin. Even though Roger had been unconscious for almost 10 hours, he had vivid memories of each musical component played and the dreams it spurned on such as a romantic interlude with Christiana and Doctor Janxel, either one seemed to have been love at first site.

As Doctor Janxel (pronounced Jan-zel) gave the wakeup gas mixture to Christiana and Roger, she informed them, "After you take care of your morning activities and freshen up, General Níngsī requests you join him for a pre-Space Battle Brunch."

Doctor Janxel also informed Christiana a few minutes later, "You are directed to wear your combat uniform since we expect enemy activity shortly after the Brunch is concluded and you will be going back on watch as Weapons Console number seventeen, operator."

"Understand, Doctor."

There was also an interesting development as Artificial Intelligence advised General Níngsī, "During Doctor Brandenhagen's dream state he was talking in his sleep and he thought he was talking to Doctor Janxel."

"You think there is some sort of attraction?"

"Yes definitely. I augmented the music he requested with synthesized voice of Doctor Janxel and did role playing with him while he was semi-unconscious to fortify his dream."

"That's outstanding. In case it doesn't work out between Doctor Brandenhagen and Christiana, our backup plan would be to help foster the beginning of a relationship between Doctor Brandenhagen and Doctor Janxel."

"Is that because you wish him to stay with you as your friend after this mission is over?"

"A general can have no friends on a command ship because of the issues involving fraternization. It gets lonely at the top."

"General Níngsī, I will do what is necessary to foster a relationship between Doctor Brandenhagen on either one the women he seems to get interested in."

"Thank you."

"General Níngsī, your guests have been notified their presence is requested. Expect to see all of them here shortly."

"Thank you."

"You are most welcome General Níngsī."

This was the most auspicious occasion in practically all of General Níngsī's life as he would be soon experiencing the most important battle in his entire career. This was the winner take all battle, that's how important it was. Not knowing for sure the outcome since the battle had not yet started, General Níngsī at least had the satisfaction of knowing he would be standing in his control room directing the battle with his new best friend standing beside him observing this massive battle.

The three arrived within a few minutes of each other. Roger now had on his space uniform and appeared like Christiana and Doctor Janxel also wearing their battle uniforms. General Níngsī looked about the same except his uniform had red trim and decorations on the moth-colored fire proof fabric.

The place settings were similar from before except now Roger faced two very beautiful women. General Níngsī secretly wanted Roger to develop a romance with either one of them and chose to remain with him as his friend long after the battle. Once victory was assured, there would be no point in him remaining in command of the Zhrakzhongs Space Fleet. He would retire, enjoy the finer things of life and introduce Roger to a whole universe that no one on Earth knew existed. General Níngsī would introduce Roger to the top brains in Zhrakzhong society, so that his remaining years would be full of the gratification of spell binding scientific achievement. He might even visit the Jupitorians with Roger so that he might be able to glean more on the destruction of Mars and what it was like before the Jupitorians did their dastardly deed.

The meal was served with music playing in the background Roger recognized. It was an obscure piece rarely played in concert halls on Earth, but nevertheless a fine beautiful example of exquisite piano concerto composition by the late Ilmari Hannikainen who lived between 1892-1955. This unique composer's life was cut short when he drowned during a sailing trip in Kuhmoinen in 1955. [Ilmari Hannikainen (1892-1955) : Piano Concerto (1917) **MUST HEAR** - YouTube.]

The food besides being utterly delicious, hit the spot really good. This could actually be their last supper. Nobody really knew for sure what the future held as they were heading for the big showdown with Admiral Aete who had ever intention on carving out a victory after his most recent disaster during the Battle of Earth.

~~~

Chapter Nineteen

The Resurrection of Admiral Aeta

Admiral Aeta had gone through several more training sessions with the Tytrone Philosophers. Admiral Aeta no doubt was a *converti*. After obtaining his gateway experience, his entire battle philosophy changed. He knew he would be at least tenfold more effective in the next battle. He was ready to now deploy his fleet and end this insane war once and for all but he had one more task to perform prior to departure.

If the Emperor Guards ever discovered their plans, Admiral Aeta, Kāiwù de Sēngrén, and Xié'è de Gōngniú would be placed before laser firing squads. The Tytrone Philosophers did all the planning and logistics support. If there was ever a deep state in the galaxy that mattered, this was it. They not only crafted policy, they carried it out. What is seen and what is not seen are two separate entities, but they are tied together in ingenious manners that precludes, detection and defenses. Emperor Shāyú would be appalled if he only knew how inept his Emperor Guards really were.

Xié'è de Gōngniú and his men knew their weaknesses and elements of their vigilance degradation. Emperor Shāyú's guards came from the best and wealthiest families in the Empire. Since they were far more affluent than most of Xīnggui society, they were more synchronized to the holidays and celebrations society experienced. It was during such festivities their vigilance was extremely poor.

The XSS (Xīnggui Security Service) knew all too well the deplorable condition the Emperor Guards lapsed into during such merriments and as a consequence routinely had to bolster Emperor Shāyú's security at those times. One could estimate the Emperor Guards vigilance went from a 10 point down to a one point, especially during the most important Holiday that certainly was exemplified.

XSS men who were slightly envious of the Emperor's Guards who got about ten times the accolades with only ten percent of the efforts. Because of the secrecy, only the XSS knew they had solved more attempts on Emperor Shāyú Shāyú's life and did not even divulge it to the Emperor Guards because of their poor security practices and lack of compartmentalization. Even Emperor Shāyú didn't know his Emperor Guards were actually detrimental to his personal security. That whole situation played heavily into mission planning. Timing could never be so perfect. In the midst of the holiday, Emperor Shāyú would be kidnapped. He would then be taken to a remote area where Kāiwù de Sēngrén and his Tytrone Philosopher Monks would convert Emperor Shāyú if all worked out to plan and there were no SNAFU's.

Admiral Aeta had his role to play in all this. Prior to his conversion he would take a laser kill shot before he would betray Emperor Shāyú. Now he would go back up to his command ship and bring back a squadron of multi-purpose combat craft. These could be fighters, bombers, or deliver forces for ground assault. In this mission they would provide protection for the XSS Sky Cars and seal off the perimeter to the safe house where Emperor Shāyú would undergo his conversion and make sure nobody interfered including the Emperor's Guards in the event they discovered his *whereabouts*.

During the holiday, Emperor Shāyú picked the most unsafe place to be: his palace. As predicted, the Emperor Guards were inebriated. Under normal regulations, 33% of them must be on duty and in a viable condition to thwart off all attacks. The Sargent of the Guard, made some very bad choices that day. His first egregious act was to only have 11% of the men on staff sending the rest of them home to be with their families, because he knew in his own mind, nobody on the planet would have the nerve to break into the Palace. Afterall the XSS had this place wired to the hilt. The alarm systems were fail-safe and they could always vector in the Space Force for reserves. There was one possibility they would never assume: the XSS would turn off all the security devices at the appropriate moment. Since they controlled security, nobody outside the Palace would know anything about what went on inside it. Attempting to activate alarms would not do them any good because all the alarms were deactivated.

Within thirty seconds of the assault all communications in the vicinity of the Palace would be jammed.

One of the XSS men who drove Admiral Aete's Space Scooter to the safe house had one of the most enjoyable rides of his life. If he could ever acquire enough credits, this would be the first thing he would buy.

The Space Scooter landed in front of the safe house about the same time Xié'è de Gōngniú escorted Admiral Aete to it. In the span of a minute or less, the XSS man hopped out of the space scooter and Admiral Aete got in it. Admiral Aete gave Xié'è de Gōngniú a thumbs up then drove it down the road about 100 feet then transitioned to flight mode and like any good Harley owner would do leaving a bar, gave it some juice and went vertical. In the span of about five minutes, it was so high up in the air, it could not be seen without the aid of a telescope with Admiral Aete enjoying feeling those G forces!

Admiral Aete had a communicator in his Scooter that allowed an encrypted conversation with his executive officer who called on his way back up to his command ship. He knew who his most trusted officers were and directed the XO to have them all gather in the ward room for a briefing followed by an immediate departure for a mission. To the XO's surprise, Admiral Aete said he planned to lead the mission and to have a squadron of twenty multi-purpose combat craft with 200 Space Marines fully armed and suited up in assault gear. In essence they would appear like cyborgs with all the equipment they wore including a few of them in exoskeleton's allowing them to carry additional equipment for the rest of the force. Those Space Marines with exoskeletons were the equivalent of truck drivers operating a vehicle with powerful legs instead of wheels.

This force could easily last 30 days with no re-supply. In reality the space marines would only be required for a few days, but anytime the space marines deployed in a multi-purpose combat craft they were always sent out with a full tactical load. This was a disciplinary measure to ensure they went on every mission as if it were important as it not only tested the marines deployed but all their logistics people that put together the package. Admiral Aete was a firm believer in training in the same manner as you would fight, so when the fighting started it would all be second nature with no guess work and no worries that some box kicker (logistics guy) screwed up a packing. Their quality control was no different than parachute packers who went out on drops. The idea there was if they were fearful in deploying for an air drop, it meant they might not have confidence in the way the packed parachutes. Even though parachuting was an ancient art of war, it actually came in good use especially for special forces parachuting behind enemy lines where loiter time for multi-purpose combat craft disgorging space marines was considered excessively risky.

One of the scariest jobs of the space marines was to be the guy who parachuted down inside an exoskeleton.

It was heavy with a full load and landed like a cat on all four absorbing some of the jar that occurred because otherwise it would be a hard landing. If there was a parachute deployment issue, death was assumed since they were usually dropped at 200 feet with only scant moments of parachute opening.

Today, there would be no parachutes. The safehouse picked was an abandoned farm house, reconditioned for decent habitability and lots of room for multi-purpose combat craft to park around a perimeter to keep everyone out.

Paramilitary XSS men were at the site with laser designators to guide the force down and to place them in a perimeter and set up road blocks and detours on the seldom used country road. The condition to start the operation in the Palace required this Space Marine force to be in place and deployed around the perimeter prior to the snatch and grab.

The Emperor Shāyú made it easy for the snatch and grab. Since today was a holiday, he would enjoy it by having a couple of his bruisers toss one of his enemies into the pool with his lovely fish.

Xié'è de Gōngniú hoped to arrive just before the toss to save the man's life. Although they might have to throw in the two bruisers to get rid of the evidence.

The emperor had a lovely lawn next to the pool that would easily accommodate four or more skycars.

As soon as Admiral Aeta reported his men were in position the four skycars came down quickly just as the two bruisers were dragging the screaming man towards the pool with the sick emperor laughing as if it was the next best thing to ice cream on a hot sunny day.

The Skycars landing caused the two big goons to suddenly drop the desperate man so they could grab their blasters out of their shoulder harness, and as the man started running away one of the men pointed his blaster at the man and was getting ready to cut him down when he met his own fate from an orbiting skycar with laser guided four barrel high velocity guns that Xié'è de Gōngniú only had to point at on the target screen and say shoot. Most of the Emperor Guards were in hiding and didn't want to be around when these horrible men did the Emperor Shāyú's dirty work and were hidden so well, they didn't know what was going on.

After watching his buddy get chewed up with over 100 high velocity rounds the other goon froze. Emperor Shāyú froze in horror as the men piled out of the four sky cars and came over and cuffed the goon and the Emperor Shāyú and hauled them away in one of the sky cars. A few of the other XSS men dressed in coveralls quickly cleaned up the mess and threw the remains into the pond to give the fish their daily diet.

The first skycar carrying Emperor Shāyú and the goon who was soon injected and knocked out, departed vertically and was quickly on its way to the safehouse.

The Space Marines had no idea who they were protecting and guarding. They would never know. This was going to be one of the best kept secrets in Xīngguī history. The staff at the Palace didn't realize Emperor Shāyú was missing until the following morning, and only after they received a visitor informing them, that Emperor Shāyú would be back in a few days, and there was to be no mention of his disappearance or the perpetrator would go for a swim in his special pool.

When the skycar arrived it drove into the attached garage and paramilitary guards shut the garage door, so nobody could see who arrived. The Space Marines set up all their positions with almost a half mile between them and the farm house that had lights on inside with shades drawn so nobody could look inside.

After some time, they could hear strange sounds coming from the farm house, but since it was patrolled by paramilitary people with uniforms on, they figured it was none of their business and that whoever the VIP in the farmhouse was, must somehow enjoyed the sounds that could be heard coming from a Tytrone Philosopher Temple.

Emperor Shāyú was led out of the skycar into the farmhouse via a door that accessed the garage. The house was nearly empty except it had some chairs arranged in a strange fashion and to Emperor Shāyú's great surprise that created instant fear were Tytrone Philosophers wearing their Kǎisà Robes. Fear struck Emperor Shāyú as his personal spies had been warning him the Tytrone Philosophers were out to get him, and here he was, one of their prisoners. He was also dumbfounded how all this happened. He evidently suffered one of the greatest breaches of security in Xīnggui Empire history. How they managed to pull off this amazing feat would probably keep him thinking for a long time if he were allowed to live. Was it a Coup and who else was involved?

Emperor Shāyú was led over to a chair in the middle of three and directed: "Sit down here Emperor Shāyú."

Nobody said anything yet, it wasn't time. Xié'è de Gōngniú had another couple of tasks to do before it was time to begin the training. He called Admiral Aeta and said, "We have one of the two men Emperor Shāyú was using to throw his enemies into the fish pool to kill them. He's been injected and is in a semi-comatose. I've sent images up to your command ship we secretly recorded showing what this man did. I want you to bring one of your multi-purpose combat craft to the garage of the farm house and load this man up. Take him up to your command ship and when he comes too, make sure he has good leg and arm restraints, show him the videos, then dump him out into space from one of your shuttle bays."

"I'll be there in a few minutes."

"When you get done with that, come back to the farm house, I want you to participate in what we do next."

"I'll be there as soon as I get done with what you requested."

Admiral Aete didn't exactly like what he was doing, but he understood this would be a deterrent to others who might want to participate in heinous crimes. He wasn't going to waste his time dumping him out a shuttle bay. He would rather put the man into a probe launch tube, that worked off the principals of shooting torpedos. After watching a couple of the videos, he would be put in the tube bound really well then ejected out of the tube just like a high-speed probe. The people launching him into space would feel no remorse for the evil deeds he did. After completing all the messy work, Admiral Aeta was back down at the farm house to see first-hand what was to happen with the Emperor Shāyú.

The room had been quiet. Emperor Shāyú assumed he would soon be executed so there was no reason to talk or ask questions. Xié'è de Gōngniú didn't say anything until Admiral Aeta returned and joined them in the farm house:

"Now that we are all here together, I'm going to explain what we are going to do. We support the Empire and would give our lives for the Empire. That means we have to support you Emperor Shāyú. But before you can continue ruling this great Empire, you need to go through the same training that Admiral Aete and I have gone through. After you complete the training, we'll take you back to the Palace where you can continue on with your duties as the our Emperor. We believe that after you receive this training, you will be a more effective Emperor and realize your spies lied to you about the Tytrone Philosophers. They wish you no harm. They are only concerned about your soul and your future journey through life and the ever after. In a few minutes the Tytrone Philosophers will begin the training session. Admiral Aeta and I will take the training with you. We all hope this process will help each of us so that we can better serve you in the future. I apologize for forcing you into this training, but I fear the Empire is at risk and unless you receive the training, the war will drag on with the Zhrakzhongs with the risk of us all being wiped out."

Xié'è de Gōngniú nodded at Kāiwù de Sēngrén who then very softly and politely explained to the Emperor what he was to do to reach this higher level of enlightenment. Then immediately on cue, the Tytrone Philosophers began their chants, and musical tones and the gong at times.

Kāiwù de Sēngrén a very experienced trainer knew that Evil men took much longer to change. Their minds are wired up differently and most lack empathy. It's through empathy that one reaches a higher level of enlightenment much quicker.

Emperor Shāyú was agitated and upset with his treatment that he felt was downright treasonous requiring them all to be shot with laser rifles. At first, he didn't want to hum and do the things that Kāiwù de Sēngrén. But after a couple sharp jabs in the rib cage by Xié'è de Gōngniú he started cooperating merely to avoid further pain. And for 10 to 20 minutes his ribs actually hurt where he took the sharp blows that should earn Xié'è de Gōngniú a firing squad by laser rifles. However around twenty minutes his mind slowly started drifting into a strange vision. His ribs no longer hurt. He actually started feeling invigorated and the more they continued the stranger he felt to finally there appeared a wavy area in front of him full of different bright colors that he seemed to pass through. Then he knew he was traveling through the Universe.

Emperor Shāyú was going places and seeing things he never imagined. It was a magical experience. Life unfolded before him. This life seemed to slip away and he entered a new life in a different time and place. Those around him were totally unfamiliar. He was absorbed in all that. And it continued longer than he could imagine. Day turned into night and night turned into day. His days sped up as if he had a new time standard. This entire trip to the Universe was beyond anything he could expect in his lifetime. As time went by, he became more and more satisfied. His new artificial world was so much more pleasant.

Emperor Shāyú was starting to feel something he doubt he ever felt in his life, empathy and love. Then slowly it all started to fade away. He struggled harder than any time in his life to try to keep it, but the challenge was just too great. Soon his artificial world slipped away and he slowly came back to reality. He looked around the room. Everyone was sitting there observing him. There was no sound. He woke into complete silence. He knew now his mind was different. He had just experienced more than any time in his life. At first, he thought it was just a few minutes possibly, then when asked how long that lasted, he was informed:

"You were gone for three hours, your excellency."

Emperor Shāyú slowly realized this was quite an event. He looked down at his arm where he had an elongated wrist band that had a communicator, a chronometer, and a dozen other devices built in. Indeed, over three hours or more had transpired. His journey around the Universe lasted over three hours.

Emperor Shāyú looked at Xié'è de Gōngniú and asked, "Did you go where I went?"

"Yes, your excellency, I too traveled to the Universe, and so did Admiral Aeta.

"This experience gives me something to think about."

"Your excellency, this is a verbal method, it's for beginners. You have a very important role for the Empire. There will be times where you will have to do this silently as to not give your enemies knowledge that your mind has gone to the Universe because you are in a very vulnerable condition. Even though you may not like the way we brought you here, we do serve you and are always worried about your safety. We want you to learn the silent meditation technique that will allow you to travel to the Universe without anyone knowing you are somewhere else so that they cannot harm you. If you work with us long enough, Kāiwù de Sēngrén will teach us a bi-mental technique where we can be traveling through the Universe but at the same time have an awareness so that you can regain your posture to avoid dangerous situations."

"How long will that take."

"Kāiwù de Sēngrén assures us he can teach us all that in 3 or 4 days."

"Will we have something decent to eat in the meantime and do I have a place to sleep?"

"Your excellency, we have a bedroom set up for you that is comfortable and clean. As far as food goes, we can bring it to you, but if you want special food made from your Palace Chefs, let us know and we will send over some XSS men to bring your personal Chef's creations to eat here, just as if you are on a picnic."

"When do we start the next training session?"

Kāiwù de Sēngrén then spoke and said, "Your excellency, your mind has been exercised far more than probably any time in your life. We want to protect you and make sure that in no way do you receive any serious injury from this training. You need to relax and not engage your mind until tomorrow. That way you will be fresh and your brain will be much better able to handle the next phase of training which you will discover is beyond what you experienced today.

"Well, I suppose I'm getting hungry. But I want some fine wine to go with it."

"Your excellency, we want you to feel the best because in doing so you will be able to better achieve the level of training and pathway to enlightenment, we hope you achieve that will make you a far more effective Emperor and in the long run will make the Empire more united and stronger," Kāiwù de Sēngrén stated in a very soft and gentle manner.

"I think I misjudged you and its apparent my spies mislead me about you Tytrone Philosophers."

"Your excellency, we do not have all the answers and every day with new discoveries we find ourselves confronted with new challenges, such as the war with the Zhrakzhongs that only brings misery and suffering to the masses."

"What do you expect me to do about the war? It started before I became Emperor?"

"Your excellency, it's not our job to advise you on what you should do. You will figure it out. Our purpose is to get you to the Universe so that you can find the answers. I feel confident you will eventually discover all the right answers and become a much more effective

Emperor and you will be able to figure it out without our help."

"You believe so?"

"Yes, I have complete faith in your excellency, and after you finish the training, you will be very successful and feel so much better in life."

"I already feel better. It's amazing."

"Your excellency, we want you to maintain good health. It's now time that you eat something and relax and rest until tomorrow when we begin the silent meditation training that you can do without allowing your enemies to know you are in a vulnerable state."

"Allright, I'm going to contact my Chef now and let him know what I want to eat. But I want someone to fly to my palace and pick up the chef and the food and bring them here so he can properly serve me."

"Your excellency, we will do that right now."

In 30 minutes, Emperor Shāyú was sitting at a table with fine settings as nice as if he were in the palace. But one thing was developing now is his paranoia was quickly declining. He was also slowly building a degree of respect for Admiral Aeta, Xié'è de Gōngniú, and Kāiwù de Sēngrén who he now fully understood were loyal, but slightly unconventional. *Perhaps had they not*

*done it this way, I never would have caught on and would
have kept listening to those people giving me bad advice?*

And as they promised, Emperor Shāyú had a
very comfortable bed and the room appeared to have
been modified with an environmental enclosure with
air filtering and conditioning to a very comfortable
level. He also had another awakening. In his bedroom
were two-armed guards to protect him.

Emperor Shāyú didn't know it yet but he really
did have enemies who gave him tainted information.
They were also the source of the assassins. War profiteers
who wanted the blood flowing through eternity and
connected with intergalactic bankers. Over the next
four days, Emperor Shāyú would realize a lot as he
traveled through the universe and discovered some of
the truths himself. Had Xié'è de Gōngniú his chief of
security informed him of all this, he would have been
skeptical and in disbelief and not taken correct actions
until it was too late.

The following day, Emperor Shāyú began his
silent meditation and learning a new approach to the
gateway. As his brain synchronized and he went to the
Universe he grew mentally faster than anyone could
imagine. After the third day of training, he now felt
more confident than ever before in his lifetime. His
metamorphism would seem astonishing to his court
and those well to do individuals who were actually his
enemies and not on his side. It's a painful experience
when you learn all these things. He learned and he also

knew Admiral Aeta and Xié'è de Gōngniú learned with him. There was a sort of bonding that developed. Some might say it was like the Earth Stockholm Syndrome where you become attracted to your captors. But this was different because the Captors were also the students. Even the Tytrone Philosophers experienced many of the phenomena these three powerful men discovered as they too traveled to the Universe.

Finally on the morning of the fourth day, Kāiwù de Sēngrén stated, "Emperor Shāyú, my observations are that you have reached a level of enlightenment. You need to now go back to your palace and administer your Empire."

"I do feel much better than I have in a long time."

"Your efforts released the demons in your mind. You will be able to think clearer and more precise in the future. The Empire now needs you go back to it. I have faith in you," Kāiwù de Sēngrén stated, leaving Emperor Shāyú in a state of awareness as well as appreciation for the transformation he manifested.

Emperor Shāyú walked over to Kāiwù de Sēngrén and placed his hands on his shoulders and said, "You are a very wise man. You have opened my eyes and for that I thank you."

"You are most welcome your excellency."

Emperor Shāyú then turned towards Xié'è de Gōngniú and said, "Take me back to the Palace and on the way, I want to discuss with you, new security arrangements."

"It will be my pleasure, your excellency."

In five minutes, they were gone and Admiral Aete was then mobilizing his troops to go back to the command ship as they all wondered, "What was that all about?"

The following day, Admiral Aete led his fleet back out into space and headed to the expected final showdown. He would go out as a winner dead or alive. He had no fear either way. The Tytrone Philosophers had modified his thinking. He would now make all the right choices and he knew the end was near and finally they had a chance to end this nightmare that had gone on far too long.

In Admiral Aete's last conversation with Emperor Shāyú, his prime orders and directives were not caustic as they were before. There were no threats or extraordinary requirements. Emperor Shāyú simply said, "Admiral Aete, I have complete confidence you will do the best you can. The results of the battle will determine our next actions, which could include another round of diplomatic attempts to end the fighting once and for all."

Those words conveyed to Admiral Aete the

obvious change in posture of Emperor Shāyú who was now ready to end this conflict. Admiral Aete wasn't quite sure there was actually a need for the battle, but common sense suggested the public would not tolerate a unilateral surrender without at least putting up a fight. Admiral Aete had one additional method at his disposal. He would perform silent meditation until someone woke him out of his gateway condition when the shooting was about to start. Hence, he had a method to prevent himself from second guessing or adopting a radical shift to his plan before all the combat commenced.

In space battles the convergence speeds are usually very fast. In many cases the enemy passes while the shooting is in progress and both sides quickly loop around in an attempt to get in the rears of the enemy. From initial detection until combat begins is usually a short duration.

Admiral Aete, explained to the tactics officer in the control room, "I'm going to my Space Cabin to meditate and reflect up this battle. Send someone to get me when you make contact with the enemy. I may be unresponsive, so inform your messenger to shake me if necessary to wake me so I can come to the Bridge immediately.

"Will do admiral, get some rest and we will come get you when we get our detects."

The Admiral's Space Cabin located just twenty

feet aft of the control room allowed fast access in the case of an emergency. It took a few moments to reach his Space Cabin that in no way compared to the opulence General Níngsī enjoyed. If he wanted to eat a meal, he had to go to the wardroom just like all the other officers. His Space Cabin had enough room for a small conference table and eight chairs for meetings with his department and division commanders.

Admiral Aete would be mildly appalled to see the opulence of General Níngsī's quarters aboard his command ship. His crew members would also be jealous to learn that each crew member had their private quarters. This was all made possible because the Zhrakzhongs constantly worked on miniaturization and artificial intelligence that eventually paid big dividends allowing them to unload over half of the equipment and replace it with much smaller and smarter processors. Because this was a high stakes war, tech refresh was the name of the game for the Zhrakzhongs, whereas the vast sums squandered by Emperor Shāyú forced his budgeteer's to often keep using obsolete equipment as long as it still functioned. The Xīngguī only stayed competitive in this war because prior Emperors built large numbers of space warships. Hence the Xīngguī tactic of overcoming the technological advantage the Zhrakzhongs exhibited was to overwhelm them with numbers. If you get a force large enough during a battle, the smaller force cannot sustain as many causalities before the technological advantage was any longer beneficial to the outcome of the battle.

Admiral Aeta, removed his shoes, but kept his

battle dress on and laid back into his comfortable bed that was still covered by temperature moderators connected to the air conditioning system to maintain set values allowing a person to pick the temperature they desired sleeping in.

Admiral Aeta then began his silent meditation. He didn't have the Tytrone Philosophers there to create the sounds that helped trigger his gateway experience, so he simply concentrated on the memories of the sounds that were now indelibly etched in his memories. Just as if he were hearing real sounds to manifest the experience, he slowly evolved into a mental hemi-synchronization and his mind then started its journey to the universe. He would live five or six lifetimes in this journey because the time reference changes. One heart beat becomes millions of seconds as his brain now produced that holographic imagery that is only theorized of how its created. Scientists will never discover how the brain produces that holographic imagery, but they know the results that leads to their speculation that could actually be way off the mark.

The Tytrone Philosopher's knew how to create those gateway holographs and how they discovered this process was long lost. Some theorized space travelers brought it here from other planets. The fact they find names of individuals similar to those found on Earth also added to the speculation, that could have been the source of the technique.

Chapter Twenty

Tough Decisions

The brunch was more of a social call than a meal. This was carefully planned as General Níngsī sensed the war was almost over and he wanted his friend Doctor Brandenhagen to go back to his home worlds with him so that he had a real friend and not a social climber seducing him using social engineering to climb the ladder of success. If things worked out well, he would also invite Sargent Hawthorne and Sally Fairbanks to leave Earth with him. But he somehow felt they had too many ties to Earth to be convinced to go on such a long journey in life. Having a physical relationship with Sally Fairbanks also crossed his mind, so there were other factors. Nevertheless, Sally's mother now 65 had many years left to live and was in great physical shape, so logic indicated she would be crushed if her daughter departed. That alone convinced General Níngsī not to pursue Sally beyond the time he spent on Earth since such a relationship would eventually come up to a dead end.

It was kind of quiet during the brunch which General Níngsī didn't like because he knew the three guests were probably spending too much time thinking about the coming battle. He had to create a scenario to get them talking and get their minds off the struggle that lay ahead probably in a few hours.

"Tell me about your journey in life, Doctor Janxel, how did you end up as part of the Zhrakzhongs Space Force?"

"General Níngsī, I grew up on the planet Práxímùs Táoshù. I was educated there and studied medical and biological research in post graduate. As you probably know Práxímùs Táoshù is very provincial and isolated by a great distance to our Capitol at Tèlándìa. Due to the ongoing war with the Xīngguī our medical physician ranks were getting depleted at an alarming rate. I was visited by a Space Force Surgeon who was tasked to survey the records of many people with my credentials and he determined I had most of the requirements to convert to a physician. He then informed me that if I was willing to leave my research post, they would send me to the Fleet's medical center at Tèlándìa where I would enter an accelerated course that focused on skin grafts, surgery, and battlefield type injuries. I worked half time assisting other physicians and was supervised in performing many different types of emergency surgery on battlefield casualties. After six months of accelerated training in the medical center working always over half a day from sun up until sun down usually, I was certified by the Space Force Chief Surgeon to deploy with the fleet as a Space Warship Surgeon and Medical

Officer."

"What kinds of things did you enjoy doing on Práxímùs Táoshù?"

"General Níngsī, Práxímùs Táoshù lacks the entertainment and rich culture that exists on Tèlándìa to the point we often had to create our own forms of entertainment. I was always close to nature so I enjoyed my time outdoors, exploring the wilderness and enjoying the strange flora and wild life that exists there."

"In your treks through the wilderness did you ever come across a Sīmǎní Hǔ?"

"No thank goodness, they have a voracious appetite. If one found me, I wouldn't be here today. I lived far north of where they exist, so it's unlikely I would ever see one."

"Doctor Brandenhagen, Doctor Janxel's planet is the only one in our empire that has the Sīmǎní Hǔ. They are extremely rare and almost extinct now from what I recently read," General Níngsī stated then added, "Us have the Artificial Intelligence put up some Sīmǎní Hǔ video so you can see what they are like."

The holograph that was soon showing a live recording of a Sīmǎní Hǔ was almost frightening to Roger as the holograph appeared real. The three-dimensional video and sound created a pulsating sensation in Roger as if it were a real-life experience.

Roger calmly told himself, it's just a holograph, calm yourself down.

After Roger regained his composure, he calmly stated, "That animal looks like Saber Toothed Tigers we had on Earth about 10,000 years ago."

"What happened to them?"

"Our scientists theorize that environmental change, decline in food supply, and human hunters lead to the extinction of the saber-tooth tiger some 10,000 years ago around the end of Earth's last glacial period."

Roger sitting directly across from Doctor Janxel with much better lighting than what exists in his private quarters, observed her very carefully. She had blonde hair that was cropped short almost to the length of a male haircut, *possibly to make sterilization and pre- and post-surgery cleaning simpler*, he thought. She was fully humanoid and would fit in Earth very easily. It was hard to gauge what her body was like with a combat space uniform on, but she seemed to be slender and well-shaped overall. Her face and complexion appeared very attractive. She looked so good there would never be the need for her to put on makeup.

On top of all that Doctor Janxel definitely had superior intelligence as a medical officer on the task force command ship. That meant she had been evaluated with superior skills, exactly what senior officers wanted. Command ships by nature always had the superior officers and crew members as the commanding officer and task force commander could cherry pick the crew they wanted. They also had the diverse capability of Artificial Intelligence doing most of their leg work.

General Níngsī an expert body language observer picked up on the subtle infatuation Doctor Brandenhagen appeared to exhibit towards Doctor Janxel. *I wonder if Doctor Brandenhagen is more attracted to Doctor Janxel vice Christiana because he's not psychologically prepared to discover the essence of a green skinned woman?*

Doctor Brandenhagen really didn't know what was really occurring and the grand scheme of things. He assumed he was just going on a joy ride and possibly see a little combat from a safe distance aboard the command ship viewing the pincer attack on the Xīngguī expected.

What Roger didn't know was General Níngsī had to use his command ship as the lure to get the Xīngguī to channelize their attack thinking that taking out the command ship and its leadership would create the victory the Xīngguī so desperately needed as their advantage in ship numbers had been voided in the Earth attack and the Battle of Wukar. General Níngsī had theorized that giving up the luxuries of his command ship and unfortunately its crew would be worth the price of finally finishing off Admiral Aeta once and for all. Based on his intelligence reports, the Xīngguī didn't have many replacement commanders with Admiral Aete's tactics and leadership because many had been exterminated in coup attempts or killed in recent battles. The loss of Admiral Aeta would have a material effect on the viability of the Xīnggui Space Force. In essence both sides had the same exact game plan: you kill a snake most efficiently by cutting off its head first.

General Níngsī was an excellent odds maker and as he sat there watching these three, he was already changing the game plan in his head. As an added measure he would soon evacuate all three and shuttle them over to the Space Warship Doctor Brandenhagen had become familiar with because of his multiple trips on it. As soon as they finished with brunch, General Níngsī would send them to their private quarters to freshen up and prepare for the battle. He would then inform his Artificial Intelligence to have the three put on a shuttle and then sent to that Space Warship that would be sent to the rears to act as a rear guard, but ostensibly keep them out of harms way.

General Níngsī asked, "Christiana, tell us about your journey, how did you end up on this command ship?"

"General Níngsī, I grew up living in the small town of Yànwéi at Plastras Nostras. My father was the mayor of this town that had a population of around three thousand people. My family is very civic minded. I had no brothers therefore my father told me I had to go into the military and serve the empire to keep our family reputation intact. I did well in school and finished half of my secondary education when I volunteered. While processing me into the Space Force I was asked if I would be willing to complete my secondary education and become an officer. I agreed so they sent me to the Space Force Academy at Tèlándìa, where I was placed as an accelerated student since I only required half the courses. In two years, I graduated earning a full commission and was sent to a Fast Frigate. That space warship participated in a number of raids on Xīngguī forward deployed bases. After post mission analysis of weapons deployment achievement credited me as causing the most enemy ships destroyed by our ship, I was given a battle field promotion and when due to the urgency of recent events I was placed in the group selected to transfer to your Command ship because an analysis of your manning situation indicated you had insufficient number of sensor operators."

"I'm glad they assigned you to my command ship."

"Thank you."

"What kinds of things did you enjoy growing up?"

"We lived in a sparsely populated area where everything was spread out, so as kids we often enjoyed long rides on Gǒumǎ's."

General Níngsī asked, "Do we have any onboard

files showing people riding Gǒumǎ's?"

Artificial Intelligence responded in the background, "General Níngsī, we do and I will start playing the video momentarily."

In a few minutes, Doctor Brandenhagen was completely enthralled. All of a sudden high-definition holographic three-dimensional video showing young people riding Gǒumǎs. They appeared to be a cross between a dog and a horse. The animals have a horse's body with a dog's head.

"The heads of those animals almost look like a Saint Bernard type of dog we have on Earth," Roger stated.

Several minutes of video played and the most astonishing thing occurred. People got off the Gǒumǎs and removed all the riding hardware that seemed similar to horse saddles on Earth. Then the apparent owners gave the Gǒumǎs commands the animals appeared to acknowledge then walked over to a feeding device and a watering device.

"It appears like these people are very fond of their Gǒumǎs," Roger Brandenhagen stated.

"Yes, Gǒumǎs love humans. We treat them like all higher order species with great respect and care," Christiana explained.

"Do you have Gŏumăs on your planet, Doctor Janxel?"

"Doctor Brandenhagen, in many cases a lot of animal life you will discover in our worlds are usually found only on that planet because we have laws against transferring any livestock between planets."

"What do you do about food and things such as that?"

"All imported food has to be processed at the point of origination. No livestock ever leaves a planet in a living condition."

Having experienced this meal with the Zhrakzhongs, Roger Brandenhagen had awareness they were also carnivore eaters. He now suddenly had some strange feelings as he started wondering if *he had eaten meat from one of those Gŏumăs?*

Roger made eye contact with doctor Janxel a few times. There was evidently something there. Several surrealistic notions flooded his thoughts. One very strange notion he had was a desire to kiss her. He didn't understand he was sitting in a cloud of pheromone explosions by two women.

Doctor Janxel had her own issues with pheromones and was tired of being a virgin. She wanted to be touched by a man. And here she was on a command ship going into one of the grandest battles in Zhrakzhong history, even far grander than the Battle of Huátiĕlú.

Doctor Janxel was a brilliant person if not a genius. She was well read and because of her role treating casualties of war, she studied battles to glean the extent of medical emergencies they created. This helped her figure out triage plans and what types of medical instruments and supplies she needed to have on hand to treat patients. Having read up on most of the great battles in the past few hundred years, she knew vividly the command ship would be the number one target. The enemy would attempt their biggest effort to decapitate the leadership that would diminish the expertise in continuing the battle giving them far superior tactical ability.

The eye contact was mutual if not more so by Doctor Janxel who stared into those alien eyes of Doctor Brandenhagen whom she thought was a handsome man and intelligent to be a friend of General Níngsī who had very few friends and very little exposure of any type of socialization. Being here with General Níngsī and observing him with his new friend from Earth who had seemingly created a bond with General Níngsī, in itself was rather remarkable to her. She knew that if it were known at the medical center back on Tèlándìa about this event, she would get a lot of questions by many female members of the staff who ostensibly were social climbers. In these precious moments that General Níngsī seemed so calm on the eye of the storm, she felt her moistness and her growing desires. She could be dead in a few hours. In her mind she was calculating her next move and even though it was highly irregular and not permitted, she knew if she acted on those notions, General Níngsī would most likely overlook it on the grounds she was pleasing his friend. She had no idea how much General Níngsī actually wanted those actions to be carried out.

Christiana had a notion to invite Doctor Brandenhagen to the recreation room if they survived this battle and while wearing the special head gear, they could communicate with each other in total privacy and she might just let her guard down and allow discovery.

After a few more minutes of conversation, with the meal long over, one of General Níngsī's requested permission to enter his Space Cabin, and upon permission walked over to General Níngsī's and whispered a codeword in his ear. General Níngsī then nodded and said, "I'm sorry to have to break up this very pleasant gathering, but I have some work to do. I would like you all to go back to your quarters and freshen up and perhaps we'll be seeing each other again sometime soon."

General Níngsī then stood up and walked out of his Space Cabin and went directly to the Control Room where he walked up the circular staircase and approached the Combat Systems Officer and said, "We have contact?"

"Yes sir, probe number A7Y just sent us a contact report of the Xīngguī Fleet approaching its position which you can see on navigation monitor above.

General Níngsī observed the flashing purple circle that was a long distance away. There were another 6 probes the Xīngguī would pass before getting into weapons range.

"It all starts now," General Níngsī said.

"Sure, appears that way General Níngsī."

"They are still a long way off. I want to let the crew rest as much as possible. As soon as they pass probe D9X then sound battle stations alarm."

"Understand sir, at D9X I will announce Battle Stations."

About that time A7Y started flashing RED on the Navigation monitor. The Combat Systems Officer commented. "We just lost telemetry on probe A7Y."

"The Xīngguī most likely destroyed it. They now know we are somewhere near them. I expect to see their transit speed slow down now as they start searching hard for us."

"I'm going back to my quarters for a few minutes to freshen up, I'll be right back, contact me right away if you discover any new surprises."

"Yes sir, General Níngsī."

General Níngsī walked down the circular stairway and went back to his Space Cabin which he knew would be empty by now as his guests were going back to their quarters to freshen up. He then likewise took care of his business then asked Artificial Intelligence, "What are my three guests doing now?"

Weapons operator Christiana went to her quarters, relieved herself then has proceeded to the control room to assume the watch. Doctor Brandenhagen is in his private quarters and Doctor Janxel is approaching his door now."

"That's good. I hope they become lovebirds before the battle starts."

"General Níngsī, it's against regulations for a doctor to have any relationship with crew members or guests."

"I'm aware of that, but because of the extraordinary circumstances we find ourselves in with this distinguished scientist, I want the two to engage in romantic proclivity and hope that will convince Doctor Brandenhagen to remain with us."

"He means that much to you as a friend?"

"Yes, as you know a General can have no friends while he's with his Fleet. All the friends I had are now dead, killed in space battles, with the exception of Captain Luōjiàn."

"Very well General, I will keep this situation completely confidential."

"Thank you."

Just as the artificial intelligence indicated, Janxel went to Doctor Brandenhagen's private quarters and was glad she did not pass Christiana along the way.

The Artificial Intelligence Randolph announced, "Doctor Brandenhagen, Doctor Janxel is at your door and wishes to enter.

"Please let her in."

As soon as the doctor arrived, Roger said, "Hello Doctor what can I do for you?"

"Doctor Brandenhagen, this is not an official visit.

I'm coming as a friend and wanted to spend some time with you before the battle."

"Thank you, I appreciate that. Could you please call me Roger?"

"Alright when we are alone, I will call you Roger but in public due to protocol I must call you Doctor Brandenhagen."

"That works. Is Janxel your full name?"

"Nobody on the ship knows my full name, Elja Brielle Janxel."

"What would you like me to call you in private."

"Please call me Elja."

"Elja Brielle Janxel is a beautiful name."

"And you are a beautiful man, Roger."

"Thank you."

"Roger was now in for one of the biggest shocks of his life."

Elja walked closer and put both her hands on the side of Rogers face. They were approximately the same height. She then smiled and pulled his head closer to him and she kissed him gently on his lips. Her pheromones were flowing out of her nose and Roger was breathing them in and that situation slowly caused Roger to transcend to a new orbit. His valence with Elja started having a covalence like he never experienced before. In all the times he was with Ami, she never invigorated him like this. *Maybe that's why their sex was so dull?*

Roger stood kind of dumbfound not knowing what to do next. His mind slowly transcended to a new emotional level. The scent, the taste, the extreme beauty of Elja slowly encapsulated his emotions into a critical mass. The attraction was mutual and powerful. Just like the spark on a car battery when you accidently touch the wrong terminal with jumper cables, the electricity flowed through Roger and he was engulfed and captivated by this stunningly beautiful Alien. The fact she was extremely intelligent added a luster uncommon to his past experiences. To be the subject of romance from someone that is either as intelligent or even more so is such an uplifting event in any man's life who has a sense of relevancy.

Roger's instinct took over, he had no idea if he was doing anything wrong, or whether the Zhrakzhongs would frown upon their actions. All the second guessing was done and not a factor in his next moves. He pulled Elja closer and he added the positivity to their kiss as it became stronger and more pronounced. Her pheromone explosion shedding a cloud like Roger never experienced before now took control of his neurological functions. He furled all his passions at her and after a longated kiss and a strong embrace, Elja pushed back to give them space and she looked directly in his eyes and smiled and asked, "Is this what you Earth people call love?"

"It must be."

Elja had to efficiently undress battle causalities especially if there were numerous cases to allow triage to figure out who can be saved and who was a lost cause. She then started to quickly unfasten Roger's battle dress uniform and surprised how quickly she could do it!

And to add to the suspense, she was out of her battle dress even quicker.

Elja had never had sex before but she studied it in medical school and understood the basics and figured Roger would fill in the blanks. She grabbed his and led Roger over to his bed and got in first and pulled Roger on top of her. He was more than ready as he furled his manliness into her and they began the most glorious lovemaking he ever experienced.

Roger didn't quite understand the gratification that Elja now felt knowing if she died in this battle, she at least got to taste a real man and even if it were temporal love, feel the exquisite nature of it. Her cloud of pheromones was driving Roger far more than his own cognitive psychophysical responses. He could have taken ten doses of Viagra and not feel this animated. His thrusts and his actions were out of character. His body was acting like it never did before because his brain had never processed the impact of the Alien's pheromones.

Roger's gratification lasted a short infinity. His emotions were elevated and his passions poured out like a volcano eruption. Elja felt that extreme gratification and said to herself, *if I survive this battle, I will follow Roger to the ends of the universe to be with him.*

After they reached their climax, their bodies then lapsed into a post orgasmic state where each would have liked to lay there for a short eternity, but Elja knew the realities of life. She was a ship's doctor and she now needed to go to her medical lab and prepare for the obvious. She hoped she would see Roger again and they would survive the battle together. And now she had to do the inevitable.

"Roger, I think I'm in love with you and I would gladly stay here and be with you as long as you desired, but I really do need to get back to my medical lab and work with my medical associates as we unpack certain materials and set up the operating room for what I fear could happen soon."

"I understand. I will look for you after this is all over."

"And I will look for you."

"Elja, thank you for giving me an incredible feeling."

"Roger, you have no idea how much you mean to me."

"Elja, I know we have only known each other for a very short time, but I have special feelings for you."

"Roger, I'm sorry but I must leave now. I will look for you as soon as this is all over."

Elja slid out of the bed and was back in her battle dress uniform ready to leave the room in fifteen seconds. As she was walking out the door, she turned back towards Roger still laying nude and in great wonder, and gave him that heart breaking smile, a man can never forget. Then she was gone.

Roger reluctantly got up and decided to try out the body washer and soon was glad he did as it gave him an invigorated feeling since the water was heavily spiked with negative ions to add to his pleasant feeling and enhance his personal psychology.

After the body wash, Roger put his Battle Dress Uniform on and was then notified by the Artificial Intelligence *Randolph,* "General Níngsī would like you to report to the control room."

"Alright."

"Do you remember how to get there from here?"

"Yes, I think so."

"If you have problems finding along the way, just say "Randolph which way do I go now. I will follow your progress and guide you as necessary."

"Thank you, Randolph."

"My pleasure Roger."

Roger had a good memory and Randolph's help wasn't necessary, as he soon found himself climbing up the circular stairway and approached General Níngsī.

"Doctor Brandenhagen thank you for promptly coming to see me. We've had a change of plans."

Roger was looking in a direction where he could see the Navigation displays and beyond, weapon's control station number 17. Someone was leaning over and said something to Christiana. She then immediately turned back and looked directly at General Níngsī with a strange look on her face.

"What's the change General?"

"Doctor Brandenhagen, you are my very good friend and I've decided I want to protect you as much as I can. Do you remember Captain Luōjiàn who took you to Mars and brought you here?"

"Yes, General Níngsī."

"I'm transferring you to Captain Luōjiàn's Space Warship and you can watch the battle from that space warship a safer distance. All our tactical video will be shown on the monitors in his private quarters. You can watch the battle from there. We'll get back together after the battle."

"If that's what you want General Níngsī, but I'm more than willing to stay here and be with you during the battle."

"I know you are Doctor Brandenhagen."

"General Níngsī, since we do not yet know how this is going to turn out, I want you to know I view you as my personal friend, and when we are in private settings, please use my first name Roger."

"I will Roger. This fine officer here is going to take you to the shuttle craft."

Roger held out his hand to shake General Níngsī's hand.

The handshake was sincere and General Níngsī knew more than Roger realized, such as his love making with *Elja*. Roger would have gladly stayed and General Níngsī realized he was a brave man willing to face the risks of the battle, but the notion of preserving his friend gave him great pleasure.

Roger was also slightly animated because he knew if General Níngsī lost this battle, Earth would be at great risk, possibly wiped out just like Cydonia was on Mars 900,000 years ago.

The Zhrakzhong officer escorted Roger down the circular staircase and back to the shuttle bay. He was soon surprised that as he arrived, Christiana was sitting in the shuttle.

Listening to the conversation between the shuttle pilot and the control room there appeared to be a major issue brewing. General Níngsī also ordered Doctor Janxel to the shuttle and she refused to be evacuated stating her medical oath precluded any special treatment. It became such a heated argument General Níngsī personally walked to the lab to confront her because they were running out of time, he only had a few more minutes to get her of his command ship before the shooting started.

"Why are you not willing to go? I know you are quite fond of Roger."

"General, I have my responsibilities to this crew and even if I love Roger and would gladly spend the rest of my life with him, I must stay here for this battle to treat casualties."

General Níngsī knew he was running out of time to launch the shuttle and he knew Artificial Intelligence was always listening to him anywhere on the command ship, so he said. Alright then. Launch the shuttle."

Artificial Intelligence in the background informed General Níngsī, "Shuttle Launch Sequence in progress. Three people aboard, pilot, Doctor Brandenhagen and Weapons Operator Christiana."

By the time Artificial Intelligence made the report, the shuttle left the command ship within just a few seconds.

Captain Luōjiàn was nervously standing by knowing this shuttle operation was a major priority for General Níngsī. His Space Warship was a short distance away, so the flight time would be very short.

As soon as got confirmation the shuttle was landed in the bay and the hatches were closing, he ordered, "Reverse Course."

The Space Warship would be classified by the waring parties as a Battle Cruiser that had a lot of self-defenses as well as its own fighter bomber squadron that could operate in the atmosphere or out in space. That Squadron would be used only as a last-ditch effort and they were all armed with very powerful nuclear devices that could make someone chasing them regret it really quickly.

An officer was waiting for them as they were exiting the shuttle. He said, "I will take you to the Captain's Space Cabin."

Roger knew it would be a short walk said, "Alright."

Christiana seemed rather confused and after they were inside the Captain Luōjiàn's private quarters, his steward asked, "Would you two like a serving of Gěnkóviàn Jiǔyàowù?"

Roger now feeling the stress of the oncoming space battle and the tactical displays showing it all replied, "I think that would be an excellent idea."

Christiana was extremely agitated to be pulled off her weapon's control console, wasn't in the mood for Gĕnkóviàn Jiŭyàowù, but started thinking, *maybe the Gĕnkóviàn Jiŭyàowù might help control my anger.* She then responded. "Sure, why not."

Right after served, Roger could now start to see the battle unfold which was now a long distance behind them, but due to the communications technology appeared as if they were right in the middle of it.

The slaughter began. Admiral Aeta just recently came out of his meditation and felt superior. He had no fear and he knew he had to win this battle at all cost or die in the process.

Xīngguī Molecular Disrupter Cannons found their marks and a few Zhrakzhong Space Warships used as decoys blew up in sparkling debris. The sight was incredible!

Zhrakzhongs Plasma Debilitater weaponry also found their marks in this slugfest that was now underway. The two flanking forces had not yet started firing. The Xīngguī slowly grew over confident and were starting to deviate from the master plan because they thought they had achieved a great victory and there ahead was the main target. General Níngsī's command ship with only a few remaining escorts that were nothing more than magnets for Xīngguī Molecular Disrupter Cannons. They had to maneuver between the enemy and the command ship and take the brunt of the punishment. In a short while most of the escorts were destroyed and the delicious target remained dead ahead slowly maneuvering on an egress course.

The Zhrakzhongs command ship had a lot of fire power itself and it disgorged its squadrons and fired numerous Plasma Debilitater weapons.

Admiral Aete knew it was going to be tough taking out the command ship, but in doing so they could end the battle before much more carnage ensued.

The Xīngguī got a hit on the command ship with their Molecular Disrupter Cannons. There was some damage but thanks to compartmentalization, no rapid depressurization.

Just when Admiral Aeta was feeling good the battle was almost over, the Zhrakzhongs flanking forces did their pincer attacks. The devastation was immense. Admiral Aeta was far enough forward of the heavy fighting his Command ship was spared the damage.

With all the alarms going off, the Combat Systems Officer said, "General Níngsī, we have some fires burning on the ship. You need to evacuate at once."

General Níngsī didn't want to go, but two other officers grabbed him and hustled him to the shuttle bays and put him aboard his flag shuttle that had a lot more speed than a normal shuttle to escape in case of a situation like this. As soon as he was in the shuttle the door closed, the officers went back through the access hatch which shut immediately. The shuttle bay then went into a rapid depressurization where they simply opened the hatches. The air pressure in the bays helped the heavy doors started a fast movement. Five seconds later the shuttle was in space going at extreme speed being sent to Captain Luōjiàn's Space Battle Cruiser.

Captain Luōjiàn now a safe distance away from the battle was then vectored by Space Traffic Controllers aboard his command ship to the rendezvous point to pick up General Níngsī.

Admiral Aete was slowly coming to grips that he was losing the battle. It was shocking to him that he had been once again humiliated by a far more talented leader. But one thing he knew, there wasn't much distance between his command ship and General Níngsī's command ship. The Zhrakzhong squadrons now attacking were beaten off like flies, their effectiveness was harassment only against this well armed and well defended Xīngguī Command ship. Admiral Aete then made the providential decision to ram the Zhrakzhong Command ship that he knew would destroy it. Xīngguī Molecular Disrupter Cannons were a blazing at the Zhrakzhong Command ship that returned a lot of fire with its Plasma Debilitater weapons.

By the time the Zhrakzhongs figured out Admiral Aete was going to ram them it was too late, they maneuvered with everything they had in propulsion, but they turned at too much of an angle, that allowed Admiral Aeta to hit them amidships right in the middle of their neutron accelerator and Antimater reactors. With that amount of mass colliding, the forces were tremendous and the Zhrakzhong command ship broke in half as it exploded. The explosion which had the energy of one thousand hydrogen bombs incinerated all the Xīngguī in their control room including Admiral Aete.

As soon as the remaining Xīngguī saw their command ship explode and loss of all telemetry, they knew they were severely beaten and immediately sent out cries of surrender.

General Níngsī standing beside Captain Luōjiàn in his control room saw the destruction of the command ships and the pleas for surrender said, "Secure firing. Proceed to assist all casualties."

The Artificial Intelligence in all the Zhrakzhong complied and the battle was ended.

"Are my visitors in your Space Cabin Captain Luōjiàn?"

"Yes General Níngsī."

"I'm going down to talk with them. Change course to the fleet and see what assistance you can give."

"Yes sir."

General Níngsī, knew his way the short distance to the Space Cabin and went inside. It was very quiet and somber.

General Níngsī could see they both had tears in their eyes. Thanks to his artificial intelligence, he knew to what extent Roger and Elja's sparky relationship quickly evolved. He had to talk with Roger alone first, so he said, "Christiana, would you mind stepping outside for a few minutes. I need to talk with Roger alone."

"Yes sir."

Christina got up and exited the Space Cabin leaving the two men alone.

"Roger, I can't tell you how I know this, but I do know that Elja was in love with you. I tried to evacuate her just like I did with you and Christiana, but she refused to leave. She placed her medical responsibilities ahead of her own personal well-being. I know you loved her too, I'm very sorry."

Rogers eyes were now flowing like a river. He knew he had tasted real love and in a manner of no time had lost it all. He sat there weeping for a few minutes. General Níngsī, gave him his space.

After a few minutes, Roger took a deep drink of his Gěnkóviàn Jiǔyàowù. That seemed to have immediate effect. General Níngsī turned towards the steward and said, give him a refill and give me one too.

"Right away General Níngsī."

After a few more calming moments when it appeared Roger had regained his composure and General Níngsī had a good dose of Gěnkóviàn Jiǔyàowù, he stood up walked to the door and asked Christiana, "Would you please come back in now."

Christina still had a few tears and meekestly walked back in the room but instead of facing the numerous tactical displays the Ship's Captain had on one wall, she sat at the other side of the table and didn't want to look at it. Her anger of being removed off the ship for the battle was now replaced by remorse and regret she didn't die with her shipmates. Christiana was a smart woman and knew that while they were together in General Níngsī's Space Cabin she could see the flirtation and the body language between Roger and Doctor Janxel. *Perhaps something happened between the two?* Roger's display of sadness went beyond empathy or circumspect, there was an emotional bond of some sort. If they had developed a relationship, then it would be obvious why Roger seemed so sad. Christiana could see the residual tears and his eyes were still watery displaying utter sadness that one who lost their lover would.

Suddenly Christiana could no longer hold her anger. It dissipated as fast as Roger's tears and she now felt an angst for Roger as she realized what he had just lost. In her own time with Roger, she too had grown and affection towards him. Now watching him mourn over the loss of Doctor Janxel further extended her own interest in Roger. She wished they had privacy so she could console him. After General Níngsī finished his Gěnkóviàn Jiǔyàowù, he knew he could leave them alone here and, in a while, set them up with some berthing. But now he needed to be in the control room with Captain Luōjiàn where he could further assess the situation and start immediate planning.

"I'm sorry but I need to go to the control room. In a while I will get you guys set up with some berthing."

"Thank you," Christiana said.

As General Níngsī was leaving he motioned to the steward to follow him. After they were outside with the door shut, General Níngsī said, "I know you would like to spend some time in the control room with me so we can give them some privacy."

"Yes, General Níngsī, I would like to go to the control room with you."

After they were alone for a brief amount of time, the emotion was so overwhelming. Christiana stood up walked around to the sofa like chair Roger was sitting in and sat down beside him and put her arms around him. His sadness hit him again and he started weeping again. Christiana knew he was going through a lot of sadness and put her arms around him and held him as he wept for fifteen minutes. It truly was the saddest day of his life on the happiest day of the Zhrakzhongs who were already celebrating their magnificent victory. The Xīnggui no longer had a fleet, a peace treaty could now be forced on them.

General Níngsī's directed Captain Luōjiàn to redirect his berthing assignments to place Roger and Christiana in staterooms next to each other. He knew what they had gone through they needed to be close to each other. Christiana would help Roger get over his tremendous loss much quicker. Later when General Níngsī was alone in his new stateroom he asked the Artificial Intelligence to show the Captain's Space Cabin video after the time he left and went back to the control room. Just as he suspected, Roger was taking Elja's demise pretty hard. Had he could do it all over again, he would have had Space Marines forcibly take Elja to the shuttle with Roger. He now hoped Christiana could fill the deep void that now must exist.

Chapter Twenty-One

Showdown at Màichōng

After a half a day, all the damaged ships were put back into some order so they could transit to home worlds. General Níngsī knew he would soon be on his way to Màichōng, but he first needed to report to Tèlándìa to leave behind the crippled ships and pick up new Space Warships with fresh crews.

This was going to be a painful journey because this operation cost the lives of many. A new Command ship would also be available to him as this Battle Cruiser was crowded since they had to spread the space refugees among all the ships that remained intact and demolish the ones that were hopeless hulks.

The best way to demolish a destroyed Space Warship is to tow it towards a nearby star and give it the velocity to continue on with the star's gravity into oblivion. Once the battlefield was all cleaned up, they departed with all remaining ships including the enemy ships that were now partially manned by Zhrakzhongs as prize crews.

In three weeks, they arrived in orbit over Tèlándìa. Enemy crew members were taken to the planet into custody until the treaty was signed, then they would be taken back up to their ships to go back to Xīngguī worlds. All the Xīngguī prisoners were informed the Zhrakzhongs were simply going to Màichōng with a full treaty. There would be no armistice allowed. When shown the contents of the treaty all the Xīngguī were very positive about the reasonable treatment by benevolent conquerors. Since Emperor Shāyú no longer had a space fleet, there wasn't much he could do but sign the treaty, otherwise the Zhrakzhongs would install a new Emperor and he would no longer have a say in matters.

Not long after the Zhrakzhongs Fleet arrived at Tèlándìa, spy networks got out the devastative information to Emperor Shāyú via Xié'è de Gōngniú. Emperor Shāyú was so distraught over the loss of Admiral Aeta, he asked Xié'è de Gōngniú to bring the Tytrone Philosophers to the Palace and set up aural meditation in his main conference room. In due time the two men underwent more Meditation with the help of Kāiwù de Sēngrén.

The two men did this meditation for several days and before they started their next session, were alerted "The Zhrakzhongs Fleet is approaching at high speed."

"What do you plan on doing?" Xié'è de Gōngniú asked Emperor Shāyú.

"When they get within communications range, invite their emissaries to the Palace. We will have a dinner party, then sign the treaty after you and I look it over and agree to its content."

"We already know what's in the treaty, our spies have informed us."

"We have to look it over and appear to act like this is the first time we saw it."

"Alright I will go make preparations."

"Us do one more session of meditation first."

"If that's what you want."

Xié'è de Gōngniú then turned towards one of his men and said, "When the Zhrakzhongs get in communications range, invite their emissaries here to the Palace. We can meet with them after we finish our meditation."

"Yes sir."

General Níngsī surprised the leaders of the Zhrakzhongs when he brought Doctor Brandenhagen down to the planet with him and explained he was his personal friend and came from Earth.

Christiana was transferred to General Níngsī's

new command ship as he wanted her to be with Roger
as much as possible to help him remove the scars of the
battle from his heart.

When General Níngsī left Tèlándì he had Doctor
Brandenhagen with him. Nobody on Tèlándì was going
to tell General Níngsī he couldn't do that after he just
accomplished something no other leader was capable
in several decades, *end the war with the Xīngguī.*

To Doctor Brandenhagen's surprise, General
Níngsī had him fitted with a diplomatic uniform. He
was going down on the planet with General Níngsī and
so was Christiana.

In route to Màichōng, General Níngsī made
one small change to the Treaty. It stipulated Earth in
the Gamulin Solar System was a protectorate of the
Zhrakzhongs and any attack on Earth would be viewed
the same as attacking if they were attacking Zhrakzhongs
and automatic abrogating the treaty. As part of one of
the most important Treaties signed in Galactic History,
there was an Earth Signature, and Doctor Brandenhagen
was signing on behalf of Earth. He would also be given
a copy to take back to the United Nations. However,
General Níngsī knew he would delay that trip to give
Roger time to fully pursue Christiana and discover the
splendid nectar this woman could give him that would
soon heal his heartache.

Xié'è de Gōngniú and Emperor Shāyú were soon
in a meditation with the Tytrone Philosophers. This

was perhaps the crowning achievement of the Tytrone Philosophers because they eliminated any anguish or fear in preparation for the big meeting.

When General Níngsī's Force arrived in orbit above Màichōng he became slightly agitated with the delays and inquired what was causing it. The answer Xié'è de Gōngniú's assistant gave him in a teleconference really surprised him and gave him great pause.

"I'm terribly sorry General Níngsī, they are in meditation right now to better help prepare for this meeting. It usually takes three hours, so they should be done really soon."

"Allright, we are ready to go to the planet now."

"General Níngsī, why don't you and your delegation come down now and by the time you get here, they should just about be done."

"Thank you for the update. We'll be launching our shuttle in a few minutes."

"We will be waiting for you General Níngsī."

One thing that General Níngsī noted was the amount of belligerence he received in the past was totally gone. A new paradigm had formed.

General Níngsī looked at Roger and Christiana

who were standing by him in the control room and said, "Please follow me to the shuttle. We leave now."

In a few minutes they were on their way down to the planet. Màichōng was one of the more opulent and greener planets in the Xīngguī worlds. Looking at the viewer screens as the shuttle hurdled down towards the planet, Roger had a strange feeling of excitement as well humbleness knowing he was now in a very highly unusual circumstance. He would no doubt get yelled at for signing a treaty for the entire planet, but based on what he just witnessed he didn't care. This treaty was the very best thing for planet Earth who by all practical measures was defenseless against the fire power of the likes of the Zhrakzhongs and the Xīngguī. It was really for their own good.

Christiana was growing fonder of Roger every day. She decided as soon as they finished this treaty business, she would ask General Níngsī for a favor to put her on administrative leave and send her and Roger to Plastras Nostras. She wanted to take him to Yànwéi and show him her world and meet her family. She also wanted at that time to consummate the relationship.

The Xīngguī Space Traffic Control System gave the shuttle all the proper coordinates and diverted traffic around it so it could come down unmolested and have a safe and secure landing at the Emperor's Palace.

The flight was straight in and in a brief period of time they landed right in front of the Emperor's Palace with his Guards in dress uniforms and a color guard to salute the distinguished visitors.

Xié'è de Gōngniú's assistant informed of their arrival went into the conference room and walked up to Kāiwù de Sēngrén's ear, "The Zhrakzhong delegation is here now, we need to end the meditation."

Kāiwù de Sēngrén lifted up both arms into the vertical and down and back up a couple of times, almost appearing like a Japanese Banzai but silent. At that time one of the Tytrone Philosophers hit the gong very loudly, then all sound stopped. Xié'è de Gōngniú didn't know it yet, but that was one of the mechanisms used to stop the meditation and bring their minds back from the temporal dimensions to the current reality of their world.

Within five minutes both men showed signs they were back to reality as they knew it. They stood up and Xié'è de Gōngniú's assistant stated, "The Zhrakzhong are at the front entrance."

The two men left the conference room and walked to the front entrance. They expected a large official delegation and were taken back to see just three. More so they were also in quite a significant discovery to see only one tall person and two normal people based on their standards, one of which is a Plastras Nostras citizen! This was utterly shocking to Xié'è de Gōngniú and Emperor Shāyú. The two smaller persons were wearing official Zhrakzhong diplomat attire. The eight-foot-tall giant was wearing a well decorated military uniform, which had to be General Níngsī.

Emperor Shāyú walked out first to greet the Zhrakzhongs and Xié'è de Gōngniú followed a respectful distance behind.

General knew the Xīnggui customs. They bowed during greeting. They did not shake hands.

"Hello I'm Emperor Shāyú, welcome to Màichōng."

"Emperor Shāyú, I'm General Níngsī. Let me introduce you to my delegates. This is Christiana from Plastras Nostras, and this is Doctor Brandenhagen from planet Earth."

Now it got interesting. Emperor Shāyú was more than perplexed. Why General Níngsī would bring just these two and not a bunch of diplomats to argue with?

"It's a pleasure to meet you all. Let me introduce you to my chief of security, Xié'è de Gōngniú."

They all took their series of bows and then Emperor Shāyú said, "Please follow me into my conference room so we can look over the documents."

Nobody directed the Tytrone Philosophers to leave the conference room, nor did Emperor Shāyú care. He did however think he should at least introduce them.

"General Níngsī, these are our Tytrone Philosophers. They help me meditate and become a better person. This is their leader Kāiwù de Sēngrén."

"It's a pleasure to meet you Kāiwù de Sēngrén."

Kāiwù de Sēngrén smiled and bowed and said, "May your future be bright and you achieve your pathway to enlightenment."

"Thank you."

They quickly had their places at the table that was set up for 20 diplomats on each side of the table.

Emperor Shāyú's 20 diplomats were soon marching into the room and found their places at the table and were mildly astonished when they hear Emperor Shāyú say, "Now that everyone is here, let's begin."

General Níngsī opened up his diplomatic pouch and handed Emperor Shāyú ten copies and said, "There is one small change from the copy sent to you in advance of our arrival. It's the last paragraph added."

Emperor Shāyú handed the copies of the treaty down to his diplomats who figured out how to share them.

Xié'è de Gōngniú kept standing and looked over Emperor Shāyú's shoulder and observed the final paragraph that Emperor Shāyú was reading. It was a simple paragraph that stated all provisions of this treaty also pertained to Earth in the Gamulin Solar System.

Even though it was probably out of protocol, Xié'è de Gōngniú asked, "What does Earth have to do with this? We have no interest in Earth."

"Your forces came very close to Earth and since we have a billion people living there, they would have been exterminated if you destroyed the planet. Earth will be protected by this treaty."

Just as Xié'è de Gōngniú was about to start arguing about placing Earth in the Treaty, Emperor Shāyú said, "I do not mind having Earth protected in this treaty. If there are no other changes, I'm ready to sign."

The twenty diplomats almost started an uproar when all of a sudden Emperor Shāyú put his finger up to his mouth and said, "Shhhhhhh."

The diplomats quickly quieted down because they didn't know this was the new and improved tolerant Emperor Shāyú. They simply assumed if they didn't abruptly quiet down, they too might be tossed in the swimming pool with the Emperor Shāyú's special meat-eating fish.

Xié'è de Gōngniú grabbed the treaty out of the hands of the diplomat closest to him and quickly read through it then he said, "I'm really glad you trimmed this down and removed all that diplomatic talk in it. This document doesn't require a lot of analysis thanks to the elegance of its simplification."

"We can always have negotiations to clear up matters peacefully," General Níngsī stated which let the air out of all the hawkish diplomats sitting at the table. Kāiwù de Sēngrén was all smiles because he could now see the fruits of his efforts. He knew that if Xié'è de Gōngniú and Emperor Shāyú agreed to the treaty, the fire breathers would lose out on their arguments to continue the war.

There were writing utensils and notebooks at each place setting at the treaty table. Emperor Shāyú grabbed one of the ink stylus and said, "Hand me your copy General Níngsī, so I can sign it.

General Níngsī handed Emperor Shāyú his copy. Emperor Shāyú signed the treaty then handed it to Xié'è de Gōngniú and said, "Sign below my name."

After Xié'è de Gōngniú finished signing he handed it back to Emperor Shāyú who in turn handed it back to General Níngsī. General Níngsī then handed the treaty to Doctor Brandenhagen and said, please sign where I have your name. Then he handed it to Christiana who also signed the document and then he handed it back to Emperor Shāyú. He then handed his copy to Emperor Shāyú to sign and the process repeated.

Before long the second copy of the treaty was signed and General Níngsī handed it to Christiana and said, "Take this out to the shuttle and have the pilot take it back to my command ship. Inform the Shuttle pilot to come back to pick us up when I give the ship our signal to do so in a couple hours.

Moments after Christiana left to give the Shuttle Pilot the Zhrakzhong copy of the Peace Treaty, Emperor Shāyú asked, "tell me General Níngsī do you possibly know how Admiral Aete perished?"

"Your excellency, Emperor Shāyú, we have live recordings of the event. When I get back up to my command ship, I will send you the video of the event."

"General Níngsī, thank you, but I would like you to tell me know what happened to him?

"Your excellency, Emperor Shāyú, I can't tell you what drove Admiral Aete to do what he did, I could only speculate."

"What exactly did he do?"

"Admiral Aete and his escorts had destroyed most of my Battle Cruiser escorts and there wasn't much between my command ship and his. My command ship had sustained some severe blows and there was a serious fire burning in the engineering spaces, therefore my senior officers demanded I evacuate myself from the ship. I refused to go, so they carried me to the shuttle which deployed as soon as I got in and the access was secured. They did an emergency air equalization allowing us to leave the semi-stricken command ship is probably 5 seconds after I was shoved inside. Admiral Aete had no way of knowing I had departed the command ship.

"Admiral Aete realized my coordinated pincer attacks was inflicting serious damage to his Fleet and he apparently assumed if he crashed his command ship into my command ship, it would do material harm to our forces by making it leaderless so that his forces might have a chance to still prevail.

"It's kind of unusual for a commander to purposely ram his ship into an opponent because it usually means he would die in the process. Admiral Aete gave his life for his Fleet in hope he would save it from its demise by this action. My command ship never thought such an intentional collision would occur and both ships were trading a heavy volley of weapon engagement, that might have resulted in the destruction, but Admiral Aete apparently wanted to make sure he accomplished destroying my ship and me. My ship did not start to perform evasive maneuvers until it was too late. Admiral Aete's command ship collided perpendicular to my command ship in the mid-section. Based on the horrific explosion that occurred, the neutron accelerator and Antimater reactors lost containment and when the Antimater made contact with other materials on the ship it caused a massive explosion that cooked off all the explosives on board which completely disintegrated my command ship and Admiral Aeta's command ship."

"No chance of any survivors?"

"We utilized the remaining assets of your fleet to help us clean up the battle field to reduce the risk to transports in the future. You can confirm with your surviving Commanding Officers we all combed through all wreckages looking for survivors and we pursued locating any distress beacons. When we left the area, all the space junk had been cleaned up and there were no remaining distress beacons to locate and rescue.

"You think Admiral Aete was killed in the explosion?"

"Your excellency, Emperor Shāyú, the collision caused a horrific explosion. None of my crew members or Admiral Aete's men survived."

"The battle wasn't worth the damage we received."

"Several of my long-distance probes were programmed to send Admiral Aete messages to please simply surrender because we did not desire a bloodbath. I suppose Admiral Aete wanted to end the war once and for all. His actions were out of character."

Emperor Shāyú knew the truth. *Admiral Aete understood he had to give his life to make sure the war ended.* The Tytrone Philosophers had made sure of it with their training of Admiral Aete by utilizing the gateway process.

Emperor Shāyú also knew one other thing, General Níngsī had lost a lot of personnel on his very large command ship. He too was now scarred from the war. Emperor Shāyú also saw the watery eyes that Doctor Brandenhagen exhibited. *There was a connection between him and the story as well.*

Emperor Shāyú never had an ounce of empathy in him until the Tytrone Philosophers gave him the meditation training. As Emperor Shāyú further observed Doctor Brandenhagen, he caught a glimpse of a tear that ran down the side of his face. That confirmed his suspicion that Doctor Brandenhagen lost someone special in the battle. In reality it was a Pyrrhic Victory at best for Doctor Brandenhagen and General Níngsī who lost a lot personally in this battle. In a way everyone sitting at the table was a loser in some way. Perhaps those losses seemed to bring them closer together. Forgiveness was insured.

When Christiana returned, she too saw a tear flowing down the side of Roger's face. It was a somber mood when all of a sudden Kāiwù de Sēngrén approached Emperor Shāyú and whispered something in his ear.

Emperor Shāyú smiled and said, "Now that we are at peace and we can get on with our lives and our daily business, I would like to invite all of you to follow me to my dining hall for a dinner to celebrate the beginning of an era of peace."

This was more than welcome as the feast would soon take people's minds off the past. The twenty-course meal was fabulous and prepared by the best chefs in the galaxy. The guests were offered wine, filtered water, or Chami Elixir.

Emperor Shāyú was pleased these people acted so reasonable. Their demure and attitude felt refreshing. He asked, "Doctor Brandenhagen, would you please sit next to me. I might like to ask you some questions about Earth."

"I would be most delighted, your excellency."

While the waiters were serving drinks, Emperor Shāyú felt for Roger, knowing he had gone through some trying times suggested, "Doctor Brandenhagen, I will advise you to try the Chami Elixir. You will like the sensation it gives you."

Doctor Brandenhagen responded, "Thank you." He then turned towards the waiter and said, "Let me have a glass of Chami Elixir."

Roger thought he had gotten over the battle, but he realized certain discussions could trigger his melancholy like just a few minutes ago, was pleased to feel the effects of the Chami Elixir.

General Níngsī was sitting directly across from Roger. Christiana sat to Roger's left and Xié'è de Gōngniú sat to the right of General Níngsī had a direct view of Christiana, the exceptionally beautiful Plastras Nostran.

Xié'è de Gōngniú had traveled to Plastras Nostras and experienced these women before. He wondered how Christiana fit into the bigger scheme of things. He could not help but recollect his experiences with sexy Plastras Nostrans. Before the dinner was over, he saw the telltale signs that Christiana and Roger had some kind of relationship going. Xié'è de Gōngniú thought, *I would feel jealous to learn they were lovers.*

Kāiwù de Sēngrén and the five other Tytrone Philosophers were asked to join the group and Kāiwù de Sēngrén was sitting across from Roger at an angle.

While they were eating and having numerous discussions, musicians played music at a low volume nearby as to not interfere with the conversations, but loud enough for everyone to hear and enjoy. Roger thought, *this music is as good as Beethoven or Liszt.* [Alina Bercu performs Beethoven's Piano Concerto No. 5 in E flat major op. 73 (full) - YouTube] [Liszt Piano Concerto No. 2 - JY Thibaudet, Sokhiev - YouTube]

Perhaps it was the music that transfixed Roger just enough so that his grief of having a true love, suddenly taken from him. It's one thing to be aced by another gentleman, but it's another to have her ripped out of your heart in the manner that just happened. Roger will never forget the horror of watching General Níngsī's command ship blow up on the monitor. Due to the horrific explosion everyone died very quickly. There was no suffering. Roger would be pleased to know Doctor Elja Brielle Janxel, was already unconscious when the explosion occurred so she didn't feel it. Her universe simply vanished. Was she born again?

Christiana started to feel better seeing Roger in a more chipper mood. The Chami Elixir was having its effect.

Kāiwù de Sēngrén was as good as General Níngsī reading body language. The discussion of Admiral Aete ramming his command ship into General Níngsī's ship triggered the emotional response in he observed in Roger, and he knew that event had terrible consequence for someone in Roger's life. To cause a grown man to exhibit this level of emotion could only mean, that person was very close to Roger and most likely his lover. After dinner if there was a chance he could get close to Roger and have a private discussion, he would offer his help in meditation which he knew would go a long way towards elevating that grief.

Kāiwù de Sēngrén also could tell General Níngsī was somewhat affected for similar reasons, *but to lose an entire crew must take a heavy toll on the commander if he survives.*

Kāiwù de Sēngrén would also approach General Níngsī and offer similar help. Kāiwù de Sēngrén a good judge of men sized up General Níngsī and was convinced, he wanted to end this Rotten War at all cost, and it came close to costing him. Had his officers not forcibly removed him from the command ship, he too would be dead, but the outcome would most likely not been any different.

When a conquering military acts as benevolent as Zhrakzhongs it creates a strange effect. It would most likely have an impact for a long-lasting peace until the next despot comes along and wrecks the arrangement. Kāiwù de Sēngrén felt he made an impact in how Emperor Shāyú evolved, otherwise, there would have not been a peace treaty, and the next space battle might have occurred as soon as he rebuilt the fleet which could only have taken ten years.

Kāiwù de Sēngrén was disappointed that Admiral Aete didn't act in the way he predicted. *Perhaps he committed suicide in the face of defeat and thought he was taking out his opponent in the process?*

The food, entertainment and small talk lasted about as long as General Níngsī desired for diplomatic reasons and he touched a couple areas of the touch sensitive face of his wrist band that signaled his command ship to send the shuttle own to pick them up.

Then he said, "Your Excellency, Emperor Shāyú, I think it's time we all leave now that this matter is settled. Our diplomats will soon be visiting each other to work out any wrinkles that happen along the way."

"General Níngsī, thank you for coming and thank you for being instrumental in this peace. Your approach to it is exactly what we needed to finally end this war."

"Your excellency, Emperor Shāyú, it's time to rebuild our civilizations and not our military. We've lost too many good years with this war."

"Now that the war is over and the Zhrakzhongs no longer need you as a Force Commander, what's your plans?"

"Your excellency, Emperor Shāyú, I need to go back to Earth and return Doctor Brandenhagen. We also will now start relocating our war refugees back to their home planets. I'm not sure I'll be need for all that, so after I see all that working smoothly, I'm going to step down and retire."

"Any plans in retirement?"

"As you can imagine being dedicated to our Space Forces for so many years, I missed out on living. I'm going to travel at a leisurely pace and visit quite a few places I always wanted to see."

"Does that include visits to Xīngguī worlds?"

"Yes, in fact Màichōng has some of the greatest artwork's collections I've seen in publications but never in person. That is on my short list of places to visit."

"You are not afraid of assassination from some disgruntled Xīngguī upset over the outcome of the war?"

"Your excellency, Emperor Shāyú, something tells me if I visited Màichōng, Xié'è de Gōngniú would be so busy doing surveillance on me, no terrorists would get near before his men would intervene."

Xié'è de Gōngniú chuckled a little but he also knew General Níngsī would be tailed the minute he arrived at Màichōng because the spy business is always live and well in peacetime. Spies in nature have excellent job security because just as soon as the ink is dry on the last peace treaty, the next war is already being planned.

"I will make sure you are safe General Níngsī when you come to Màichōng."

Kāiwù de Sēngrén then jumped in with his opportunity to speak and said, "General Níngsī, when you visit Màichōng, I would like you to see us at the Tytrone Philosophers Temple and try some of meditation techniques. You are war weary and carried a lot of burden on your shoulders. I think it will help you.

"Kāiwù de Sēngrén, when I visit Màichōng, I would like to spend some time with you."

"General Níngsī, you be welcomed and we look forward to your visit."

"Thank you."

General Níngsī did a deliberate and respectful long bow. Then he stood upright and turned towards the front entrance as his arm band device just signaled him the shuttle was waiting outside.

Roger and Christiana instinctly followed General Níngsī.

As Kāiwù de Sēngrén observed the three leaving, he knew they each carried a lot of burden. Even though it was unspoken, it was unmistakable as he had seen these examples many times before. Wounded souls that needed healed.

As the three reached the shuttle with door opened ready to go, General Níngsī turned around. Roger and Christiana followed his example and the three did a long and deliberate respectful bow at Emperor Shāyú, Xié'è de Gōngniú and Kāiwù de Sēngrén who all stood there with a sense of fondness towards General Níngsī who they now knew was a compassionate and decent man. The peace treaty offered was more than they could bargain for considering the fact they really were vanquished and not in any position to bargain.

It was puzzling to them why General Níngsī didn't place on them burdensome reparations of forfeiture of a large part of their Empire. Kāiwù de Sēngrén now had a chance to feel out General Níngsī and knew he had figured out the only way to secure a long-lasting peace was to do exactly the way he did. To the point he set up fabulously elaborate traps to ensure the events all unfolded in the manner they did. Nobody in either the Zhrakzhong or Xīngguī Empires realized the elaborate plan General Níngsī conducted and its apparent he probably had enemies withing he also had to deal with.

Kāiwù de Sēngrén knew what this cost General Níngsī. He truly hoped he would visit Màichōng because he knew he could help him remove the burden off his shoulders. He may have had to sacrifice thousands of lives, but in doing so he saved billions on both sides of the issue.

When General Níngsī straightened up and was just about to turn around and step into the shuttle craft, Kāiwù de Sēngrén copied his long respectful bow. Xié'è de Gōngniú standing between Kāiwù de Sēngrén and Emperor Shāyú saw him bow and followed his actions.

Out of th corner of his eye Emperor Shāyú saw the other two men bow, so he also followed and waited for Kāiwù de Sēngrén to rise up before he did. That resulted in the longest bow in Emperor Shāyú's life. And when he stood tall and saw General Níngsī smiling, he knew it was one of happiness and satisfaction. This meant a lot to Emperor Shāyú feeling really bad about the outcome of Admiral Aete's foray into a poorly planned and executed attack.

Life would go on and the Xīngguī would go back to a peaceful and happy period. Emperor Shāyú would live the rest of his life in peace thanks to General Níngsī. This day he would never forget.

Once the shuttle was airborne, Xié'è de Gōngniú turned towards Emperor Shāyú and said, "I was looking forward to you telling our distinguished guests the fish they had for dinner came out of your swimming pool."

"Somethings are best left unknown."

Chapter Twenty-Two

Plastras Nostras

On the shuttle rid back to command ship, Christiana asked, "General Níngsī, I would like to take some leave when I get back to Tèlándìa. I would like to take Roger there and show him my world and meet my parents.

General Níngsī had a small task force with him. The Xīnggui were no longer a threat. He smiled and said, "Since I'll be retiring soon, there isn't much they can do to me now, so I have a better idea."

"What is that General Níngsī?"

I will take you there now, give my troops some rest and recreation there since most of them were involved in the space battles with the Xīnggui they need some rest."

"That would be wonderful sir."

"Plus, it's sort of on our way to Tèlándìa."

Christiana turned towards Roger who was taking this all in and said, "Roger, I like you a lot. I want you to meet my parents."

"Sure, I would be happy to meet them." Roger said then he started thinking about some of the issues that could grip her parents. He wasn't a Plastras Nostran, and they may think he's slightly too old for her.

Christiana was suddenly filled with joy. She had a secret crush on Roger and even though he might have had an affair with Doctor Elja Brielle Janxel, she still had that attraction to him.

The past was the past and Doctor Elja Brielle Janxel could now only be part of the past, there was no way Roger could ever go back to it. Its sometimes best to bury the past.

It didn't take long to get back to the command ship. Everyone went their separate way. As soon as General Níngsī was in his Space Cabin, he spoke, "Have the Navigator report here right away."

"General Níngsī, the Navigator has been informed," Artificial Intelligence stated.

Two minutes later General Níngsī's door opened and the Navigator walked in.

"Here as requested General Níngsī."

"We have a change of plans. We are going to transit from here to Plastras Nostras."

"May I inquire the reason for the change sir?"

"Navigator, almost all the men aboard this ship was involved in the recent space battles. Many of them are lucky to be alive. They were up against one of the greatest commanders in Galactic History and we only got lucky because we allowed him to drive into his arrogance and be destroyed. Half the crew came off burning hulks or ships that barely made it back to Tèlándìa. I'm going to repay them for their personal sacrifice by giving them a couple weeks of rest and relaxation at Plastras Nostras."

"I'm sure the crew will love that, but you realize you will be in trouble when you get back to Tèlándìa.

"Nav, I'm going to retire when I get back to Tèlándìa. There is nothing they can do to me."

"Our Fleet will be missing a great leader if you leave us."

"I will probably be asked to stay on a bit longer to help start the process of bringing home all our war refugees."

"After that you will leave?"

"Affirmative."

"Alright sir, I need to go back to NAV CENTER and lay down our new track."

"Nav, I want to get there quickly, you do not have to plan for normal transit speeds, plan as if we are going on another battle and get us there quickly."

"When are we going to inform Plastras Nostras we are coming?"

"When we reach their star system, you can let them know we are on the way. We don't want to give Tèlándìa heads up we are diverting from our flight plan."

"I understand. It's always better to ask for forgiveness than permission in a deal like this."

"You got that right."

What would normally take two weeks cruising at normal transit speeds was cut down to three and a half days. Plastras Nostras Space Defense Command was utterly stunned to discover General Níngsī was arriving semi-un announced.

The small fleet slid into orbit around the planet

and leave arrangements were organized. Only half the crews could be gone in case they had to do an emergency departure, even if this was assumed peace time. The other factor was not to inundate the planet with a lot of men who had not spent time with women for quite a while.

By General Níngsī's orders, Roger and Christiana were put aboard the first shuttle down to the planet. Also with his direction, the shuttle pilot was to drop them off first in front her parents' home. The only catch was she had to depart in uniform and return in the same manner. Roger dressed in a similar fashion so they each appeared to be Zhrakzhong Space Force members. Christiana would not divulge the other details of Roger came from a very distant start system far from their empire in the area referred to as the wilderness.

It was never expected that a Zhrakzhong Space Transport/Shuttle would land on the street in front of their home. No such activity ever occurred before on this planet, so it was highly unusual.

Christiana's mother was working in their front yard doing some landscaping in her lovely flower bed. She saw some glitter come out of the sky and there it was sitting in the middle of the street. The door opened and out walked her daughter. Closely behind her was a man and each were carrying a small bag, for change of clothes.

Christina's mother stood up and looked upon

her daughter with great interest. Her father was gone for the moment but would be arriving home in a short while. Being the chief executive for the town, he had one of the few skycars which allowed him to access nearby cities very easily and often took members of the community with him where they could purchase ample wares and make it home in a reasonable time frame.

The women approached each other, teers were flowing. When news that General Níngsī's Command Ship was destroyed, Christiana's mother was heart sick for a few days. Due to the distance and operational security her family was not informed she was a survivor until the fleet returned to Tèlándìa.

Her mother was so glad to hold her baby in her arms. With the grace of God, she made it back alive.

Now the second astonishment revealed itself. There was a plain skin man with her daughter. About the same time the shuttle took off into the air, Christiana's mother with her strong intuition surmised, her daughter was bringing home her boyfriend to meet them. But he was a grown mature man. By his looks he would be in his late 30's compared to people that lived around there. Her mother at first didn't like the notion of some dirty ole man rocking the cradle so to speak.

But being a wise person, she said to herself, *don't jump to any conclusions until you find out what that's all about.*

Mother, I would like to introduce you to my good friend Doctor Roger Brandenhagen.

Roger had been schooled by Christina to bow and not shake hands.

Pleased to meet you Doctor Brandenhagen. My name is Starhwā.

"I'm very happy to meet you Starhwā."

"Why don't we go inside and have a cool drink," Starhwā suggested.

This would be an eye opener for Roger. He knew one thing, he's the first human from Earth to go inside the home of people that lived far away in another solar system. This would be an eye opener for him and an experience he never would expect.

The home probably had as much room as a typical Earth home, but he also knew this was not in a city, where there was more density and congestion, where it was possible to build a house with a yard. Had he looked like a Xīnggui that had more of an Asian like appearance, he might not be allowed to enter because there was animosity left over from their last invasion.

Starhwā understood from gossip and their equivalent to tabloids, the lure Plastras Nostras women had towards the plane skin people. She hoped Roger had not yet sampled the forbidden fruit of her daughter. She would feel very uncomfortable if she knew they had crossed the line and enjoyed such celestial feasts.

Starhwā knew nothing about Roger and this sudden visit added a whole new dimension to her relationship with her daughter Christiana. The fact she brought Roger here alone means she had already developed some type of bonding to her. The fact the Zhrakzhongs brought them directly here also speaks volumes about the probability Roger was someone special. Starhwā hoped Roger wasn't going to break Christina's heart and leave forever. However, she would give her daughter credit for bringing Roger here to meet her parents. If this was the beginning of a serious relationship it would soon quickly unfold. There was a story to all this and she would eagerly await to hear it all.

"Were you two together during the Space Battles?"

"For some of it yes."

Starhwā would later tell them where to place their hand bags, but first it was time to have a refreshing drink and get to know one another.

"We were terrified when the news reported General Níngsī's command ship was destroyed with all crew members on board."

"I can understand how you feel since we were also shocked to observe the ship blow up ourselves. We both lost friends on that ship."

Christiana then said to Roger, "I need to talk with my mother for a few minutes in our language, please forgive me, because my mother does not speak English."

Christiana then explained to her mother, "I have a fondness for Roger and am ready to make the next step with him.

Her mother Starhwā instantly knew what that meant and this was a very serious visit. She hadn't had time to think about this before she expected her mate Narzhack to return home.

Christiana then filled in a few more blanks that gave Starhwā new insights in all this situation, "General Níngsī evacuated me off the command ship before the battle started because he suspected Roger and I were lovers. He wanted to protect Roger and he wanted to protect me. If it were not for Roger, I would not be alive today. I owe my life to Roger."

"Did General Níngsī have good reason to believe you were lovers?"

"We were very attracted to each other, but we had not reached that level in our relationship."

"Have you reached it now?"

"On this trip we will, that's why I brought him home to meet you before we go to that next level."

"I fear your father may not approve."

"Mother, you realize I'm in a very dangerous profession. I could be dead next week and I'm extremely lucky to have survived the space battles. In previous battles before I was evacuated, I witnessed a lot of combat and was particularly involved. It was a sobering and horrifying event. I'm not daddy's little girl anymore. I'm now a space warrior with deadly space combat under my belt."

"What if your father doesn't approve."

"Mother, because of my profession its possible you might not see me for another 10 years as we have no idea where our fleet will go and what it will do. We have just finished a war with one enemy. Let me remind you we also have other enemies."

Starhwā felt very uncomfortable now because if Roger stayed at their home, its quite possible that consummation of that relationship could happen in their guest bedroom which she knew her husband would most likely utterly oppose because of some of his more poignant comments in the past about plain skinners.

Unless her male companion had green skin her father would never accept him. Starhwā was slowly sinking into a melancholic state because she feared that real soon this would end up in a heart breaking episode.

Starhwā would be interested in observing how her husband responded to this visitor. Narzhack was a complicated man. But as a politician, he always wore a poker face and he always let the public drive the narrative. He was never going to stick his neck out as an activist. Because of its remoteness, Yànwéi had seldom received plain skin visitors.

Cities on the otherhand often had visitors from off world places such as Tèlándì and Màichōng mainly as tourists or import/export traders. A lot of intergalactic bankers and war profiteers often brought their special clients to Plastras Nostras for fleshly desires of young women just reaching their periods of explosive pheromone shedding. Evil organized criminals often drugged the young women with special narcotics that caused explosive release of pheromones and enzymes that when absorbed by men during copulation gave them very lengthy periods of gratification.

This abusive exploitation of young Plastras Nostras left Christiana's father Narzhack in a constant state of resentment and disdain for any plane skinner he saw.

Narzhack's day was typical, enjoying taking some political activists into the Plastras Nostras City to do their shopping and a few leisure events including a brief stop at an art exhibit. He had just dropped off the last of the city travelers and pulled his skycar into the driveway a short period after his daughter arrived. He like his spouse did not expect Christiana and the last thing in the world he would ever expect was to see Christiana bring a plane skinner home to meet her parents.

Roger quickly discovers after Narzhack arrived; he was not to receive a warm welcoming. Because of the afternoon lighting and the position of where everyone was sitting, the greatest lit up space in the room was exactly where Roger sat. It not only showcased him but it accentuated his plane skin.

Perhaps had Roger been sitting in a shaded area of the room, the emotions might not have gripped Narzhack so terribly. However, walking into a room and observing to him what appeared to be a dirty old plain skinner and soon to learn his daughter's lover, almost sent him into a rage.

Starhwā knew when Narzhack was extremely agitated. By the grace of god he held back all his fury as he decided he needed to calm down and find out what all this really meant.

"Hello."

Roger stood up immediately and bowed and as schooled by Christiana, said in well delivered standard

Plastras Nostras dialect, "Greetings Narzhack, I'm Doctor Brandenhagen and a friend of your daughter Christiana."

Roger then gave a standard respectful bow that lasted approximately five seconds as Christiana had schooled him. Then he straightened up and smiled at Narzhack.

Narzhack responded in standard Plastras Nostras dialect assuming Roger was acquainted with thee language: "What brings you here Doctor Brandenhagen?"

Christiana wanted to intervene and make sure there was no mishap in communications jumped in and translated for Roger then explained to Roger in English that she knew from her training for the Earth Mission, "Father, Doctor Brandenhagen's first name is Roger. He's my personal friend." She then repeated in English for Roger what she just said.

Seeing they each had on standard Zhrakzhongs official dress uniforms, Narzhack assumed they were both military officers. He then asked, "Were you with the Fleet during the space battles?"

"Yes, we were on General Níngsī's command ship that blew up and were evacuated before the explosion. Because of OPSEC she could not explain how or why they were evacuated.

"Doctor Brandenhagen, what exactly did you do on the command ship?"

"I'm a personal friend of General Níngsī and a diplomatic observer from planet Earth."

"I've never heard of Earth before. Is it some far off planet in our Empire?"

"No, we are not part of the Empire. Earth exists in a solar system far away from your empire."

"Then why are you wearing an Empire Uniform?"

"I'm wearing it out of respect for General Níngsī who requested I wear it because of my interactions with him and as a signatory to the treaty just signed with the Xīngguī."

"Why did you sign the treaty?"

"My planet Earth is a signatory to the treaty. The last clause in the treaty covers planet Earth."

"What is so special about Planet Earth?"

"The major portion of the battle took place as the Xīngguī were approaching it to wipe it out."

"Why is that?"

"That's where General Níngsī's headquarters is."

"It is?"

"Well, it was. Its now moving back to Tèlándìa."

"So, you are just a diplomat?"

"No, I'm a scientist and a researcher."

"Then how did you get selected as a diplomat for your planet?"

"It pays to be General Níngsī's personal friend."

"How does my daughter fit into all of this?"

"She is also General Níngsī's personal friend as well as my own."

Starhwā knew this conversation was soon going to go somewhere that would make them all uncomfortable so she quickly intervened: "Narzhack, please come to me to the kitchen so we can prepare dinner."

"I never help you prepare dinner."

"You will today, we need to talk about something."

Now it hit Narzhack hard. In his speculation

he now figured Doctor Brandenhagen may be his daughter's lover. He almost felt like fainting. But he figured out in the Kitchen that had a door between them, he would get to the bottom of it.

Starhwā stood up and Narzhack followed her into the Kitchen. If he thought his blood pressure was high, it would get much higher in a few minutes.

Like a master chef Starhwā started pulling things out of the food chiller and setting up a dinner they would all enjoy in a while. She also realized the longer she kept Narzhack away from Roger things would be better.

"We didn't expect her visit. There was no indications she was coming."

"Why did she come?"

"It's obvious General Níngsī wanted her to see her parents and meet her special friend."

"What do you mean by special friend?"

"Are you that dumb Narzhack?"

"You mean with that plain skinner?"

"I know its probably going to be hard for you to accept, but you need to realize she's in love with that man."

"How could that possibly happen?"

"Narzhack, she's no longer your little girl. She's just been through huge space battles and she's a personal friend of General Níngsī the most important person in the Empire next to the Emperor himself."

"How long will they be here?"

"She didn't say exactly but reporters say General Níngsī plans to be at Plastras Nostras for two weeks to rest his crews."

"Where will he be staying?"

"Right here."

"What are you talking about?"

"Get used to it, you just looked at the man your daughter is in love with."

"He can't stay here."

"Where can he stay?"

"After dinner I'll fly him to the city where he can get a hotel room."

"If you do that you will make your daughter very unhappy and resentful. You need to remember we do not know what all transpired, but we do know they just went through a war together and have great affection for each other."

"I'm not going to have a plain skinner spend the night here."

"If that's your final decision be ready to live with it if in another year you lose your daughter in a space battle and you screwed up one of her rare visits to her parents."

"So be it. He's not staying here and tell her not to come back again with him. I'm not hungry, I need to go to my office."

Narzhack stormed out of his house and went to the mayor's office where he sat and contemplated for a long while.

Eventually when he started feeling hunger pains, he slipped back into his sky car and drove home.

When he arrived Christiana and her friend were not around and Starhwā sat in her chair where she watched a lot of videos quiet and obviously in a sour mood.

"Where's Christiana and the plain skinner?" The

thought hit him they could be in the bedroom copulating and that would really piss him off and he would toss the jerk out of his home, naked if necessary.

"Why should you care?"

"I wanted to see her."

"She doesn't want to see you."

"She's not here."

"Where did she go?"

"Why should you care after the way you embarrassed her in front of her special person?"

"What do you mean by that?"

"You of all people have complained this home has poor acoustics and people can hear each other in the other room. Christiana overheard everything you said. Your daughter just came back from a major war where a bunch of her best friends were killed and you had to pick this of all time to be a jerk."

"Well, where did she go?"

"Out the door."

"Where too?"

"She didn't say."

"She walked out of here on foot?"

"Yes, she's with Roger and they took their small suitcases with them. Don't expect her to come home any time soon."

"I'm going to get in my skycar and find them. They could not have gone far on foot."

Since Roger is in reality General Níngsī's true only friend still living besides Captain Luōjiàn, he wanted him protected. Roger and Christiana had no idea the level of surveillance on them. When they left the home carrying their small suitcases still wearing their uniforms, one of the surveillance men spotted them and reported: "Roger and Christiana are leaving her parents home still wearing their uniforms and appear to be walking up the street. Christiana is crying.

"Pick them up and bring them to my hotel immediately," General Níngsī replied immediately.

The unmarked skycar lifted off and flew down the street a couple blocks and stopped in front of the two walking and two men got out and approached Roger and Christiana.

This was unexpected and slightly unnerving for both and it was evident Christiana was still weeping.

Doctor Brandenhagen and Christiana, "General Níngsī asked me to give you a ride to his hotel. I think he has some rooms set aside for you."

"Sure," Roger said not appearing to chipper as he had just learned first-hand, a modern society on this Alien planet was no further along socially advanced than where he just came from.

They got in the skycar and headed for the city a seemingly short ride that would have been a long walk otherwise.

By the time they were long gone by the time it was sundown, Narzhack had flown all over town and along all major streets and transportation stops and saw no sign of them and went home.

The kitchen was clean, all the food was placed in cold storage and his wife was not around. Narzhack peeked in the bedroom and saw his wife laying in bed seemingly weeping.

Narzhack was not in a good mental state now so he walked over to his Elixir Cabinet and pulled out a bottle of one of his favorite fermented beverages and poured a full glass and sat down and slowly drank it. He knew better than to go into his bedroom as his wife was very upset. After almost polishing off the bottle he laid back and fell asleep.

General Níngsī made arrangements to get Roger and Christiana separate hotel rooms as to not create a scandal since there were a number of their space warriors staying in the hotel, some of whom knew Christiana. Protecting Christiana's reputation was important to General Níngsī.

In the morning Christiana's mother did not leave the bedroom. Christiana's last words to her broke her heart. "Tell daddy to have a nice life, I doubt I will be coming back."

Narzhack didn't want to face his wife that morning so he left wearing the same clothes he had on the day before, went out to his sky car and flew to his Mayor's Office.

In many ways now, Roger Brandenhagen was glad he and Christiana had not copulated. Its one thing to be rejected by her family as a close friend verse being rejected if they had consummated the relationship. They still had the ability to go their separate ways with disappointment which is a lot better than leaving with a broken heart.

It is a very unique feeling to be rejected by a father when you are in love with his daughter. There are other types of rejections people go through. In most cases it's just normal people with normal life styles. But sometimes its special people who have gone through hellish experiences and by the grace of God, due their Karma or for some other reasons life sometimes seems so unfair.

The Governor of Plastras Nostras was extremely happy the first planet General Níngsī stopped at after one of the most important events in Zhrakzhong History, was his planet. He decided to pay General Níngsī a personal visit at his hotel he provided for him.

"Hello General Níngsī, I'm very delighted you decided to stop here on the way back to Tèlándìa."

"I'm sorry Governor, but I think we'll be leaving much earlier than planned."

"How much sooner."

"Tomorrow."

"Why the sudden departure?"

"I only stopped here for one reason."

"What was that?"

"My only friend, Doctor Brandenhagen is with me. He's a good friend with one of my crew members from Plastras Nostras. No doubt she was in love with him. She took him yesterday when we first arrived to meet her parents and her father flatly rejected him to the point it was an embarrassment. There is no point in us remaining here on this unfriendly planet."

"Please don't leave early, this will be a terrible disaster for my planet. Let me look into the matter."

"I'll give you a day."

"Who is it who rejected him?"

"The mayor of the small town Yànwéi."

General Níngsī had a long talk with Roger the night before after they arrived at the Hotel, so he was able to provide the Governor a lot of private information of exactly what transpired.

The Governor who had to exist in a secular society knew this information could be damaging to their tourist business. But also, when this got reported to the media that a small town mayor pissed off General Níngsī so the fleet left, would have a serious negative impact on the reputation of the entire planet.

"General, please let me look into this. There must have been a misunderstanding."

The Governor of Plastras Nostras was soon in his Skycar followed by several other skycars that made up his security detachment. Since he controlled the speed limits, they wasted very little time in their souped up skycars to get to Yànwéi. His computer controlled Skycar went directly to the Mayor's Office where pedestrians were all amazed at the number of skycars that descended down upon the parking in front of the mayor's office and for those that didn't have a parking spot, they simply stopped on the street since they also were the predominate law enforcement.

Unfortunately, the damage was already done and Roger analyzed the situation and determined he could not take the relationship to the next step.

The Major wasn't expecting this and when the Governor of the planet stormed into his office, he sat almost paralyzed. The Governor knew this was a very delicate matter and looked around at the 15 people that came with him into the office so he turned around and asked everyone to leave so that he and the mayor could have a little talk. The crowd left leaving them alone.

"Hello Governor, what can I do for you?"

"Mayor, I know a lot about what happened yesterday when your daughter and General Níngsī's best friend, Doctor Brandenhagen arrived at your home."

"What about it?"

"Your actions not only disenfranchised your daughter who you may possibly never see again, but you also put this entire planet in a bad light."

"Mayor, didn't it dawn on you the hell your daughter just went through?"

"She's in the space force, that's their business."

"She went through hell, and she and Doctor Brandenhagen lost very special people in that battle."

"Okay so what?"

"Are you such a dimwit to not understand you just upset General Níngsī to the point he's going to leave with the fleet tomorrow?"

"That's his business."

"It's now your business."

"Why do you say that?"

"You know all those organized crime people in the city that will lose billions of credits when the fleet pulls out of here 2 weeks early because you decided to be a jerk, may come pay you a visit."

"Are you threatening me?"

"No, I don't need to threaten you. I will simply say I know if the fleet leaves 2 weeks early because you decided to be a jerk, those bad guys will come pay you a visit and I have no way of protecting you if they want to do you harm."

"They are not going to come after me, this is a small town, they have no interests in me."

"You do not think a few billion credits might anger them?"

"I'm just a small-town mayor."

"Okay wise guy I'm going to tell it to you like it is. I've seen these guys cut the heads off their spouse and send it to them for a lot less that even thousands of credits. You dummy, you are risking them billions of credits. Are that dumb?"

"So, you say they will come and kill me?"

"No, they will cut your wife had off then they will kill you."

"What do you expect me to do about it?"

"I think there is only one way you can save your own life and your wife's life now."

"What can I do?"

"You will accompany me to their hotel and you

will get down on your hands and knees if necessary and apologize for being a jerk, then you will try to be a good daddy again instead of a jerk. Then maybe General Níngsī may stay. He's given me 24 hours to get you to do the right thing."

"I'm kind of dirty now, I didn't take a shower before I left home and I need to change my clothes."

"All right, I'll take you there now to clean up. I suggest you bring your wife with you; she may be able to help you out of this mess you got yourself."

"You really think they would cut my wife's head off?"

"You are a small-town idiot; you have no idea how fast these guys operate plus they got infiltrators within my offices and police forces. There is no way we can protect you. I really want you to know this because as the Governor, I know a lot I can't tell you about, but assume if General Níngsī leaves in 24 hours like he says he is, I doubt you and your wife will live another 48 hours."

"All right, take me home so I can get cleaned up."

"Be careful what you say from now on, because I'm absolutely sure if you upset Doctor Brandenhagen, General Níngsī leaves in 24 hours."

The Governor and his group with the mayor in tow went out to their skycars and immediately headed for the mayor's home.

The last person in the world the major's wife wanted to see then was the mayor who really screwed things up with his stupidity. But with the Governor whom she only saw on video with him kept her from unloading.

"We need to get cleaned up; we are going to visit our daughter in a few minutes. The Governor is taking us."

The wife looked rather strange taking it all in.

"Come with me to our bedroom we need to have a quick talk."

Inside the bedroom he informed her: "We need to bring our daughter home and her friend Doctor Brandenhagen. Our lives depend on it. This is very scary situation. I'm terribly sorry I caused this mess."

The mayor's wife had never heard her husband talk like this before and having the Governor of the planet in their home really created a lot of stress. She meekly complied.

In about 30 minutes they were scrubbed and presentable and exited their bedroom with the Governor patiently waiting. He was glad he brought the mayor home because he looked disheveled this morning. Now he looked distinguished.

"Okay Governor, we are ready."

As soon as the group left, they mayor's house, General Níngsī's spies in a skycar not far away made the report which made General Níngsī smile knowing he might be able to salvage this situation afterall.

Roger was in his hotel room watching an entertainment holograph. Christiana was in the next room crying intermittently feeling really bad. General Níngsī figured the two love birds who had not been together and surveillance video showed Christiana was still weeping sent one of his female aides-de-camps down to Christiana's room to tell her to pull herself together that her parents and the Governor of the planet would be arriving soon. He also sent word to the Governor to bring her parents up to his room to have a little talk to give them time to clean up their daughter.

Roger was also notified of the meeting and asked to get himself in a presentable fashion.

As they arrived at the hotel, one of the Governor's security men said, "General Níngsī wants to talk with Christiana's parents in private first."

They were ushered up to the General's room for a private meeting. Meanwhile the Aide-de-Camp helped to work the magic on Christiana to get rid of the baggy crying eyes and disheveled appearance. She didn't have much to work with but in 30 minutes pulled off a miracle as she also embellished a few things to get Christiana's mind off her heartbreak. Learning her parents were there and wanted to take her and Roger back to their home had in interesting effect on her.

The Governor of Plastras Nostras introduced Christiana's parents to General Níngsī, then he took the nod and stepped outside the room and waited patiently.

"Hello Mayor Narzhack and Starhwā, I wanted to talk with you a few minutes before you meet with Christiana and Doctor Brandenhagen."

The two nodded and Narzhack was now starting to be slightly terrified as he realized the corner, he painted himself in. When reality struck home and he suddenly heard from the Governor of the entire planet, that organized crime would cut off his wife's head and kill him after he was forced to watch it, knew he was now deep in over his head.

"Mayor Narzhack, the only reason why I brought the fleet to this planet was so that your daughter could introduce you to her close friend Doctor Brandenhagen. You have no idea what those two have just gone through."

"I lost an entire ship, everyone killed. Those were the only two I could save. It was unavoidable and it was a supreme sacrifice that saved our Empire and ended the war."

"As a General in charge of the expedition, I cannot fraternize with crew members. A leader has to keep a distance from his crew. The force commander is the loneliest person on the ship."

"I was most fortunate I was able to bring along my best friend Doctor Brandenhagen. Before the battle started, he had already gone through a lot. You have no idea. They survived the battle but saw first hand the horror of my command ship blowing up killing everyone onboard. Your daughter's life was saved a few mere moments, and had it not been for Doctor Brandenhagen she would not be alive today. You owe her existence to Doctor Brandenhagen my very best friend."

"Narzhack, I'm not sure why the two of you got off on such a rocky start, but I want you to try to find some compassion not only for your daughter after what she has been through these past few months but also Doctor Brandenhagen who lost a lot in that battle. You have no idea how badly he grieves for the loss.

"As the commander who gave your world peace for the first time in 100 years, I'm asking you to be considerate of Doctor Brandenhagen. Also, I've instructed my staff to make you this copy of the Treaty to end the war with the Xīngguī Empire on this etched gold tablet I'm giving to you now. You will notice your daughter signed for your planet and Doctor Brandenhagen signed for the planet Earth where currently one billion Zhrakzhong live among the Earth people who have been a very generous host to our refugees."

"What do you want us to do General Níngsī?" Narzhack asked.

"In a few minutes I'm going to bring your daughter and Doctor Brandenhagen here, I want you to take them home and spend the day with them and give your daughter the love she desperately needs and be courteous to Doctor Brandenhagen who earned the right to be my best friend for what he has done. He's an extraordinary person and I hope he and I can remain close for the rest of my life. I have no other friends except a couple back at Earth that will likely decline to move here with me. Consider Doctor Brandenhagen an extension of my personal family.

"We will be happy to do that General Níngsī," Narzhack said.

General Níngsī then tapped on his wrist strap communicator which signaled his aide-de-camp via the communicator to come into the room.

"What do you desire General Níngsī?"

"Bring the couple in now."

"They are on the way."

Moments later the two came into General Níngsī's Hotel room and the tension was high, as Narzhack understood his life depended upon what transpired in the next few minutes.

As soon as they were in the room, General Níngsī said, "I'm going to step outside for a couple minutes to give you all time to talk."

Narzhack fully fearing for his life now as he realized the gravity of the situation started first speaking in standard Plastras Nostras dialect: "Doctor Brandenhagen, I'm very sorry the way I mistreated you yesterday. I have no excuses for my deplorable behavior, I'm very sorry."

Christiana was very proud that her father could show such humbleness knew Roger probably didn't understand a lot of what he said so she translated it.

He then turned to Christiana and said, "I had no idea what you went through in those space battles. Now I know and I'm very sorry. I want you and Roger to come home with us and start over. We love you and want you to have happiness.

Tears were coming down Christiana who had a hard time translating it but she got it out. It was a very difficult moment and Roger who had recently had his love ripped out of his heart as he watched General

Níngsĩ's command ship explode had some emotions and a few tears as well. It was a very emotional moment.

Christiana jumped at her father and threw her arms around him and started wheeping profusely. It struck Roger real hard in the gut and when Starhwā observed that behavior she was very touched. She too had tears rolling down her face.

The tough guy Narzhack had his own tears. And as his daughter weeped holding and crying, he realized she had a broken wing and Roger really was the spirit that kept her alive. She had gone through a lot, but so had Roger. Narzhack was a changed man. His almost fatal blunder was stereotyping Roger and not giving him a chance.

It took a while for them all to regain their composure. General Níngsĩ waited patiently outside with the Governor and his aide-de-camps looking on. It was quite astonishing to them. But they had no idea General Níngsĩ would wait for hours for Roger.

In about 15 minutes they slowly regained their composure and Narzhack said, "Us all go home now."

Roger said, "I'm ready to go with you," then walked over and opened the door and walked into the hallway and said, "General Níngsĩ, we are going to Christiana's home now."

"Excellent, I'll give you all a ride."

The others followed Roger and General Níngsī to the elevator that took them to the ground floor a mere thirty feet from the main entrance where General Níngsī's transporter/shuttle was parked for a quick get-away if necessary.

The ride back to Christiana's home was quick. The mayor was delighted to see his skycar parked in his driveway, then he wondered, *how did that get here?*

General Níngsī dropped the group off and realized they needed some privacy and time alone, to heal some wounds, and headed back to his Hotel, where the people who would have cut off Christiana's mother's head had several young, green skin, purple eyes, with red hair Plastras Nostras women there to entertain General Níngsī and convince him not to leave tomorrow.

General Níngsī knew their masters expected them to please him so after they were in the privacy of his hotel room he said, "Us get in bed. He slipped in bed with the two girls and said, I'm very tired. I need to get some sleep, just hold me nearby. The girls complied with his request and soon discovered this was a wonderful gentleman who only wanted their company. Nothing else was necessary and he later told the businessmen who provided them, those two girls were utterly fantastic. Every time I come back here; I want exclusive access to the two.

"Not a problem General Níngsī."

General Níngsī gave the two young women substantial tips and they were relived they could spend time with this caring gentleman and spent the full two weeks with him, enjoying every moment. They would be more than willing to be with this wonderful kind man anytime. All the other working girls were surprised the nice reports these two superstars had to say about General Níngsī. In the underworld and organized crime, they too took a liking to General Níngsī because when the working girls talk fondly of you, that means you are a special person. In reality the two girls were on a fabulous 2-week paid vacation and enjoyed every moment of it.

That night Christiana's parents pulled her into their bedroom for a private meeting.

"We want you and Roger to spend the night in the hotel."

"Why?"

"You can have more fun and we do not want to hear it, the walls are too thin here."

Christiana smiled walked out of the bedroom walked over and grabbed Roger's hand and said, "Honey we get to sleep in the hotel again tonight."

"Why is that?"

"It's a secret, I'll tell you when we get there."

"How we getting there?"

"I think our watcher is outside will offer us a ride again."

"Alright."

Christiana grabbed Roger's hand and took him to the door, but as soon as they got to the door her mother came and walked up and gave Christiana a big hug and said, "I love you."

"I love you too mother."

Then she surprised Roger and grabbed him and hug him too. It was a sensual moment for Roger. As he left the home he had some emotions that were quite genuine and unique. As expected the watcher alarmed at them leaving again pulled up and asked, "Are you going somewhere?"

"Yes back to the Hotel, can you give us a ride?"

"Absolutely."

"Today it was different, they were all smiles, not crying like yesterday."

As soon as he dropped them off at the front entrance of the hotel, he called General Níngsī: "General I just dropped the two lovebirds off at the hotel. They were all smiles; I think it's a positive change."

"Thank you for keeping me informed."

"My pleasure sir, I'm sorry for disrupting you, but I know you wanted the report right away."

"Not a problem you did right. Good night and thanks for the heads up."

"Your welcome sir."

Roger went up to his room but Christiana had other ideas, "We need to go to my room."

"Why?"

"To protect my reputation. I can't be seen leaving your hotel room in the morning, but nobody will pay attention to you leaving mine."

"Allright."

General Níngsī speculated that after tonight Roger would be a changed man and most likely willing to stay in the Zhrakzhong Empire.

Roger was soon doing what Christina's mother feared yesterday, eating the forbidden fruit. When a Plastras Nostras has an emotional spike caused by the activity they now started they have pheromone explosion followed by the vaginal chemicals that were a freak of nature. Roger was soon experiencing that rarified resplendence wealthy people spent fortunes to obtain. And as General Níngsī speculated by morning, Roger was a changed man and his sad memories of Elja Brielle Janxel were buried deep into his psyche to stay dormant for decades.

The two weeks were what the doctor ordered. General Níngsī's forces were not at the mutiny stage but they were certainly war weary. When you see huge spacecraft blow up not far from your position it's a psychological intensifier because they all knew it easily could have been them. Had they flown directly back to Tèlándìa, many of them would already be back out in space, facing a breaking point. The rest the crews received was more than beneficial because now they would soon be starting the next phase of repatriating long separated Zhrakzhong back to their home worlds.

General Níngsī's punishment for the unauthorized stop over at Plastras Nostras was to be sent back to Earth to start the movement of all those currently in Mexico using high speed transports while the mother ship that deposited them was now vectored back to Tèlándìa where they would pick of various dispersed population on the trip back while obtaining higher speeds since they didn't have to hide their presence and generate ion trains and X-ray emanations easily tracked long distance.

As the two-week vacation rapped up, Christiana's family was now whole again. The mayor realizing his daughter and potential future son-in-law's signature as on the Treaty of Wukar as it was titled to recognize the largest galactic space battle of all time.

In two weeks there were a lot of happy people as it appeared the peace was holding and diplomats hadn't screwed it up.

It was now time to gather the troops and head back out into deep space and head for Tèlándìa. As ships in the task force were fully loaded up with their crews they slowly slid out of orbit and out of the solar system. The fleet would rendezvous at a point (Q) then all fly in formation back to Tèlándìa and receive long delayed accolades they all deserved.

Doctor Brandenhagen and Christiana could not share the same quarters but were next to each other. In reality since Roger didn't stand a watch, and spent most of his time hanging out with General Níngsī, he was always available to Christiana. In essence she often kept his bed warm and General Níngsī directed artificial intelligence, "They are a couple all but married." Regulations did not apply to the VIP and if he invited Christiana to sleep with him as far as General Níngsī was concerned it was authorized.

If and when the two decided to have a permanent

unification, General Níngsī knew the perfect place to do it: The Tytrone Philosophers Temple in Màichōng. When the time and date materialized, he would send a request to Kāiwù de Sēngrén and ask him to also give him some meditation training at the same time.

General Níngsī soon received a special notification through secret channels, the two girls on Plastras Nostras wanted to marry him and organized crime said he earned them both by creating peace which allowed their business to now flourish. When he responded he liked them equally and didn't want to break a heart of one over the other, the response was unique: the two women would agree to be co-wives. He accepted and thus determined a double wedding was in order and the fact he and Roger would each have Plastras Nostras spouses made even more ideal.

In no time at all Kāiwù de Sēngrén started planning the event, but he insisted, all members go through meditation training prior to the unification ceremonies. General Níngsī gladly accepted, the two Plastras Nostras women would do anything to buy their freedom were more than happy to take meditation training if that's all it took. And Roger having the inquisitive mind, knew the theory of Hemi-Sync and thought it would be interesting to try it. Christiana was so deeply in love that if that's what Roger wanted to do, she would be happy as well.

Xié'è de Gōngniú and Emperor Shāyú were informed about the VIP coming for such an event.

Through Kāiwù de Sēngrén, they requested to attend which was just fine with General Níngsī.

Weeks later they all converged on Màichōng and met Kāiwù de Sēngrén and six Tytrone Philosophers. The two young ladies from Plastras Nostras were now free and looking forward to an interesting life being tied to VIP's.

The Meditation chapel had plenty of room. However, as it turned out the two former Plastras Nostras working girls were sitting between General Níngsī and Xié'è de Gōngniú who asked to receive the training with them. Everyone seemed open minded and in search of spiritualistic symmetry. Hence, these were overall the best students Kāiwù de Sēngrén could ever hope to have in a single setting.

The theory is the larger the group if they are willing and interested participants, the stronger the results of the meditation that can be achieved. There was also the possibility of intersections and cross influences between others. The working girls with new found freedoms were so happy they merely melted in the proximity of their benefactor gentleman who up to this time had never laid a hand on them or made any demands. With all the enthusiasm and positive valence, the meditation proceeded very quickly achieving its results. The working girls were the first to enter a Hemi-Sync experience. In due time they all went to the universe and experienced several lifetimes. And like before after 3 or 4 hours they slowly came out of it with a high degree of satisfaction on their experience.

There was an extraordinary development of an intersection. One of the working girls intersected strongly with Xié'è de Gōngniú. In front of General Níngsī and the others she made the comment: "While I was traveling through the universe, I meet Xié'è de Gōngniú. We fell in love and I lived several lifetimes with him. General Níngsī I truly thank you for my freedom. You saved my life, but I want to unify with Xié'è de Gōngniú. She then turned around and looked into Xié'è de Gōngniú's eyes who was now having an emotional moment as he had a strange feeling for this stranger. He didn't quite understand it, but he said, "If she will have me, I will be hers."

General Níngsī was actually delighted with this development because he felt it would be too awkward with two spouses and responded. "If you two desire each other and want to be unified, I give you, my blessing."

The two spontaneously embraced, it truly was remarkable. This was another one of those mysteries Kāiwù de Sēngrén would file away in the back of his mind as he had now witnessed the total transcendence of Xié'è de Gōngniú one of the evilest men in the galaxy to one of the kindest and gentlest.

By agreement the group went through four sessions then it would be time to do the unification event.

Not very many people were invited but Christiana's parents came to the ceremony. As word leaked out of the grand event, there was a line wrapped around the block to see General Níngsī unification and to a lesser degree, Xié'è de Gōngniú. The only thing that could be done was to set up outside speakers so that the vast sprawling crowd could at least hear what went on. The 100 people close to the Temple were all XSS men who respected Xié'è de Gōngniú because without him, they never could have got Emperor Shāyú to end war.

There was an empty seat next to Christiana's parents in the front row. Nobody seemed to figure out who it was reserved for.

As the Monks were all stationed with musical devices to give off strange sounds as part of the process it was anticipated it would all start momentarily. About one minute before the ceremony the side door to the Temple opened and in walked Emperor Shāyú wearing an ornate Emperor gown and escorted by one of the Monks to the empty seat.

Ten Emperor Guardsmen were stationed on each side of the Temple for his protection as his enemies had not given up. The war profiteers and the intergalactic bankers were upset he cut off their multiple boondoggles paid for by the horrors of war. Within just the past few weeks, Xié'è de Gōngniú had shown him secretly over 30 videos showing some of the assassins they foiled. Xié'è de Gōngniú also gave him proof that some of his "spies" were actually agents of the intergalactic bankers constantly implicating the Tytrone Philosophers to cover their own tracks. This was all being sorted out now by Emperor Shāyú who by now had placed his Emperor Guardsmen under the control of Xié'è de Gōngniú because they were getting too sloppy and their vigilance decrement coefficients were now really bad.

Emperor Shāyú was quite animated to see General Níngsī's unification of all places here in Màichōng. When Emperor Shāyú was informed by Xié'è de Gōngniú the entire wedding party received meditation training, he truly was astonished. He had a growing respect for General Níngsī who really was what he portrayed, a wise General who wanted peace and end the suffering. The fact he would come here, get meditation training, and go through a unification clearly demonstrated his real essence that Kāiwù de Sēngrén observed.

The ceremony had a series of statements and sound effects that resonated with everyone observing. Kāiwù de Sēngrén had prepared all of these participants through his meditation process. He now saw the fruits of his labor as two of the most powerful people in the galaxy stood before him to achieve their unifications. In a parallel process Kāiwù de Sēngrén established the legal transcendence to unified couples. The only person here today who would not benefit was Emperor Shāyú because it was out of the question for his unification with anyone other than Xīngguī. The bloodline to the throne had to remain pure with only Xīngguī blood lines.

Emperor Shāyú felt these three men were the luckiest guys on the planet because three plain skinners marrying three Plastras Nostras women in a group unification was unheard of nor were there very many inter-racial couples in the Xīnguī Empire. Emperor Shāyú would almost give up the throne to be up there with a Plastras Nostras woman. His enemies would certainly love to see his departure.

Because of the strange sounds the Tytrone Philosopher Monks created during meditation training, the couples were sensitive to this cacophony of intricate design now presented to them, it had a long-lasting effect on their unification. Each one of them felt the love pouring in from their mate. This surreal effect humbled each and every one of them. The most powerful General in the Galaxy was now merely a Noble Savage. They each clearly understood they were nothing more than mere mortals which they understood by their meditation training. Filled with empathy and love and beauty now around them seemingly everywhere. The special lighting synchronized with the unique sounds the Tytrone Philosopher Monks resonated their souls added the fabric of transcendence they now sensed. General Níngsī, causally looked towards his friend Roger Brandenhagen who really was responsible for all this.

Coincidences sometimes manifest outcomes terribly unpredictable. Here General Níngsī was standing next to a woman he cared for and loved would not have been possible had he not befriended Roger out of desperation for friendship that escaped him because of his dedication to resolving the biggest issues of their lives by ending the war. His happiness from his friendship with Roger was thus now multiplied by a huge factor as this all resulted in him discovering the love of his life. For this he would always owe Roger a great deal of gratitude.

Roger heartbroken from the loss of Elja Brielle Janxel was now healed. Roger had a devastating loss, the same as a bird having both its wings broken. General Níngsī's intervention made this all possible. Roger knew General Níngsī gave him his biggest happiness in his life by his intervention. Now Roger would be faced with another heart-breaking affair. He would have to go back to Earth and inform Ami who was not the most ideal girlfriend by a long stretch and who really didn't appreciate the man she knew by her numerous selfish acts, would discover Roger was now irrevocably lost for the rest of her life. Roger wasn't looking forward to that trip but knew it had to be done. It would be the final chapter of his life on planet Earth because in Roger's heart, he belonged out searching the galaxy with new sights and scenes and experiences that would never be possible for him back on Earth.

After the ceremony ended and the newly unified couples turned and faced the packed temple all smiling from the greatest achievements in their lives, Emperor Shāyú stood and walked up to the platform and made a pass down by each couple and in a very uncharacteristic fashion grabbed each of their hands, not for a shake, but for an endearing moment. It was a very strange affair as the emperor had tears enveloping his eyes. He truly was touched be each of them and as he touched each person, he felt a strange electricity. He knew in his heart he loved each one of them.

At the very end of the group of course was Kāiwù de Sēngrén who was equally astonished when Emperor Shāyú reached out and grabbed his hand and said, "Kāiwù de Sēngrén, I want you to come with me back to my Palace, I need to consult you on some important matters I need your help with."

"Your excellency, I would be very happy to accompany you to your Palace."

As the newlyweds walked out the front of the Tytrone Philosopher Temple, Kāiwù de Sēngrén and Emperor Shāyú exited the side entrance and walked twenty steps into the courtyard where his skycars and security apparatus was patiently waiting. Moments later they were airborne heading for the Palace where the strangest conversations began.

By now the XSS men had cordoned off an area directly in front of the Tytrone Philosopher Temple the crowd had no idea why, and in the most elaborate choreographed fashion a series of skycars sequenced down and picked up the various parties and skedaddled away to their retreats where they would begin their new journeys in life.

Chapter Twenty-Three

Ami

Roger understood long before th Zhrakzhongs arrived that Ami was changing. The first time he saw her up in Nicholas-Nicholas Restaurant and Night Club atop the Alamoana Hotel in Waikiki, Hawaii, he thought she was the most beautiful woman he had seen in his life time. But he felt an inward sadness because he didn't believe he would ever be able to know this incredibly beautiful Japanese lady.

As time passed, he eventually met and got to know Ami. She was very hard to get. She wasn't interested in anything that wasn't going to lead to a permanent relationship.

All was well and it seemed they were slowly becoming a couple. Roger lived every day to see Ami and time seemed to fly. In due time their life travels brought them to the Washington DC Beltway area and the relationship seemed to flourish. They had their own homes and lived apart. Roger pursued Ami with great determination and it appeared that eventually they would become a couple with the sights set on a permanent relationship.

Then disaster struck. One night Ami's best friend took her out to a club and they ended up drunk and in bed with two dudes set on one-night stands. The dude obviously lied profusely to Ami. She didn't know the brutal truth the man wasn't interested in any spare baggage.

For the next couple of months Ami and her friend ran into the two gentlemen out in town and received a cold shoulder. It was utterly disgusting to her. Meanwhile before she realized the truth she had given Roger the indication she needed some time by herself to think things over as she wrongly assumed that suave new Prince Charming would be her future partner until the brutal truth became apparent.

In these past couple of months, Roger didn't see much of Ami and got the feeling she didn't want to see him anymore. Then the Zhrakzhongs arrived and Roger made no further attempt to contact Ami who he felt didn't want to see him again. Ami was of course going through a period of personal humiliation and feeling violated by a stinking liar. And the truth be told she really actually forgot about Roger for well over a month. Just before she was about to contact Roger, he appeared on that well televised event and all the negativity surrounded by it quickly diminished any desires Ami had to contact him.

In due time Ami got curious as to why Roger stopped calling and texting her. One morning while she was drinking her morning coffee, she looked at her cell phone text records because she was curious the last time, she saw a text from Roger. That's when it hit her, he had not texted her for over two months. She then looked at her email old mail and found the same thing. Roger had not sent her an email for quite some time. She sort of understood because she had blown him off. *She probably hurt his feelings.*

One thing Ami knew for sure about Roger, he was kind and courteous and always treated her in high regards. She now felt miserable she had treated Roger so badly and let some rascal get her splendid female gratification at the same time denied the real gentleman she should have been with all along. In a way she hated her friend for taking her and setting her up for a personal disaster. She wondered; *how should I approach Roger now. What if he saw me with this other man?*

It took Ami a few days to get the nerve up and do a cold call on Roger. She was actually willing to confess to him she made a huge blunder and had sex with another man. She wondered how Roger would react to it. She really felt like a rotten bitch she often accused other women of being. The day of reconning happened and she put on some nice-looking clothes, made herself up really nice and drove over to Roger's home. When she got there, a couple news crew vehicles with antenna's were parked on the street near Roger's home and two guys in suits were standing out front.

Ami drove past all this then turned at the end of the block and shortly turned and drove down the alleyway. Posted in the back of Roger's house was two more guys in suits. Ami didn't stop, she went home then when she got the nerve up called his cell phone. There was no answer. She sent him some text messages and he didn't respond to them as well.

Ami wondered if Roger knew what happened to her and he simply wrote her off. Afterall what she did wasn't very nice, anyone would be hurt under the circumstances. What puzzled her was the TV vans and the guys guarding his house. *Was his TV appearance such a big deal?*

Ami tried a few more times to text Roger and call him but got no answers. A month later she drove by Roger's house. The TV Vans were gone but the suits were still guarding his home.

There were several empty parking spots nearby, so Ami parked her car and walked up to Roger's home where she had experienced some nice dinners, glasses of wine and even a few bouts of recreational sex. But she never told Roger she loved him and she never offered any words of exclusivity and permanence. She now felt how she had badly screwed up.

Ami walked up to the porch and one of the men in suits asked, "Can I help you?"

"I would like to see Roger. I'm his friend Ami."

"He's not home."

"Do you know when he will be home?"

"We don't expect him any time soon."

"Will he be home later today?"

"No."

"Any idea when he might come home."

"No."

"Can I give you my business card and as Roger to call me when he gets back?"

"Sure."

Ami went home without good vibrations because of the implied secrecy and the around the clock security people.

Is Roger in some kind of trouble? Ami asked herself.

After a month of not hearing from Roger, she drove by his home again and the men in suits were still there. *Whatever it is, this sure is a mystery.*

Sally Fairbanks was also wondering what

happened to Doctor Brandenhagen and after a couple trips back out to Arizona, learned he went away with General Níngsī and nobody had seen him since. When Sally confronted the Zhrakzhongs they simply said, he should be coming home soon and everything was fine.

Days later Mike Barnes notified Sally Fairbanks she needed to be prepared because the SAC Director Mark Rebman would be coming back from leave soon and also the men guarding Doctor Brandenhagen's home had a business card from a woman who ostensibly was Roger's girlfriend and appeared worried because she was unable to contact him.

Sally knew she had to handle this second matter real fast because if she waited until the SAC Director Mark Rebman returned, he would most likely screw it up.

Sally called the phone number on Ami's business card.

"Hello."

"Ami?"

"Yes, what can I help you with?"

"Ami, I'm a friend of Roger Brandenhagen and I was informed by the security men guarding his home that you are concerned about his whereabouts?"

"Yes, I was attempting to contact Roger."

Sally pulled up Roger's dossier and a person of interest like Roger has an extensive catalog of pictures and events in their lives. Thanks to CIA's artificial intelligence, everything associated with Ami was tabularized and laid out in a most recently used fashion. It did not take but a few minutes for Sally to conclude Ami was probably Roger's girlfriend. She felt compelled to give Ami some reassurances but knew they could not discuss it over the phone.

"Ami, would it be possible to meet you somewhere, and I can give you some information about Roger I think you should know about."

"All right. Do you know the Starbucks over at K street near the water front west of the Kennedy Center?"

"Yes."

"Could we meet there?"

"Sure."

"I'll be wearing some black slacks and a blue top."

"I know how you look; I've seen your pictures."

"Okay, thanks, say 11:00 A.M.?"

"Allright."

This situation is something the CIA had to deal with all the time especially when husbands whose wives think they are some white color workers are delayed for a few weeks in places like Honduras.

Sally dressed very toned down. She didn't want to convey by any means she was some sort of risk for Ami. This no doubt would probably not be a pleasant time for Ami and they were near a place they could go for a walk and have some privacy. There were numerous foot paths along the Georgetown Waterfront Park they could take because it was obvious if Ami pressed for answers, Sally might have to divulge some sensitive information to calm Ami down. The big shot SAC Director Mark Rebman that would be back in the office in a few days would no doubt fire Sally Fairbanks if he knew what she was willing to disclose to Ami. Time was important, this meeting had to happen while Mike Barnes was still acting Director of SAC.

Sally hopped in her white supped up BMW she wanted horsepower in the event she got tagged by some enemies. Sally transitioned off the Whitehurst Freeway onto K Street and made her way to the Washington Harbor shopping mall and pulled into Colonial Parking and walked over to the Starbucks about a block away. She went inside about five minutes to Eleven and looked around and Ami had not arrived. Ami was very punctual and exactly at 11:00 A.M. a hot looking Japanese lady that most men would say was smoking hot walked in. The tall shoes helped the image quite a bit reducing the dragon ass by a great margin.

Sally knew this was Ami so she approached her and said, "Hello Ami, I'm Sally Fairbanks, can I buy you a coffee?"

"Sure, why not."

After they got their two coffees with all the appropriate ingredients, they left Starbucks and proceeded a short distance walking towards Senator Charles H. Percy Plaza and the park area. There was quite a bit of privacy at this time as the daytime joggers had not yet appeared in numbers.

"Thanks for meeting with me. I was getting kind of concerned about Roger."

"Ami, I've worked with Roger for several months and he never discussed you. Had I known you had some interest in Roger, I would have contacted you earlier."

"Well, we kind of have been going through some rough times and I'll be the first to admit I didn't treat Roger very fairly."

"How long has it been since you talked to Roger?"

Ami said, "I might as well be honest with you. I really screwed up badly with Roger. And at first, I knew he was hurt and had good reason to not call me, but when I tried contacting him to apologize and try to work things out, he never called me back. I doubt he knows what happened so there should have been no reason why he abruptly cut me off."

Ami was disgusted with herself and her own behavior and thought Sally was a decent person and explained what transpired. Sally could tell Ami was hurting inside and her guts were all tangled up because you often don't know what you lost until its gone forever.

"Sally said, "I have no idea how Roger feels about all this because quite frankly he's not discussed you. Truly, Roger has been extremely busy and involved in a lot of serious things I can't tell you about. You might as well assume he's under cover somewhere and we will not know his status until he returns."

"So, he's not avoiding me?"

"No, he has no way of contacting you."

"Do you know where he went?"

"Yes, I do, but its something you are not prepared to hear and my superiors would not appreciate me divulging that to you since you are not his spouse and have no legal connections to him."

"Do you have any idea when he might be coming home?"

"There are a lot of things we do not know. We have no way of contacting him now. But I'm sure he'll return home in the near future."

"Can you contact me when he gets back?"

"In a few more days my status may be changing. I have a revengeful boss who hates my guts. But I will leave word to the men guarding his home to notify you if Roger is home. I would suggest you simply drive by about once a week and ask them if Roger has returned. I will make sure they know what you look like and to answer that important question."

"I appreciate that."

"Roger has been through a lot lately. He needs some down time without a lot of emotion. You have no idea what that man has been through. Give him some space and be patient, and I hope things work out for you in the future."

"Thank you, I appreciate that."

"Ami, I really got to go back to work now. I think Roger will be okay and when he returns you can work things out. He's a very reasonable person."

"Yes I learned that the hard way."

"Goodbye Ami, I wish you the best."

"Thank you."

Sally left and one thing she knew based on Hubble and KH-14 there was a lot of space warfare that went on. Now it was very quiet, but neither has General Níngsī or Roger returned. She feared her answers my lie where those explosions occurred and they may never see Roger again.

~~~

Roger was having the time of his life with his new bride. Her chemicals that entered Roger's blood stream during their coitus, had a remarkable effect on his general health and youthfulness. Roger simply slowed down his aging. His health improved and he became far more energetic and able to focus and concentrate far better than he remembered in his lifetime. His meditation created a whole new psyche for him. The personification of his being now resonated with the aura of Christiana. He evolved.

In and out of that small town of 3,000 Roger created a lot of positive vibrations with Narzhack who was now a very humbled man. Prior to Roger's arrival the town was just about to dump him as a mayor because his attitudes created a lot of enemies and didn't make many new friends. But now with Roger's apparent influence, Narzhack was becoming far more socially adept and he was slowly winning back friends. As the community learned about the treaty sighing by his daughter and their new son-in-law, the family slowly became far more popular in the community and the mayor was spoken well of more often.

One day Roger could tell by Narzhack's attitude, he had crossed over an artificial boundary and Narzhack slowly grew fonder of Roger. Christiana also witnessed the change in her father which she was forever grateful. The way Roger treated Christiana also built a fabric of love and respect towards Roger from Christiana's mother. In life people are not always on your side. But when you realize those few that are, you appreciate them even more so.

Unfortunately, all this wonderful recreation and celestial feasts had to come to an end. Reality struck, Roger had to go back to Earth and make some major decisions.

Roger didn't think his relationship with Ami was much of one, especially in the later days when she started to exhibit the cold shoulder and needed her space. He didn't even realize how long it had been since he last communicated with Ami. But he had to face the fire and inform Ami of his change in life and the fact what ever relationship they did have, was irrevocably gone forever. Roger was hoping the fire had completely gone out and Ami would have little interest otherwise.

As part of General Níngsī's punishment for the joy ride to Plastras Nostras he was not allowed to retire and was slated to go back to Earth and start the process of returning everyone home. In reality as the task force commander, he could take any VIP with him he desired. He had to return Roger to Earth until he sorted out his future and since Christiana was a member of his crew, her passage was guaranteed. However, Roger and General Níngsī's new wife Dragée would come along as VIP guests. Since Roger was one of the three signers to the Treaty of Wukar, he was now considered a historical figure in Zhrakzhong Society. Nobody could deny he was a VIP.

The last embraces at Christiana's parents' home were a bitter sweet moment. Her father now wished he had behaved differently when Roger first arrived because over the course of the past few weeks with the initial two weeks followed by leave period and the wedding and subsequent honeymoon, Narzhack learned a lot about Roger and as he dwelled on the conditions his daughter and Roger experienced, he realized what a colossal jerk he had been in the beginning. But now the healing had occurred and Roger was friendly and showed no signs of resentment. Roger was truly an extraordinary person and to discover he was also a nuclear physicist added to the luster of the man.

It was well known that Roger was also perceived as General Níngsī's best friend. It didn't take the mayor long to figure out the extent to which Roger and now his daughter was protected. All-important men have enemies. General Níngsī's was no exception including attacks and reprisals from people associated with events long ago. Even the intergalactic bankers and war profiteers would love to see General Níngsī's as well as Emperor Shāyú disposed of. Xié'è de Gōngniú knew he was a target and always needed ample protection to stay one step ahead of the assassins. It was a never-ending battle.

In some ways, General Níngsī was glad he was taking Roger and his new wife with him to Earth because that would give them an added layer of security. It would be much easier for his enemies to whack them in Tèlándìa.

After the last round of hugs, the Zhrakzhongs Space Force transport/shuttle parked nearby on the street was ready to go. Christiana and Roger both wearing Zhrakzhong Space Force Dress Uniforms with dozens of neighbors looking on, walked deliberately to the shuttle and got inside. The shuttle took off and went vertical and in a brief period of time was out of sight as it was quickly leaving the atmosphere flying up to the waiting Command Ship.

Upon docking, they were ushered into General Níngsī's private quarters where his gracious wife, Dragée was waiting for them.

By now Dragée and General Níngsī had consummated their marriage. Dragée was extremely relieved that while she and Xié'è de Gōngniú's wife Cerise Sucrée were alone with General Níngsī and if he wanted sex with them, they would be required to perform it, didn't and was fully reserved gentleman who paid them great respect. He was like fresh air, sweet and desireable, and now Dragée knew she was in love with this powerful man General Níngsī.

When Xié'è de Gōngniú questioned Cerise Sucrée about her involvement with General Níngsī, she informed him, "There was never a physical relationship. He was a very kind soul and treated us with great respect and only desired our company."

"How could you agree to marry him without ever having sex?"

She went on to say, "He was going to marry us to insure our freedom. We know that was his intentions. I'm glad we didn't have sex with him because in the future when I meet Dragée, we know we didn't soil that relationship. We have no regrets and can always look back at it with a very positive memory."

"You would have married him if I didn't step forward and request?"

"Yes."

"Any regrets now?"

"No, I love you. You are more than I could ever ask for."

"You really feel that way."

"Yes, you own my heart now."

It took three weeks for General Níngsī to reach Earth. As he was sending people to the planet he informed Roger, "I'm putting Christiana on permanent administrative leave until you guys decide what you want to do."

"Allright."

"Do you wish me to take you directly to your home?"

"General Níngsī, if it would be possible, I would like to first stop at the *Béésh Łigaii Atsu* (Silver Eagle) Native American Tribe so I can introduce my wife to *Binii 'łigaii* (screeching owl) medicine man and his wife *Nizhóní Ch'ilátah Hózhóón* (beautiful flower) medicine man's wife.

"That's a great idea. I would also like to introduce Dragée to them as well."

After giving his executive officer his directions, General Níngsī turned towards the group he had join him on his command pedestal in the Combat Information Center including Roger and their wives and said, "Us proceed to the shuttle so we can go down and visit our friends."

The women were wearing Plastras Nostras attire that made them look more like dancers from Fiji. Their allure was rather incredible. As General Níngsī looked down into the CIC from his elevated platform he could see that just about every male and half the female crewmembers were observing them. Its very seldom any plain skin is allowed to marry a Plastras Nostras female and here were two of them on their command ship dressed in a manner that would make most of the men observing weak at their knees.

As the entourage walked down the circular stares to get to the shuttle bay, Roger observed the massive attention they were getting. He had no idea this was *just the beginning*.

In a very short while the shuttle departed the command ship and headed to Earth at the same time it was causing NORAD to give off multiple alarms.

NORAD tracked the unexpected visitors down to Arizona. It was more or less a foregone conclusion that's where they were heading.

The shuttle pilot was directed by General Níngsī to pay extra attention for children playing and cattle and also notify the compound he was coming down at the *Béésh Łigaii Atsu* (Silver Eagle) Native American Tribe to pay a personal visit, then he would be going to his command center.

As luck would have it, Sargent Hawthorne was there with *Binii 'łigaii* (screeching owl) medicine man working in their new garden, pulling weeds and working the soil around the plants and laying down additional straw to help keep the moisture in the soil. Nobody was expecting visitors when the shuttle suddenly came down and landed a mere 40 feet from them.

Sargent Hawthorne looked directly at the shuttle and said, *"Binii 'łigaii,* it looks like we got visitors."

Within moments the door opened up and General Níngsī stepped out first followed by his wife Dragée. Soon following was Roger and Christiana.

Binii 'łigaii and Sargent Hawthorne approached the group obviously taking in the incredible view of the green skinned women who had the luster and appeal that only magnified as soon as the two men were hit with the Pheromones these women were shedding because of their recent sexual activity.

"Hello Sargent Hawthorne and *Binii 'łigaii,* there has been some changes since the last time I saw you. First of all I would like to introduce you to my significant other, Dragée.

Just like rehearsed privately, Dragée a very intelligent woman stepped forward and held her hand out to *Binii 'łigaii* and said, "General Níngsī informed me how you helped him win the Battle of Wukar, I'm so very pleased to meet you. I would also like the privilege of meeting your wife *Nizhóní Ch'ilátah Hózhóón.*"

"Let me go get her I think she would like to meet you too. *Nizhóní Ch'ilátah Hózhóón* had been looking out her kitchen window and saw all this unfold and saw *Binii 'łigaii* walk towards her home. He opened the door and said, *"Nizhóní,* please come out with me. General Níngsī and his new wife would like to meet you."

Nizhóní Ch'ilátah Hózhóón had been cleaning up after a meal and dried her hands and laid the towel on the kitchen table top and said, "I'm coming."

Nizhóní Ch'ilátah Hózhóón was taken back slightly from the two glorious green skinned women and approached with a degree of trepidation.

Hello *Nizhóní Ch'ilátah Hózhóón*, since the last time I saw you, I've been wed with this wonderful lady, Dragée I wanted to introduce her to you."

Dragée feeling comfortable being around the most powerful men in th galaxy, was very politically astute as well as a social engineer and pleasure perfectionist, stepped forward and said, "*Nizhóní Ch'ilátah Hózhóón*, I'm so very pleased to meet my husband's best friends. He has informed me much about your friendliness and how your husband assisted him in the Battle of Wukar. I want to thank you for what you have done and your husband who helped General Níngsī develop tactics that took our enemies by surprise. Your husband holds one of the highest awards in Zhrakzhong History. He's now in our history books. He will never be forgotten."

Nizhóní Ch'ilátah Hózhóón had tears forming, it was an emotional roller-coaster what she went through worrying about her husband and if Sally Fairbanks had not stayed with her, she might have broken down.

Dragée spotting the emotional overload, was a very sensitive person realized that emotional spike and moved forward and put her arms around *Nizhóní Ch'ilátah Hózhóón* and hugged her while that emotional spike transcended into a few brief moments of weeping. As soon as she regained her composure, she smiled at the lovely lady who gave her very positive vibes.

Dragée then quickly thinking, said, *"Nizhóní Ch'ilátah Hózhóón,* while Doctor Brandenhagen was away he met this lovely woman Christiana and they were married the same day as me and General Níngsī in a group marriage. Please let me introduce you to my very good friend Christiana."

Christiana a very positive person always carrying a positive aura with her stepped forward and held her hand out and said, *Nizhóní Ch'ilátah Hózhóón* it is a great pleasure that I'm able to meet some of my husbands' friends here on Planet Earth. Also I am privileged to meet *Binii'łigaii* and Sargent Hawthorne. *Nizhóní Ch'ilátah Hózhóón* could not help it, she was feeling so emotional she reached out and hugged Christiana who reciprocated. It was such a glorious meeting for her.

And it all came back to *Nizhóní Ch'ilátah Hózhóón's* trek in life marrying her good friend and medicine man who seemed to have caused much of these moments. Her love for her husband grew even more that day, because he had done things that no Earth people had done before. And as she figured it out, the greatest general in the galaxy coming directly here to meet them and introduce their new wives was very important to them.

Binii'łigaii figured now was as good a time as ever to get out his pipe and load it up and share it with his friends. He took a big puff on it and handed it to General Níngsī took the pipe and copied *Binii'łigaii* then handed it to Roger who took a deep toke then handed it to Sargent Hawthorne who followed suit.

General Níngsī then spoke, "Sargent Hawthorne,

I'm very proud of you for all that you have done. I notice you are a single man like I used to be. If you would like to leave with me on a trip, I would be happy to take you to Plastras Nostras and introduce you to one of Christiana or Dragée's friends so that you have a very good wife.

Nizhóní Ch'ilátah Hózhóón then spoke up, "General Níngsī, these women are gorgeous creatures, and I'm sure Sargent Hawthorne would love to be with one for the rest of his life, but what he doesn't know is I already have five Navajo women that want to meet him. All he has to do is ask them and they would marry him immediately just on my recommendations of how good a man he is."

General Níngsī then spoke, "See that Sargent Hawthorne, you are already set up but let me know if you want to take that trip and we will go."

"Thank you General Níngsī, but I have a lot to do here and even though I know I would love to be married to a woman like these two, I'm more concerned about getting that vegetable garden up to tip top shape."

"You know how to reach me if you ever decide you want to make that trip."

"Yes, I do General Níngsī, and perhaps one day I will make that call, but for now I just want to see these projects around here get completed."

"Sargent Hawthorne, I've led millions of our Space Warriors in battles over the years. I know how to spot a reliable person. You are reliable and I am always available for you."

"Thank you General Níngsī."

"Binii 'łigaii, even though I would like to stay here and smoke your pipe with you for a few more hours, I need to take Roger to his home so he can figure out what he needs to do. I'll come back tomorrow and you can show me your garden and we can smoke the pipe together."

"General Níngsī, I will be looking forward to your visit and I'm very happy that you found love in your life."

"Binii 'łigaii, so am I."

"General Níngsī, then turned toward Dragée and said, "Us take Roger to his home."

"I'm ready when you are."

The four got back into the shuttle and it went airborne and skipped above the atmosphere and came straight down on the street in front of Rogers home. This time however they were not alone. Just in case there were itchy trigger fingers, a dozen combat assault ships came down and parked on the street in front of General Níngsī's and behind his shuttle. Fifty-eight-foot giants got out of those combat assault ships and got into an exact formation. General Níngsī's got out first with Dragée and Roger and Christiana followed closely behind.

The two CIA men on the porch were stunned especially seeing the green skinned women that appeared to be the sexyist things they ever saw in their lifetimes. General Níngsī marched up on the porch with the group followed by 20 or more eight-foot giants loaded with combat gear.

"I do not want Doctor Brandenhagen and his bride disturbed tonight. I'm going to leave five of those craft parked on the street and blocking it to keep everyone away."

He then turned towards Roger and said, "I would like you to give us a tour of your home."

"It will be my pleasure."

They went inside Roger's home and the place was spic and span. Obviously, the CIA agents were getting bored. The dishes were clean, the laundry done, and no dust anywhere. Roger wasn't necessarily a pig, but in all honesty the place had never been this clean before. Plus, none of the bushes were in any serious condition!

Christiana had no basis to understand what to expect. She was obviously animated by what she discovered how Roger lived. First impressions are important and compared to her family in Plastras Nostras, Roger appeared to be wealthy.

But by now she also learned he was respectful and sweet to her. She could ask for nothing more. Roger was far nicer to her than her father ever was to her mother. There was a message in all that.

Roger never divulged to Christiana his life travels and the terrible events in his life including the discovery on Mars. He tried to make life as comfortable as possible for her.

General Níngsī lived in much more splendor but understood he was with a typical Earth person of no major stature. To him this was enough for him to see. He was happy that Roger obtained one of the best wives anyone could in the galaxy and business men back in Tèlándìa would pay billions of credits for a mail order bride like Christiana. He was glad to see Roger understood he had a very special prize in his marriage. He already knew just like a drug, Roger was already addicted to Christiana, so he would have a lifelong happy relationship.

General Níngsī said, "I'm sorry Roger, but I'm a busy man. I have a lot of things to do. I'll meet up with you and your lovely bride in a couple days. I have a surprise for you.

"Thank you General Níngsī, I really appreciate everything you have done for me. I owe my happiness to you. I had a chance of a lifetime. I will always be very grateful for what you did for me."

"Roger, you don't know how much you helped me. I owe you a lot too, more than you can imagine. You have provided me with happiness like no man has ever earned before. I will always be grateful for what you did for me."

In a very impressive manner, the two men bowed to each other for a good five or six seconds. Christiana and Dragée had substantial social skills understood the significance of this sincere posture. They each knew Roger was very special to General Níngsī, and woe be it to anyone who ever hurt Roger.

General Níngsī and Dragée were escorted out of the home by Roger and Christiana and quickly surrounded by 50 or more eight-foot-tall giants who took them to their shuttle that quickly departed. Five minutes later the street was empty.

The CIA men made all the appropriate reports. Sally Fairbanks was called into the office in the late afternoon in the task force conference room and Mike Barnes was still in charge. The idiot would not be back for a couple more days as it was put out.

"Okay everyone, the Aliens are back in force and General Níngsī brought Roger home with a green skin woman. It's the opinion of the men on the watch there that this woman is Roger's new spouse."

With Ami fresh in Sally's mind, there would soon be an interesting development. Sally understood Ami, a woman who cheated on Roger and now fully regretted her behavior and hoped she could mend fences because she had no idea what she just lost if the INTEL is accurate. She then made a statement.

"Mike there are some things people in this room do not know about. I would like permission to go to Roger's home this evening and have a talk with him."

Mike realized this was a serious situation and Sally visiting Roger Brandenhagen might be a good idea, said, "Okay Sally, pay Roger a visit and let us know if there are any new developments."

Sally immediately stood up and headed out the door. This would not be a good night for Roger especially if the reports were true, he had a green skinned alien up in his bedroom. This time in the evening with all the TV vans gone there was ample parking along Roger's Street as Sally pulled her BMW into a spot near his home.

Sally was wearing her CIA badge outside her clothing as she walked up the sidewalk to Roger's home. One of the CIA men on th second shift knew her and asked, "Are you here to visit Roger?"

"Yes I am."

"Let me ring the doorbell for you."

Roger was laying in sweat slowly recovering from a journey to splendid gratification on a theme from Paganini when he heard the doorbell ring.

"That's odd, I thought General Níngsī explained to those men out front not to disturb us. I better go down and see who it is."

Roger put on his house coat and soon walked down the stairs and too the front door and discovered Sally Fairbanks there, wearing her CIA badge.

"Hello Sally, what can I do for you?"

"We need to talk."

"Please come in."

Roger took Sally to the side to a family room where there was ample room to sit and large screen TV existed.

"Reports are you are married."

"Yes, Christiana and I were recently married."

"What about Ami?"

"She blew me off a few months ago and simply said she didn't want to see me for a while and didn't contact me for quite some time so I figured she dumped me."

"Roger there are some things we probably need to talk about."

About that time Sally looked up and saw the exquisite green creature the CIA guards mentioned in their report and asked, "Are you going to introduce me Roger?"

Roger saw Sally was looking toward the stairway and he turned and saw a scantly clothed Christiana. Roger immediately stood up and said, "Christiana, let me introduce you to Sally Fairbanks who works for America's Central Intelligence Agency."

Christiana had been fully briefed on the CIA and acted coy as if this was something new to her. She knew by intelligence briefings how to react in situations like this.

Christiana walked forward and held her hand out. Sally took it and they had a very warm and respectful hand shake.

"You know Roger well?"

"Yes, Roger and I were the first people on this planet to meet General Níngsī. I've spent some time with General Níngsī and dealt with him on a number of issues.".

"I see, so you are professional contacts."

"Yes, we are. Roger has been through a lot since the Zhrakzhongs arrived."

"This is a business visit?"

"Yes, it is and I apologize."

"One of these days I'll fill you in on Sally Fairbanks. She certainly knows her business and the early days dealing with General Níngsī and the arrival was scary times for us."

"I can imagine since I was scared too."

"Sally, Christiana and I went through a unification, which on Earth would be called a marriage. She is my spouse and the love of my life."

"Christiana, you are a very beautiful woman. I like Roger, he's my friend and I'm very happy that he met you and you are now together. Roger is a very good man and you should be proud of him."

"I am. He's been through a lot."

"I bet he has and that's why I'm here Christiana. Would it be possible for us to borrow Roger for a few hours tomorrow so we can discuss what's all happened since he left?"

"Yes, I think its very important that Roger addresses your government on a few items that has happened."

"Roger, what is the state of the war with the Xīngguī?"

Christiana jumped in because she wanted to leave her mark on Roger in case Sally or anyone else had any notions, "The treaty was signed. The war is over. Earth is safe and the Zhrakzhongs are now going to leave your planet."

"How do you know this?"

"I'm an officer in the Zhrakzhong Space Force."

"Yes, she's a weapons deployment officer on General Níngsī's Command ship."

"I was Roger until I became your bride. Now I'm a civilian like you."

This conversation was definitely peaking Sally Fairbank's interest and she offered: "Roger, I know this is your first night home with your new bride, so I don't want to take up too much of your time. I plan to leave you alone for the rest of the night. I'm glad you made it back safely and I would like to talk to you a couple hours tomorrow to get an understanding of what all happened and what the treaty means."

"Sure I'll be happy to visit your office for a couple hours tomorrow."

"I'll send a car over to pick you up."

"All right."

Sally stood up and approached Christiana and said, "Christiana, you are very beautiful. Roger is a very nice guy and I'm glad he met you. I think very highly of Roger and I know he would not have picked you as his mate if you too were not special. So, I will always hold you in my mind as a special person and if there is anything I can ever do for you, I will try to help as much as I can. Here is my business card you can contact me any time. Roger will explain how to get in touch with me. Welcome to Earth and I want you to know I am your friend and will help you anyway I can."

"Thank you Sally, that means a lot to me."

"Take good care of Roger, he's really a very good guy and he deserves a princess like you."

Christiana could not hold back she grabbed Sally Fairbanks and hugged her. She knew she was a genuine friend and the embrace was mutual. Women seem to know when other women care about them. Christiana had super sensitivity in this regard and was glad that all the Earth women she met until now were seemingly very sweet. This was unlike poor Roger's reception but she understood that's how things are in the galaxy.

Sally left, drove home and called Mike Barnes and said, "Roger Brandenhagen will be visiting us in the morning. I will arrange to send a car over to pick him up."

"Any new revelations?"

"Yes, the war is over, we can breathe easy now."

"That's good to know. See you in the morning."

The Zhrakzhong intelligence people watched Sally Fairbanks come and go. In between they aimed a device at the windows and recorded all the conversations and immediately made their reports to General Níngsī's head of intelligence and after review decided it was nothing to warn General Níngsī about.

Roger and Christiana went back up to his bedroom and went back to bed, this time to sleep. Christiana who had received special intelligence briefings was feeling a lot better now because her early experience with these Earth people was very positive. She was also astonished how Sally Fairbanks held Roger in high esteem. In her experience, when women feel like towards a male that is a good sign, he's a good person. Roger had been through a lot including the disaster when he first arrived at Plastras Nostras to meet her family. She knew she loved Roger. He truly made her heart feel love every day. He was a kind and gentle soul. It was apparent to her now why General Níngsī felt the way he did towards Roger. As they clinged together that night in celestial love, the compassion and the satisfaction could reach no higher levels.

Roger woke up in the morning for two reasons. He seriously had to urinate and the smell of bacon. Roger had on his house coat and went down stairs and his trusty CIA watcher was there.

"Ready for some bacon boss?"

"You realize you need to cook some extra bacon this morning?"

"Why is that?"

"Let me go get her."

Roger went back up the stairs and shook Christiana and said, "I want you to go downstairs with me and have some bacon a CIA guy is cooking for us."

"Okay dear, if that's what you want."

Roger handed Christiana a bathrobe so she would not have to waste a lot of time dressing, and a minute later they went down the stairs.

A minute later they were making that CIA tough shit very nervous as he had never met an alien in his life and here was this green skin goddess!

"Hey buddy, I want to introduce you to my wife Christiana."

The CIA guy was almost paralyzed and his value system was seriously challenged.

The CIA cook had never seen such a beautiful woman in all his life. Roger knew this guy was unaware that Aliens would pay almost a Trillion USD$ for a mail order bride like Christiana. Yes, she was rare and most male emotions that came in contact with Plastras Nostras women appeared more than exuberant.

The twelve CIA guys who spent a lot of time protecting Roger had grown somewhat affectionate towards him. His directions to them simplified their watches by a huge degree. And his friendly mannerisms were infectious. He truly was a positive guy. A person that Ami threw away so amazingly astonishing. She had no idea she had the prince of her lifetime. But in general sense you do not know what you do not know. Its all part of the mystery of life.

Roger enjoyed watching this CIA consummate professional go through mental twists and turns as his faith was now thrown out the door. Roger just created another secular entity by the presence of Christiana. But it was going to get far more exciting as the day wore on.

Roger was in love, Christiana was in love, this new experience in life begets far more than this mere mortal deserved. But as a noble savage Roger evolved and transcended in this new reality, he felt the satisfaction of few men ever knew about. Christiana's chemical equilibrium she gave Roger every day changed him. Roger didn't recognize the subtle changes. The CIA did. Roger was now the most watched and person of interest that ever existed and the fun was just starting.

Roger truly liked these CIA guys especially the one who cooked the bacon, provided the orange juice and the eggs. Roger didn't know it quite yet, the feeling was mutual.

After finishing breakfast and taking care of morning evolutions, Roger was in his family room with Christina when is cell phone rang. It was Sally Fairbanks who said, "Roger I'm sending over a car to pick you up to bring you in here for debriefing."

After Roger was certain Christiana knew how to change Cable TV channels, he informed her what their day would be like but he had to go away with the CIA for a few hours. Being a weapons officer of the Zhrakzhongs Space Force with lot of INTEL training, this was not a big deal for Christiana who already understood Roger. She simply remained home and observed humans through their cable TV.

By the intelligence briefings, Christiana already knew Earth was a backwards planet. If it were not for the fact, she evolved in her relationship with Roger during their periods with General Níngsī, she would not be here today. She didn't seek out Roger it was how it all manifested beyond her wildest imagination.

No Earth person had ever gone where Roger went. He really was the full recipient of all Alien information off the planet. Nobody had any idea of galactic awareness like Roger. Nor did anyone please

Christiana any where near Roger. Their emotions were now tied together legally as well as morally. Christiana knew her future resided in Roger. Being a sophisticated individual with quite a lot of experience she didn't expect Roger to remain on this backwards planet.

Roger transferred files to his email system. He wasn't going to allow the CIA to wipe out his memories again. He figured a CIA expert would be bleaching his cell phone memory later this morning and there was not much he could do about it.

In about 15 minutes one of the two CIA agents posted on his front porch rang his door bell. Roger instinctively knew, *his ride was here.*

"I'll be away for a few hours then I will take you somewhere and do some fun things."

"Allright Roger, I know you have things you need to do." Christiana was very sweet in her delivery.

Roger walked out his front door and stopped and looked at the two CIA guys who had the day shift and said, "Be sure and keep my wife safe while I'm gone. If something happens to Christiana, I'll make sure General Níngsī has you barbecued and I'll eat your flanks with great satisfaction."

The two CIA men had seen the eight-foot tall giant and knew Roger wasn't making idle threats. "She will be safe Roger."

"Thank you."

Roger walked down the sidewalk and hopped in the waiting SUV.

It was back out to that all too familiar building next to Dulles international airport. Roger was led back up to the conference room where 20 stuffy CIA types were waiting for him. He had a big surprise for them because he had a copy of the treaty of Wukar with him.

"Good morning, Roger," Mike Barnes said as soon as he entered the room.

"Thank you."

Sally Fairbanks was sitting there smiling. She already had a head start on all the rest and knew this might turn into an interesting meeting.

As soon as Roger sat down in the empty seat at the table facing Mike Barnes, the questions began.

"Roger, it was reported you brought an Alien into your home an possibly violated a lot of medical protocols in doing so."

"That's true, that means those four CIA agents I had breakfast with might die any moment."

There was some slight chuckling in the room which helped to agitate Mike Barnes a notch or two.

"Don't you think what you did was a little selfish?"

"No I do not, my wife Christiana has fewer germs in her body than anyone in this room. All of you live with inferior medical technology. The Zhrakzhongs are thousands of years more advanced in medical technology that we are. The planet is not at risk from her. It's the other way around. She's at risk from this planet."

"We will have to quarantine her."

"No, you do not need to do that. She is already medically certified. And if you get near her, she'll contact General Níngsī and you will have a very bad day. My advice to you is make sure you stay the hell away from her if you know what's good for you."

"Are you threatening me?"

"Listen dumbshit, I'm sick and tired of your bullshit. Now here's something you do need to look at and then I'll be ready to discuss it with you."

The room was quiet. No civilian had ever talked to a SAC Director in the way Roger just did.

Roger handed Mike Barnes a copy of the treaty of Wukar and said, "Yes, I signed for this planet."

Mike Barnes started looking at the document that was printed in three languages: standard Zhrakzhong, Xīnggui, and English. The room was eerily quiet as Mike Barnes read through the document and showed a sign of utter surprise when he looked at the signatories with Roger's name on the bottom of the list.

"Do you think other countries will appreciate you speaking for them?"

"Be sure and let them know the planet is safe, only because my name is on the bottom of that list."

"I'm sure the President and a few others are not going to be happy with this document."

"Listen Mr. Barnes, you have no idea what I have been through. I'm not going to put up with CIA BS any more. I can leave the planet any time I like and never come back. I might even make sure you leave with me because under Zhrakzhong customs and cooking expertise, I'm sure your flanks would taste very good barbecued."

Mike Barnes was now severely agitated with that *in-your-face business.*

Sally Fairbanks decided she needed to immediately intervene:

"Mike, there are a number of things you are not aware of. I suggest that before we continue with this discussion, that you and I have a private meeting with Roger in your office. There are some developments that we need to discuss to determine the classification and the sensitivity of it."

"Allright everyone, please go back to your tasks. Sally and I will talk with Doctor Brandenhagen privately to determine if we need any further inputs from him before we put together the assessment to give to the DCI for the next Presidential briefing."

The room emptied out fairly rapidly, nobody wanted to be around when the fir was about to fly.

Thanks to Sally's intervention Mike Barnes calmed down and regained his composure and said, "Sally, everyone is gone so us just stay here and continue the discussion."

Roger then said, "I have a lot of videos on my cell phone that you probably want to take a look at so you will know what happened and you will understand, this planet is a pushover and has no way to deal with these galactic powers."

"Allright let me go get my laptop we can upload them into."

With Rogers help identifying the files in one of his

file directories exclusively set up, the upload process was rather quick. Then based on Rogers recommendation's they started looking at them on the large screen video displays.

The final battle was showing. Roger could sense based on Mike Barnes reaction, it was utterly frightening to watch, and Roger narrated the action since he had seen it all a couple times before.

"Now we are going to shortly see General Níngsī's command ship get blown up."

"You obviously were not on it since you survived the battle."

"Yes, General Níngsī's ship blew up after he and my wife got off with me."

Right after the combat video Mike Barnes was looking at pictures of Roger's wife. On the large screen she was almost her real size. Even Mike Barnes could appreciate the majestic quality of the incredibly beautiful woman.

"If I met that lady, I would have brought her home as well. Wow she is incredibly beautiful."

"Thank you."

Sally knew that she needed to get Roger together with Ami before she took him home, to close out that chapter in his life. This was going to be a tough day for Roger.

But Sally knew one thing for sure. Ami brought it on to herself by going out and getting plastered and listened to a bullshit artist who only wanted a quick fuck and put another notch on his belt buckle. Had she simply stayed reasonably sober and went home like a good girl, Roger would not have arrived home with another wife. Sally knew that Ami was going to take it real hard and they needed to close that chapter really quick because strange things can happen in love and war.

Ami would simply have to learn how to cope with the fact she screwed up a relationship with a viable future mate and perhaps will learn from it and not do a repeat in the future. Sally Fairbanks also was going to privately suggest Ami go see a therapist because she knew she was going to take it really hard when she discovered Roger was now a married man to an exotic princess and the odds of him ever leaving her were slim. If Sally knew anything about Plastras Nostras women, she would quickly figure out Ami would not be in the running. Once a plane skinner tasted the fruits of Plastras Nostras woman, he most likely could never be satisfied again by women of his own race.

At the conclusion of the debriefi ng, Mike Barnes said, "Roger I'm sorry I came off the way I did at the beginning of the meeting. I know its no excuse but we have been going through a lot of pressure here lately thanks to Sally's trip to Russia and China. I'm sorry I lost my cool with you."

"No problem, I understand."

"Sally, would you mind giving Roger a lift home."

"I would be delighted, there are some things I want to talk with him about."

"Okay thanks, and thank you both for stopping

in for the meeting."

"You're welcome."

The three stood up and Mike grabbed his laptop and headed out the door back to his office to lock up the laptop in secure storage rated for TS-SCI in his office.

"Us go to my car," Sally stated.

"Allright."

Soon they were in the car and Sally Fairbanks dropped it on Roger: "I recently met with Ami. She was upset she could not contact you. I think it would be a decent thing if you met her and explained your situation."

"I thought she was not interested in me. Just before I left with General Níngsī she was giving me the cold shoulder and wanted to have her space. I figured she had met someone else and no longer desired my presence."

"That is partially true, however she screwed up and let some fast talker get to her that only wanted to use her for cheap gratification."

"Then why bother meeting her?"

"Roger sometimes we lose special people in our lives for the dumbest reasons. She didn't really lose her feelings for you. They were just temporarily clouded by a misadventure that she terribly regrets. I know there is no way to salvage that relationship because you now have someone special and permanent in your life, but I think if you met with her and explained what happened, it will be easier for her to heal and move on with her life."

"Do you mind coming with me. I don't want to be alone with her."

"Sure, if that's what you want."

"Yes, it is."

"May I call her now and set up an appointment?"

"Go for it but I would like it be today and ASAP and get this over with."

"Okay, I'm going to call her now."

"Alexis please call Ami."

The phone rang a couple times and Ami answered not sounding too chipper.

"Ami?"

"Yes?"

"Hello this is Sally Fairbanks. Do you have some spare time now?"

"I suppose why?"

"Could you meet me at that Starbucks we met recently."

"Sure, it's not far from where I work."

"Ami, I want you to brace yourself. I'm bringing someone with me."

"Alright, I can be there in about thirty minutes."

"See you then."

Thank goodness it was early and not rush hour. Sally was able to glide down the Interstate and get back to DC quickly. About 30 minutes later all three of them converged upon Starbucks and met outside.

Sally knew nobody was there for coffee and suggested, "Why don't we just walk over to the park?"

"That's fine Ami said not looking to assure of herself. Roger was obviously acting strange to her and there was no affectionate greeting. But she knew she was the person who put the distance between them she now terribly regretted, but it was going to quickly get a lot worse.

After they got a distance into the park with nobody around Sally suggested, "Roger I know this is going to be a delicate moment, so why don't you and Ami walk on ahead and I'll wait here for you. I know you will want a private moment."

"Allright."

Ami didn't know what to make of Sally's comment but perhaps she figured they might end up in an argument especially if Roger had some ideas what really happened to them.

About 25 to 30 steps Roger stopped and looked into Ami's eyes that were already starting to water up.

"Ami I'm very-very sorry."

"You don't have to be sorry, I'm the one who should be sorry."

Ami's eyes were really watering up now.

"Ami, I was gone a long time and something happened I need to tell you about."

"Okay, I'm a big girl tell me, then I'll tell you something."

"Ami, I had some extraordinary experiences that would be almost unbelievable to you, but because of these extenuating circumstances I ended up meeting another woman. She is with me now. I'm in a permanent relationship with her. I'm sorry, but we can never go back to what we once had."

Those words hit Ami like a ton of bricks in the gut. Ami was a very sensitive woman and terribly regretted what she had done, and now her regret was even worse in that it cost her really good partner, the man she should have married a long time ago and *not dilly dallied around waiting for a better deal.*

Ami broke down hard and fast. Her sobbing turned into a torrent of passionate explosion. Sally observed Ami was miserating just like someone might who lost a love one in the hospital.

Roger stood back and did not reach out to comfort her. He was more or less paralyzed watching Ami bawl like a child with utter sadness.

Sally rushed forward and grabbed Ami and held her. Ami cried profusely for five minutes or longer. It did have an effect on Roger in that he had tears as well. He didn't understand Ami before and he didn't understand her now. He was confused by all this, but now it was too late. His world had changed. He wasn't even sure he was going to stay on this planet. He didn't have many relatives and had no relationship with the ones he did have. At least on Plastras Nostras he had the feeling he was surrounded by family and friends. And he knew vividly from all his experiences, General Níngsī was a true friend and manifested a lot of happiness for him by his personal interventions. He wasn't sure he deserved a friend like General Níngsī, but he was humbled that such an illustrious figure would have anything to do with a Noble Savage possibly qualified to be a cosmic cockroach.

When you love someone for what ever reason that relationship ends, the love does not totally go away. Roger had a great deal of empathy and he felt really-really bad watching Ami break down. It was almost gut wrenching for him to watch. It would be a sight he would never forget the rest of his life. And God help him if he ever went through this again.

Eventually Ami regained her composure and said, "I think I need to go back to work."

"Why don't you just go home for the day, Ami?"

"My boss will get mad at me."

"I'll talk to your boss; would you like me to drive you home?"

"I can't leave my car here."

"I'll drive your car for you. You are not in good shape now. Roger can follow us in my car and we can take you home."

"Allright."

There it was another chapter in Roger's life closed.

His bitter sweet memories of Ami and Elja Brielle Janxel took a lot out of him. Ami had no idea the utter sadness he felt. Sally Fairbanks had no idea about Elja Brielle Janxel until later that evening she received a phone call from General Níngsī inviting him to dine with him and his new wife!

She then informed General Níngsī who she knew took a lot of interest in Roger what transpired today.

"Sally, Roger has been through a lot. There are some things I need to tell you about. Roger probably needs more help than you can imagine."

General Níngsī then explained, "Roger lost the love of his life, Elja Brielle Janxel when my command ship blew up. Roger was watching the display monitor and saw the explosion. He was truly heart broken. We are very lucky that Christiana was there for him or I fear he might have had a tremendous mental breakdown."

"When Christiana took Roger to meet her family, her father initially utterly rejected him and more or less told him what you Earth people would say: get lost."

"Christiana who is the only surviving crew member of my command ship lost a lot of friends when it blew up. She was a very sad person there. She and Roger healed each other. I had to use organized crime on Plastras Nostras to put the fear of God in Christiana's father to force him to accept his new future son-in-law. Roger and Christiana do not know how I intervened and please keep this confidential between us."

"Are they getting along now?"

"I knew once her father gave Roger a chance, he

would discover he's a great individual and someone to be proud of. Also, I think when he discovered his daughter and Roger are signatories on the Treaty of Wukar, it had an impact on his disposition because his son-in-law is now a national hero on Plastras Nostras."

"That's good to know. I'll have to work harder to protect Roger because the former SAC Director Mark Rebman is due to return and I think he has it in for me and Roger because we affected his career path."

"Please pass this onto the Director Dipshit as you Earth people like to say: If I ever find out he hurts Roger in any way I will immediately take him out into space and dump his dead body in a trajectory towards your sun. That's how wee dispose of our war dead."

"He will not like me talking to him that way."

"Tell him you are just the messenger. I'm not going to bother calling your President and demand he fire the SAC Director Mark Rebman. I will personally handle the matter."

"That will be tough for me to do, but I'm ready to look for another job anyway."

"Sally, one more thing. Plastras Nostras women are very special. The entire galaxy wants them. I won't get into reasons why with you, but I think in due time, Christiana will not be comfortable living on planet Earth. I'm here to remove all the settlements and take all the Zhrakzhongs back to their home worlds. The war is over, we have peace now. In about six months you will not know we were even here. Any traces of our presence will be cleaned up. I want to take Roger back with me because I think he would flourish on Plastras Nostras where his wife's family has taken a keen liking to him as well as their community.

"I hope he will want to go."

"Once Christiana finds out about Ami, she will want to leave Earth, I'm sure of that. Roger is very attached to Christiana, he will do anything possible to keep her. He will no doubt willingly follow her to Plastras Nostras where I will arrange for her to have a very lucrative business and she can socialize with my wife Dragée and their other friend Cerise Sucrée."

"I hope that all works out."

"Sally, I just came up with an idea. Since the dipshit SAC Director Mark Rebman is returning this week, I want Roger and Christiana out of harms way. I've dealt with snakes before and the only way to kill them is to cut their heads off. So, us do this: I want you to bring Roger and Christiana to dinner with us tonight.

"I want the three of you to stay here for the night, we can also entertain my friends the *Béésh Łigaii Atsu* (Silver Eagle) Native American Tribe. I'll contact Sargent Hawthorne and have him help me set it all up."

"That sounds great."

"Could you please call Roger and ask him to get ready and call me back when you are all ready to get picked up."

"General Níngsī, you have helped me out of some jams in the past and I do appreciate everything you have done. I consider you a real friend if you don't mind."

"Sally I do not mind at all. I cherish your friendship."

"Thank you."

"You are most welcome and please make those calls now so Roger has time to get ready."

Sally quickly called Roger which is good because they were contemplating uber eats and Roger wasn't too happy about the selections available. He already had a sense of the kinds of food that Christiana liked and sadly they were going to have to go to an upscaled restaurant to get what they needed and Roger wasn't emotionally ready after his ordeal with Ami today, to deal with what might turn into a freak show tonight taking Christiana with him and he certainly could not leave her home alone. The phone call was thus well received.

Just like on previous times, a Limo pulled up and picked up Sally Fairbanks at her home, then went to Roger's home and picked up him and Christiana.

When Roger and Christiana walked out the front door, the CIA men were so infatuated with her posterior and getting a blast of pheromones since the couple had recently had sex and Christiana was shedding clouds of very powerful pheromones. When they eventually got home from their shifts their wives were going to be very happy as their husbands suddenly had some strong desires.

Back to the Amtrack station, the three got out of the Limo and hopped into General Níngsī's personal transport. 15 minutes later they were in Arizona and also alerting NORAD.

Chapter Twenty-Four

Snake

Sally would be very unhappy if she knew what transpired after she left the office in the Early afternoon. The snake (SAC Director Mark Rebman) returned off of administrative leave and he was on the warpath and had an agenda. Later when NORAD reported the UFO movement and the snake got his briefings in the Skiff, he attempted to contact Sally and soon the SAC Director Mark Rebman received a report she left in a Limo that later picked up Doctor Brandenhagen and a green skinned Alien.

This all dovetailed nicely into the Snake's Agenda.

Sally and the group met up with the dinner party sitting at lavish table settings in the Tribes area next to the red barn and their new garden. The Aliens had constructed platforms during the day and after Sargent Hawthorne provided a head count of everyone in the tribe, the nine long tables and plush chairs as well as a couple kiddy tables with alien day care providers supervising them were getting on of the best meals of their life.

All the tribe's people were dressed in ornate native wear only worn on special occasions. The sensory perception of green exotic illustrious Plastras Nostras females setting next to these beautiful native creatures was a sight to behold. Plastras Nostras and native wear comingled so amazingly well and it also brought out the exquisite beauty in all the women. Tribe members were proud of their women who looked glorious tonight and it added tremendously to the great feelings everyone had that was further enhanced by the medicine man's pipe and some drinks like Gĕnkóviàn Jiŭyàowù and special wines produced on Plastras Nostras that induced pheromone explosions.

During the lovely dinner, Sally Fairbanks got phone calls from the SAC watch officer which she ignored knowing she would be in deep shits tomorrow but didn't care. She was going to enjoy the night with her wonderful friends, the Aliens as well as her now close friends within the Tribe and Sargent Hawthorne who she liked more and more. He had proven himself to her. She in fact admired him to the point she didn't mind flirting with him.

Each time the SAC texted her she ignored it until all of a sudden, she got a text from Mike Barnes that greatly distressed her. General Níngsī could see Sally twist her face up and shift from the bubbly person having a wonderful time flirting with Sargent Hawthorne to a sterile and quiet personality.

General Níngsī then knew in his mind the snake had just pulled some crap. He knew his own watch officer would soon be arriving to council him on new developments they were monitoring. And just as he predicted two minutes later the gate opened and a hover craft came out and stopped a good distance away as to not stir up any dirt for the feast. General Níngsī stood up and said, "excuse me for a minute I need to go find out why they are here," even though he already suspected what it was.

General Níngsī in his dress dinner uniform looked very distinguished. The tribal kids looked in awe at this impressive looking eight-foot-tall giant. He walked to the Hovercraft and the officer handed him some type of portable device. One could say it was equivalent to a touchpad Earth people used.

He read copies of all he transactions on Sally Fairbanks cell phone. Mike Barnes had just notified her the SAC Director Mark Rebman was back and he had issued arrest warrants for her, Roger, and an undisclosed apparently green skinned alien. The arrest warrant said, "These are dangerous individuals, Lethal Force is authorized." General Níngsī suspected the snake would pull off a stunt like this, he already had an assault force prepared just for this moment.

"Go get the SAC Director Mark Rebman and place him in the Brigg until I find time to deal with him."

"Yes sir, we will deploy the teams right away."

"Do you know the whereabouts of the SAC Director Mark Rebman now?"

"Yes, we have an observer nearby. He arrived home to his residence about five minutes ago and is apparently drinking a beer, eating a snack and chuckling."

"Okay go pluck him and bring him to the Brigg right away.

General Níngsī then walked over to Sally and said, "May I have a moment with you."

"Sure."

They walked towards the alien compound and when they were far enough away to talk so the others could not hear them, he informed Sally, "Your SAC Director Mark Rebman is back. We know he has issued arrest warrants for you and with directions you are a dangerous person meaning shoot on sight. He apparently intends to assassinate you tonight. You can't go home. You will have to wait here with Roger and Christiana because they too would be assassinated if they return home.

A chill went up Sally's spine as she realized General Níngsī would probably kill the SAC Director Mark Rebman tonight. This was all getting very nasty quickly.

Don't spoil the fun, you are now safe, I will protect you. Smile. In a few more days all this will be taken care of. Also please don't inform Roger until after the party is over. You will all come to my command center where I will inform Roger and Christiana. I'm also going to offer to take them back with me for their own protection. I do not think it would be safe for Christiana to live here on this planet. Earth is not ready to have the luster of such an incredible Plastras Nostras woman here."

"I suppose you are right."

"If you noticed, Christiana and Dragée are almost like sisters. They truly like each other a lot. And when you see them socializing with Cerise Sucrée, you will know they like to be in the company of each other."

"Yes, I can sense that."

They walked back to their table and Sally was happy again. She knew General Níngsī more an anyone else could protect her and she had made up her mind. She was done and this time when she handed in her resignation, its final. She was not going to work for a Tyrant that just ordered her assassination.

Flirting with Sargent Hawthorne recommenced and happiness flourished.

Events were now happening in DC tonight. To say the SAC Director Mark Rebman had pissed someone off was an understatement.

The FBI was soon contacted by representatives of a major law firm representing the Zhrakzhongs who all knew too well legal theory.

They had to do this because the FBI would normally assume someone calling them with what the Zhrakzhongs wanted to discuss would be blown off as some idiot calling with BS. But when the legal team of one of Washington DC's most prestigious law firms approaches the FBI, they immediately take it seriously.

"What do you want to discuss, special agent Keeney asked?"

"The CIA's SAC Director Mark Rebman last night ordered the assassination of Sally Fairbanks, Doctor Roger Brandenhagen and his wife Christiana."

"And why are you interested in this matter?"

"We have been hired by the Alien Zhrakzhongs out in Arizona. We are just the messengers."

"What kind of Bullshit is this?" Special Agent Keeney asked.

I think you need to call the Assistant SAC Director Mike Barnes and explain to him the Zhrakzhongs have taken SAC Director Mark Rebman into custody and if you FBI do not investigate his attempted assassination plot, they plan on giving the 900 million SAC files to Vladimir Putin and Chairman Xi of China. By the way you of all people should be concerned about the largest data breach in U.S. History.

"This has to be some kind of bullshit story," Special Agent Keeney stated.

"Special Agent Keeney, you can check our credentials with the DOJ and we plan on filing a brief with the AG about your deplorable behavior. So, I suggest you start doing your job or you may soon find you don't have one. By the way, does the FBI Director know you just bad mouthed one of the leading attorneys for the most prestigious law firm in Washington?"

"I need to look into this."

"I think when you confront Mike Barnes with the knowledge the top law firm in Washington DC knows about the data breach and that the aliens are going to hand over 900 million files to our enemies unless you do your job, he might want to have a meeting with you."

"Okay I will contact him."

"Here's his phone number call him now and inform him the Aliens have taken SAC Director Mark Rebman into custody and if the bureaucracy doesn't start moving bad things are about to happen especially when Xi reads some of those juicy details concerning Taiwan and Korea."

"I said I would call him."

"We are going to stay right here and watch you call him and if you don't then we are required to inform our client. Unless we report back in 30 minutes, consider those 900 million files in the hands of the enemy you as a special agent could have prevented if you just did your job."

The agent was obviously pissed off to the point he wanted to punch out the lawyer doing all the talking, but figured he didn't have anything to lose by making a quick phone call.

"Hello"

"Mike Barnes?"

"How did you get this phone number?"

"The attorneys sitting in front of me gave it to me?"

"What are those attorneys doing and who are they?"

"We don't have much time Mike, let me ask you, have you seen your SAC Director Mark Rebman lately?"

"No, we got a manhunt looking for him he came up missing last night."

"These lawyers know where he's at?"

"And where is that?"

"Apparently the Aliens took him into custody last night."

"Shit! That can't be!"

Up until that moment the special agent thought

the alien talk was all nonsense. Now the agent sprung the next detail that really got Barnes fired up:

"These lawyers claim they were hired by the Aliens to represent them."

"In what capacity?"

"They have alleged the SAC Director Mark Rebman initiated actions to assassinate a woman named Sally Fairbanks, Doctor Brandenhagen and his wife."

"They can't really say it was an assassination. All he did was initiate their arrest warrants with special circumstances."

"What are the special circumstances?"

"Deadly Force is authorized."

"That sure as hell sounds like an assassination to me and oh by the way Mr. Barnes, its against the law for the CIA to take any actions against any citizen within CONUS. We now are going to put out an arrest warrant for the SAC Director Mark Rebman. Do you think the Aliens would release him to us?"

"I have no way of knowing; I'll have to send someone out to Arizona to talk with them."

"Mr. Barnes are you aware of the 900 million file data breach?"

"Yes, I'm aware."

"You need to inform the DCI I will be immediately contacting our FBI Director the Aliens plan on releasing those 900 million files to Vladimir Putin and Chairman Xi in 30 minutes unless you cancel the arrest warrant with special circumstances."

"I'll be god damn. This is going to get real sticky."

"Yea the fact is, you assholes are illegally operating in the USA will make it real sticky."

"Alright, I will go make the appropriate reports to proper channels."

"Mr. Barnes it sounds like we got less than thirty minutes, first thing you need to do is cancel that highly illegal assassination attempt so I can inform these attorneys otherwise the DCI will have to explain that data breach to the President later today after the FBI director finishes talking with the President about this matter."

"I'm at my computer keyboard now. I'm sending out an emergency order cancelation. Anyone with any jurisdiction in the case or tasking must respond within five minutes of receipt of the new orders. Consider it canceled within five minutes."

"I got you on speaker phone. The lawyers have been duly informed."

"Allright thank you."

"Mr. Barnes, could I ask you one more question?"

"Sure."

"How's come the FBI doesn't know about Aliens in Arizona?"

"We kept that operation highly compartmentalized to protect the sensitive information."

"You mean as safe as the 900 million files you lost?"

The lead lawyer sent a text message to General Níngsī's chief of security: "The assassination order has been rescinded. What do you plan on doing with the SAC Director?"

Reply: "General Níngsī says the SAC Director Mark Rebman will receive special communications training, then will be taken back to his home."

The lead attorney then informed the special agent who was taking it all in for his report.

The special agent then said, "I'm very sorry the way I treated you, but its not every day four high priced attorneys come in here and tells us we got extraterrestrial aliens out in Arizona. I hope you know I had reasons to be skeptical at first."

"Special Agent Keeney, we understand completely and we didn't have much time so we had to cut to the chase and dish it all out abruptly."

"What are the Aliens going to do with those files?"

"Their representative informed us in six months they will all be gone. They were here hiding a billion people out in Arizona because of the intergalactic war that just ended. They live a very far distance from Earth and will likely never come back, so the information is of no use to them. However, they did study it out of curiosity via artificial intelligence. By the time they leave here in six months all that information will be discarded."

"How are they militarily compared to us?"

"You don't know this because the CIA and the Air Force are covering it up. We sent F22's after them when they first showed up. With their much more advanced technology they shot half those F22's down like shooting ducks in a barrel. We are no match for them."

"We could have dropped a hydrogen bomb on them."

"Their technology is far more advanced than ours. None of our weapons would ever get near them."

The attorney then dropped a doozy on the FBI special agent: "While we were meeting with the Zhrakzhong, they showed us three-dimensional video of the recent space war. You should ask your friend Mike Barnes over at the CIA to show you the video the Aliens provided them copies."

Chapter Twenty-Five

Communications Training

Captain Luōjiàn arrived with his Zhrakzhong Space Warship the same day the snake had to be dealt with. The reason why Captain Luōjiàn arrived late is General Níngsī requested he stop at Màichōng and ask his new friend Xié'è de Gōngniú to arrange for Kāiwù de Sēngrén and six Tytrone Philosopher Monks to be sent to Earth with Captain Luōjiàn because General Níngsī felt he needed additional meditation training.

Kāiwù de Sēngrén was delighted to receive the invitation and as he was leaving the Temple to get in Captain Luōjiàn's shuttle, he turned to Xié'è de Gōngniú and said, "I am impressed with your friend General Níngsī who wants to lead himself to the pathway of enlightenment."

"Kāiwù de Sēngrén, we have learned a lot from you. I want to thank you for improving my life by a huge margin."

"Are you sure you are happy about meditation? It seems to me Cerise Sucrée is a source of a lot of your inspiration."

"Kāiwù de Sēngrén, had you not done the group meditation I would never have the realization that I could bring Cerise Sucrée into my life."

"Xié'è de Gōngniú, you have also added hugely to Cerise Sucrée. She came from a living hell and you have given her new life. That's why she adores you. She knows what you have done for her."

"You think she loves me?"

"I spent a lot of time in the past at Plastras Nostras. The Plastras Nostras women are like a special flower in nature, they glow when they are in love. Cerise Sucrée glows every day and she feels like you are her dream come true. Yes in fact I know she is in total love of you."

"Thank you for taking this trip. It means a lot to General Níngsī who is one of the forces behind keeping the peace. I'm afraid without him, the dirty rotten intergalactic bankers and war profiteers would start up a war as soon as they could."

"One of the reasons why I'm willing to go is eventually General Níngsī will retire and someone like Captain Luōjiàn would be promoted and possibly replace him. I intend to give Captain Luōjiàn meditation training on the trip to planet Earth and hopefully he will be prepared to take over when General Níngsī is no longer in command.

"Have a safe trip, and when you get back, please contact me, I would like to see you and hear your stories about your trip."

"I will."

Kāiwù de Sēngrén and six Tytrone Philosopher Monks walked over to the waiting shuttle and stepped into it. Moments later the door was shut and the craft went vertical.

As he promised he gave Captain Luōjiàn meditation training and instantly started seeing the results. All the Monks were proud of their accomplishments.

~~~

After the party at the *Béésh Łigaii Atsu* (Silver Eagle) Native American Tribe wound down, General Níngsī took his friends to his command bunker that had very nice berthing accommodations for senior offi cers. Since there was no war going on, half of those offi cers were now gone and the nice rooms were available for his friends.

Those people were sleepy and soon sound asleep in very comfortable beds. General Níngsī then departed in a shuttle and went up to his command ship where he soon received his distinguished guests, Kāiwù de Sēngrén and six Tytrone Philosopher Monks.

"Hello Kāiwù de Sēngrén, I'm very glad you arrived. I'm not going to do any training today, but I have a person now in the Brigg who ordered the assassination of Roger, Christiana, and an Earth person Sally Fairbanks who is a personal friend of mine. He's a tough character and rotten to the core. I would like you to start training him as soon as you feel you are ready."

"We are ready now General; we just finished our sleep period just a couple hours ago."

"All right let me take you down to the Brigg and introduce him. I'll have our personnel carry all your instruments down there momentarily."

"Thank you, we appreciate that."

It took less than three minutes to get to the Brigg. The snake was alone in the cell which was designed to hold up to 50 POW's so there was plenty of room to setup.

Kāiwù de Sēngrén knew how to spot evil. However, he would rather convert an evil person than to spend a lot of time training good people. If he can accomplish that, then it is more beneficial to society.

The snake was coiled up almost into a ball leaning up against the wall. He had great fear knowing he was facing a death penalty for attempting to assassinate General Níngsī's personal friends. Charges were read to him and the only thing left to learn was exactly when they planned to dump his body into the sun.

When he saw the clerics, he assumed this was the final hour he would be executed real soon.

They all marched promptly into the Brigg cell all smiling. That agitated the snake even more because it pissed him off, they were happy about him getting executed.

He ignored them pondering his fate.

A translator was with them to inform him in English what was going on.

A chair was placed somewhat in the middle of the cell and suddenly these strange musical instruments and a gong were being set up.

The translator said, "Would you please sit in this chair."

"Why?"

"We will explain it to you after you sit there."

The snake stood up and walked over and sat down at the chair.

The translator then informed him, "General Níngsī has decided that instead of killing you, if you agree to take meditation training, he will then have you sent back to your home alive."

"How long will this take?"

"Let me ask Kāiwù de Sēngrén."

The translator who was a linguist who also spoke standard Xīngguī asked the question then informed the snake, "If you cooperate, no longer than a week."

"Allright tell me what I got to do."

The session began, and like most untrained people, the snake was skeptical this would amount to much. Four hours later he was a changed man. It was like a new berth to him. It was an incredible experience.

Kāiwù de Sēngrén an absolute expert in this process knew the exact moment the snake went to the universe. Mark Rebman came back as a director with a great deal of enlightenment. His whole life went before him very quickly and he suddenly had more questions than answers. That's usually how it starts out and then in subsequent sessions they discover answers and have fewer questions.

The SAC Director Mark Rebman then received his next big surprise. He was taken to a stateroom where he was given a change of clothes and a green skin female crewmember demonstrated the body washer and the toilet. He was rather astonished when she disrobed and went into the body washer nude to demonstrate it. She then put her clothes back on and said, "After you get a body wash and change your clothes, I will be taking you somewhere that we have a meal planned for you."

As soon as the SAC Director Mark Rebman was ready, the Randolph Artificial Intelligence holograph suddenly popped up and said, your escort is ready to take you to dinner. The door suddenly opened and there she was. A different woman with green skin, purple eyes and red hair!

"Please follow me."

The escort took the SAC Director Mark Rebman to General Níngsī's private quarters where Kāiwù de Sēngrén and six Tytrone Philosopher Monks were seated and waiting for him. His place at the table had a placard with his name, Mark Rebman. When he was abducted, he had on a pair of shorts and a tee-shirt with no identity on him. *I wonder how they knew my name?*

Kāiwù de Sēngrén and six Tytrone Philosopher Monks were enjoying the way the Zhrakzhongs were spoiling them especially with the special wine from Plastras Nostras that was extremely expensive gave them one hell of a buzz.

Tell me Mark Rebman, how did you like the meditation training today? Kāiwù de Sēngrén asked.

"What is your name?"

"I'm Kāiwù de Sēngrén. I'm the Abbot for the Tytrone Philosopher Temple in the city of Màichōng the capitol of the Xīngguī civilization.

"Kāiwù de Sēngrén, I will admit I was skeptical at first. But then something happened as if I went into a magical dream."

"Do you think it benefitted you?"

"I want to experience it some more. It had an effect on me."

"Tomorrow we will continue. We can't do these sessions too quickly or you could have some serious side effects."

The monks were all very silent. What Mark didn't know is they always went to the universe with their clients. They would spend this time eating and reflecting. It wasn't as if they were not sociable, but when a person goes to the universe as often as they do, the amount of enlightenment is rather extreme. They simply had to take time to let their brains cool down and spin down. The wine seemed to help a lot.

SAC Director Mark Rebman was starting to realize, Doctor Brandenhagen had spent a lot of time with these aliens and came home with a green skin wife who probably looked like his escort.

SAC Director Mark Rebman was a very smart guy, just like Doctor Brandenhagen and some of the others they recently converted. Hence his brain was already wired in such a manner to facilitate the meditation and the Hemi-Sync he obtained but didn't realize what it was.

The evening was well planned for Mark Rebman. He would now be systematically psychologically programmed.

There was music, dancers, and then towards the end of the entertainment, he was shown the final battles of the war and on the 40-foot holograph it appeared terrifying. He already knew the statistics on the size of those monster ships. Were they showing this to send me a message?

Mark didn't know it quite yet but he was also being systematically drugged and he slowly felt very sleepy and eventually passed out. He was then put on a gurney and back to his sleeping compartment where he was undressed and put into sleeping clothes and tucked into his bed. He would be out for twelve hours to make sure his brain and a cool down period to enhance the next session.

Randolph was watching in the background and as soon as Mark Rebman stirred Artificial Intelligence knew he was coming too and soon his door opened and a couple delightfully looking women came in and said, "We are here to help you get ready for the next session. After you use the toilet, please undress and step into the body washer."

After he took care of his business, he stepped nude into the body washer. Five minutes later Mark was scrubbed and dried and feeling really good from all the extra negative ions.

The training started a short time later. Today, Mark slipped into that almost narcotic state and his two brain halves synchronized and his mind went to the Universe. He lived six or seven lifetimes, he lost track. As soon as it started fading, he struggled to keep it going. He came out of that dream like state and looked around. Kāiwù de Sēngrén and six Tytrone Philosopher Monks were gone he stood up and looked around and behind him was that green skinned woman again. Unknown to Mark this woman was having a pheromone explosion. It was her time of the month. She was in full ovulation. And she wanted a mate badly.

"I'm to take you to your quarters so you can freshen up and change your clothes we have prepared for you."

"Alright lead the way."

Mark Rebman didn't know on Plastras Nostras, women picked the men. Not the other way around. This woman had gone to General Níngsī to confess.

"General, I'm not sure of why it happened, but somehow I have discovered I have an emotional attachment from Mr. Mark Rebman. I know I am probably not the right person to deal with him so if you wish to relieve me now, I will understand, and I'm very sorry for my conduct."

"Táozi you were observing the Tytrone Philosopher's train Mark Rebman, correct?"

"Yes General, as a security officer it was my responsibility to remain with him at all times and make any necessary reports."

"Táozi, I know this is going to sound strange to you, but I've actually witnessed it myself. Sometimes when you are physically near a person going through this meditation training, your souls may intersect. What you don't know if you haven't been trained is Mark Rebman lives 6 or 7 complete lives while in that state. He may have lived 6 or 7 lifetimes with you without even you knowing it. If you think you love Mark Rebman then you need to explore it further and test the waters. As the commander of this ship I give you permission to bypass those protocols with the person of interest. If Mark Rebman takes interest in you and contemplates a unification, I will personally sponsor you and take you back to Plastras Nostras with Mark to meet your family."

"What if my parents are opposed to me unifying with a plane skinner?"

"I just went through this with Roger Brandenhagen and Christiana. I know how to solve that problem if it develops that way. Now Christiana's parents like Roger. At first it's a big shock to them. But as time passes and they get to know him, they will come around. I promise."

"Thank you general, this means a lot to me."

"You more than earned this in the war. I'm sorry I had to steal you from Captain Luōjiàn, but when my command ship was destroyed with the entire crew except for Christiana, I was hard pressed and had to go rob some of the best people in the fleet from all the ships in order to quickly put together a new crew so that we could get the peace treaty signed before others convinced Emperor Shāyú to change his mind. Artificial Intelligence now knows you have permission to proceed with Mark Rebman and I do hope you are successful because I'm very grateful for all your assistance.

"Thank you general."

When Táozi and Mark Rebman reached his stateroom, she said, "Mark may I come into your room I want to talk to you about something."

"Sure."

There was only one chair in his room and Mark asked, "Would you like to sit down?"

"No. I want you to sit down."

"Okay. What is it you want to talk about?"

"Mark, do you think I'm pretty?"

"Yes, you are beautiful."

"Are you married?"

"No."

"Would you consider marrying a green skin woman?"

"If she's as beautiful as you are, yes I would."

"What if I wanted to marry you?"

"Actually, that would please me."

Artificial Intelligence was giving General Níngsī reports and it pleased him. He could always use more friends, especially if they all ended up living on Plastras Nostras.

When she reached down and softly kissed Mark Rebman on his lips her pheromones were shedding at an incredible amount. This was quickly having an effect on Mark and he knew he was losing control and didn't know if he should make a move on Táozi. But before he could think about making the first move, she started undressing him and quickly got him nude and undid her own clothes and pulled him over to the bed and soon taught Mark a huge lesson in life. Once her body chemicals started reacting with his, Mark was going into a new plateau. Mark was also starting to realize he saw Táozi some place before as if it were in his dreams. For some very strange reason he knew he loved this woman but felt dumbfounded because he couldn't remember where and when, he just knew it happened. After their glorious lovemaking and they snapped back to temporal reality, Táozi said, we need to get our bodies into the body washer and get our change of clothes on because they are expecting you up in General Níngsī's quarters."

"Okay but first I want to tell you something."

"Yes?"

"I know I'm in love with you and want to be with you forever."

"Then we will stay together. I'm sure General Níngsī will facilitate us after you finish your meditation training."

In a brief period of time, they were dressed and ready to proceed up to General Níngsī's quarters. But just then Randolph's Artificial Intelligence holograph popped up and said, "Táozi, General Níngsī would like you to report to your quarters and someone else will be there to escort Mark Rebman up to General Níngsī's quarters."

Thirty seconds later the door opened and another crew member was there to escort Mark.

Táozi didn't have very far to go to her quarters

and she was surprised there was Dragée, General Níngsī's wife and she was carrying some clothes.

"Táozi, we need to have a little talk."

"Okay come on in."

As soon as the women were in Táozi's room, and the door closed, Dragée said, "My husband informed me that you want a unification with Mark Rebman."

"Yes, I do."

"I brought some nice dresses I want you to try on because you are General Níngsī official VIP guest for dinner. You will be seated with Mark Rebman, and my husband and I will do everything in our power to make sure you have a smooth transition into Marks life."

Táozi grabbed Dragée and started crying. Dragée suspected something like this might happen after she talked with her husband who asked Dragée to help out. Dragée loved her husband very much and would do anything for him and this was such a nice request she loved doing it.

"Táozi, we do not have time for you to cry, you can do that later. Now just smile and be happy because I think Mark will love you."

"He already does."

"How do you know that?"

"He told me he loves me and we have already made love together."

"Oh, that's wonderful. Now us get some nice clothes on you so you can show him how cute you really can get. I'm an expert on makeup. I'll make you look very pretty but you have to promise me not to cry and screw it up!"

"I promise."

It did not take long for Dragée to turn Táozi into an incredibly beautiful princess. Mark was going to get a huge surprise. He had no idea how much better she could look when she "cleaned up."

"Okay dear, I think you are ready. I think Mark will melt when he sees you."

"You are so fantastic, I can't believe what you did. You truly are an artist."

"Okay, us go see Mark. If he had any doubt before, this will finish the deal."

"I'm so happy. Thank you."

"It's my pleasure Táozi you earned it many times over."

The two women proudly marched up to General Níngsī's quarters and the room was stunned when they walked in. Táozi walked over and sat down next to Mark who was utterly stunned. He knew it was Táozi and incredibly animated. They looked into each other's eyes and it was easily determined by everyone present, these two were lovers. General Níngsī had a broad smile on his face and Kāiwù de Sēngrén smiled as he knew Mark Rebman was a newborn man in love with this beautiful princess sitting next too him.

They had no idea how long they stared into each other's eyes. It was as if their minds were locked together totally oblivious to the world. They probably would have set there staring into each other's eyes except General Níngsī tapped his wine glass with a spoon and said, Here-here."

They quickly snapped out of it and regained their consciousness to the room full of people with lots of stares.

"Thank you for joining us Táozi."

"Thank you for inviting me General Níngsī."

"Who would all like wine?" the chief steward asked.

Soon the group was dining and during the course of events, Kāiwù de Sēngrén asked, "General Níngsī, when do you plan on receiving more meditation training?"

"I think I will wait until Mark has completed his training. He's a busy man and I'm sure has a lot of issues he needs to attend to back down on the planet."

"He's progressed very rapidly; I think maybe one or two more sessions is all he needs."

This is what I would like to do, after Mark finishes his training, I want to take him down and introduce him to my friends at the *Béésh Łigaii Atsu* (Silver Eagle) Native American Tribe. I want to have another dinner like the one we had the other night because if I guess things correctly, I think Mark will be making an announcement.

"General Níngsī, it's a custom for my people to give a woman a ring when he asks her to marry him. I do not have a ring, but I would like to ask Táozi to marry me."

That was it. Táozi broke down and started crying. Dragée stood up and walked around and put her arms around Táozi and hugged her and slowly rocked her back and forth and said, "Its okay, let it out. Everyone here understands you."

Dragée looked up at General Níngsī who gave her the signal to come over to him.

"Yes dear?"

"Take Táozi back to her room for an hour to give her a chance to unwind. She's in an emotional roller-coaster now."

As soon as the women left, General Níngsī stood up and said, "Mark come with me please."

General Níngsī then said to his head steward, "Please serve everyone I know they are hungry because Mark and I will be gone for about an hour."

As General Níngsī was leaving his quarters he said, "Intel Officer meet me at the shuttle bay."

By the time they got there the Intel Officer was waiting.

"Do you have a lot of American Cash with you?"

"Yes General, I always make sure in case I need it for an operation."

"Good, take me and Roger down to the planet we need to find a ring store open so we can get him a ring to give to Táozi, and we only have an hour."

"We'll have to fly down to the West Coast of America because a lot of stores in the East are closing about now."

"That's fine. Where do you recommend?"

"Do you want a really nice ring?"

"Yes of course."

"We'll have to go to Rodeo Drive then."

"Allright."

"General, I also have numerous credit cards so we do not need cash."

"However, it works is fine with me."

The shuttle pilot was directed to drop them off on the top of a high rise building with a helicopter landing pad. The Intel Officer said, "This building has a number of upscaled jewelry stores."

Within 20 minutes of leaving the space craft they were walking into a ring store. Back on the command ship, Dragée had the ship's doctor give Táozi a medication to help control her emotions. She wanted her all smiles for the rest of the night. Once Táozi took the happy juice all the crying ended for the evening.

Twenty minutes after arriving, the men walked out of the jewelry store with a 2.5 carrot European cut diamond ring and went back up to the helicopter pad where the shuttle came back down and picked them up.

The police helicopter flying around spotted the shuttle that made no noise and went straight up in the air and out into space. People back at the police station thought they were nuts until they replayed the video the helicopter is always recording just in case; they need it and the police body cams also captured the image. The next day after the local police that were flying over Rodeo Drive shared the video with their FBI buddies, special agent Keeney was sent out to investigate.

Fifty-five minutes after leaving the command ship, the men returned to General Níngsī's quarters with a few minutes to spare before the women returned all smiles. The Tytrone Philosophers were finishing up their meals but had no indication they were ready to leave because they expected an event to unfold, they all wanted to see the fruits of their efforts, changing an evil person into Prince Charming.

The women were all smiles and arrived back and sat down at their prospective places.

General Níngsī got the ball rolling quickly because he was getting hungry and wanted this to be completed first, "Táozi, I think Mark has something he wishes to tell you."

Mark reached into his pocket and pulled out the ring box and said, "Táozi, I know that I love you and somehow I managed to get a ring. Will you please marry me?"

Mark then grabbed Táozi's hand and put the ring on and it fit utterly perfect. She threw her arms around Mark and said, "Yes, Yes, Yes."

Now Dragée started crying and all General Níngsī could do is shake his head it was out of his control.

The Tytrone Philosophers sat there enjoying and observing all this unfold. They were eternally proud that their efforts were so successful so quickly. They also grew an even greater respect for General Níngsī who did a lot for these people as well as restoring happiness for half of the galaxy.

In the days to come they had their big party at the *Béésh Łigaii Atsu* (Silver Eagle) Native American Tribe. There were several revelations there that left many of the Tribe members in total awe. They got to meet another friend of General Níngsī, Sally Fairbanks had quit the CIA and was moving in with Sargent Hawthorne which was absolutely perfect as far as *Nizhóní Ch'ilátah Hózhóón* (beautiful flower) medicine man's wife was concerned.

Tytrone Philosophers sat and smoked the pipe with *Binii'łigaii* (screeching owl) medicine man. It was a glorious evening. Six months later they were all gone. There was no trace of the Zhrakzhongs other than the water makers they left behind for the tribe with plenty of spare parts.

Author's Notes:

This book is a work of fiction. There is no real person in this book. If names are found that seem familiar, it's merely coincidental.

This book describes a scenario where aliens bring a billion people down on the planet to hide them from their enemies in a galactic scale war.

I know it seems like it's a wonderful idea to reach out to aliens and tell all the other planets we are here and we constantly expose ourselves. But let me ask you this question: "What if we reach out to the bad aliens. How would we know which alien is good and which is the bad? How would we know more advanced aliens view us as cosmic cockroaches and decide to bring in the big can of RAID and wipe us out?

We need to stop broadcasting to possible future enemies. We need to find them before they find us and study them for a while to really determine if its in our best interest to go in that direction.

Paul D. Escudero

November 14, 2021

San Diego California